# MORGAINE

"The world is going . . . and the end of the world comes, not for us, perhaps, but soon. And we have always loved monuments.

"Know that it was Morgaine who wrought this ruin. Morgen-Angharan, Men named her: the White Queen, she of the white gull feather, who was the death that came on us. It was Morgaine who extinguished the last brightness in the north, who cast Ohtij-in down to ruin, and stripped the land of inhabitants.

"Even before this present age she was the curse of our land, for she led the Men of the Darkness, a thousand years before us; her they followed here, to their own ruin; and the Man who rides with her and the Man who rides before her are of the same face and likeness— for now and then are alike with her.

"We dream dreams, my queen and I, each after our own fashion. All else went with Morgaine."

*—A Stonē, on a barren isle of Shiuan.*

# FIRES OF AZEROTH

## by
## C. J. Cherryh

**DAW BOOKS, INC.**

DONALD A. WOLLHEIM, PUBLISHER

New York

To Audrey, who is Kurshin at heart . . .
and to Brad, who asked the right question.

FIRST PRINTING, JUNE 1979

3 4 5 6 7 8 9

 DAW TRADEMARK REGISTERED
U.S PAT. OFF. MARCA REGISTRADA.
HECHO EN U.S.A.

PRINTED IN U.S.A.

# Prologue

The qhal found the first Gate on a dead world of their own sun.

Who made it, or what befell those makers, the qhal of that age never knew or learned. Their interest was in the dazzling prospect it offered them, a means to limitless power and freedom, a means to short-cut space and leap from world to world and star to star—instantaneous travel, once qhalur ships had crossed space at real-time, to carry to each new site the technology of the Gates and establish the link. Gates were built on every qhalur world, a web of eye-blink transport, binding together a vast empire in space.

And that was their undoing . . . for Gates led not alone WHERE but WHEN, both forward and backward along the course of world's and suns.

The qhal gained power beyond their wildest imaginings: they were freed of time. They seeded worlds with gatherings from the far reaches of Gate-spanned space . . . beasts, and plants, even qhal-like species. They created beauty, and whimsy, and leaped ahead in time to see the flowerings of civilizations they had planned—while their subjects lived real years and died in normal span, barred from the freedom of the Gates.

Real-time for qhal became too tedious. The familiar present, the mundane and ordinary, assumed the shape of a confinement no qhal had to bear . . . the future promised escape. Yet once that journey forward had been made, there could be no return. It was too dangerous, too fraught with dire possibilities to open up backtime: there was the deadly risk of changing what was. Only the future was accessible . . . and qhal went.

The first venturers found pleasure for a time, learned the age and tired of it, and restlessly migrated again, stage by

5

stage, joined by their own children's children, confounding law and society. In greater and greater numbers they moved on, evading tedium, forever discontent, seeking pleasures and lingering nowhere long—until they crowded into a future where time grew strange and unstable.

Some went further, pursuing the hope of Gates which might or might not remain where they were predicted to be. More lost their courage utterly and ceased to believe in further futures, lingering until horror overwhelmed them, in a present crowded with living ancestors in greater and greater numbers. Reality began to ripple with unstable possibilities.

Perhaps some desperate soul fled back; or perhaps the very weight of extended time grew too much. Might-have-been and was were confounded. Qhal went mad, perceiving things no longer true, remembering what had never been.

Time was ripping loose about them—from ripplings to vast disturbances, the overstrained fabric of time and space undone, convulsed, imploded, hurling all their reality asunder.

Then all the qhalur worlds lay ruined. There remained only fragments of their past glory . . . stones strangely immune to time in some places, and in others suddenly and unnaturally victim to it . . . lands where civilization managed to rebuild itself, and others where all life failed, and only ruins remained.

The Gates themselves, which were outside all time and space . . . they endured.

A few qhal survived, remembering a past which had been/ might have been.

Last came humans, exploring that vast dark desert of the qhalur worlds . . . and found the Gates.

Men had been there before . . . victims of the qhal and therefore involved in the ruin; Men looked into the Gates, and feared what they saw, the power and the desolation. A hundred went out those Gates, both male and female, a force never meant to know a homecoming. There could only be forward for them: they must seal the Gates from the far side of time, one and the next and the next, destroying them, unweaving the deadly web the qhal had woven . . . to the very Ultimate Gate or the end of time.

World after world they sealed . . . but their numbers declined, and their lives grew strange, stretched over millennia of real-time. Few of them survived of the second and third generations, and some of those went mad.

*Then they began to despair that all their struggle was hopeless, for one Gate omitted would begin it all again; one Gate, anywhen misused, could bring down on them the ruin of all they had ever done.*

*In their fear, they created a weapon, indestructible save for the Gates which powered it: a thing for their own protection, and containing knowledge of Gates, all that they had gained—a doomsday force against that paradoxical Ultimate Gate, beyond which was no passage at all—or worse.*

*They were five when that Weapon was made.*

*There was one who survived to carry it.*

*"Records are pointless. There is a strange conceit in making them when we are the last—but a race should leave something. The world is going . . . and the end of the world comes, not for us, perhaps, but soon. And we have always loved monuments.*

*"Know that it was Morgaine kri Chya who wrought this ruin. Morgen-Angharan, Men named her: the White Queen, she of the white gull feather, who was the death that came on us. It was Morgaine who extinguished the last brightness in the north, who cast Ohtij-in down to ruin, and stripped the land of inhabitants.*

*"Even before this present age she was the curse of our land, for she led the Men of the Darkness, a thousand years before us; her they followed here, to their own ruin; and the Man who rides with her and the Man who rides before her are of the same face and likeness—for now and then are alike with her.*

*"We dream dreams, my queen and I, each after our own fashion. All else went with Morgaine."*

> —*A stone, on a barren isle of Shiuan.*

# Chapter One

The plain gave way to forest, and the forest closed about, but there was no stopping, not until the green shadow thickened and the setting of the sun brought a chill to the air.

Then Vanye ceased for a time to look behind him, and breathed easier for his safety . . . his and his liege's. They rode farther until the light failed indeed, and then Morgaine reined gray Siptah to a halt, in a clear space beside a brook, under an arch of old trees. It was a quiet place and pleasant, were it not for the fear which pursued them.

"We shall find no better," Vanye said, and Morgaine nodded, wearily slid down.

"I shall tend Siptah," she said as he dismounted. It was his place, to tend the horses, to make the fire, to do whatever task wanted doing for Morgaine's comfort. That was the nature of an *ilin*, who was Claimed to the service of a liege. But they had ridden hard for more than this day, and his wounds troubled him, so that he was glad of her offer. He stripped his own bay mare down to halter and tether, and rubbed her down and cared for her well, for she had done much even to last such a course as they had run these last days. The mare was in no wise a match for Morgaine's gray stud, but she had heart, and she was a gift besides. Lost, the girl who had given her to him; and he did not forget that gift, nor ever would. For that cause he took special care of the little Shiua bay—but also because he was Kurshin, of a land where children learned the saddle before their feet were steady on the earth, and it sat ill with him to use a horse as he had had to use this one.

He finished, and gathered an armload of wood, no hard task in this dense forest. He brought it to Morgaine, who had already started a small fire in tinder—and *that* was no hard task for her, by means which he preferred not to handle.

8

They were not alike, she and he: armed alike, in the fashion of Andur-Kursh—leather and mail, his brown, hers black; his mail made of wide rings and hers of links finely meshed and shining like silver, the like of which no common armorer could fashion; but he was of honest human stock, and most avowed that Morgaine was not. His eyes and hair were brown as the earth of Andur-Kursh; her eyes were pale gray and her hair was like morning frost . . . *qhal*-fair, fair as the ancient enemies of mankind, as the evil which followed them—though she denied that she was of that blood, he had his own opinions of it: it was only sure that she had no loyalty to that kind.

He carefully fed the fire she had begun, and worried about enemies the while he did so, mistrusting this land, to which they were strangers. But it was a little fire, and the forest screened them. Warmth was a comfort they had lacked in their journeyings of recent days; they were due some ease, having reached this place.

By that light, they shared the little food which remained to them . . . less concerned for their diminishing supplies than they might have been, for there was the likelihood of game hereabouts. They saved back only enough of the stale bread for the morrow, and then, for he had done most of his sleeping in the saddle—he would gladly have cast himself down to sleep, well-fed as he was, or have stood watch while Morgaine did so.

But Morgaine took that sword she bore, and eased it somewhat from sheath . . . and that purged all the sleep from him.

*Changeling* was its name, an evil name for a viler thing. He did not like to be near it, sheathed or drawn, but it was a part of her, and he had no choice. A sword it seemed, dragon-hilted, of the elaborate style that had been fashioned in Koris of Andur a hundred years before his birth . . . but the blade was edged crystal. Opal colors swirled softly in the lines of the runes which were finely etched upon it. It was not good to look at those colors, which blurred the senses. Whether it was safe to touch the blade when its power was thus damped by the sheath, he did not know nor ever care to learn—but Morgaine was never casual with it, and she was not now. She rose before she drew it fully.

It slipped the rest of the way from its sheath. Opal colors flared, throwing strange shadows about them, white light. Darkness shaped a well at the sword's tip, and into that it was even less wholesome to look. Winds howled into it, and what that darkness touched, it took. *Changeling* drew its power from Gates, and was itself a Gate, though none that anyone would choose to travel.

It forever sought its source, and glowed most brightly when aimed Gate-ward. Morgaine searched with it, and turned it full circle, while the trees sighed and the howling wind grew, the light bathing her hands and face and hair. An imprudent insect found oblivion there. A few leaves were torn from trees and whipped into that well of darkness and vanished. The blade flickered slightly east and west, lending hope; but it glowed most brightly southward, as it had constantly done, a pulsing light that hurt the eyes. Morgaine held it steadily toward that point and cursed.

"It does not change," she lamented. "It does not change."

"Please, *liyo*, put it away. It gives no better answer, and does us no good."

She did so. The wind died, the balefire winked out, and she folded the sheathed sword in her arms and settled again, bleakness on her face.

"Southward is our answer. It must be."

"Sleep," he urged her, for she had a frail and transparent look. "*Liyo*, my bones ache and I swear I shall not rest until you have slept. If you have no mercy on yourself, have some for me. Sleep."

She wiped a trembling hand across her eyes and nodded, and lay down where she was on her face, caring not even for preparing a pallet on which to rest. But he rose up quietly and took their blankets, laid one beside her and pushed her over onto it, then threw the other over her. She nestled into that with a murmur of thanks, and stirred a last time as he put her folded cloak under her head. Then she slept the sleep of the dead, with *Changeling* against her like a lover: she released it not even in sleep, that evil thing which she served.

They were, he reflected, effectively lost. Four days past, they had crossed a void the mind refused to remember, the *between* of Gates. That way was sealed. They were cut off from where they had been, and did not know in what land they now were, or what men held it—only that it was a place where Gates led, and that those Gates must be passed, destroyed, sealed.

Such was the war they fought, against the ancient magics, the *qhal*-born powers. Their journey was obsession with Morgaine, and necessity with him, who served her . . . not his concern, the reason she felt bound to such a course; his reason was his oath, which he had sworn to her in Andur-Kursh, and beyond which he had stayed. She sought now the Master Gate of this world, which was that which must be sealed; and had found it, for *Changeling* did not lie. It was the selfsame Gate by which they had entered this land, by which their enemies had entered, behind them. They had fled that place for their lives . . . by bitter irony, had fled that which they had come to this world to find, and now it was the possession of their enemies.

"It is only that we are still within the influence of the Gate we have just left," Morgaine had reasoned in the beginning of their flight northward, when the sword had first warned them. But as the distance widened between them and that power, still the sword gave the same disturbing answer, until there remained little doubt what the truth was. Morgaine had muttered things about horizons and the curving of the land, and other possibilities which he by no means comprehended; but at last she shook her head and became fixed upon the worst of her fears. It was impossible for them to have done other than flee. He tried to persuade her that; their enemies would surely have overwhelmed them. But that knowledge was no comfort to her despair.

"I shall know for certain," she had said, "if the strength of the sending does not diminish by this evening. The sword can find lesser Gates, and it is possible still that we are on the wrong side of the world or too far removed from any other. But lesser Gates do not glow so brightly. If I see it tonight as bright as last, then we shall know beyond doubt what we have done."

And thus they knew.

Vanye eased himself of some of the buckles of his armor. There was not a bone of his body which did not separately ache, but he had a cloak and a fire this night, and cover to hide him from enemies, which was better than he had known of late. He wrapped his cloak about him and set his back against an aged tree. His sword he laid naked across his knees. Lastly he removed his helm, which was wrapped about with the white scarf of the *ilin*, and set it aside, shaking free his hair and enjoying the absence of that weight. The woods were quiet about them. The water rippled over stones; the leaves sighed; the horses moved quietly at tether, cropping the little grass that grew where the trees were not. The Shiua mare was stable-bred, with no sense of enemies, useless on watch; but Siptah was a sentinel as reliable as any man, war-trained and wary of strangers, and he trusted to the gray horse as to a comrade in his watch, which made all the world less lonely. Food in his belly and warmth against the night, a stream when he should thirst and surely game plentiful for the hunting. A moon was up, a smallish one and unthreatening, and the trees sighed very like those of Andur's lost forests—it was a healing thing, when there was no way home, to find something so much like it. He would have been at peace, had *Changeling* pointed some other way.

Dawn came softly and subtly, with singing of birds and the sometime stirring of the horses. Vanye still sat, propping his head on his arm and forcing his blurred eyes to stay open, and scanned the forest in the soft light of day.

All at once Morgaine moved, reached for weapons, then blinked at him in dismay, leaning on her elbow. "What befell? Thee fell asleep on watch?"

He shook his head, shrugged off the prospect of her anger, which he had already reckoned on. "I decided not to wake you. You looked overtired."

"Is it a favor to me if you fall out of the saddle today?"

He smiled and shook his head yet again, inwardly braced against the sting of her temper, which could be hurtful. She hated to be cared for, and she was too often inclined to drive herself when she might have rested, to prove the point. It should of course be otherwise between them, *ilin* and *liyo*, servant and liege lady . . . but she refused to learn to rely on anyone . . . *expecting I shall die*, he thought, with a troubling touch of ill-omen, *as others have who have served her; she waits on that.*

"Shall I saddle the horses, *liyo?*"

She sat up, shrugged the blanket about her in the morning chill and stared at the ground, resting her hands at her temples. "I have need to think. We must go back somehow. I have need to think."

"Best you do that rested, then."

Her eyes flicked to his, and at once he regretted pricking at her—a perversity in him, who was fretted by her habits. He knew that temper surely followed, along with a sharp reminder of his place. He was prepared to bear that, as he had a hundred times and more, intended and unintended, and he simply wished it said and done. "It likely is," she said quietly, and that confounded him. "Aye, saddle the horses."

He rose and did so, troubled at heart. His own moving was painful; he limped, and there was a constant stitch in his side, a cracked rib, he thought. Doubtless she hurt too, and that was expected; bodies mended; sleep restored strength . . . but most of all he was concerned about the sudden quiet in her, his despair and yielding. They had been travelling altogether too long, at a pace which wore them to nerve and bone; no rest, never rest, world and world and world. They survived the hurts; but there were things of the soul too, overmuch of death and war, and horror which still dogged them, hunting them—to which now they had to return. Of a sudden he longed for her anger, for something he understood.

"*Liyo,*" he said when he had finished with the horses and she knelt burying the fire, covering all trace of it. He dropped down, put himself on both knees, being *ilin.* "*Liyo,* it comes to me that if our enemies are sitting where we must return, then sit they will, at least for a time; they fared no better in that passage than we. For us—*liyo,* I beg you know that I will go on as long as seems good to you, I will do everything that you ask—but I am tired, and I have wounds on me that have not healed, and it seems to me that a little rest, a few days to freshen the horses and to find game and renew our supplies—is it not good sense to rest a little?"

He pleaded his own cause; did he plead his concern for her, he thought, then that instinctive stubbornness would harden against all reason. Even so he rather more expected anger than agreement. But she nodded wearily, and further confounded him by laying a hand on his arm—a brief touch; there were rarely such gestures between them, no intimacy . . . never had been.

"We will ride the bow of the forest today," she said, "and see what game we may start, and I agree we should not overwork the horses. They deserve a little rest; their bones are showing. And you—I have seen you limping, and you work often one-armed, and still you try to take all the work from me. You would do everything if you had your way about it."

"Is that not the way it is supposed to be?"

"Many the time I have dealt unfairly with you; and I am sorry for that."

He tried to laugh, passing it off, and misliked more and more this sudden sinking into melancholy. Men cursed Morgaine, in Andur and in Kursh, in Shiuan and Hiuaj and the land between. More friends' lives than enemies' were to the account of that fell *geas* that drove her. Even him she had sacrificed on occasion; and would again; and being honest, did not pretend otherwise.

"*Liyo,*" he said, "I understand you better than you seem to think—not always *why,* but at least *what* moves you. I am only *ilin*-bound, and I can argue with the one I am bound to; but the thing you serve has no mercy at all. I know that. You are mad if you think it is only my oath that keeps me with you."

It was said; he wished then he had not said it, and rose and found work for himself tying their gear to saddles, anything to avoid her eyes.

When she came to take Siptah's reins and set herself in the saddle, the frown was there, but it was more perplexed than angry.

Morgaine kept silent in their riding, which was leisurely and followed the bendings of the stream; and the weariness of his sleepless night claimed him finally, so that he bowed his head and folded his arms about him, sleeping while they rode, Kurshin-style. She took the lead, and guarded him from branches. The sun was warm and the sighing of leaves sang a song very like the forests of Andur, as if time had bent back on itself and they rode a path they had ridden in the beginning.

Something crashed in the brush. The horses started, and he came awake at once, reaching for his sword.

"Deer." She pointed off through the woods, where the animal lay on its side.

Deer it was not, but something very like unto it, oddly dappled with gold. He dismounted with his sword in hand, having respect for the spreading antlers, but it was stone-dead when he touched it. Other weapons had Morgaine besides *Changeling,* *qhalur*-sort also, which killed silently and at distance, without apparent wound. She swung down from the saddle and gave him her skinning-knife, and he set to, minded strangely of another time, a creature which had been indeed a deer, and a winter storm in his homeland's mountains.

He shook off that thought. "Had it been to me," he said, "it would have been small game and fish and precious little of that. I must have myself a bow, *liyo.*"

She shrugged. In fact his pride was hurt, such of it as remained sensitive with her, that he had not done this, but she; yet it was her place to provide for him, her *ilin*. At times he detected hurt pride in her, that the hearth she gave him was a campfire, and the hall a canopy of branches, and food often enough scant or lacking entirely. Of all lords an *ilin* could have been ensnared to serve, Morgaine was beyond doubt the most powerful, and the poorest. The arms she provided him were plundered, the horse stolen before it was given, and their provisions likewise. They lived always like hedge-bandits. But tonight and for days afterward they would not have hunger to plague them, and he saw her slight hurt at the offense behind his words; with that he dismissed his vanity and vowed himself grateful for the gift.

It was not a place for long lingering: birds' alarm, the flight of other creatures—death in the forest announced itself. He took the best and stripped that, with swift strokes of the keen blade—skill gained in outlawry in Kursh, to hunt wolf-wary in the territories of hostile clans, to take and flee, covering his traces. So he had done, solitary, until a night he had sheltered with Morgaine kri Chya, and traded her his freedom for a place out of the wind.

He washed his hands from the bloody work, and tied the hide bundle on the saddle, while Morgaine made shift to haul the remnant into the brush. He scuffed the earth about and disposed of what sign he could. Scavengers would soon muddle the rest, covering their work, and he looked about carefully, making sure, for not all their enemies were hall-bred, men of blind eyes. One there was among them who could follow the dimmest trail, and that one he feared most of all.

That man was of clan Chya, of forested Koris in Andur, his own mother's people . . . and of his mother's close kin; it was at least the shape he lately wore.

It was an early camp, and a full-fed one. They attended to the meat which they must carry with them, drying it in the smoke of the fire and preparing it to last as long as possible. Morgaine claimed first watch, and Vanye cast himself to sleep early and wakened to his own sense of time. Morgaine had not moved to wake him, and had not intended to, he suspected, meaning to do to him what he had done to her; but she yielded her post to him without objection when he claimed it: she was not one for pointless arguments.

In his watch he sat and fed the fire by tiny pieces, making sure that the drying was proceeding as it should. The strips had hardened, and he cut a piece and chewed at it lazily.

Such leisure was almost forgotten in his life—to have a day's respite, two—to contemplate.

The horses snuffed and moved in the dark. Siptah took some interest in the little Shiua mare, which would prove difficulty did she breed; but there was no present hazard of that. The sounds were ordinary and comfortable.

A sudden snort, a moving of brush . . . he stiffened in every muscle, his heart speeding. Brush cracked: that was the horses.

He moved, ignoring bruises to rise in utter silence, and with the tip of his sword reached to touch Morgaine's out-flung hand.

Her eyes opened, fully aware in an instant; met his, which slid in the direction of the small sound he had sensed more than heard. The horses were still disturbed.

She gathered herself, silent as he; and stood, a black shape in the embers' glow, with her white hair making her all too much a target. Her hand was not empty. That small black weapon which had killed the deer was aimed toward the sound, but shield it was not. She gathered up *Changeling*, better protection, and he gripped his sword, slipped into the darkness; Morgaine moved, but in another direction, and vanished.

Brush stirred. The horses jerked madly at tethers of a sudden and whinned in alarm. He slipped through a stand of saplings and something he had taken for a piece of scrub . . . moved: a dark spider-shape, that chilled him with its sudden life. He went farther, trying to follow its movements, cautious not least because Morgaine was a-hunt the same as he.

Another shadow: that was Morgaine. He stood still, mindful that hers was a distance-weapon, and deadly accurate; but she was not one to fire blindly or in panic. They met, and crouched still a moment. No sound disturbed the night now but the shifting of the frightened horses.

No beast: he signed to her with his straight palm that it had gone upright, and touched her arm, indicating that they should return to the fireside. They went quickly, and he killed the fire while she gathered their provisions. Fear was coppery in his mouth, the apprehension of ambush possible, and the urgency of flight. Blankets were rolled, the horses saddled, the whole affair of their camp undone with silent and furtive movements. Quickly they were in the saddle and moving by dark, on a different track: no following a spy in the moonless dark, to find that he had friends.

Still the memory of that figure haunted him, the eerie movement which had tricked his eye and vanished. "Its gait was strange," he said, when they were far from that place and able to talk. "As if it were unjointed."

What Morgaine thought of that, he could not see. "There are more than strange beasts where Gates have led," she said.

But they saw nothing more astir in the night. Day found them far away, on a streamcourse which was perhaps different from the one of the night before, perhaps not. It bent in leisurely windings, so that branches screened this way and that in alternation, a green curtain constantly parting and closing as they rode.

Then, late, they came upon a tree with a white cord tied about its trunk, an old and dying tree, lightning-riven.

Vanye stopped at the evidence of man's hand hereabouts, but Morgaine tapped Siptah with her heels and they went a little farther, to a place where a trail crossed their stream.

Wheels rutted that stretch of muddy earth.

To his dismay Morgaine turned off on that road. It was not her custom to seek out folk who could as easily be left undisturbed by their passing . . . but she seemed minded now to do so.

"Wherever we are," she said at last, "if these are gentle people we owe them warning for what we have brought behind us. And if otherwise, then we shall look them over and see what trouble we can devise for our enemies."

He said nothing to that. It seemed as reasonable a course as any, for two who were about to turn and pursue thousands, and those well-armed, and many horsed, and in possession of power enough to unhinge the world through which they rode.

Conscience: Morgaine claimed none . . . not altogether truth, but near enough the mark. The fact was that in that blade which hung on the saddle beneath her knee, Morgaine herself had some small share of that power, and therefore it was not madness which led her toward such a road, but a certain ruthlessness.

He went, because he must.

# Chapter Two

There were signs of habitation, of the hand of some manner of men, all down the road: the ruts of wheels, the cloven-hoofed prints of herded beasts, the occasional snag of white wool on a roadside branch. *This is the way their herds come to water*, Vayne reasoned. *There must be some open land hereabouts for their grazing.*

It was late, that softest part of afternoon, when they came upon the center of it all.

It was a village which might, save for its curving roofs, have occupied some forest edge in Andur; and a glamour of forest sunlight lay over it, shaded as its roofs were by old trees, a gold-green warmth that hazed the old timbers and the thatched roofs. It was almost one with the forest itself, save for the fanciful carving of the timbers under the eaves, which bore faded colors. It was a cozy huddle of some thirty buildings, with no walls for defense . . . cattle pens and a cart or two, a dusty commons, a large hall of thatch and timbers and carved beams, no proper lord's hold, but rustic and wide-doored and mainly windowed.

Morgaine stopped on the road and Vanye drew in beside her. A boding of ill came on him, and of regret. "Such a place," he said, "must have no enemies."

"It will have," said Morgaine, and moved Siptah forward.

Their approach brought a quiet stirring in the village, a cluster of dusty children who looked up from their play and stared, a woman who looked out a window and came out of doors drying her hands on her skirts, and two old men who came out of the hall and waited their coming. Younger men and an old woman joined that pair, with a boy of about fifteen and a workman in a leather apron. More elders

18

gathered. Solemnly they stood, . . . human folk, dark-skinned and small of stature.

Vanye looked nervously between the houses and among the trees that stood close behind, and across the wide fields which lay beyond in the vast clearing. He scanned the open windows and doors, the pens and the carts, seeking some ambush. There was nothing. He kept his hand on the hilt of his sword, which rode at his side; but Morgaine had her hands free and in sight . . . all peaceful she seemed, and gracious. He did not scruple to look suspiciously on everything.

Morgaine reined in before the little cluster that had gathered before the hall steps. All the folk bowed together, as gracefully and solemnly as lords, and when they looked up at her, their faces held wonder, but no hint of fear.

*Ah, mistrust us,* Vanye wished them. *You do not know what has come among you.* But nothing but awe touched those earnest faces, and the eldest of them bowed again, and addressed them.

Then Vanye's heart froze in him, for it was the *qhalur* tongue that these Men spoke.

*Arrhthein,* they hailed Morgaine, which was *my lady;* little by little as they rode, Morgaine had insisted to teach him, until he knew words of courtesies and threat and necessities. Not *qhal* in any case, these small dark folk, so courteous of manner . . . but the Old Ones were clearly reverenced here, and therefore they welcomed Morgaine, taking her for *qhal,* which she was to the eye.

He reasoned away his shock: there was a time his Kurshin soul would have shuddered to hear that language on human lips, but now it passed his own. The speech was current, Morgaine had persuaded him, wherever *qhal* had been, in whatever lands Gates led to, and it had lent many words to his own language—which disturbed him to realize. That these folk spoke it nearly pure . . . that amazed him. *Khemeis,* they addressed him, which sounded like *kheman:* accompany . . . *Companion,* perhaps, for *my lord* he was not, not where *qhal* were honored.

"Peace," he bade them softly in that language, the appropriate greeting; and "How may we please you and your lady?" they asked in all courtesy, but he could not answer, only understand.

Morgaine spoke with them, and they with her; after a moment she looked across at him. "Dismount," she said in the *qhalur* tongue. "Here are friendly people." But that was

surely for show and for courtesy; he dismounted as she ordered him, but he did not let down his guard or intend to
leave her back unguarded. He stood with arms folded, where
he could both see those to whom she spoke and keep a furtive watch on the others who began to join the crowd—too
many people and too close for his liking, although none of
them seemed unfriendly.

Some of what was said he followed; Morgaine's teaching
with him had encompassed enough that he knew they were
being welcomed and offered food. The accent was a little different than Morgaine's, but no worse than the shift from Andurin to Kurshin in his mother tongue.

"They offer us hospitality," Morgaine said, "and I am
minded to take it, at least for tonight. There is no immediate
threat here that I can see."

"As you will, *liyo*."

She gestured toward a handsome lad of about ten. "He is
Sin, the elder Bythein's grandnephew. He is offered to care
for the horses, but I had rather you did that and simply let
him help you."

She meant to go among them alone, then. He was not
pleased at that prospect, but she had done worse things, and,
armed, she was of the two of them the more dangerous, a
fact which most misjudged. He took *Changeling* from her
saddle and gave it to her, and gathered up the reins of both
horses.

"This way, *khemeis*," the boy bade him; and while Morgaine went into the hall with the elders, the boy walked with
him toward the pens, trying to match his man's strides and
gawking at him like any village lad unused to arms and
strangers . . . perhaps amazed also at his lighter complexion
and his height, which must seem considerable to these small
folk. No man in the village reached more than his shoulder,
and few that much. Perhaps, he thought, they reckoned him
halfling *qhal*, no honor to him, but he did not mean to dispute it with them.

The boy Sin chattered at him busily when he reached the
pens and began to unsaddle the horses, but it was conversation all in vain with him. Finally the realization seemed to
dawn upon Sin, who asked him yet another question.

"I am sorry; I do not understand," he answered, and the
boy squinted up at him, stroking the mare's neck under her
mane.

"*Khemeis?*" the boy asked of him.

He could not explain. *I am a stranger here,* he could say; or *I am of Andur-Kursh;* or other words, which he did not intend to have known. It seemed wisest to leave all such accountings to Morgaine, who could listen to these people and choose what to reveal and what to conceal and argue out their misconceptions.

"Friend," he said, for he could say that too, and Sin's face lighted and a grin spread across it.

"Yes," Sin said, and fell to currying the bay mare with zeal. Whatever Vanye showed him, Sin was eager to do, and his thin features glowed with pleasure when Vanye smiled and tried to show satisfaction with his work . . . a good folk, an open-handed people, Vanye thought, and felt the safer in their lodgings. "Sin," he said, having composed his sentence carefully, "you take care for the horses. Agreed?"

"I shall sleep here," Sin declared, and adoration burned in his dark eyes. "I shall care for them, for you and for the lady."

"Come with me," Vanye told him, slinging their gear on his shoulder, saddlebags which held things they needed for the night, and food that might draw animals, and Morgaine's saddle kit, which was nothing to be left to the curiosity of others. He was pleased in the company of the boy, who had no shyness or lack of patience in speaking with him. He set his hand on Sin's shoulder and the boy swelled visibly with importance under the eyes of the other children, who watched from a distance. They walked together back to the hall, and up the wooden steps to the inside.

It was a high-raftered place, the center filled with a long row of tables and benches, a place for feasts; and there was a grand fireplace, and light from the many wide windows which—like the unwalled condition of the village—betokened a place that had never taken thought for its defense. Morgaine sat there, a bit of pallor black-clad and glittering with silver mail in the dusty light, surrounded by villagers both male and female, young and old, some on benches and some at her feet. At the edge of that circle mothers rocked children on their laps, keeping them still, themselves seeming curious to listen.

Way was made for him, folk edging this way and that to let him through at once. He found a bench offered him, when his place was sitting on the floor, but he took it; and Sin managed to work eelwise to his feet and settle there against his knee.

Morgaine looked at him. "They offer us welcome and whatever we have need of, equipage or food. They seem most amazed by you; they cannot conceive of your origins, tall and different as you are; and they are somewhat alarmed that we go so heavily armed . . . but I have explained to them that you entered my service in a far country."

"There are surely *qhal* here."

"I would surmise so. But if that is the case, they must not be hostile to these folk." She made her voice gentle then, and lapsed back into the *qhalur* tongue. "Vanye, these are the elders of the village: Sersein and her man Serseis; Bythein and Bytheis; Melzein and Melzeis. They say that we may shelter in this hall tonight."

He inclined his head, assenting and offering respect to their hosts.

"For now," Morgaine added in Andurin, "I only ask questions of them. I counsel thee the same."

"I have said nothing."

She nodded, and speaking to the elders, turned again to the *qhalur* language, with fluency he could not follow.

It was a strange meal they took that night, with the hall aglow with torches and with firelight from the hearth, and the board laden with abundance of food, the benches crowded with villagers young and old. It was the custom here, Morgaine explained, that all the village take the evening meal together as if they were one house, as indeed was the custom of Ra-koris in Andur, but here even children attended, and played recklessly among their elders, suffered to speak at table with abandon that would have fetched a Kurshin child, be he lord's son or peasant, a ringing ear and a stern march outside to a more thorough chastisement. Children here filled their bellies and then slid down from table to play noisily in the pillared wings of the hall, laughing and shouting above the roar of conversation.

It was not, at least, a hall where one feared an assassin's knife or poison. Vanye sat at Morgaine's right—an *ilin* should stand behind, and he would rather have tasted the food that she was offered to be certain, all the same; but Morgaine forbade that, and he gave up his apprehensions. In the pen outside, the horses fed on good hay, and they sat in this bright, warm hall amid folk who seemed more inclined to kill them by overfeeding than by ill will. When at last no one could eat any more, the children who did not wish to be quiet were cheerfully dismissed into the dark outside, the oldest of that company leading the youngest, and there seemed no thought in any one that the children might be in any danger in the dark outdoors. Within the hall, a girl began to play on a tall, strangely tuned harp, and sang beautifully with it. There was a second song which everyone sang, save themselves; and then they were offered the harp as well—but playing was long-past for him. His fingers had forgotten whatever childish skill they had once had, and he refused it, embarrassed. Morgaine also declined; if there was ever a time when she had had leisure to learn music, he could not imagine it.

But Morgaine spoke with them instead, and they seemed pleased by what she said. There followed a little discussion, in which he could not share, before the girl sang one last song.

Then dinner was done, and the villagers went their own way to beds in their houses, while oldest children were quick to make their guests a place nearest the fire . . . two pallets and a curtain for privacy, and a kettle of warm water for washing.

The last of the children went down the outside steps and Vanye drew a long breath, in this first solitude they had enjoyed since riding in. He saw Morgaine unbuckle her armor, ridding herself of that galling weight, which she did not do on the trail or in any chancy lodging. If she were so inclined, he felt himself permitted, and gratefully stripped down to shirt and breeches, washed behind the curtain and dressed again, for he did not utterly trust the place. Morgaine did likewise; and they settled down with their weapons near them, to sleep alternately.

His watch was first, and he listened well for any stirring in the village, went to the windows and looked out on this side and on the other, on the forest and the moonlit fields, but there was no sign of movement, nor were the village windows all shuttered. He went back and settled at the hearth in the warmth, and began to accept finally that all this bewildering gentleness was true and honest.

It was rare in all their journeying that there awaited them no curse, no hedge of weapons, but only kindness.

Here Morgaine's name was not yet known.

The morning brought a smell of baking bread, and the stir of folk about the hall, a scatter of children who were hushed to quiet. "Perhaps," Vanye murmured, smelling that pleasant aroma of baking, "a bit of hot bread to send us on our way."

"We are not going," Morgaine said, and he looked at her in bewilderment, not knowing whether this was good news or ill. "I have thought things through, and you may be right: here is a place where we can draw breath, and if we do not rest in it, then what else can we do but kill the horses under us and drive ourselves beyond our strength? There is no surety beyond any Gate. Should we win through—to another hard ride, and lose everything for want of what we might have gathered here? Three days. We can rest that long. I think your advice is good sense."

"Then you make me doubt it. You have never listened to me, and we are alive, all odds to the contrary."

She laughed humorlessly. "Aye, but I have; and as for my own plans, some of the best of those have gone amiss at the worst of times. I have ignored your advice sometimes at our peril, and this time I take it. I reckon our chances even."

They broke fast, served by grave-faced children who brought them some of that hot bread, and fresh milk and sweet butter besides. They ate as if they had had nothing the night before, for such a breakfast was not a luxury that belonged to outlawry.

Three days went too quickly; and the courtesy and gentleness of the folk brought something that Vanye would have given much to see: for Morgaine's gray eyes grew clean of that pain which had ridden there so long, and she smiled and sometimes laughed, softly and merrily.

The horses fared as well: they rested, and the children brought them handfuls of sweet grass, and petted them, and combed their manes and curried them with such zeal that Vanye found nothing to do for them but a bit of smithing— in which the village smith was all too willing to assist, with his forge and his skill.

Whenever he was at the pens with the horses, the children, particularly Sin, hung over the rails and chattered merrily to him, trying to ask him questions of the animals and Morgaine and himself, little of which he even understood.

"Please, *khemeis* Vanye," said Sin, when he leaned to rest on the edge of the watering-keg, "please may we see the weapons?" At least so he put the words together.

He recalled his own boyhood, when he had watched in awe the *dai-uyin*, the high-clan gentlemen with their armor and their horses and weapons . . . but with the bitter knowledge of bastardy, which—for he had been a lord's bastard, gotten on a captive—made the attainment of such things desperate necessity. These were only village children, whose lives did not tend toward arms and wars, and their curiosity was that which they might hold toward the moon and stars . . . something remote from them, and untainted by understanding.

"Avert," he murmured in his own tongue, wishing harm from them, and unhooked the side ring of his sheathed sword, slipped it to his hand. He drew it, and let their grimy fingers touch the blade, and he let Sin—which filled the boy with delight—hold the hilt in his own hand and try the balance of it. But then he took it back, for he did not like the look of children with such a grim thing, that had so much blood on it.

Then, pointing, they asked to see the other blade that he carried, and he frowned and shook his head, laying his hand on that carven hilt at his belt. They cajoled, and he would not, for an Honor-blade was not for their hands. It was for suicide, this one, and it was not his, but one he carried, on his oath to deliver it.

"An *elarrh* thing," they concluded, in tones of awe; and he had not the least idea of their meaning, but they ceased asking, and showed no more desire to touch it.

"Sin," he said, thinking to draw a little knowledge from the children, "do men with weapons come here?"

At once there was puzzlement on Sin's face and in the eyes of the others, down to the least child. "You are not of *our* forest," Sin observed, and used the plural *you*—surmise which shot all too directly to the mark. Vanye shrugged, cursing his rashness, which had betrayed him even to children. They knew the conditions of their own land, and had sense enough to find out a stranger who knew not what he should.

"Where are you from?" a little girl asked. And, wide-eyed, with a touch of delicious horror: "Are you *sirren?*"

Others decried that suggestion in outrage, and Vanye, conscious of his helplessness in their small hands, bowed his head and busied himself hooking his sword to his belt. He pulled on the ring of the belt that crossed his chest, drawing the sword to his shoulder behind, hooked it to his side. Then: "I have business," he said, and walked away. Sin made to follow. "Please no," he said, and Sin fell back, looking troubled and thoughtful, which in no wise comforted him.

He walked back to the hall, and there found Morgaine, sit-

ting with the clan elders and with some of the young men
and women who had stayed from their day's work to attend
her. Quietly he approached, and they made place for him as
before. For a long time he sat listening to the talk that flowed
back and forth between Morgaine and the others, understanding occasional small sentences, or the gist of them. Morgaine
sometimes interrupted herself to give him an essential
word—strange conversation for her, for they spoke much of
their crops, and their livestock and their woods, of all the affairs of their village.

*Like,* he thought, *a village discussing with its lord their
state of affairs.* Yet she accepted this, and listened more than
she spoke, as was ever her habit.

At last the villagers took their leave, and Morgaine settled
next the fire and relaxed a time. Then he came and rested on
his knees before her, embarrassed by what he had to confess,
that he had betrayed them to children.

She smiled when he had told her. "So. Well, I do not think
it much harm. I have not been able to learn much of how
*qhal* may be involved in this land, but, Vanye, there are
things here so strange I hardly see how we could avoid re-
vealing ourselves as strangers."

"What does *elarrh* mean?"

"It comes from *arrh,* that is *noble,* or *ar,* that is *power.*
The words are akin, and it could be either, depending on the
situation . . . either or both: for when one addressed a *qhal-
lord* in the ancient days as *arrhtheis,* it meant both his status
as a *qhal* and the power he had. To Men in those days, all
*qhal* had to be *my lord,* and the power in question was that
of the Gates, which were always free to them, and never to
Men . . . it has that distressing meaning too. *Elarrh* something belonging to power, or to lords. A thing—of reverence
or hazard. A thing which . . . Men do not touch."

*Qhalur* thoughts disturbed him, the more he comprehended
the *qhalur* tongue. Such arrogance was hateful . . . and other
things Morgaine had told him, which he had never guessed,
of *qhalur* maneuverings with human folk, things which hinted
at the foundations of his own world, and those disturbed him
utterly. There was much more, he suspected, which she dared
not tell him. "What will you say to these folk," he asked,
"and when—about the trouble we have brought on their
land? *Liyo,* what do they reckon we are, and what do they
think we are doing among them?"

She frowned, leaned forward, arms on knees. "I suspect

that they reckon us both *qhal*, you perhaps halfling, . . . but after what fashion or with what feeling I can find no delicate means to ask. Warn them? I wish to. But I would likewise know what manner of thing we shall awaken here when I do so. These are gentle folk; all that I have seen and heard among them confirms that. But what defends them . . . may not be."

It well agreed with his own opinion, that they trod a fragile place, safe in it, but perilously ignorant, and enmeshed in something that had its own ways.

"Be careful always what you say," she advised him. "When you speak in the Kurshin tongue, beware of using names they might know, whatever the language. But henceforth you and I should speak in their language constantly. You must gather what you can of it. It is a matter of our safety, Vanye."

"I am trying to do that," he said. She nodded approval, and they occupied themselves the rest of the day in walking about the village and the edge of the fields, talking together, impressing in his memory every word that could be forced there.

He had expected that Morgaine would choose to leave by the next morning, and she did not; and when that night came and he asked her would they leave on the morrow, she shrugged and in talking of something else, never answered the question. By the day after that, he did not ask, but took his ease in the village and settled into its routine, as Morgaine seemed to have done.

It was a healing quiet, as if the long nightmare that lay at their backs were illusion, and this sunny place were true and real. There was no word from Morgaine of leaving, as if by saying nothing she could wish away all hazard to them and their hosts.

But conscience worried at him, for the days they spent grew to many more than a handful. And he dreamed once, when they slept side by side—both slept, for sitting watch seemed unnecessary in the center of so friendly a place: he came awake sweating, and slept again, and wakened a second time with an outcry that sent Morgaine reaching for her weapons.

"Bad dreams in such a place as this?" she asked him. "There have been places with more reason for them."

But she looked concerned that night too, and lay staring into the fire long afterward. What the dream had been he could not clearly remember, only that there seemed something as sinister in his recollection as the creeping of a serpent on a nest, and he could not prevent it.

*These folk will haunt me,* he thought wretchedly. They two had no place here, and knew it; and yet selfishly lingered, out of time and place, seeking a little peace . . . taking it as a thief might take, stealing it from its possessors. He wondered whether Morgaine harbored the same guilt . . . or whether she had passed beyond it, being what she was, and impelled by the need to survive.

He was almost moved to argue it with her then; but a dark mood was on her, and he knew those. And when he faced her in the morning, there were folk about them; and later he put it off again, for when he faced the matter, the odds against them outside this place were something he had no haste to meet: Morgaine was gathering forces, and was not ready, and he was loath to urge her with arguments . . . when the *geas* fell on her, she passed beyond reason; and he did not want to be the one to start it.

So he bided, mending harness, working at arrows for a bow which he traded of a villager who was an excellent bowyer. It was offered free, once admired, but in his embarrassment Morgaine intervened with the offer of a return gift, a gold ring of strange workmanship, which must have lain buried in her kit a very long time. He was disturbed at that, suspecting that it might have meant something to her, but she laughed and said that it was time she left it behind.

So he had the bow, and the bowyer a ring that was the envy of his companions. He practiced his archery with the young folk and with Sin, who dogged his tracks faithfully, and strove to do everything that he did.

In the pen and agraze on the grassy margin of the fields, the horses grew sleek and lazy as the village's own cattle . . . and Morgaine, always the one who could not rest in an hour's delay, sat long hours in the sun and talked with the elders and the young herders, drawing on a bit of goatskin what became a great marvel to the villagers, who had never seen a map. Though they had the knowledge of which it grew, they had never seen their world set forth in such a perspective.

Mirrind, the village was named; and the plain beyond the forest was Azeroth; the forest was Shathan. In the center of the great circle that was Azeroth, she drew a skein of rivers, feeding a great river called the Narn; amid that circle also was written *athatin*, which was *the Fires*—or plainly said, the Gate of the World.

So peaceful Mirrind knew of the Gate, and held it in awe: *Azerothen Athatin*. Thus far their knowledge of the world did extend. But Morgaine did not question them on it closely. She made her map and lettered it in *qhalur* runes, a fine fair hand.

Vanye learned such runes . . . as he learned the spoken language. He sat on the step of the meeting hall and traced the symbols in the dust, learning them by writing all the new words that he had learned, and trying to forget the scruples in such things that came of being Kurshin. The children of Mirrind, who thronged him when he would tend the horses or who had such zeal to fetch his arrows that he feared for their safety, quickly found this exercise tedious and deserted him.

"*Elarrh*-work," they pronounced it, which meant anything that was above them. They had awe of it, but when there was no amusement to come of it, and no pictures, they drifted away—all but Sin, who squatted barefoot in the dust and tried to copy.

Vanye looked up at the lad, who worked so intently, and poignant recollection stirred in him, of himself, who had never been taught, but that he had sought it, who had insisted on having the things his legitimate brothers were born to have—and thereby gained what learning his mountain home could offer.

Now among all the children of Mirrind, here sat one who reached and wanted beyond the others, and who—when they had taken their leave—would be most hurt, having learned to desire something Mirrind could not give. The boy had no parents; they had died in some long-ago calamity. He had not asked into it. Sin was everyone's child, and no one's in particular. *The others will be only ordinary,* he thought, *but what of this one?* Remembering his sword in Sin's small hand, he felt a chill, and blessed himself.

"What do you, *khemeis?*" Sin asked.

"I wish you well." He rubbed out the runes with his palm and rose up, with a great heaviness on him.

Sin looked at him strangely, and he turned to go up the steps of the hall. There was a sudden outcry somewhere down Mirrind's single street . . . not the shrieks of playing children, which were frequent, but a woman's outcry; and in sud-

den apprehension he turned. Hard upon it came the shouting
of men, in tones of grief and anger.

He hesitated, his pulse that had seemed to stop now quick-
ening into familiar panic; he hung between that direction and
Morgaine's, paralyzed in the moment, and then habit and
duty sent him running up the steps to the shadowy hall,
where Morgaine was speaking with two of the elders.

He needed not explain: *Changeling* was in her hand and
she was coming, near to running.

Sin lingered at the bottom of the steps, and tagged after
them as they walked the commons toward the gathering knot
of villagers. The sound of weeping reached them . . . and
when Morgaine arrived the gathering gave way for her, all
but a few: the elders Melzein and Melzeis, who stood trying
to hold back their tears; and a young woman and a couple in
middle years who knelt holding their dead. To and fro they
rocked, keening and shaking their heads.

"Eth," Morgaine murmured, staring down at a young man
who had been one of the brightest and best of the village:
hardly in his twenties, Eth of clan Melzen, but skilled in
hunting and archery, a happy man, a herder by trade, who
had laughed much and loved his young wife and had no enemies. His throat had been cut, and on his half-naked body
were other wounds that could not have brought death in
themselves, but would have caused great pain before he was
killed.

*They gave him his death,* Vanye thought fearfully. *He
must have told them what they wanted.* Then he reckoned
what kind of man he had become, who could think foremost
of that. He had known Eth. He found himself trembling and
close to being sick as if he had never looked on the like.

Some of the children were sick, and clung to their parents
crying. He found Sin against his side, and set his hand on the
boy's shoulder, drew him over to his clan elders and gave him
into their care. Bytheis took Sin in his arms and Sin's face
was still set and stricken.

"Should the children look on this?" Morgaine asked, shock-
ing them from their daze. "You are in danger. Set armed
men out on the road and all about the village and let them
watch. Where was he found? Who brought him?"

One of the youths stepped forward—Tal, whose clothes
were bloody and his hands likewise. "I, lady. Across the
ford." Tears ran down his face. "Who has done this? Lady—
*why?*"

Council met in the hall, the while the Melzen kindred prepared the body of their son for burial; and there was unbearable heaviness in the air. Bythein and Bytheis wept quietly; but Sersen-clan was angry in its grief, and its elders were long in gathering the self-possession to speak. The silence waited on them, and at last the old man of the pair rose and walked to and fro across the fireside.

"We do not understand," he cried at last, his wrinkled hands trembling as he gestured. "Lady, will you not answer me? You are not our lady, but we have welcomed you as if you were, you and your *khemeis*. There is nothing in the village we would deny you. But now do you ask a life of us and not explain?"

"Serseis," Bytheis objected, his old voice quavering, and he put a hand on Serseis' sleeve to restrain him.

"No, I am listening," Morgaine said.

"Lady," said Serseis, "Eth went where you sent him: so say all the young folk. And you bade him not tell his elders, and he obeyed you. *Where* did you send him? He was not *khemeis;* he was his parents' only child; he never went to that calling. But did you not sense that the desire was in him? His pride made him take risks for you. To what did you send him? May we not know? And who has done so terrible a thing?"

"Strangers," she answered. Not all the words could Vanye understand, but he understood most, and filled in the rest well enough. At the feelings which gathered in the air of this hall now, he stood close to Morgaine. *Shall I get the horses?* he had asked her in his own tongue, before this council met. *No,* she had answered, with such distraction that he knew she pulled both ways, with anxiety to be moving and guilt for Mirrind's danger. She lingered, and knew better; and he knew better, and sweat gathered on his sides and trickled under the armor. "We had hoped they would not come here."

"From where?" Sersein asked. The old woman laid her hand on the rolled map that lay atop the table, Morgaine's work. "Your questions search all the land, as if you are looking for something. You are not our lady. Your *khemeis* is not of our village nor even of our blood. From some far land you surely come, my lady. Is it a place where things like this are common? And did you expect such a thing when you sent Eth out against it? Perhaps you have reasons that are too high for us, but, o lady, if it takes the lives of our children—

and you knew—could you not have told us? And will you
not tell us now? Make us understand."

There was utter stillness for a time in which could be
heard the fire, and from somewhere outside the bleating of a
goat, and the crying of a baby. The shocked faces of the
elders seemed frozen in the cold light from the many windows.

"There are," Morgaine said at last, "enemies abroad; and
they are spread throughout Azeroth. We watch here and rest,
and through your young men, I have kept watch over you as
best I could . . . for your young folk know these woods far
better than we. Yes, we are strangers here; but we are not of
their kind, that would do such a thing. We hoped to have
warning—not a warning such as this. Eth was the one—as
you say—who ranged farthest and risked himself most. I
knew this. I warned him. I warned him urgently."

Vanye bit his lip and his heart beat painfully in anger that
Morgaine had said nothing of this to him . . . for he would
have gone, and come back not as Eth did. She had sent inno-
cents out instead, boys who little knew what quarry they
might start from cover.

But the elders sat silent now, afraid more than angry, and
hung on her words.

"Do none," asked Morgaine, "ever come from Azeroth?"

"You would best know that," Bythein whispered.

"Well, it has happened," Morgaine said. "And you are near
to the plain, and there are Men massed there, strangers,
armed and minded to take all the plain of Azeroth and all
the land round about. They could have gone in any direction,
but they have chosen this one. They are thousands. Vanye
and I are not enough to stop them. What befell Eth was the
handiwork of their outriders, seeking what they could find;
and now they have found it. I have only bitter advice to give
now. Take your people and walk away from Mirrind; go
deep into the forest and hide there; and if the enemies come
farther, then flee again. Better to lose houses than lives; better
to live that way than to serve men who would do what was
done to Eth. You do not fight; and therefore you must run."

"Will you lead us?" Bythein asked.

So simple, so instant of belief: Vanye's heart turned in
him, and Morgaine sadly shook her head.

"No. We go our own way, and best for you and for us if
you forget that we have ever been among you."

They bowed their heads, one after the other, and looked as if their world had ended . . . indeed it had.

"We shall mourn more than Eth," said Serseis.

"This night you will rest here," said Sersein. "Please."

"We ought not."

"Please. Only tonight. If you are here, we shall be less afraid."

It was truer than Sersein might understand, that Morgaine had power to protect them; and to Vanye's surprise, Morgaine bowed her head and consented.

And within the same degree of the sun, there was renewed mourning in Mirrind, as the elders told the people what they had learned and what was advised them to do.

"They are naive people," said Vanye heavily. "*Liyo*, I fear for what will become of them."

"If they are simple enough to believe me utterly, they may live. But it will be different here." She shook her head and turned away for the inside of the hall, for there came the women and children down the midst of the commons, to begin the preparation of the evening meal.

Vanye went to the horses, and made sure that all was in readiness for the morning. He was alone when he went, but when he reached the gate, he heard someone behind him, and it was Sin.

"Let me go where you go," Sin asked of him. "Please."

"No. You have kin who will need you. Think of that and be glad that you have them. If you went where we go, you would never see them again."

"You will never come back to us?"

"No. Not likely."

It was direct and cruel, but it was needful. He did not want to think of the boy building dreams about him, who least deserved them. He had encouraged him too much already. He made his face grim, and attended to his work, in the hope that the boy would grow angry and go away.

But Sin joined him and helped him as he always had; and Vanye found it impossible to be hard with him. He set Sin finally on Mai's back, which was Sin's constant hope, whenever they would take the horses out to graze, and Sin stroked the mare's neck, and suddenly burst into tears, which he tried to hide.

He waited until the boy had stopped his crying, and helped him down again, and they walked together back to the hall.

Dinner was a mournful time. There were no songs, for they had buried Eth at sundown and they had no heart for singing. There was only hushed conversation and few even had appetite, but there were no animosities, no resentment shown them, not even by Eth's closest kin.

Morgaine spoke to the people in the midst of dinner, in a hush in which not even a child cried: babes slept in arms, exhausted by the day's madness, and there was a silence on all the children.

"Again I advise you to leave," she said. "At least tonight and every day hereafter, have your young men on guard, and do what you can to hide the road that leads here. Please believe me and go from this place. What Vanye and I can do to delay the evil, we will do, but they are thousands, and have horses and arms, and they are both *qhal* and Men."

Faces were stricken, the elders themselves undone by this, which she had never told them. Bythein rose, leaning on her staff. "What *qhal* would wish us harm?"

"Believe that these would. They are strangers in the land, and cruel, even more than the Men. Do not resist them; flee them. They are too many for you. They passed the Fires out of their own land, that was ruined and drowning, and they came here to take yours."

Bythein moaned aloud, and sank down again, and seemed ill. Bytheis comforted her, and all clan Bythen stirred in their seats, anxious for their elder.

"This is an evil we have never seen," said Bythein when she had recovered herself. "Lady, we understand then why you were reluctant to speak to us. *Qhal!* Ah, lady, what a thing is this?"

Vanye filled his cup with the ale that Mirrind brewed and drank it down, trying with that to wash the tautness from his throat . . . for he had not shaped what followed them and now threatened Mirrind, but he had had his hand on it while it formed, and he could not rid himself of the conviction that somehow he might have turned it aside.

One thing of certainty he might have done, and that regarded the Honor-blade which he carried, a kinslaying that might have averted all this grief. In pity, in indecision, he had not done it. To save his life, he had not.

And Morgaine: indeed she had launched what pursued them, more than a thousand years ago as Men reckoned time . . . men who had not trespassed in Gates. Her allies once, that army that followed them—the children's children of men that she had led.

There was much that wanted drowning this night. He would have gotten himself drunk, but he was too prudent for that, and the time was too hazardous for self-indulgence. He stopped short of it, and, likewise in prudence, ate—for the wolves were at their heels once more, and a man ought to eat, who never knew whether the next day's flight would give him leisure for it.

Morgaine too ate all that was set before her, and that, the same as his, he thought, was not appetite but common sense. She survived well . . . it was a gift of hers.

And when the hall was clear, she gathered up what supplies they could possibly carry, and made two packs of it . . . more than to distribute the weight: it was their constant fear that they could be separated, or one fall and the other have to continue. They carried no necessity solely on one horse.

"Sleep," she urged him when he would have stood watch.

"Trust them?"

"Sleep lightly."

He arranged his sword by him, and she lay down with *Changeling* in her arm . . . unarmored, as they had both slept unarmored since the first night in Mirrind.

# Chapter Three

Something moved outside. Vanye heard it, but it was like the wind, stirring the trees, and did not repeat itself. He laid his head down again and shut his eyes, drifted finally back to sleep.

Then came a second sound, a creak of boards; and Morgaine moved. He flung himself over and came up with his sword in hand before his eyes were even clear; Morgaine stood beside him, doubtless armed, confronting what suddenly appeared as three men.

And not Men. *Qhal.*

Tall and thin they were, with white hair flowing to their shoulders; and they bore that cast of features that was so like Morgaine's, delicate and fine. They carried no weapons and did not threaten, and they were not of that horde that had come through at Azeroth: there was nothing of that taint about them.

Morgaine stood easier. *Changeling* was in her hand, but she had not unsheathed it. Vanye straightened from his crouch and grounded his blade before him.

"We do not know you," said one of the *qhal.* "The Mirrindim say that your name is Morgaine and your *khemeis'* is Vanye. These names are strange to us. They say that you send their young men into the forest hunting strangers. And one of them is dead. How shall we understand these things?"

"You are friends of the Mirrindim?" Morgaine asked.

"Yes. Who are you?"

"Long to tell; but these folk have welcomed us and we would not harm them. Do you care to protect them?"

"Yes."

"Then guide them away from this place. It is no longer safe for them."

There was a moment's silence. "Who are these strangers? And who, again, are you?"

"I do not know to whom I am speaking, my lord *qhal.* Evidently you are peaceloving, since you come empty-handed; evidently you are a friend of the Mirrindim, since they raised no alarm; and therefore I should be willing to trust you. But call the elders of the village and let them urge me to trust you, and then I may answer some of your questions."

"I am Lir," said the *qhal,* and bowed slightly. "And we are where we belong, but you are not. You have no authority to do what you have done, or to tell the Mirrindim to leave their village. If you would travel Shathan, then make clear to us that you are friends, or we must consider that what we suspect is the truth: that you are part of the evil that has come here, and we will not permit you."

That was direct enough, and Vanye clenched his hand on the hilt of his sword and held his senses alert, not alone for the three who stood before them in the hall, but for the undefended windows about them. In the firelight, they were prey for archers.

"You are well-informed," said Morgaine. "Have you spoken with the Mirrindim? I think not, if you consider us enemies."

"We have found strangers in the woods, and dealt with them. And we came to Mirrind and asked, and so we were told of you. They speak well of you, but do they truly know you?"

"I will tell you what I told them: your land is invaded. Men and *qhal* have come through the Fires at Azeroth, and they are a hungry and a dangerous people, from a land in which all law and reason has long since perished. We fled them, Vanye and I . . . but we did not lead them here. They are prowling, hunting likely prey, and they have found Mirrind. I hope your dealing with them let none escape back to their main force. Otherwise they will be back."

The *qhal* looked disturbed at that, and exchanged looks with his companions.

"Have you weapons," Morgaine asked, "with which you can protect this village?"

"We would not tell you."

"Will you at least take charge of the village?"

"It is always in our keeping."

"And therefore they welcomed us . . . not knowing us, save as *qhal.*"

"Therefore you were welcomed, yes."

Morgaine inclined her head as in homage. "Well, I understand a great many things that puzzled me. If Mirrind shows your care, then it speaks well for you. This I will tell you: Vanye and I are going back to Azeroth, to deal with the folk who have it now . . . and we go with your leave or without it."

"You are arrogant."

"And are not you, my lord *qhal?* You have your right . . . but no more right than we."

"Such arrogance comes of power."

Morgaine shrugged.

"Do you ask leave to travel Shathan? You must have it. And I cannot give it."

"I should be glad of your people's consent, but who can give it, and on what authority, if you will forgive the question?"

"Wherever you go, you will be constantly under our eye, my lady—whose speech is strange, whose manners are stranger still. I cannot promise you yea or nay. There is that in you which greatly alarms me, and you are not of this land."

"No," Morgaine admitted. "When we began our flight, it was not at Azeroth. It is your misfortune that the Shiua horde chose this direction, but that was not our doing. They are led by a halfling *qhal* named Hetharu; and by a halfling man named Chya Roh i Chya; but even those two do not fully control the horde. There is no mercy in them. If you try to deal with them face to face, then expect that you will die as Eth did. I fear they have already shown you their nature; and I wish above all else that they had come against me and not against Eth."

There were looks, and at last the foremost inclined his head. "Travel north along the stream; north, if you would live. A little delay to satisfy our lord may save your lives. It is not far. If you will not, then we shall count you enemies with the rest. Friends would come and speak with us."

And without further word the three *qhal* turned—the one in the shadow was a woman. They departed as noiselessly as they had come.

Morgaine swore softly and angrily.

"Shall we take this journey?" Vanye asked. He had no eagerness for it, but likewise he had no eagerness to gather more enemies than they had.

"If we fought, we would work enough ruin that these innocent folk would lie exposed to the Shiua; and probably we would lose our own lives into the bargain. No, we have no choice, and they know it. Besides, I do not completely believe that they came here unasked."

"The Mirrindim? That is hard to think."

"We are not theirs, Sersein said. This afternoon when Eth was killed and they doubted us—well, perhaps they sought other help. They were anxious to keep us here tonight. Perhaps they saved our lives by holding us here. Or perhaps I am too suspicious. We shall go as they asked. I do not despair of it; I have felt from the beginning that the *qhalur* hand on this place was both quiet and not greatly remote."

"They are gentler than some *qhal* I have met," he said, and swallowed heavily, for he still did not like proximity to them. "It is said, *liyo*, that in a part of Andur's forests that are called haunted, the animals are very tame and have no fear . . . having never been hunted. So I have heard."

"Not unapt." Morgaine turned back toward the fire. She

stood there a moment, then laid down *Changeling* and gathered her armor.

"A leave-taking?"

"I think we should not linger here." She looked back at him. "Vanye, gentle they may be; and perhaps they and we act for similar reasons. But there are some things—well, thee knows. Thee well knows. I trust no one."

"Aye," he agreed, and armed himself, drew up the coif and set on his head the battered helm he had not worn since their coming to Mirrind.

Then they departed together to the pen where the horses were.

A small shadow stirred there as they opened the gate . . . Sin, who slept near the horses. The boy came forth and made no sound to alarm the village . . . shed tears, and yet lent his small hands to help them saddle and tie their supplies in place. When all was done, Vanye gave his hand as to a man . . . but Sin embraced him with feverish strength; and then to make the pain quick, Vanye turned and rose into the saddle. Morgaine set herself ahorse, and Sin stood back to let them ride out.

They rode the commons quietly, but doors opened along their way all the same. Sleepy villagers in their nightclothes turned out to watch, silent in the moonlight, and stood by with sad eyes. A few waved forlornly. The elders walked out to bar their way. Morgaine reined in then, and bowed from the saddle.

"There is no need for us now," she said. "If the *qhal*-lord Lir is your friend, then he and his will watch over you."

"You are not of them," said Bythein faintly.

"Did you not suspect so?"

"At the last, lady. But you are not our enemy. Come back and be welcome again."

"I thank you. But we have business elsewhere. Do you trust yourselves to them?"

"They have always taken care for us."

"Then they will now."

"We will remember your warnings. We will post the guards. But we cannot travel Shathan without their leave. We must not. Good journey to you, lady; good journey, *khemeis*."

"Good fortune to you," Morgaine said. They rode from the midst of the people, not in haste, not as fugitives, but with sadness.

Then the darkness of the forest closed about them, and they took the road past the sentries, who hailed them sorrowfully and wished them well in their journey—then down to the stream, which would lead them.

There was no sign of any enemy. The horses moved quietly in the dark; and when they were far from Mirrind, they dismounted in the last of the night, wrapped themselves in their blankets and cloaks and slept alternately the little time they felt they could afford.

By bright morning they were underway again, travelling the streamside by trails hardly worthy of the name, through delicate foliage that scarcely bore any mark of previous passage.

From time to time there came a whispering of brush and a sense that they were being watched: woodswise, both of them, so that it was not easy to deceive their senses, but neither of them could catch sight of the watchers.

"Not our enemies," Morgaine said in an interval when it seemed to have left them. "There are few of them skilled in woodcraft, and only one of them is Chya."

"Roh would not be here; I do not think so."

"No, I do doubt it. They must be the *qhal* who live here. We have escort."

She was uneasy in it; he caught that in her expression, and agreed with it.

A hush hung all about them as they went farther. The horses moved with their necessary noise, breaking of twigs and scuff of forest mold . . . and yet something insisted there was another sound there, wind where it should not be, a whispering of leaves. He heard it, and looked behind them.

Then it was gone; he turned again, for the trail bent with the stream, and they were entering a place not meant for riders, where often branches hung low and they must lean in the saddle to pass under . . . a wood wilder and older than the area where they had entered the forest, or that which surrounded Mirrind's placid fields.

Again something touched at hearing, leftward.

"It is back," he said, becoming vexed at this game.

"Would it would show itself," she said in the *qhalur* tongue.

They had ridden hardly around the next bending when an apparition stepped into their path—a youth clad in motley green, and tall and white-haired . . . empty-handed.

The horses snorted and shied up. Morgaine, in the lead, held Siptah, and Vanye moved up as close as he could on the narrow trail.

The youth bowed, smiling as if delighted at their startlement. There was at least one more; Vanye heard movement behind, and his shoulders prickled.

"Are you one of Lir's friends?" Morgaine asked.

"I am a friend of his," said the youth, and stood with hands in his belt, head cocked and smiling. "And you wished for my company, so here I am."

"I prefer to see those who share a road with me. You are also going north, I take it."

The youth grinned. "I am your guard and guide." He swept an elaborate bow. "I am Lellin Erirrhen. And you are asked to rest tonight in the camp of my lord Merir Mlennira, you and your *khemeis*."

Morgaine sat silent a moment, and Siptah fretted under her, accustomed to blows exchanged at such sudden meetings. "And what of that one who is still watching us? Who is he?"

Another joined Lellin, a smallish dark man armed with sword and bow.

"My *khemeis*," said Lellin. "Sezar." Sezar bowed with the grace of the *qhal*-lord, and when Lellin turned to lead the way, taking for granted that they would follow, Sezar went at his heels.

Vanye watched them ghost through the brush ahead, somewhat relieved in his apprehensions, for Sezar was a Man like the villagers, and went armed while his lord did not. *Either well-loved or well-defended*, he thought, and wondered how many more there were thereabouts.

Lellin looked back and grinned at them, waiting at a branching of the way, and led them off again on a new track, away from the stream. "Quicker than the other way," he said cheerfully.

"Lellin," Morgaine said. "We were advised to stay by the streamside."

"Think nothing of that. Lir gave you a sure road; but you would be til tomorrow on that track. Come. I would not mislead you."

Morgaine shrugged, and they went.

They called halt of their guides at noon, and rested a time; Lellin and Sezar took food of them when it was offered, but disappeared thereafter without a word, and did not reappear until they grew tired of waiting and began to follow the dim

trail on their own. Now and again came birdsong which was
unnatural with so much moving; now and again either Lellin
or Sezar would disappear from the trail, only to reappear at
some far turning ahead . . . there seemed even shorter ways,
though perhaps none that a horseman could take.

Then in late afternoon there was the faint scent of wood-
smoke in the air, and Lellin returned from one of his and
Sezar's absences to stand squarely in their path. Hands in
belt, he bowed with flippant grace. "We are near now. Please
follow me closely and do nothing rash. Sezar has gone on to
advise them we are coming in. You are quite safe with me; I
have the utmost concern for your safety, since I stand so
close to you. This way, if you will."

And Lellin turned and led them onto a trail so overgrown
that they must dismount and lead the horses. Morgaine
delayed to take *Changeling* from her saddle and hook it to
her shoulder-belt, the matter of an instant; and Vanye took
not only his sword but his bow and quiver, and walked last,
looking over his shoulder and round about him, but no threat
was visible.

It was not quite a clearing, not in the sense of Mirrind's
broad circle. Tents were placed here among wide-spaced
trees—and one tree dwarfed all the tents: nine or ten times a
man's height it rose before it even branched. Others at the far
side of the camp soared almost that high, and spread wide
branches, so that shadow dappled all the tents.

Their coming brought a stir in the camp, with *qhal* and
Men lining the aisle down which they walked, where the light
came greenly down, and the only sky showed golden-white in
comparison to the shadowing branches.

None threatened them. There were tall, white-haired *qhal*,
male and female; and small dark human-folk . . . a few
elders of both kindreds stood among them, robed, old Men
and old *qhal*, alike even to the silver hair at the last, though
Men were sometimes bearded and *qhal* were not; and Men
balded, and *qhal* seemed not to. The younger folk whatever
their sex or kind wore breeches and tunics, and some were
armed and some were not. They were a goodly-looking folk
together, and walked with a free step and cheerfully, moving
along with the strangers who had come to them as if all that
animated them were curiosity.

But Lellin stopped and bowed before they had quite
crossed the camp. "Lady, please leave your weapons with
your *khemeis,* and come with me."

"As you have remarked," said Morgaine softly, "we two have outlandish ways. Now, I have no objection to handing my weapons to Vanye, but how much more are you going to ask?"

*"Liyo,"* Vanye said under his breath, "no, do not allow it."

"Ask your lord," said Morgaine to Lellin, "whether he will insist on it. For my own opinion, I am minded not to agree, and to ride out of here . . . and I can do that, Lellin."

Lellin hesitated, frowning, then strode away to the largest of the tents. Sezar remained, arms folded, waiting, and they waited, holding the reins of the horses.

"They are gentle-seeming," Vanye said in his own tongue, "but first they separate us from our horses, and you from your arms, and me from you. If they go on, we shall be divided into very small pieces, *liyo.*"

She laughed shortly, and Sezar's eyes flickered, puzzled. "Do not think I mean to let that start," she said. "But bide easy until we know their minds; we need no unnecessary enemies."

It was a longish wait, and all about them the folk of the camp stood staring at them. No weapon was drawn, no bow bent, no insult offered them. Children stood with parents, and old ones remained in the forefront of the gathering: it was not the aspect of a people who expected violence.

And at last Lellin returned, frowning still, and bowed. "Come as you wish. Merir will not insist, only I do ask you leave the horses; you cannot expect to take them too. Sezar will see that they are safe and cared for. Come with me, and see that you keep peace and do not threaten Merir, or we will show you quite another face of us, strangers."

Vanye turned and took from Siptah's saddle Morgaine's personal kit, and shouldered the strap of that. Sezar took the reins of both horses and led them away, while he trailed Morgaine, and she walked beside Lellin to the green tent, that largest one of all in the camp.

The flaps were back, reassuring, indicating less chance of outright ambush; and the *qhal* inside were elders, robed and unarmed, with old Men, who looked too advanced in years to use the daggers they generally wore. In their midst sat an old, old *qhal,* whose white hair fell thickly about his shoulders, confined with a gold band about his brow in the manner of a human king. His cloak was green as the spring leaves, the shoulders done in layers of gray feathers, smooth and minutely black-edged, a work of remarkable skill and beauty.

"Merir," said Lellin softly, and bowed, "lord of Shathan."

"Welcome," Merir bade them, a low and gentle voice, and a chair was unfolded and offered Morgaine. She settled, while Vanye stood at her shoulder.

"Your name is Morgaine; your companion's is Vanye," said Merir. "You stayed in Mirrind until you took it upon yourself to bid its young folk venture into Shathan, and lost one of them. You say now that you are going to Azeroth, and you warn of invasion out of the Fires. You are not Shathana, neither of you. Are all these reports true?"

"Yes. Do not expect, my lord Merir, that we understand much of what passes in your land; but we are enemies of those who have massed out on the plain. We are on our way to deal with them, such as we can; and if we must have your permission, then we ask it."

Merir gazed on her a long time, frowning, and she on him, nothing yielding. At last Merir turned and spoke briefly to one of the elders. "You have ridden far," he said then. "You are at least due hospitality while we talk, you and your *khemeis*. You seem impatient. If you know of some imminent attack, say, and I assure you we will act; or if not, then perhaps you will take the time to speak with us."

Morgaine said nothing, and sat easily, the while such hospitality was arranged, and while the old lord gave instruction for the preparation of a tent and shelter for them. For his part, Vanye stood with his hand on the back of Morgaine's chair, watching every move and listening to every whisper . . . for they two had knowledge of Gates, and of the powers of them, knowledge which some *qhal* had lost and which some would kill to learn. Whatever the gentleness of the folk, there was that to fear.

Drink was brought and offered them both; but Vanye leaned forward and took the drink from Morgaine's hand sipped at it first and gave it back to her before he took a drink of his own. She simply held the cup in her hand, though Merir drank of his.

"Are these your customs?" Merir asked.

"No," said Vanye out of turn, "but they are, among our enemies."

The other *qhal* looked displeased at that forwardness with the old lord. "No," Merir said. "Let be. I shall speak with them. Go, all who should. We shall speak," he added then, "of things belonging to the inner councils of our people. Although you have insisted that your *khemeis* must remain with you, still it might be well if you dismissed him as far as the outside of the tent."

"No," said Morgaine. Not all the *qhal* had departed. Those remaining settled, some on the mats and the oldest ones in chairs. "Sit down," she said aside. Vanye unslung his bow and tucked his sword aside to sit crosslegged at her feet. It was a posture less than formal, and he kept the cup in one hand the while, sipped at it a second time, for he had felt no ill from the first taste. Morgaine tasted hers then, and crossed her booted ankles and extended her legs before her, easy in her attitude and bordering on too much casualness for the *qhal's* liking. She did it deliberately; Vanye knew her well enough to sense the tension in her. She sought their limits and had not yet found them.

"I am not accustomed to be summoned," she said. "But this is your land, lord Merir, and I do owe you the courtesy I have paid in coming here."

"You are here because it is expedient . . . for both of us. As you say: it is my land, and the courtesy I ask is an accounting of your purpose in it. Tell us more of what you told the Mirrindim. Who are these folk that have come here?"

"My lord, there is a land called Shiuan, the other side of the Fires . . . I think you understand me. And it was a miserable place, the people starving, Men first, and then *qhal*. *Qhal* had wealth and Men lived in poverty . . . but the floods that threatened their land were going to take them both all the same. Then came a Man named Chya Roh, who knew the workings of the Gates, which the *qhal* in that land had forgotten completely. He was not himself from Shiuan, this Chya Roh, but from beyond Shiuan's own Gates. From Andur-Kursh, as we two are. And that is how we came to be in Shiuan: we were following Roh."

"Who taught a Man these things?" one of the elders demanded. "How is it in the land called Andur-Kursh . . . that Men make free of such powers?"

Morgaine hesitated. "My lord, it is possible . . . that man and man may change by those powers. Is that known here?"

There was utter silence, and looks exchanged: terror; but Merir's face remained a mask.

"It is forbidden," Merir answered. "We do know; but we do not permit that knowledge outside our high councils."

"I am encouraged to see so many—*elder* folk in places of power among you. Old age evidently takes its course here; perhaps I am among people of restraint and good sense."

"It is an evil thing, this changing."

"But one known to a few ruthless folk in Andur-Kursh. Chya Roh . . . There was once a great master of the powers of the Gates . . . *qhal*, at least in the beginning, although I have no proof of it: all the guises I have known him to use were Men. Man after man he has murdered, taking bodies for his own use, extending his life over many generations of Men and *qhal*. He was Chya Zri; he was Chya Liell; and lastly he took the body of Chya Roh i Chya, a lord of his land —Vanye's own cousin. So Vanye's knowledge of Gates, my lord, is a bitter one.

"After that, Roh fled us, because he knew that his life was in danger from us . . . life: I do not know how many lives he has known from the begining, or whether he was first male or female, or whether he was born to Andur-Kursh or arrived there from beyond. He is *old*, and very dangerous, and reckless with the powers of the Gates. So for one reason and the next, we pursued him to Shiuan, and there he found himself trapped . . . in a land that was dying—a thing fearful enough for the people who were born there, who might have had several generations more before the end; but for a being who looked to live forever . . . that death was imminent enough. He went among the *qhal* of that land, and among Men, and declared to them that he had the power to open the Gates that had been so long beyond their own knowledge, and to bring them through to a new land, which they might take for their own . . . thus he had a way out and an army about him.

"We failed to stop him, Vanye and I. He was ahead of us on the road, and we simply could not overtake him in time. It was all we could do to come through the passage ourselves. We were exhausted after that, and we ran . . . until we chanced into the forest, and then into Mirrind. We rested there, trying to find out what manner of land this is and whether there was any force in it that could stop this horde from its march. We did not want to involve the Mirrindim; they are not fighters and we saw that: our watch was meant to protect them. Now we see that there is no more time left, and we are going back to Azeroth to see to the matter as best we can. That is the sum of it, my lord."

There was dismay among them, murmurings, distressed looks cast to Merir. The old *qhal* sat with dry lips pressed tautly, the mask at last broken.

"This is a terrible tale, my lady."

"Worse to see than to tell. Whether Vanye and I can do anything against them, well, we shall see. There is little hope that the horde will not reach for Mirrind. They would have come there sooner or late . . . and on no account did I urge the Mirrindim to meet them. What I should have realized is that the Mirrindim would fear them no more than they feared us. I warned them; I warned them. But likely Eth walked innocently into their hands, fearing them no more than me, and that thought grieves me."

"You had no authority," said another, "to send Men into Shathan. They thought that you did, and they went, as they would go for us . . . eager to please you. You sent that Man to his death, beyond doubt."

Vanye glowered at that elder. "The Man was warned."

"Peace," said Merir. "Nhinn, could one of us have done better, alone and with a village to defend? We were at fault too, for these two moved so skillfully and settled so peacefully among the Mirrindim that we never realized their presence until this violence came. There could have been a far worse result . . . for this evil could have come on Mirrind utterly by stealth, with no one there to protect them. We were remiss; let us not pass the blame to them. These two and the others passed our defenses in small numbers, and that was my fault."

"Eth may have been questioned," Morgaine said. "If so, that means some of the *qhal* of the horde came into Shathan, for only they could have spoken to Eth: Men in Shiuan do not speak the same language. Your folk speak of invaders killed; you might judge how much the horde now knows by knowing if *qhal* were among them and if any escaped. But either a report from Eth's murderers or the mere failure of that force to return to the main body of the horde . . . will prick the interest of their leaders. Whatever else they are, they are not the sort to retreat from challenge. You might ask Lir. And I understand that you do not permit the Mirrindim to travel; if you have regard for them, I hope that you will reconsider that, my lord. I am very much afraid for their future there."

"My lord." It was Lellin, who had come in unnoticed, and all eyes turned to that young and uninvited voice. "By your leave."

"Yes," said Merir. "Go tell Nhirras to tend to that matter. Take no chances." The old *qhal* settled back in his chair. "No light thing, this uprooting of a village; but the things you tell

us are no light matter either. Tell me this. How do you two
alone think to reckon with these enemies of yours?"

"Roh," Morgaine said without hesitation. "Chya Roh is the
principal danger, and next to him is Hetharu of Ohtij-in in
Shiuan, who leads the *qhal*. First we must be rid of Roh; and
Hetharu next. Leaderless, the horde will divide. Hetharu murdered his own father to seize power, and ruined other lords.
His folk fear him, but they do not love him. They will split
into factions without him, and turn on each other or on the
Men, which is more likely. Men in the horde likewise have
three factions at least: two kindreds which have always hated
one another, the Hiua and the marshlands folk; and there are
the Men of Shiuan, for the third. Roh is the piece that holds
the whole together; Roh must be dealt with first . . . and yet
not so simply done; the two of them are surrounded by thousands, and they sit securely by the Gate in Azeroth. It is the
Master Gate, is it not, my lord Merir?"

Merir nodded slowly, to the consternation of his people.
"Yes. And how have you means to know that?"

"I know. And there is a place which governs it . . . is
there not, my lord?"

There was a stir among the elders. "Who are you," one
asked, "to ask such questions?"

"Then you do know. And you may believe me, my lords,
or you may go and ask Chya Roh his side of the tale . . .
but I do not advise that. He has skill to use such a place; he
has force to take it when he locates it . . . as he will. But for
me, I come asking you: *where*, my lords?"

"Do not be in haste," said Merir. "We have seen your
handiwork and theirs, and thus far prefer yours. But the
knowledge you ask . . . ah, my lady, you do well understand
what you ask. But we—we cherish our peace, lady Morgaine.
Long and long ago we were cast adrift here . . . perhaps you
understand me, for your skill in the ancient arts must be considerable to make the passage you have made and to ask
questions so aptly, and your knowledge of the past may
match it. There were Men here, and ourselves, and our power
had been overthrown. It could have been the end for us. But
we live simply, as you see. We do not permit bloodshed
among ourselves or quarrels in our land. Perhaps you do not
understand how grievous a thing you do ask, even in seeking
permission to pursue your enemies. We enforce the peace
with our law; and shall we yield up our authority to keep order in our own land, and give you leave to hunt across the

face of it and dispense life and death where and as you will? What of our own responsibility to our people? What then when another rises up from among *us* and demands similar privilege outside the law?"

"First, my lord, neither we nor our enemies are of this land; this quarrel began outside it and you are safest if it is contained in Azeroth and never allowed to affect your people at all. That is my hope, faint as it is. And second, my lord, if you mean that your own power is sufficient to deal with the threat entire, and to stop it at once, pray do so. I like not the odds, the two of us against their thousands, and if there were another way, believe me that I would gladly take it."

"What do you propose?"

"Nothing. My intent is to avoid harming the land or its people, and I do not want any allies of your people. Vanye and I are a disharmony in this land; I would not do it hurt, and therefore I would touch it as little as possible."

She bordered on admitting something they would not like to hear, and Vanye grew tense, though he tried not to betray it. Long Merir considered, and finally smoothed his robes and nodded. "Lady Morgaine, be our guest in our camp tonight and tomorrow; give us time to think on these things. Perhaps I can give you what you ask: permission to travel Shathan. Perhaps we shall have to reach some further agreement. But fear nothing from us. You are safe in this camp and you may be at ease in it."

"My lord, now you have asked me much and told me nothing. Do you know what passes at Azeroth now? Do you have information that we do not?"

"I know that there are forces massed there, as you said, and that there has been an attempt to draw upon the powers of the Gate."

"Attempt, but not success. Then you do still hold the center of power, apart from Azeroth."

Merir's gray eyes, watery with age, looked on her and frowned. "Power we do have, perhaps even to deal with you. But we will not try it. Undertake the same, lady Morgaine, I ask you."

She rose and inclined her head, and Vanye gathered himself to his feet. "On your assurance that there is yet no crisis, I shall be content to be your guest, . . . but that attempt of theirs will be followed by worse. I urge you to protect the Mirrindim."

"They are hunting you, are they not, these strangers? You

fear that Eth betrayed your own presence there, and therefore you fear for the Mirrindim."

"The enemy would wish to stop me. They fear the warning I can give of them."

Merir's frown deepened. "And perhaps other things? You had a warning to give from the very beginning, and yet you did not give it until a man was dead at Mirrind."

"I do not make that mistake again. I feared to tell them, I admit it, because there were things in the Mirrindim that puzzled me . . . their carelessness, for one. I trust no one whose motives I do not know . . . even yours, my lord."

That did not please them, but Merir lifted his hand and silenced their protests.

"You bring something new and unwelcome about you, lady Morgaine. It adheres to you; it breathes from you; it is war, and blood. You are an uncomfortable guest."

"I am always an uncomfortable guest. But I shall not break the peace of your camp while your hospitality lasts."

"Lellin will see to your needs. Do not fear for your safety here, from your enemies or from us. None comes here without our permission, and we are respectful of our own law."

"I do not completely believe them," Vanye said, when they had been settled in a small and private tent. "I fear them. Perhaps it is because I cannot believe that any *qhal's* interests—" He stopped half a breath, held in Morgaine's gray and unhuman gaze, and continued, defying the suspicion that had lived in him from the beginning of their travels, "—that any *qhal's* interests could be common with ours . . . perhaps because I have learned to distrust all appearances with them. They seem gentle; I think that is what most alarms me . . . that I am almost moved to think they are telling the truth of their motives."

"I tell thee this, Vanye, that we are in more danger than in any lodging we have ever taken if they are lying to us. The hold we are in is all of Shathan forest, and the halls of it wind long, and known to them, but dark to us. So it is all one, whether we sleep here or in the forest."

"If we could leave the forest, there would still be only the plains for refuge, and no cover from our enemies there."

They spoke the language of Andur-Kursh, and hoped that there was none at hand to understand it. The Shathana should not, having had no ties at all to that land, at whatever time Gates had led there; but there were no certainties about it, . . . no assurance even that one of these tall, smiling *qhal* was not one of their enemies from off the plains of Azeroth. Their enemies were only halflings, but in a few of them the blood brought forth the look of a pure *qhal*.

"I will go out and see to the horses," he offered at last, restless in the little tent, "and see how far we are truly free."

"Vanye," she said. He looked back, bent as he was in leaving the low doorway. "Vanye, walk very softly in this spider's web. If trouble arises here, it may take us."

"I shall cause none, *liyo*."

He stood clear, outside, looked about him at the camp—walked the tree-darkened aisles of tents, seeking the direction in which the horses had been led away. It was toward dark; the twilight here was early and heavy indeed, and folk moved like shadows. He walked casually, turning this way and that until he had sight of Siptah's pale shape over against the trees . . . and he walked in that direction with none offering to stop him. Some Men stared, and to his surprise, children were allowed to trail after him, though they kept their distance . . . *qhal*-children with them, as merry as the rest; they did not come near, nor were they unmannered. They simply watched, and stood shyly at a distance.

He found the horses well-bedded, with their saddle-gear hung well above the damp of the ground, suspended on ropes from the limb overhead. The animals were curried and clean, with water sitting by each, and the remnant of a measure of grain . . . *Trade from villages,* he thought—*or tribute: such does not grow in forest shade, and these are not farmer-folk by the look of them.*

He patted Siptah's dappled shoulder, and avoided the stud's playful nip at his arm . . . not all play: the horses were content and had no desire for a setting-forth at this late hour. He caressed little Mai's brown neck, and straightened her forelock, measuring with his eye the length of the tethers and what chance there was of entanglement: he could find no fault. Perhaps, he thought, they did know horses.

A step crushed the grass behind him. He turned. Lellin stood there.

"Watching us?" Vanye challenged him.

Lellin bowed, hands in belt, a mere rocking forward. "You are guests, nonetheless," he said, more sober than his wont. *"Khemeis,* word has passed through the inner councils . . . how your cousin perished. It is not something of which we may speak openly. Even that such a thing is possible is not

knowledge we publish, for fear that someone might be drawn
to such a crime . . . but I am in the inner councils, and I
know. It is a terrible thing. We offer our deep sorrow."

Vanye stared at him, suspecting mockery at first, and then
realized that Lellin was sincere. He inclined his head in respect to that. "Chya Roh was a good man," he said sadly.
"But now he is not a man at all; and he is the worst of our
enemies. I cannot think of him as a man."

"Yet there is a trap in what this *qhal* has done—that at
each transference he loses more and more of himself. It is not
without cost . . . for one evil enough to seek such a prolonged
life."

Cold settled about his heart, hearing that. His hand fell
from Mai's shoulder, and he searched desperately for words
enough to ask what he could not have asked clearly even in
his own tongue. "If he chose evil men to bear him, then part
of them would live in him, ruling what he did?"

"Until he shed that body, yes. So our lore says. But you
say that your cousin was a good man. Perhaps he is weak;
perhaps not. You would know that."

A trembling came on him, a deep distress, and Lellin's
gray eyes were troubled.

"Perhaps," said Lellin, "there is hope—that what I am
trying to tell you. If anything of your cousin has influence,
and it is likely that it does, if he was not utterly overwhelmed
by what happened to him, then he may yet defeat the man
who killed him. It is a faint hope, but perhaps worth holding."

"I thank you," Vanye whispered, and moved finally to pass
under the rope and leave the horses.

"I have distressed you."

Vanye shook his head helplessly. "I speak little of your
language. But I understand. I understand what you are saying. Thank you, Lellin. I wish it were so, but I—"

"You have reason to believe otherwise?"

"I do not know." He hesitated, purposing to walk back to
their tent, knowing that Lellin must follow. He offered Lellin
the chance to walk beside him. Lellin did, and yet he found
no words to say to him, not wanting to discuss the matter
further.

"If I have troubled you," Lellin said, "forgive me."

"I loved my cousin." It was the only answer he knew how
to give, although it was more complicated than that simple

word. Lellin answered nothing, and left him when he turned off on the last aisle to the tent he shared with Morgaine.

He found his hand on the Honor-blade he carried: Roh's . . . for the honorable death Roh had been given no chance to choose, rather than become the vessel for Zri-Liell. An oath was on him to kill this creature. Lellin's hope shattered him, that the only kinsman he had yet living . . . still might live, entangled with the enemy who had killed him.

He entered the tent and settled quietly in the corner, picked up a bit of his armor and set to adjusting a lacing, working in the near dark. Morgaine lay staring at the ceiling of the tent, at the shadows that flickered across it. She cast him a brief look as if she were relieved that he was back without incident, but she did not leave her own thoughts to speak with him just them. She was given, often, to such silences, when she had concerns of her own.

It was false activity, his meddling with the harness—he muddled the lacing over and over again, but it gave him an excuse for silence and privacy, doing nothing that she would notice, until the trembling should leave his hands.

He knew that he had spoken too freely with the *qhal*, betraying small things that perhaps it was best not to have these folk know. He was almost moved to open his thoughts utterly to Morgaine, to confess what he had done, confess other things: how once in Shiuan he had talked alone with Roh, and how even then he had seen no enemy, but only a man he had once owned for kinsman. The weapon had failed his hand in that meeting, and he had failed her . . . self-deceived, he had reasoned afterward, seeing what he had wished to see.

He wanted now desperately to seek Morgaine's opinion on what Lellin had said to him . . . but deep in his heart was suspicion, long-fostered, that Morgaine had always known more of Roh's double nature than she had told him. He dared not, for the peace which was between them, challenge her on that, or call her deceitful . . . for he feared that she had deceived him. She might not trust him at her side if she thought his loyalties might be divided, might have misled him deliberately to have Roh's death: and something would sour in him if he learned her capable of that. He did not want to find out such a thing, more than he longed to learn the other. Roh's nature could make no difference in his own choices; Morgaine wanted Roh dead for her own reasons, which had nothing to do with revenge; and if she meant to have it that way, then there was an oath to bind him: an *ilin* could not refuse an order, even against friend or kinsman: for his soul's sake he could not. Perhaps she thought to spare him knowledge . . . meant her deception for kindness. He was sure it was not the only deception she had used.

There was, he persuaded himself at last, no help for himself or Roh in bringing the matter up now. War was ahead of them. Men died, would die—and he was on one side and Roh on the other, and truth made no difference in that.

There would be no need to know, when one of them was dead.

# Chapter Four

By night, fires blazed fearlessly throughout the camp, and in a clear space there burned a common-fire, where songs were sung to the music of harps. Men sang tunes that at times minded one of Kursh: the words were *qhalur,* but the burden of them was Man, and some of the tunes seemed plain and pleasant and ordinary as the earth. Vanye was drawn outside to listen, for their tent was near to that place and the gathering extended to their very door. Morgaine joined him; and he brought out their blankets, so they might sit as most did in the camp, and listen. Men came and brought them food and drink along with all the others as they sat there, for dinner was prepared in common as in Mirrind, and served in this fashion under the stars. They took it gratefully, and feared no drug or poison.

Then the harp passed to the *qhalur* singers, and the music changed. Like wind it was, and the harmony of it was strange. Lellin sang, and a young *qhalur* woman kept him harmony, that ranged the eerie scale fit to send chills coursing down a human back.

"It is beautiful," Vanye whispered at last to Morgaine, "for all it is not human."

"There was a time when thee could not have seen it."

It was true, and the realization weighed on him, the more when he considered Morgaine, who saw beauty in what she came to destroy . . . who had always been able to see it.

*This will pass,* he thought, looking out over all the camp of *qhal* and Men. *It will pass when she and I have done what we came to do, and killed the power of their Gates. It cannot help but change them. We will destroy all this no less than we shall destroy Roh.* It saddened him, with that sadness he had often seen in Morgaine's eyes and never understood until now.

There came a stirring at their backs. Morgaine turned, and so did he; it was a young Woman who bowed to speak with them. "Lord Merir sends," she whispered, not to disturb the listeners nearby. "Please come."

They rose up and followed the young Woman, delaying to put their blankets inside, and Morgaine took her weapons, though he did not. Their guide brought them into Merir's tent. One light burned there, and within were only Merir and a young *qhal*. Merir dismissed her and the Woman, so that they were quite alone.

Both trust and power, it was . . . that this frail elder received them thus; Morgaine bowed courtesy, and Vanye did.

"Sit down," Merir offered them. He was himself wrapped in a cloak of plain brown, and a brazier of coals smoldered at his feet. Two chairs sat vacant, but Vanye took the floor out of respect: an *ilin* did not insult a lord by sitting on a level with him.

"There is refreshment by you, if you wish," said Merir, but Morgaine declined it, and therefore Vanye refused it also. His place was comfortable, on the mat nearest the brazier, and he settled at his ease.

"Your hospitality has been kind," said Morgaine. "We have been served all that we can use; your courtesy encourages me."

"I cannot call you welcome. Your news is too grim. But for all that, your steps lie easily on the forest; you bruise no branch nor harm its people . . . and therefore we make place for you here. For the same reason I am encouraged to believe that you do oppose the invaders. You are perhaps—dangerous to have for enemies."

"And dangerous to have for friends. I still ask nothing more than leave to pass where I must."

"Secrecies? But this is our forest."

"My lord, we perplex each other. You look on my work and I on yours; you create beauty, and I honor you for that. But not all that is fair is trustworthy. Forgive me, but I have not come so far as I have by scattering all that I know to every wind. How far, for instance, does your power extend? How much could you help me? Or would you be willing? And the Men here: do they support you out of love or of fear? Could they be covinced to turn on you? I do doubt it, but my enemies are persuasive, and some of them are Men. What skill have there *khemi* of yours in arms? Things here look to be peaceful, and it might be that they would scatter in terror from the first moment of conflict; or if they are practiced in war, then where are your enemies, and what would befall me at their hand if I took your part? How is this community of yours ordered, and where are decisions made? Have you power to promise and to keep your word? And even if the answer to all these questions should please me, I am still reluctant to let this matter pass into other hands, which have not fought this battle so long or so hard as I."

"Those questions are direct and very apt. And I do read much of the nature of you and your enemies in the suspicions you hold of us. I do not think that I like that accounting. As for answers . . . my lady, that someone has passed the Fires and come here frightens me in itself. We have not found it good to make use of that passage."

"Then you are wise."

"Yet you have done so."

"Our enemy has no reluctance in the matter. And he must be stopped. You know of other worlds. You are too knowledgeable of the Gates not to know where they lead. So you will understand me if I say that the danger is to more worlds than this one. This is a man who will not scruple to use Gates recklessly in all their powers. How much more need I say to a man who understands?"

A great fear crept into Merir's eyes. "I know that much passing of that barrier may work calamity. One such disaster came on us, and we abandoned use of that passage, and made peace with Men, and gave up all that tempted us to that evil. So we have remained at peace . . . and there is none hungry but that we will feed him, none harmed—no thief or murderer nor abuser of his people. We live in the consciousness of what we can do . . . and do not. That is the foundation on which all law rests."

"I was at first amazed," said Morgaine, "that here *qhal* and Men are at peace. It is not so elsewhere."

"But it is the only sanity, lady Morgaine. Is it not very evident? Men multiply far more rapidly than we. Shorter lives, but ever more of them. And should we not have respect for that abundant vitality? Is it not a strength, as wisdom is a strength, or bravery? They can always overcome us . . . for war with them we can never win, not over the passing of much time." He leaned forward and set his hand on Vanye's shoulder, a gentle touch, and his gray eyes were kind. "Man, you are always the more powerful. We reached beyond our knowledge in bringing your kind among us, and though you were not the beginning of our sorrow, you have the power to be the end-all of it . . . save we make you our adopted sons, as we have tried to do. How is it that you travel with lady Morgaine? Is it for revenge for your kinsman?"

The heat of embarrassment rose to his face. "I swore her an oath," he said: half the truth.

"Long ago, Man, there was your like here. You are reckless in your lives, having so much life. But we took *khemi*, and that life agreed well with such Men and left others free to lead quiet lives in the villages. The hands of the *khemi* administer justice and do unpleasant things that want doing, and sometimes brave things, risking themselves in the aid of others. Such recklessness is natural to Men. But when a *qhal* dies young, he often leaves none behind him, for once and perhaps twice do we bear, and that after some years. In hostile times our number shrinks rapidly. It is always in our interest to keep peace, and to deal fairly with those who have such an advantage over us. Do you not see that it is so?"

The thought amazed him; and he realized how seldom he had seen children of the *qhal*, even among halflings.

Merir's hand left his shoulder, and the old lord looked across at Morgaine. "I shall lend you help, lady, asked or unasked. This evil has come, and we must not let it touch Shathan. Take Lellin with you, him and his *khemeis*. I send my heart with you. He is my grandson, my daughter's child, of a line that is fast fading. He will guide you where you will to go."

"Has Lellin consented in this? I would not take anyone who did not clearly reckon the danger."

"He asked to be the one, if I reached the conclusion that I should send someone."

She nodded sorrowfully. "May he come home safely to

you, my lord. I will watch over him with all the force that I have."

"That is much, is it not?"

Morgaine did not answer that probing, and silence hung between them a moment. "My lord, I asked you once for help to reach the master-hold, that would control the Gate at Azeroth. And I still ask that."

"Its name is Nehmin, and it is well defended. I myself would not be allowed to pass there freely. What you ask of me is—more than difficult."

"That comforts me. But Roh's allies spend lives recklessly, and they will simply spend them until they have broken its defenses. I must have access there."

Merir sat a moment, the fires of the lamp leaping upon his downcast features. "You ask power over us."

"No."

"But you do . . . for with your hand there, you have choices, regarding more than your enemy. Perhaps you would choose what we would choose . . . but you are utterly a stranger, and I wonder if that is likely. And might you not, in that power, be as deadly to us as the enemy you fight?"

Morgaine had no answer, and Vanye sat still, fearful, for Merir surely understood . . . if not the whole truth, surely truth enough. But the old *qhal* sighed heavily. "Lellin will guide you; and there will be others along the way who will help you."

"And yourself, my lord? Surely you will not be idle . . . and should I not know where you will be? I have no wish to harm you or to expose you to the enemy by mistake."

"Trust to Lellin. We will go our own way." He rose stiffly. "The Mirrindim were amazed at your map-making. Bring the lamp, young Vanye, and let me show you a thing that may help you."

Vanye gathered up the lamp from its hook and followed the ancient *qhal* to the tent wall. There was a map hung there, age-faded, and Morgaine came and looked on it.

"Here is Azeroth," said Merir, stretching forth his hand to the great circle in the center "Shathan is all the forest; and the great Narn and its tributaries feed the villages—see: each has accessible water. And this is a walk of many days—Mirrind is here."

"Such circles cannot be natural."

"No. In some places the trees fail, and yet there is water; and Men have cleared the rest. And where forest fails too much, thy have planted hedges and thickets to change the land so that trees may grow and wild things have their place. The circles are orderly and boundaries between farm and forest are thus distinct. It gives quiet passage for our folk . . . we do not like the open lands; and Men do, who farm and herd. Also . . ." he added, and laid his hand on Vanye's shoulder, "it has prevented war and strife over boundaries Once men rode in great hordes where they would, and there was war. They endangered us . . . but the vitality of Shathan itself is even greater than that of Men; they turned fire against us, and that was worst . . . always we are vulnerable to that kind of attack. But the woods regrew in the end; and the barricades of hedges were maintained by Men who sheltered with us. We are not the only forest or the only place where such a thing has been done; but we are the oldest. There are places outside, where Men have run to themselves, and make wars and ruin and—in some places—make better things, beautiful things. Of these folk too we have hope, but we cannot live as their neighbors; we are too fragile. We cannot admit them here above all, to the place of power: *that* must remain outside their reach. The *sirrindim*, we call them, these Men outside; they are horsemen and avoid our forests. But do you perceive why I am distressed, lady Morgaine, with the like of the *sirrindim* suddenly camped about Azeroth?"

"Nehmin is one dire concern, and I suppose that it is somewhere close about Azeroth, though I do not see it on your map. But the Narn itself . . . could become a threat, a road to lead them through your heart."

"Indeed you do see. It leads too close to the land of the *sirrindim*. It is a threat much beyond Mirrind . . . we do see that. In war, we would swiftly decline and die. The invaders must be held in Azeroth . . . above all they must not open a way to the northern plains. Of all directions they might have gone, that is the most deadly to us . . . and I think that is the direction they will choose, for you are here, and they will surely find that out."

"I understand you."

"We will hold them." There was sorrow etched deep in the old *qhal's* face. "We shall lose many of our numbers, I fear, but we shall hold them. We have no choice. Go now. Go and sleep. In the morning you will go with Lellin and Sezar, and we shall hope that you keep faith, lady Morgaine: I have shown you much that could greatly harm us."

She inclined her head, respecting the old *qhal*. "Good
night, my lord," she murmured and turned and left. Vanye
replaced the lamp carefully on its hanging chain near the old
lord's chair, thinking of his comfort, and when the aged *qhal*
sat down, he bowed too, the full obeisance he would have
shown a lord of his own people, forehead to the ground.

"Man," said Merir gently, "for your sake I have believed
your lady "

"How, lord?" he asked, for it bewildered him.

"Your manner—that you are devoted to her. Self-love
shows itself first that *qhal* and Man cannot trust one another.
But neither you nor she is afflicted by that evil. You serve,
but not because you fear. You affect the manner of a servant,
but you are more than that. You are a warrior like the *sirrindim*, and not like the *khemi*. But you show respect to an
elder, and him not of your blood. Such small things show
more truth than any words. And therefore I am moved to
trust your lady."

He was stricken by this, knowing that they would fail that
trust, and he was frightened. All at once he felt himself utterly transparent before the old lord, and soiled and unclean.

"Protect Lellin," the old *qhal* asked of him.

"Lord, I will," he whispered, and this faith at least he
meant to keep. Tears stung his eyes and choked his voice,
and a second time he inclined himself to the mat, and sat
back again. "Thank you for my lady, for she was very tired
and we are both very weary of fighting. Thank you for this
time you have given us, and for your help to cross your
lands. Have I leave to go, my lord?"

The old *qhal* dismissed him with a soft word, and he rose
and left the tent, sought Morgaine's in the dark, on the rim
of the gathering. The merriment there still continued, the
eerie sounds of *qhalur* singing.

"We shall both sleep," Morgaine said. "And the armor is
useless. Sleep soundly; it may be some time before we have
another chance."

He agreed, and put up a blanket for a curtain between
them, suspended from the cross-pole; gladly he stripped of
the armor, and of clothing, wrapped himself in a blanket and
lay down, and Morgaine did likewise, a little distance away
on the soft furs provided for their beds. The makeshift curtain did not reach the floor, and the light of the fires outside

cast a dim glow within. He saw her gazing at him, head pillowed on her arm.

"What kept thee with Merir?"

"It would sound strange if I said it."

"I ask."

"He—said that he trusted you because of me . . that if there were evil in us, it would show—between you and myself; of course they take you for one of their own."

She made a sound that might have been a laugh, bitter and brief.

"*Liyo,* we shall ruin these people."

"Be still. Even in Andurin, I would not discuss that; Andurin is laced with *qhalur* borrowings, and I do not feel secure in it. Besides, who knows what tongue these *sirrindim* speak, or whether some *qhal* here may not know it? Remember that when we travel with Lellin."

"I shall."

"Yet thee knows I have no choice, Vanye."

"I know. I understand."

Her dim face seemed touched by that, and a great sorrow was on it.

"Sleep," she said, and closed her eyes.

It was the best and only counsel in the matter.

# Chapter Five

Their setting out was by no means furtive or quiet. The horses were brought up before Merir's tent, and there Lellin took leave of his grandfather and his father and mother and great-uncle . . . grave, kind-eyed folk like Merir. His parents seemed old to have a son as young as Lellin, and they took his leaving hard. Sezar too they bade an affectionate farewell, kissing his hands and wishing him well, for the *khemeis* seemed to have no kinfolk among the Men in the camp: it was of Lellin's family that he took his leave.

They were offered food, and they took it, for it was well-prepared for keeping on the trail. Then Merir came forward and offered to Morgaine a gold medallion on a chain, intricate, beautiful work. "I lend this," he said. "It is safe passage." And another he brought forth and gave to Vanye, a silver one. "With either of these, ask what you will of any of our people save the *arrha*, who regard no authority of mine. Even there it might avail something. These are more protection in Shathan than any weapon."

Morgaine bowed to him in public respect, and Vanye likewise . . . Vanye at his feet, and not grudgingly, for without the old lord's help, the passage which now lay so easily before them would have been a terrible one.

Then they went to their horses, Siptah and Mai glistening from a bath and content with good care. Someone had twined star-like blue flowers in long chains from Siptah's mane, and white in Mai's—the strangest accouterment that ever a Kurshin warrior's horse bore, Vanye thought . . . but the gesture was like these graceful folk, and touched him.

There were no horses for Lellin or Sezar. "We will have," Lellin explained, "farther."

"Do you know where we are going?" Morgaine asked.

"Where you will, after I have taken you clear of this camp. But the horses will be there."

And by this it was clear that they would be under more eyes than Lellin's during their journey.

They set out down the main aisle of the camp, while the people both Men and *qhal* inclined to them in a bow like the rippling of wind through tall grass—as if they honored old friends; the rippling flowed with their passage almost to the edge of the wood.

There Vanye turned and looked back, to convince himself that such a place had been real at all. There was the forest shade on them, but a golden-green light fell over the encampment, which was all tents and movable—and would, he suspected, swiftly vanish from the place.

They entered the forest then, where the air was at once cooler. They took a different path than that by which they had come: Lellin avowed they must follow it until noon. And Lellin strode along by Siptah's head, while Sezar vanished shadow-wise into the brush. The *qhal* whistled a few clear notes from time to time, which were echoed from ahead, evidence where Sezar might be . . . and sometimes, for what seemed Lellin's own joy, the notes trilled into a snatch of *qhalur* song, wild and strange.

"Do not be too reckless," Morgaine bade him after one such. "Not all our enemies are unskilled in the forest."

Lellin turned as he walked and swept a slight bow . . . he seemed too happy by nature to keep the spring from his step, and a smile came naturally to his face. "We are surrounded at the moment by our own people . . . but I shall remember your warning, my lady "

He had a fragile look, this Lellin Erirrhen, but today, against what seemed the habit of his people, he went armed . . . with a smallish bow and a quiver of brown-feathered arrows. It was probable, Vanye reckoned to himself, that this tall, delicate-looking *qhal* could use them, with the same skill that he and his *khemeis* could travel the woods unheard. Doubtless the noise they must make in riding seemed so loud to their young guide that he felt he might as well whistle songs into the bargain . . . but thereafter he heeded Morgaine's wish and signaled only. He still seemed cheerful, songs or no.

They rested at noon, and Lellin called Sezar back, to sit beside them at a streamside, while the horses drank and they took the leisure for a bit to eat. They had become well-fed in their recent travels, accustomed to meals at regular times and abundant provisions, when before, their travelling and their scant rations had worn them so that they had made new notches in their armor straps. Now they were back to the old, and rested in a patch of warm sun. It would have been easy to fall under Shathan's whispering sell. Morgaine's eyes were half-lidded and lazy, but she did watch, and observed their two guides as if her thoughts much turned upon them.

"We must move," she declared sooner than they would have wished, and rose; dutifully they gathered themselves up, and Vanye took up their saddle-kits.

"My lady Morgaine says our enemies are forest-wise," Lellin said then to Sezar. "Be most careful in your walking."

The Man set his hands in his belt and gave a short nod. "It is quiet all about, no sign of trouble."

"There is bloodshed likely before we are done with this journey," Morgaine said. "And now we come to a point where we are clear of your camp and choose our own way. How far will you two be with us?"

The two looked at her with apparent dismay, but Lellin

was the first to recover himself, and bowed ceremoniously. "I am your appointed guide, wherever you will go. If we are attacked, we will defend; if you attack others, we will stand aside, if it is a matter of going into the plains: we do not go there. Yet if your enemies come into Shathan—we will deal with them and they will not come to you."

"And if I bid you guide us to Nehmin?"

Now Lellin faced her with more directness than he was wont, and his look was sad. "I was warned that this was your desire, and now I warn you, my lady: the place is dangerous, and not alone because of your enemies. It has its own defenders, the *arrha*, against whom my grandfather warned you. Your safeconduct is not valid there "

"But it will take me there."

"So will I, my lady, but if you attack that place—well, you would not be wise to do that."

"If my enemies attack it, it may not stand; and if it falls, then Shathan will fall. I have discussed it with my lord Merir, and he likewise warned me, but he set me free to do what I would in the matter. And he set you to watch me, did he not?"

"Yes," said Lellin, and now all joy and lightness in his face was replaced by dread. "If you have deceived us, doubtless Sezar and I could not stand against you, for you could always take us by stealth if nothing else. Yet I wish to believe that this is not the case."

"Believe that it is not. I have promised lord Merir that I will see you come home safely, and I will keep that promise to the best of my ability."

"Then I shall take you where you wish to go."

"Lellin," said Sezar, "I do not like this."

"But I cannot help it," said Lellin. "If Grandfather had said do not go to Nehmin, then we should not be going; but he did not, and therefore I must do this."

"At your—" Sezar began to say, and stopped; and all froze in each small movement. A horse moved, untimely, drowning the faint sound that had come to them, a bird calling. It was caught up again, nearby.

"We are not safe any longer," said Lellin.

"How do you reach such signs?" Vanye asked, for it seemed a good thing to know; and Lellin bit his lip in reluctance, then shrugged.

"It is in the pulses. The more rapid the trill, the more certain and imminent the hazard. There are other songs for other purposes, and some carry words, but this was a watch-song."

"We should be moving," said Sezar, "if we wish to avoid the matter, and I hope that is your wish."

Morgaine frowned, and nodded, and they quit the place and rode farther.

There were warnings sometimes about them, and all that day they tended east, bending about the arc of Azeroth . . . and it seemed, though the route they took was different, the lay of the land was familiar. "We are near Mirrind," Morgaine observed finally, which agreed with Vanye's own sense of direction, abused though it was by their crooked journeyings and the strangeness of another sky.

"You are right," Lellin said. "We are north of it; best we stay as much withdrawn from the rim of Azeroth as possible. So the signals advise."

By evening they had passed the vicinity of Mirrind and crossed one little stream and another, hardly enough to wet the horses' hooves. Then they came upon a stand of trees many of which were bound with white cords, a-flutter in the breeze.

"What are those?" Vanye asked of Lellin, for he had seen them about Mirrind; and because they had ominous meaning in Shiuan, he had avoided asking. Lellin smiled and shrugged.

"Cut-mark. We are nearing the village of Carrhend, and so we mark the trees for them that are proper to cut, for wood at need, so that the best trees live and they take the least shapely. This we do throughout Shathan, for their use and ours."

"Like tenders of gardens," Vanye observed, amazed by such a thought, for in Andur, forested as it was, and even in Kursh, men cut where they would and the trees still outpaced them.

"Aye," said Lellin, and seemed amused and pleased by such a thought. He patted the shadowy trunk of an old tree they passed in the gathering dusk. "We wander, but I have wandered more in this wood than in any other, and I daresay I know these trees as villagers know their goats. That old fellow has guided me since I was a boy and he was a little slimmer. Gardeners indeed! And if weeds spring up, why, we tend to that too."

That, Vanye thought, had a chilling undertone to it, having nothing at all to do with trees.

"It is coming time for camp," Morgaine said. "And have you a place in Mind, Lellin?"

"Carrhend. They will take us into their hall."

"And shall we endanger another village? I would rather the woods than that."

Lellin sketched a bow, a backward step as they walked. "I believe you would, my lady, but there is no need. Our horses will find us there in the morning, and everything there is quite secure. You will find folk there you know: some of the Mirrindim have elected to come to Carrhend for their safety, such as did not choose to stay by their own fields."

Morgaine looked to Vanye, and he ventured no opinion, but he was privately glad when she accepted. More than two years he had spent under the open sky, but Mirrind had re-taught him the luxuries he had put from his mind forever, being Morgaine's companion. In his mind was a strong memory of Mirrind's mornings, and fine hot bread and butter, so vivid he could taste it. He was, he thought, losing his keen edge. The Shathana style of travel seemed all too easy . . . and yet they had covered much ground in the day's ride, and evaded some manner of trouble.

Sezar turned up again in their path, walking with them in the gathering dark. Soon enough they saw the forest's edge and a broad expanse of fields. They skirted that open space, keeping within the forest shade, and came into Carrhend at the very last of the daylight.

The village spilled out to meet them. "Sezar! Sezar!" the children cried with abandon, and they trooped round the *khemeis* and caught his hands and made much of him.

"This is Sezar's village," Lellin said as they dismounted. "His parents an sister and four brothers live here, so you see we could not pass by this hospitality; I would not be forgiven."

They had been maneuvered, but not to their hurt, and even Morgaine took it in good humor, smiling as the elders of Carrhend presented themselves. Three clans lived here: Salen, Eren, and Thesen . . . and Sezar, who was of clan Thesen, kissed his elders both, and then his parents, and his brothers and sister. There was not overmuch astonishment in this visit, as if it were a frequent thing; but Vanye felt for the young *khemeis* they took perforce into danger with them, and reckoned why he would have been anxious to make this particular stop on their way to Nehmin.

Lellin also had his welcome with them. Neither young nor

old had much awe of him. He took the hands of the kin of Sezar, and was kissed on the cheek by Sezar's mother, which gesture he repaid in kind.

But suddenly there were the Mirrindim, spilling down the steps of the common-hall, as if they had waited on their hosts' courtesies. Now they came, Bythein and Bytheis, and the elders of Sersen and Melzen, and the young women . . . some of them running in their joy to greet them.

There was Sin, among the other children. Vanye caught him up out of their midst and the boy grinned with delight when he lifted him up to Mai's back. Sin set himself astride and looked quite dazed when Vanye passed him up the reins . . . but Mai was too tired to give him trouble and would not leave Siptah.

Morgaine received the elders of Mirrind—embraced old Bythein, who had been their staunchest friend, and there was a chorus of invitations to hall and meal.

"Some of the men are still in Mirrind," Bytheis explained when Morgaine asked after their welfare. "They will keep the fields. Someone must. And the *arrhendim* are watching over them. But we know that our chidren are safest here. Welcome, welcome among us, lady Morgaine, *khemeis* Vanye."

And perhaps the Mirrindim were no less pleased to find them now in the company of their own legitimate lords, assurance that they had not given their hospitality amiss.

"See to the horses," Morgaine said, when all the turmoil was past; and Vanye took Siptah's reins and Sin followed on Mai, the proudest lad in Carrhend.

Sezar walked with him to show him the way, while a cloud of children walked about them, Carrhendim and Mirrindim, male and female. They crowded in behind as they put the horses in the pen, and there was no lack of willing hands to bring them food or curry them. "Have care of the gray," Sin was quick to tell them, lord over all where it concerned the horses. "He kicks what surprises him," which was good advice, for they crowded too close, disrespecting the warhorse's iron-shod heels; but Siptah as well as Mai had surprising patience in this tumult, having learned that children meant treats and curryings. Vanye surveyed all that was done and clapped Sin on the shoulder.

"I will take care of them as always," Sin assured him; he had no doubt this would be so.

"I will see you in hall at dinner; sit by me," Vanye said, and Sin glowed.

He started back to the hall then, and Sezar waited for him at the gate, leaning on the rail of the pen. "Have a care. You may not know what you do."

Vanye looked at him sharply.

"Do not tempt the boy," said Sezar, "to seek outside. You may be cruel without knowing."

"And if he wishes to go outside?" Anger heated him, but it was the way of Andur-Kursh itself, that a man was what he was born . . . save himself, who had always fought his own fate. "No, I understand you," he admitted.

Sezar looked back, and a thoughtful look was in his eyes. "Come," he said then, and they walked back to the hall with a few of the children at their heels, trying to imitate the soft-footed stride of the *khemeis*. "Look behind us and understand me fully," Sezar said, and he looked, and did. "We are a dream they dream, all of them. But when they grow past a certain age—" Sezar laughed softly, "they come to better sense, all but a few of us . . . and when the call comes, we follow, and that is the way of it. If it comes to that boy, let it come; but do not tempt him so young. He may try too early, and come to grief for it."

"You mean that he will walk off into the forest and seek the *qhal*."

"It is never said, never suggested . . . forbidden to say. But those who will come, grow desperate and come, and there is no forbidding them, then, if they do not die in the woods. It is never said . . . but it is a legend among the children; and they say it. At about twelve, they may come, or a little after; and then there is a time that it is too late . . . and they have chosen, simply by staying. We would not refuse them . . . no child dies on his journey that we can ever help. But neither do we lure them. The villages have their happiness. We *arrhendim* have ours. You are bewildered by us."

"Sometimes."

"You are a different kind of *khemeis*."

He looked down. "I am *ilin*. That—is different."

They walked in silence, almost to the hall. "There is a strangeness in you," said Sezar then, which frightened him. He looked up into Sezar's pitying eyes. "A sadness . . . beyond your kinsman's fate, I think. It is about both of you. And different, for each. Your lady—"

Whatever Sezar would have said, he seemed to think better of saying, and Vanye stared at him resentfully, no easier in his mind for Sezar's intimate observations.

"Lellin and I—" Sezar made a helpless gesture. "*Khemeis*, we suspect things in you that have not been told us, that you— Well, something weighs on you both. And we would offer help if we knew how."

*Prying after information?* Vanye wondered, and looked on the man narrowly; the words still afflicted him. He tried to smile, but it was effort, and did not come convincingly. "I shall mend my manner," he said. "I did not know that I was such unpleasant company."

He turned and climbed the wooden stairs into the hall, where dinner was being prepared, and heard Sezar on the treads behind him.

The village had already begun the cooking before they came, but there was enough for guests and to spare . . . a prosperous place, Carrhend, and the Mirrindim in their well-ordered fashion took a share of the word as well as of food. Cooks laughed together and children made friends, and old ones smiled and talked by the fireside, sewing. There seemed no strife from the mixing: the elders could lay down stern edicts when they must, and the *qhalur* law was clearly set forth and respected.

"We have so much to exchange," said Serseis. "We long for Mirrind already, but we feel safer here." Others agreed, though clan Melzen still mourned for Eth, and they were very few here: most of the younger folk of Melzen, male and female, had elected to stay in Mirrind, a determination for Eth's sake, and showing a tough-mindedness that lay deep within the Men of Shathan.

"If any of these evil strangers pass through," Melzein said, "they will not pass back out again."

"May it not happen," Morgaine said earnestly. To that, Melzein inclined her head in agreement.

"Come to the tables," called Saleis of Carrhend then, desperate effort to restore cheer. Folk moved in eagerly, and the benches filled.

Sin scurried in and wedged himself into his promised place. The lad had no words during the meal, contenting himself with quick looks and much listening. He was there; that was enough for Sin; and Sezar caught Vanye's eye during the meal and flicked a glance at the boy, strangely complacent— as if he had seen something clear to be seen.

"It will come," Sezar said then, which Vanye understood and none else might. A weight lifted from him. He saw Mor-

gaine puzzled by that exchange, and felt strange to have one
single thought in which she had no part, a single concern that
did not touch her affairs—to that extent their lives were
bound together.

Then a chill came on him. He remembered what he was,
and that no good had ever come of friendship with those
along their way; most that they touched—died of it.

"Vanye," Morgaine said, and caught his wrist, for he laid
down his spoon of a sudden and it clattered even amid the
noise of voices. "Vanye?"

"It is nothing, *liyo*."

He calmed himself, tried not to think of it, and tried not to
let himself go grim with the boy, who had no thought of
what fear passed in him. Food went down with difficulty for
a time, and then more easily; and he put it from his mind, almost.

A harp silenced the talk after dinner, announcing the accustomed round of singing. The girl Sirn, who had sung in
Mirrind, sang here; then a boy of Carrhead sang a song
for Lellin, who was their own *qhal* they teased Lellin for it,
fondly.

"My turn," said Lellin afterward, took the harp and sang
for them a human song.

Then, still holding the harp, he struck a chord to silence
them, looked round at them all, strangely fair as all his folk,
pale in that dim hall, among their faces. "Take care," he
wished them. "With all my heart, Carrhendim, take care in
these days. The Mirrindim can have told you only a part of
your danger. You are guarded, but your guards are few and
Shathan is wide." His fingers touched the strings nervously,
and the strings sighed in that silence. " 'The Wars of the Arrhend' . . . I could harp you that, but you have heard it
many times . . . how the *sirrindim* and the *qhal* warred, until
we could drive the *sirrindim* from the forest. In those days
Men fought against Men, and they fought us with fire and
axe and ruin. Be on your guard. There are such *sirrindim* at
Azeroth, and renegade *qhal* are with them. It is the old war
again."

There was a frightened murmuring in the hall.

"Ill news," Lellin said. " I grieve to bear it. But be alert and
be ready to walk away even from Carrhend if it comes to
you. Possessions are nothing. Your children are precious. The
*arrhead* will help you rebuild with stone and wood, with our
own hands and of all that we have; so must you be ready to

aid any village that should be in need. Trust at least that we are moving to deal with it; the *arrhendim* are not always there to be seen, and so they serve you best. Let us do what may be done in the way we know; it may suffice. If not, then it will be your arrows that defend us." The strings sighed softly into a *qhalur* song, and folk listened as if it cast some spell over them. There was neither outcry nor debate. When it was done, the hush remained. "Go to your homes, Carrhendim, and Mirrindim to your sheltering; we four guests will leave early in the morning. Do not disturb yourselves to see us go."

"Lord," said one of the young Carrhendim. "We will fight now if we can help."

"Help by defending Carrhend and Mirrind. Your help in that is much needed."

That one bowed, and joined his friends. The Carrhendim left, each bowing to their guests; but the Mirrindim stayed, for they were bedded down in the wings of the hall.

Only Sin departed. "I shall sleep by the horses," he declared, and Vanye did not deny him that.

"Lellin," said Sezar, and Lellin nodded. Sezar left, likely to his kinfolk for the night, or perhaps to some young woman.

The hall was long in settling. There were fretful children and restless young folk. Blankets hung on cords curtained the wings, making a sort of privacy, and leaving the area nearest the fire for their guests.

At last there was quiet, and they settled comfortably, without armor, sharing with Lellin a few sips of a flask that Merir had sent with him.

"Things are well done here," Morgaine said, in the whisper the hour and the sleeping children demanded. "Your folk are very well organized to have lived so long at peace."

The *qhal's* eyes flickered, and he cast off the sober mood that had lain on him like a mantle. "Indeed, we have had fifteen hundred years to meditate on the errors we made in the wars. So long ago we settled on what we would do if the time came; it has, and we will do it swiftly."

"Is it," asked Vanye, "that long since a war in the land?"

"Aye," answered Lellin, compassing with that more than the known history of Andur-Kursh, where strife was frequent. "And may it be longer still."

Vanye thought on that long after they had taken to their pallets, with the *qhal*-lord resting beside him.

Fifteen hundred years of peace. In some measure the thought distressed him, who was born to warfare. To be locked within such long and changeless tranquility, in Shathan's green shadow—the thought distressed him; and yet the pleasantness of the villages, the safety, the order—had their appeal.

He turned his head and looked on Morgaine, who slept. Theirs was a heavy doom, endlessly to travel . . . and they had seen enough of war for any lifetime. *Might we not stay here?* he wondered, brief traitor thought: and pushed it aside, trying not to think of their existence and Mirrind side by side.

Morning was not yet sprung where there came a sound of horses in Carrhend. Vanye rose, and Morgaine, sword in hand; Lellin padded after them to the windows.

Riders had come in, with two saddled horses in tow; they tied them to the rail of an empty pen and rode away.

"Well," said Lellin, "they came in time. They have ridden in from the fields of Almarrhane, not far from here, and I hope they have care riding home."

At the doorstep of one of the nearest houses Sezar appeared, lingering to kiss his parents and his sister, and then, slinging his bow and his gear to his shoulder, he walked across the commons, waved back at his family and then came toward the hall.

They went back to the fireside and armed, quietly gathering their belongings, trying not to disturb the sleeping Mirrindim. Vanye slipped out to saddle the horses and found Sin awake, already beginning that task.

"Are you going to Azeroth to fight *sirrindim?*" Sin asked, the while they both worked . . . no longer innocent, the Mirrindim: they had seen Eth's fate, and had been driven from their homes.

"Where I go next I can never say. Sin, seek the *qhal* when you are old enough; I should not tell you that, but I do."

"I would go with you. Now."

"You know better. But someday you will go into Shathan."

The fever burned in the dark young eyes. The Men of Shathan were all smallish. Even so, Sin would never be tall among them, but there was a fire in him that began already to burn away his childhood. "I will find you there, then."

"I do not think so," Vanye said; sorrow settled deep in Sin's eyes, and all at once a pain stabbed him to the heart.

*Shathan will not be the same for him,* he thought. *We will go, and destroy the Gates; and it is his hope we are going to kill. It will all change, in his lifetime . . . either at our ene-mies' hand—or ours.* He gripped Sin's shoulder then, gave him his hand.

He did not look back.

They were not quiet enough for the village; despite their wish to depart quickly and quietly, there was no preventing the Mirrindim, who rose to bid them farewell; or Sezar's mother, who brought them bread hot from the ovens—she had risen long before dawn, baking for them; and Sezar's fa-ther, who offered them some of his finest fruit wine for their journey; and the brothers and sister who turned out to bid Sezar farewell. They laughed gently when Lellin planted a kiss on the sister's cheek, picking her up and setting her down again, for though she was a budding woman, she was tiny next a *qhal*. She laughed at the kiss, but glanced down shyly and up again with a look that held her heart in her eyes.

Then they mounted up and rode out quietly among the trees, past sentries who were themselves little more than shadows in the trees. Leaves curtained them from Carrhend, and they soon had only the sound of the forest about them.

Sezar was downhearted after the leavetaking, and Lellin looked at him in frowning concern. His mood needed no in-quiry, for surely Sezar and perhaps Lellin would have been glad to stay for Carrhend's protection, and the duty which drew them off lay heavy on them at the moment.

Finally Lellin gave a low whistle . . . and in time there came an answer, slow and placid. At that Sezar looked some-what cheered, and they all felt better for his sake.

# Chapter Six

They kept to the streamcourse for a road after Carrhend and made good time. The horses that the two *arrhendim* had acquired . . . both bays, Lellin's with three white stockings . . . kept well from Siptah's vicinity, so that Lellin and Sezar generally kept the lead by some small space.

The two talked together in soft voices which they, who rode behind, could not quite hear, but they had no distrust for it, and sometimes conversed themselves in private, though usually in the *qhalur* tongue. Morgaine was never inclined to conversation, not in all the time he had known her, but she spoke idly and often since they had come to this land . . . teaching, at first, deliberately making him speak, correcting him often. Then she seemed to have fallen into the habit of talking more than she once would. He was glad of it, and though she never spoke of her own self beyond Andur-Kursh, he found himself speaking of home, and of the better moments of his youth in Morija.

They could speak of Andur-Kursh now, as one finally could speak of the dead, when the pain was gone. He knew his own age; she knew that of a hundred years before his birth; and grim as some of the tales they passed back and forth might be, there was pleasure in it. Time-wanderer she was; and now he was of her kind, and they could speak of it.

But once she mentioned Myya Seijaine i Myya, clan-lord of the Myya when she had led the armies of Andur-Kursh . . . and then her eyes clouded and she fell silent, overcome by memory—for that was one of the scatterings in time which had begun what sat at Azeroth, clan Myya, clan Yla, clan Chya—men who had served her once, and who had become lost in Gates and time. Myya survived. Their children's children a thousand years removed had dwelt in Shiuan, re-

calling her only as an evil legend, confounding her with myth
. . . until Roh came to rouse them.

"Seijaine was a fell sort," she said after a moment, "but
good and generous to his friends. So are his children, but I
am not among their friends."

"It looks," he said with desperate irrelevance, "as if it
might rain."

She looked perplexed by his bent of thought, then looked
up at the clouds that were only slightly gray-edged, and at
him again. She laughed. "Aye. Thee's good for me, Vanye.
Thee is—very good."

She went sober after, and found something to look at
which did not necessitate meeting his eyes. Something swelled
up in him that was bitter and sweet at once. He savored it
briefly, but then, his eyes on Lellin's back—Lellin, whose
pale, spidery grace was the very like of Morgaine's—he
despaired, and put a different interpretation on what she had
said to him . . . recovered the good sense which had long
saved him from making a mistake with her which would
sever them.

He laughed aloud at himself, which drew from her a
strange look. "An odd fancy," he explained, and quickly led
the talk to stopping for noon rest; she did not probe more
deeply.

The rain proved an empty threat. They had feared a wet
camp and a hard night, but the clouds passed over with only
a slight sprinkling at evenfall, and they lay down on the
streamside having made good progress during the day, well-
fed, and under a clear sky on dry ground. It was as if all the
wretchedness that had attended their other rides were a bad
dream, in this land too kindly to do them harshness.

Vanye chose first watch . . . even in this matter they were
more comfortable, for the four of them sharing watches
meant longer sleep. He yielded his post afterward to Lellin,
who rubbed his eyes and propped himself against a tree,
standing, while he lay down to sleep without a qualm or apprehension of treachery.

But he was roused again by a touch on his back, and at
once terror seized on him. He rolled over and saw Lellin likewise touch Morgaine: Sezar was already awake. "Look," Lellin whispered.

Vanye strained his eyes against the dark, following the fix
of Lellin's stare. A shadow stood among the trees on the

other side of the stream. Lellin gave a low trilling whistle, and it moved . . . manlike, but not a Man. It waded the stream with soft splashes, long-limbed and jerking in its precise movements. A chill tightened Vanye's skin, for he knew now that he had seen such a creature before, and in the same vicinity.

Lellin arose, and so did they all, but they stayed where they were, while Lellin walked to the stream and met the creature. Its height was greater than Lellin's; its limbs were arranged like those of a Man, but the articulation was different. When the creature looked up, the eyes were all dark in the starlight, and the features were thin and the mouth pursed, very small for the enormity of the eyes. The legs when it moved flexed like those of a bird, knees bent opposite the direction of a Man's. Vanye crossed himself at the sight, and yet more in awe than in fear, for there seemed less menace in it than difference.

*"Haril,"* Morgaine whispered in his ear. "Only once have I seen the like."

It came onto the bank, wary, and looked them all over with its large eyes. Whether it was male or female was impossible to tell. The body, dusky-hued, was ambiguous under its thick, fibrous robes, which were short and matched the shade of its skin, whatever the color was in daylight. Lellin spoke softly and signed to it. The *haril* answered in a lisping chitter and made a gesture of its own. Then it turned and waded the stream, heron-like in its cant of body and its movements.

"There are strangers," said Lellin. "It is distressed. Something is fearfully amiss that a *haril* has approached us. It wants us to follow."

"What are they?" Vanye asked. "How much can you understand of what it wants?"

"They are from long ago. They live in the deepest parts of Shathan, the wild parts where we seldom go, and generally they have nothing to do with *qhal* or Men. Their speech is their own; we cannot learn it and they cannot learn ours . . . nor wish to, I suppose . . . but they will sign—and if a *haril* has come asking us to do something, then we should do it, my lady Morgaine. There is something vastly amiss to urge it to that."

The *haril* waited, across the stream.

"We will go," Morgaine said. Vanye spoke no word of objection, but there was a tightness at his belly that settled in like an old friend. He gathered up their gear and started for the horses in haste and quietly. Whatever they had evaded in these last slow days was suddenly upon them, and from now on, there seemed no hope of coming peacefully to Nehmin.

They rode across the stream, moving as quietly as the horses might, and the *haril* went before them, a shadow that the horses did not like. It chose ways difficult for riders, and often they must bend beneath branches or negotiate difficult slopes. At each delay the *haril* waited, silent, until they had overcome the obstacle and began to close the gap.

"Madness," Vanye said under his breath, but Morgaine did not regard him. The *haril* stayed in sight, but now and again there was another presence: the horses detected it and threw their heads and would as gladly have fled. It flitted now on this side and now on the other, a tail-of-the-eye presence that was gone before one could turn the head, or which rustled a leaf and stopped before one could fix the place of it.

Another, Vanye reckoned . . . or maybe more than one. He slipped the ring which let his sword fall to his hip, and ducked low against Mai's neck as they took a new turn through dense branches and down a slope.

The trees thinned. Their guide brought them out into the midst of an almost-clearing, where something like a white-butterfly seemed suspended above a shadowy form . . . a little nearer and they saw it for a body, *haril*, and dead. The butterfly was the fletching of the arrow in its back. Their guide chittered a string of words that seemed to reproach them.

Lellin dismounted and signed what looked like a question. The *haril* stood still and did not respond.

"It is no arrow of ours," said Sezar; and while Morgaine and Sezar stayed ahorse, Vanye slid down and went carefully to the dead *haril*, examined the arrow more closely in the starlight. The feathering it bore would not give it near the accuracy of the *arrhendim's* brown-fletched shafts at long range. This was the feather of a sea-bird, here in Shathan woods.

"Shiua," he said. "Lellin, ask them: *where?*"

"I cannot be—" Lellin began, and then looked about in alarm. Morgaine's hand went to her back, where she carried the lesser of her weapons, for all about them were tall, stalking shadows, heron-like in their movements. No brush rustled. They were simply there.

"Please," Lellin breathed, "do not do anything. Do not

move." He faced the first *haril,* and repeated the question-sign, adding to it several others.

The *harilim* chittered reply all together. There was anger in that sound, which was that of mice or rats, but deeper. One came forward to stand by the dead, and Vanye backed a step, but only a step, lest they mistake it for flight. He stood very close to that one, and dark, enormous eyes flickered over him minutely. A spidery arm extended and it touched him; fingers ran lightly over his clothing, clinging slightly at each touch. He did not move. Starlight shone on the creature's smooth dark skin, showed the gauzy weave of its thick garments. He shuddered involuntarily as it moved behind him and touched his back, and he cast a glance at Morgaine, seeking counsel. Her face was pale and set, and in her hand was the weapon which had killed the deer. If she used it, he thought, then he would not be riding out with her: he much feared so.

Signs passed between the *haril* and Lellin, angry on the *haril's* part, urgent on Lellin's. "They believe you part of the strangers' force," Lellin said. "They ask why we ride with you. They have seen you two here before, alone."

"Near Mirrind," Vanye said very quietly, "there was one. I know what it was now. It ran away when we chased it." The *haril's* hand descended on his shoulder from behind, gentle as wind, and tightened, betraying enormous strength, wanting him to turn. He did so, and faced it, heart beating wildly as he stared up into that dark, strange face.

"It is you," Sezar said from horseback. "It is you that disturb them . . . a tall Man, and too fair for a Shathana. They know that you are not of our blood."

"Lellin," said Morgaine, "I advise you do something before I do."

"Please, lady, do nothing. We are all alone here. Our folk have given no warning of this, and I do not think there are any of the *arrhendim* in the vicinity . . . little they could help if they were. These woods are the *harilim's* just now, and our chances of escape are not good. They are not violent . . . but they are very dangerous."

"Bring one of my arrows," Vanye said; and when no one moved: "Bring it!"

Lellin did so, moving very carefully. Vanye held it so that the *haril* could see it and indicated the feathering, which was brown; and pointed at the arrow in the corpse, which bore white feathers. The *haril* spoke something to its fellows; they responded in tones that seemed at least less angry.

"Tell him," Vanye asked of Lellin, "that those Men out there in Azeroth are not our friends; that we come to fight them."

"I am not certain I can," Lellin said in despair. "There is no system to the signs; subtleties are almost impossible."

But he tried, and perhaps succeeded. The *haril* spoke to its fellows, and some of them gathered up the body of their dead and bore it into the woods.

Then the one behind set hand on Vanye and began to draw him away too. He resisted, planting his feet, and now he was very frightened, for the thing was strong and they were still completely surrounded.

Lellin put himself in the *haril's* path and signed a negative. The *haril* spat back a chittering retort, and beckoned.

"They want us all to come," Lellin said.

"*Liyo*—get out of here."

She did not. Vanye turned his head, trying to reckon his chances of breaking for his horse and living to reach it. Morgaine did not move, doubtless weighing other considerations.

Sezar muttered something he did not hear clearly. "Their weapons are poisoned," Morgaine said more loudly. "Vanye, their darts are poisoned. I think Lellin has been persuaded by that from the beginning. We are in somewhat of a difficulty, and I fear that there are more of them that we do not see."

Sweat trickled down his face, cool as it was in the night. "This is a ridiculous situation. I apologize for it. What do you advise, *liyo?*"

"Vanye asks for advice," she said to Lellin.

"I think we have no choice but to go where they wish . . . and not to do anything violent. I do not think they will harm any of us unless they are threatened. They cannot speak to us; I think that they want to assure themselves of something or to demonstrate something. Their minds are very different; they are changeable and excitable. They rarely kill; but we do not enter their woods, either."

"Are these their woods, where you have led us?"

"They are ours, and we are now nearer Azeroth than I would have liked to come, following this one. Your enemies have roused something that we may all regret. *Khemeis* Vanye, I do not think they will let you go until they have what they want, but I do not think they will harm you."

"*Liyo?*"

"Let us go with this a little way and see."

Lellin translated an affirmative sign. The *haril* tugged
gently at Vanye's arm, and he went, while the others were allowed to go ahorse: he heard them following. The *haril's*
hand slid to his wrist, a gentle grip, dry as old leaves and unpleasantly cold. The creature turned and chittered at him
now and again as they came to rough ground, helped him up
slopes, and when a time had passed in their journey, it let
him go seeming to judge that he would stay with it. Then his
fear diminished despite the strangeness of the face which occasionally turned to him in the dark. They were being urged
to haste, but not threatened.

He looked back more than once, to be sure that they had
not lost the others; but the riders stayed with them, more
slowly and by a course the horses could follow. Sezar brought
Mai along, which he was glad to see. But when his looking
back delayed him, a touch came on his shoulder: shuddering,
he faced the *haril*, which seized him a time and hurried him
on.

He tried signs of his own, making what among Andurin
signed for *where?*—A pass of the open palm back and forth
supine. The *haril* seemed not to comprehend. It touched his
face with clinging, spidery fingers, replied with a sign he did
not understand, and hurried him on, through the thicket and
up slopes and on and on until he was panting.

They came briefly into the open between trees. The *haril*
seized his arm again to be sure of him, for suddenly there
was a dead man at their feet, and another, as they crossed
that area, bodies almost hidden in the dark and the leaves.
He saw the leather and cloth in the starlight and knew them
for the enemy. One carried arrows, white-feathered. He
resisted the *haril* enough to bend and gather one up, showing
the creature the nature of the feather. The *haril* seemd to
understand, and took the arrow from him and threw it down.
*Come, come,* it beckoned him.

He glanced over his shoulder and for a moment panicked,
for he no longer saw the others. Then they came into view,
and he yielded to the *haril's* pulling at him. It began to go
very quickly, so that he was rapidly exhausted by the pace,
for he was in armor and the creature strode wide with its
stalking gait.

Then they were at a complete break in the forest: trees
ceased, and starlight fell clearly across a wide plain. Something else glowed there, the glare of fires spangled across the

open. Where they stood there was wood hewn, trees felled, their wounds stark in the faint light. The *haril* pointed to those, to the camp, and signed at him, at *him*, accusingly.

*No,* he signed back. Whatever it wanted or suspected that had to do with himself and that camp, the answer was not. Morgaine and the others overtook them now, and *harilim* were all about them. He looked up at her, and she gazed at the campfires of the enemy.

"This is not their main strength," she whispered for Lellin's benefit; and that was true, for the camp was not nearly large enough—nor would Roh or Hetharu likely give up possession of the Gate of Azeroth's center.

"This is what the *harilim* brought us to see," Lellin said. "They are angry . . . for the trees, for the killing. They blame us that this has been allowed."

"Vanye," Morgaine said softly. "Try; mount up quickly."

He moved, without prelude or hesitation, flung himself for Mai's side and scrambled into the saddle. There was a stir among the *harilim*, but none moved to stop him. He remembered the poisoned weapons and sat the nervous horse with his heart pounding against his ribs.

Morgaine turned Siptah slowly, to regain the shelter of the woods. *Harilim* stood gathered in the way, stick-like arms uplifted, refusing them passage.

"We are not wanted here," Lellin said. "They will not harm us, but they do not want us in the area."

"Will they cast us out onto the plains?"

"That seems their intent."

*"Liyo,"* Vanye said for of a sudden he read her mind and liked not what he read. "Please. If we strike at them, then we will not ride far in the forest before there are others. These creatures are too apt to ambushes."

"Lellin," she said, "why have not your people been hereabouts? Where are the *arrhendim* who should have warned us of this intrusion of enemies?"

"The *harilim* probably forced them out . . . as they mean to do with us. We do not dispute passage with the dark folk. Lady, I fear for Mirrind and Carrhend. I fear greatly. That is surely where the other *arrhendim* have retreated, to protect and warn those places with all haste; they would not have come this far when they knew the dark folk were here. Lady, forgive me. I have failed miserably in my charge. I led you into this and I do not see a way out. None of the *arrhendim* hereabouts had reason to suspect there were those who would ride past their warning-signals. They gave them, but we rode through. I thought only of *sirrindim,* that we could resist. I did not reckon that the *harilim* had taken possession here. Lady, it may be that the keepers of Nehmin have stirred them up."

"The *arrha?*"

"There is rumor that the keepers of Nehmin can call them. It is possible that they are part of Nehmin's defense, summoned against *that.* If that is so, then I myself would be surprised; they are as difficult to reason with as the trees themselves; and they hate both Men and *qhal.*"

"But if it is true, then it is possible that Nehmin itself is under attack."

"It is possible, lady, that this is so."

She said nothing for a moment. Vanye felt it too, the sense that beneath the peace of Shathan, which had wrapped them securely thus far, things had been going dangerously, utterly amiss.

"Beware, all of you," she said, and slipped *Changeling* from her shoulder to her hip. Holding one palm aloft, in a gesture which somewhat stilled the *harilim's* chittering apprehension, she unhooked the sheath.

Then, two-handed, she drew it slowly, and the opal light of the blade swirled softly in the dark. The light glittered in the dark eyes of the *harilim,* and grew as she drew it forth. Suddenly it blazed full, and the well of darkness at the tip burst into being. The *harilim* drew back, their large eyes reflecting it, red mirrors of that cold light. The wind of otherwhere stirred the trees and whipped at their hair. The *harilim* covered their faces with spidery hands and backed and bowed at that howling sound.

She sheathed it then. Lellin and Sezar slid from their horses and came and bowed at Siptah's hooves. The *harilim* kept their distance, chittering softly in fear.

"Now do you understand me?" she asked.

Lellin looked up, his pale face stark with dread. "Lady, do not—do not loose that thing. I understand you. I am your servant. I was given to be, and I must be. But has my lord Merir knowledge of that thing?"

"Perhaps he suspects. He gave you for my guide, Lellin Erirrhen, and he did not forbid my seeking Nehmin. Tell the *harilim* we will go through their forest and see what their mind is now."

Lellin rose and did so, signing quickly; the *harilim* melted backward into the trees.

"They will not stay us," he said.

"Get to horse."

The *arrhendim* remounted, and slowly Morgaine urged Siptah forward. The gray horse threw his head and snorted his displeasure at the *harilim*, but they passed freely back into the forest, while the *harilim* stayed with them like shadows.

"Now I know the grief that is on you," Sezar whispered as they came near in the dark. Vanye looked at him, and at Lellin, and a weight sat at his heart, for it was true that the *arrhendim* began to understand them, who carried *Changeling* . . . recognized the evil of it, and the danger.

But they served it, as he did.

## Chapter Seven

The *harilim* moved about them still, shadows in the first fading of the stars. They rode as quickly as they could in the tangled wood, and the *harilim* did not hinder, but neither did they help; while Lellin and Sezar, beyond the woods that they knew, could only guess at the quickest way.

Then at the very last of the night the forest gave way before them, and dark waters glistened between the trees.

"The Narn," Lellin said as they drew rein within that last fringe of trees. "Nehmin lies beyond it."

Morgaine stood in the stirrups and leaned on the saddle-bow, stretching. "Where can we cross?"

"There is supposedly a ford," Sezar said, "halfway between the Marrhan and the plain."

"An island," said Lellin. "We have never ridden this far east, but we have heard so. It should be only a little distance north."

"Day is coming on us," Morgaine said. "The riverside is exposed. Our enemies are likely near at hand. We cannot af-

ford errors in judgment, Lellin . . . nor can we linger over-
long and risk being cut off from Nehmin."

"If they have hit Mirrind and Carrhend," Vanye reasoned,
"they will have learned which way we rode, and some of
them would not be long at all in understanding the meaning
of that." He saw Sezar's stricken face as he said it; the *khemeis* knew well his meaning and understood the danger his
people were in. "Can we find an answer of the *harilim*,
whether the strangers have crossed the Narn?"

Lellin looked about; there was nothing behind them, not a
breath, not a whisper of leaves . . . no sign, suddenly, of
their shadowy companions.

Morgaine swore softly. "Perhaps they do not like the coming daylight; or perhaps they know something we do not.
You lead, Lellin. Let us come to this crossing as quickly as
we can, and if there is night enough left, we will try it."

Lellin eased his horse into the lead northward, trying to
keep within the trees as they rode, but there were washes and
flood-felled trees that made their progress slow. At times they
must go down onto the bank, exposing themselves to view of
any watchers on the far side. At others they must withdraw
far into the forest, almost losing sight of the river.

And they were tired, the better part of the night without
sleep, constantly tried by obstacles, the branches of the trees
tearing at them, the horses stumbling often over impossible
ground, or exhausting themselves in climbs up and down
tributary washes. Dawn began, almost enough that they could
see color on the forest's edge.

Yet in that first coloring they came to their islet, a long
bar, bearing a crown of brush, with logs piled up at the up-
stream end.

They hesitated. Morgaine sent Siptah forward, down that
slope toward the crossing. Vanye put the spurs to Mai and
followed, little caring whether Lellin and Sezar stayed with
them or no; but he heard them coming. Morgaine hastened:
the fever was on her now . . . enemies behind, the thing
which they sought ahead of them; in any doubt, he knew
what she would choose, and that was to go, to make ground
while they could, nothing hesitating.

The horses slowed as they hit the water, fighting current
which rose about their knees. Siptah hit a hole, struggled out
of it; Vanye rode around it, with the *arrhendim* in his wake.
The horses waded breast-deep now, the water dark and
strong. Mai slipped often, struggling after Siptah . . . shoul-

dered into Sezar's horse. Almost Vanye dismounted then, but
she found firmer footing, and the water fell briefly as they
passed the halfway mark, the point of the isle. Siptah kept
going, strongest of their mounts, and in anxiety Vanye used
the spurs to force the mare into the second half of the
crossing, cursing Morgaine's stubbornness. Soon the gray
horse began to rise from the water a second time, coming out
on the bank. Morgaine reined about to look back at them.

Something flew, hissing, and hit; she went over, flung
nearly out of the saddle. Siptah shied wildly, and Vanye cried
out and rammed spurs into the mare. Somehow, by desperate
strength, Morgaine was still ahorse, clinging by the mane and
by one heel across the saddle, her pale hair a wild banner
against the shadow, a white-feathered arrow driven somewhere the armor was not. Siptah spun once, confused, then
ran, arrows hailing fater. Vanye bent low and drove the mare
in desperate flight down the bank after her . . . somehow
Morgaine pulled herself back into the saddle, enough to hold
on.

"Riders!" Sezar shouted behind him.

He did not turn to look. His eyes were only for Morgaine,
who slumped now across Siptah's neck, and the sand over
which the mare's hooves flew was spotted with dark drops.

The mare slowed, faltered, froth spattering her and him.
Sezar and Lellin overtook him—passed him now as the mare
broke stride. Sezar started to draw back for him. "No!" Lellin cried, and Sezar whipped the horse on to stay with Lellin.
Further and further the distance widened between him and
*arrhendim.*

"Get her to safety!" Vanye screamed after them. To do
that, they had come within reach, he would have cast one of
them from the saddle and thrown him to the enemy. Perhaps
Lellin sensed it, and would not delay in his reach. "Help
her!"

Mai was done, staggering badly. In desperation he turned
for the trees up the incline of the bank, drove her for that, to
dismount and run for cover afoot.

But she betrayed him at the last. Her strength failed in the
loose sand and she went down nose-first while they were still
on the flat. He sprawled, and she heaved down on him before
he cleared the saddle, rolled as dead weight, neck broken,
limp.

He twisted round as he heard the riders bearing down on

him—grimaced, for his leg was pinned and he could not drag it free nor get leverage against Mai's heavy body.

He had no hope of anything further, even that all would give up the chase and delay for him; they did not. Most of them thundered past, spraying him with sand and gravel, but four reined back to deal with him. He had his sword still, and managed to get it into his hand, reckoning even so that it was futile, that they would put an arrow into him at safe distance and end it.

They were not halfling Shiua, but Men. He recognized them as they left their horses and came to him, and he cursed as they grinned in triumph, making a half-ring about him, out of his reach.

Myya Fihar i Myya . . . Mija Fwar, a Hiua accent made the name: there was no mistaking that face, scarred and twisted about the lips with a knife-mark. Fwar had been Morgaine's lieutenant once, before their ways parted in violence. The others were Fwar's kinfolk, all Myya, all with blood-debt against him.

They laughed at his plight, and he bided quietly, no longer anticipating the arrow, hoping that Fwar in particular would come within reach. "Bring that branch over here," Fwar ordered one of his cousins, Minur. The man brought it, a sandy length of still-sound wood, tall as a Hiua and thick as a man's wrist.

Not for levering, that; they were wiser. Vanye saw the intent in Fwar's eyes and tucked down as the blow came . . . clutched the sword against him, but blow after blow to his helmed skull stunned him, and finally they rammed the end of the branch at him and broke his grip on the sword. They were on him then; he tried for the dagger, and though he had it from sheath and put a wound on at least one of them, they pinned him and wrested it from him. Then they found cords and tried to bind his hands back; but he fought that wildly, and twice they had to daze him before that was done.

Then he was finished, and knew it . . . lay still with his face against the dry sand, gathering his forces for whatever came next. One kicked him in the belly for good measure, and he doubled reflexively, not even focusing his eyes to look at them. They were Myya, of a cold and vengeful clan, which had hated him in Kursh and sworn his death there. But these descendants of the proud Kurshin Myya, lost in Gates a thousand years and more . . . knew nothing of honor, despised it as they despised everything beyond themselves. Fwar hated him with a burning and personal hatred.

They levered Mai off him finally. He had thought that the leg might be broken where she had fallen on him, but the sand had saved him from that. He had some hope then; but the knee gave with a stab of blinding pain when they seized him up and expected him to stand, and not all their blows and curses could amend that. Then he gave up all hope of winning free of them.

"Put him on a horse," Fwar said. "There might be friends of his hereabouts . . . and we want time to pay you your due, Nhi Vanye i Chya, for all my brothers and our kinfolk that you killed."

Vanye spat at him. It was all the recourse he had left, and that too failed of the mark. Fwar's eyes raked him over and calculated . . . not stupid, this man: Morgaine would not have had a dull-witted man in her service. "He would like us to stay near here as long as possible, I suppose. But the *khal*-lords will see to *her*, and we can deal with them later. We had better take our prize downriver a ways."

One of them brought a horse near. Vanye kneed the hapless beast in the flank and sent it screaming and plunging away from him; but the Hiua had an answer for that too, and bound his ankles and flung him over another saddle belly down, lashed him in place so that he could not further delay them. The helm fell; one of them gathered it up and set it mockingly on his own head.

Then they started off down the riverside, moving rapidly, and from that head-down jolting Vanye began to slip from consciousness . . . now wholly unaware, but there were long darknesses in which he found no refuge.

And worse than other pain was the thought of Morgaine, whether the Shiua riders had overtaken her or whether she had fallen to her wound . . . he recalled the blood on the sand, sick at heart. But he must live, then. If she were alive, she needed him. If she were dead, he still must contrive to live; he had sworn so.

He had not been reckoning of that when he had fought the Hiua, trying to win of them a quick death and honest; but when he had had time to think of what she had set on him by oath, he gave up fighting his enemies and gathered his strength for another and longer fight, in which there was no honor at all.

The Hiua stopped at mid-morning. Vanye was aware of the horse slowing, but of little else until they freed him of the saddle and flung him roughly to the sand. There he lay still and ignored them, staring at the dark waters of the Narn which flowed a stone's throw away . . . a black thread that still bound this place to that where she was: the sight of it comforted him, that they were not yet lost, one from the other.

One of the Hiua seized hold of him and lifted his head, put a flask to his lips: water. He drank what they would give him; they poured more of it on his face and struck him, trying to restore him. He reacted little to either, although he was aware enough.

Fwar came, seized him by the hair, shook at him until his eyes fixed on him. "Ger, Awan," he named his dead brothers, "and Efwy. And Terrin and Ejan and Prafwy and Ras, Minur's kin here; and Eran, that was Hul's brother; and Sithan and Ulwy that were Trin's . . ."

"And our wives and our children and all those that died before that," said Eran. Vanye looked at him, reading there a hate which equalled Fwar's. He had killed Fwar's brothers with his own hand. Perhaps he had killed the others they named too: many had died in pursuit of them. The women and children had died with their dead hold, no doing of his . . . but that made no difference in their minds. He was a hate they could seize upon, an enemy they had in hand, and for all the grief they had ever suffered, for Morgaine who had led their ancestors to grief in Irien and tried to bind them in drowning Shiuan—for her too they had such burning hate: but he was Morgaine's, and he was in hand.

He gave them no answer; none would serve. Trin hit him a dazing blow, and Vanye twisted over and spat blood on him, with more accuracy than before. Trin hit him a second time, but Fwar stopped him from a third.

"We have all day, and all night and after that."

They looked pleased at that thought, and the talk afterward was foul and ugly, at which Vanye simply set his jaw and stared at the river, ignoring their attempts to bait him. A great deal of their threatening was wasted on him, for they spoke a rough sort of Kurshin well-laden with *qhalur* and marshlands borrowings, much changed from his own tongue . . . and he had learned Hiua of a young woman whose speech was gentler. He could guess at enough of it.

He was angry. That fact dully amazed him, in the far distance to which his thinking mind had retreated . . . that he would feel more rage than terror. He had never been a brave man. He had come to every grief that had driven him from home and hold and honor because he imagined pain too vividly and came undone at his kinsmen's slow tormenting . . . a boy's misery: he had been all too vulnerable then, loving them more than he had understood.

He had no love for these, these scourings of Hiuaj's Barrow-hills, these fallen Myya. He seethed with anger that of all the enemies he had, he had fallen to them . . . to Fwar, whose worthless life he had spared, being too much Nhi to kill a downed enemy. Now he had his reward of that mercy. Morgaine too they attacked with their foul laughter, and he had to bear it, still hoping that somewhere in their confidence they would make the mistake of freeing his hands with Fwar in reach.

They did not. They had learned him too well, and devised to get him from his armor without freeing him, throwing a noose about his ankles and suspending him from the limb of one of the trees like a slaughtered deer. They amused themselves in that too, pushing him to and fro while the blood pounded in his head and his senses were near to leaving him. Then they had easier work to free his hands and take the armor from him. Even so he succeeded in getting his hands on Trin, but he could not hold him. They struck him for their amusement until the blood ran down his arms and spotted the sand beneath him. Eventually his senses faded.

Horsemen, in number.

He hears the thunder of the hooves that merged with the pulse in his ears. Bodies rushed about him, with panting and blowing of horses.

More of them, returned from upriver. He remembered Morgaine and struggled back to consciousness, trying to focus his blurred eyes to see whether they had found her or not. Upside down in his vision, all the horses were dark shadows: Siptah was not there. One rider came near, aglitter with scale, white-haired.

*Khal.* Shiua *qhal.* "Cut him down," the *khal*-lord ordered. Finally there came a sawing at the rope. Vanye tried to lift his stiffened arms to protect his head, knowing that he must fall. But armored riders locked arms beneath him, eased him to the ground upright. He did not struggle after he realized their support . . . fell less hard than he might. They were not

Fwar's: no more his friends than Fwar's men, and likely crueler; but their immediate purpose involved his living, and he accepted it. He lay still on the sand at the horses' feet, while the blood flowed back to his lower limbs and his heart labored with the strain of it. In his ears were the *khal*-lord's curses for the Men who had almost killed him.

*Morgaine*, he thought, *what of Morgaine?* But nothing they said gave him any clue.

"Ride off," the lord bade Fwar and his cousins. "He is ours."

Eventually—for in Shiuan as here, *qhal* were the more powerful—Fwar and his men mounted and rode away, without a word of a threat of vengeance . . . and that, in a Barrows-man and a Myya, boded ill for an enemy's back when the time came.

Vanye struggled to his elbows to see them go; but he had view of nothing but horses' legs and a few *khal* afoot, scale-armored and wearing helms which gave them the faces of demons—all helmed, save their lord, who remained ahorse, his white hair flowing in the wind. It was not one of the Shiua lords he knew.

The men-at-arms cut the cords that bound his ankles and tried to make him stand. He shook his head at that. "The knee . . . I cannot walk," he said hoarsely and as they spoke . . . in the *qhalur* tongue.

They were startled at that. Men in Shiuan did not speak the language of their masters, although *khal* spoke that of Men; he remembered that they were Shiua when one hit him across the face for his insolence.

"He will ride," said the lord. "Alarrh, your horse will bear this Man. Gather up all that is strewn here; the humans have no sense of order. They will leave all this for enemies to read. You"—for the first time he spoke directly to Vanye, and Vanye stared up at him sullenly. "You are Nhi Vanye i Chya."

He nodded.

"That means yes, I suppose."

"Yes." The *khal* had spoken the language of Men, and he had answered again in *qhalur*. The lord's pale, sensitive face registered anger.

"I am Shien Nhinn's-son, prince of Sotharrn. The rest of my men are hunting your mistress. The arrow that took her was the only favor for which we thank the Hiua cattle, but it is a sorry fate for a high-born *khal*, all the same. We will try to better it. And you, Vanye of the Chya—you will be welcome in our camp. Lord Hetharu has a great desire to find you again . . . more desire for your lady, to be sure, but you will find him overjoyed to see you."

"I do not doubt," he murmured; but he did not resist when they bound his hands and brought a horse for him, heaving him into the saddle upright. The pain of his wounds almost took his senses from him; he swayed with dizziness as the horse shied off, and the Shiua began to dispute bitterly who should foul his hands and his person in seeing that he stayed ahorse, bloody and half-naked and human as he was. "I am Kurshin," he said then between his teeth. "While the horse stays under me, I shall not fall off. I will have no *khal's* hands on me either."

They muttered at that and spoke of teaching him his place; but Shien bade them to horse. They started off down the sandy bank with speed that jolted, likely malice rather than needful haste. They gave it up after a time, and Vanye bowed his head and gave to the horse's moving, exhausted. He roused only when they made the fording of the Narn, and the wide plain of Azeroth lay open before them.

After that it was grassland under the horses' hooves, and they went smoothly and easily.

He lived: that was for now the important thing. He smothered his anger and kept his head down as they expected of a Man awed by them. They would not anticipate trouble of him, these folk who marked their own hold-servants with brands on the face, to know them from other Men . . . reckoning no Man much more than animal.

It was not uncharacteristic of them that they found a means to splint his knee at their first rest, caring for him with the same detachment that they might have spent on a lame horse, no gentler and no rougher than that; yet no one would give him a drink because it meant his lips touching something they must use. One did throw him a morsel of food when they ate, but it lay on the grass untouched, for they would not unbind his hands and he would not eat after that fashion, as they wished. He sullenly averted his face, and was no better for that stop except that he could at least stand once he had been put on his feet. They saw to that, he reckoned, simply because it saved them having to work so much getting him on and off a horse.

"There was a *khal* with you besides your mistress," Shien said to him, riding close to him that afternoon. "Who?"

He did not look up or give indication that he had heard.

"Well, you will find time to think of it," Shien said, and spurred disdainfully ahead, giving up the question with an ease curious in his kind.

And that *who* seemed to desire a name in answer, as if they had taken Lellin to be one of their own, renegade to them. As if—he thought, hope stirring in him—as if they had not yet realized the existence of the *arrhend*, or realized a presence in this land besides that of Men. Perhaps Eth had held back more than seemed likely; or perhaps his killers had not left Shathan alive.

He lifted his head despite himself, and looked at the horizon before him, which was grassy and flat as far as the eye could see, an expanse unbroken save for a few bushes or thorn-thickets randomly scattered. The unnatural shape of Azeroth was not evident to the man who stood amid it: it was too vast to grasp at once. Perhaps there was much still secret from the Shiua . . . indicating that as yet none of Lellin's folk had fallen into their hands, and that the Mirrindim might yet be safe.

He hoped so with a fearful hope, although he held out little for himself.

They camped in the open that night, and this time they yielded to practicality and freed his hands briefly, standing over him with swords and pikes as if he could run, lame as he was. He ate a little, and one of them condescended to pour a little water into his hands that he might drink, thus saving the purity of his waterflask. But they restored the bonds for the night, hand and foot, securing him to one of their heavy saddles on the ground, so that he could not slip off into the dark. Lastly they threw a cloak over him, that he not freeze, for he had no clothing on his upper body.

Then they slept, insolently secure, posting no guard. He fretted long, trying his bonds, with an eye to stealing a horse and running for it; but the knots were out of his reach and the cords were too tight. Exhausted, he slept too, and woke in the morning with a kick in the ribs and a *khal's* curse in his ears.

It was more of the same the next day: no food nor water until the evening, enough to keep him alive, but little more. He nursed his anger, for it kept him fed the same as the food did; but he kept his senses too, and bore their arrogance without resistence. Only once it failed him, when a guard seized

him by the hair; he rounded on the halfling . . . and the
guard stepped back at what he saw in him. They struck him
to the ground then, for no more than that—that he had dared
look one of them in the eyes. Their treatment of him wor-
sened thereafter. They began to torment him with mindful
spite when they must handle him, and began to talk among
themselves, for they knew that he could understand, of what
might befall him at their hands.

"You have the grace of your Barrows-ancestors," he said to
them finally, and in their own tongue. One of them struck
him for this. But Shien frowned, and curtly bade his own
men to silence, and to let him be.

That night, when they made camp by a new tributary of
the Narn, Shien stared at him long and thoughtfully after the
others had begun to settle to sleep, stared with a concentration which began to disturb him . . . the more so when Shien
roused his men and dismissed them out of hearing.

Then Shien came and settled at his side.

"Man." It was an inflection that only a *khal* could give
that word. "Man, it is said that you are close kin to the halfling Chya Roh."

"Cousin," he answered, unnerved by this approach. No
word before this had they drawn from him in questions. He
resolved to say nothing more. But Shien stared at him in pen-
sive curiosity.

"Fwar's handiwork has disturbed the resemblance, but it is
there; I see it. And this Morgen-Angharan . . ." he used the
name by which Morgaine was known to them, and laughed.
"Can Death die?" he asked, for Angharan was a deity among
the marshlanders of Shiuan, and that was her nature, the
white queen.

He knew *khalur* humor, which believed in nothing and reverenced no gods, and he shut his ears to this pointless baiting.
But Shien drew his dagger and laid it along his cheek, turning
his face back with that, lest he soil his hands. "What a prize
you are, Man . . . if you know what Roh knows. Do you realize that you could become both free and comfortable if you
hold what I think you may? Man who speak our language.
And I would not disdain to seat you at my table and give
you—other—privileges. Gods, you have some grace of bearing, more than some who go boasting their tiny portion of
*khalur* blood. You are not of the Hiua's kind. Do you know
how to be reasonable?"

He stared into Shien's eyes . . . pale gray they were by daylight, as so few of the halflings' were: near full-blood, this prince. He was shaken to reckon that he could be what Shien said, a prize among *khal*, a commodity of value among the powerful: he had knowledge of Gates, the lore which they had lost, knowledge by which Roh himself had gained power among these folk.

"What of Roh?" he asked.

"Chya Roh has made mistakes, which may well prove fatal to him. You might avoid those same mistakes. You might even expect that Hetharu could be persuaded to forget his vexation with you."

"And you will present that solution to Hetharu, is that it? I work at your orders, give what I know to you, and you regain what power Hetharu has taken from you."

The blade turned, and bit slightly. "Who are you to talk of our affairs?"

"Hetharu brought all the Shiua lords to their knees because he had Roh to give him power. Do you love him for it?"

He thought for an instant that Shien would kill him outright. His expression was ugly. Then Shien flipped the knife back into sheath at his belt. "You have need of a patron, Man. I could help you. But you want to play games with me."

"If there is a way out of my situation, make it clear to me."

"It is very clear. Give me the knowledge that you have, and I will be able to help you. Otherwise not."

He stared into Shien's eyes and read it for half-truth. "And if I give you knowledge enough to contest with Hetharu and Roh, then my usefulness is ended there, is it not? Give you knowledge so that you can politic with it and trade influence with your brother-lords? Not in Hetharu's game. Be braver than that, Shiua lord, or do not think that you can use me for a weapon. Break with them both and I will serve you and give you the power that you want; but not otherwise."

"The *khal* who rode with you . . . who?"

"I will not tell you."

"You think that you are in a position to refuse?"

"Those men of yours . . . how well can you trust them? You think there is not one among them who would bear information to Hetharu for reward? How you killed me out here, trying for knowledge Hetharu would not approve you having . . . why else did you send them out of hearing? No.

If you are going to break with Hetharu, you need me alive
and healthy. I will *tell* you nothing; but I will help you get
what you want."

Shien sat on his heels and stared at him, arms folded. He
knew that he had gone very far with this *khalur* prince. He
saw a veil come over Shien's eyes, and hope failed him.

"It is said," Shien murmured, "that you killed Hetharu's
father. And do you hope to deal with him after that?"

"A lie. Hetharu killed his father, and blamed me for it to
save his reputation."

Shien laughed wolfishly. "Aye, so do we all think. But that
is the kind of lord Hetharu is, and so he dealt with you once
when you trifled with him . . . so he dealt with his own lord
and father; and now do you propose that if I refuse your
mad scheme you will throw yourself on his mercy again? You
do not learn readily, Man."

A chill came on him, remembering, but he shook his head
nevertheless. "Then you also know him well enough to know
that you will never profit by serving him. Take my way, lord
of Sotharrn, and have what you want—or have nothing. I
learn too readily to hand any *khal* the only thing that makes
my life valuable."

Shien's white brows knit into a frown. For a moment
thoughts passed visibly through his eyes, none of them good
to behold. "You assume that you know how to deal with us,
and how I must deal with the other lords. You do not know
us, Man."

"I know that I am dead when you have what you want."

Shien's frown bent slowly into a smile. "Ah, Man, you are
too unsubtle. One does not accuse his possible benefactor of
lying. I might even have kept my word."

"No," he said, though the doubt was planted in him.

"Think of it, tomorrow, when we deliver you to Hetharu."

And Shien rose then and settled some distance away.
Vanye turned his head to stare at him, but Shien poured himself a cup from his flask and sat with his face averted, drink-
ing delicately.

Beyond him sat the others, halflings aping *khal*, with
bleached hair and coarse arrogance, and a hate for Men that
was the greater because of their own human blood.

Shien turned his head and smiled at him thinly, lifting the
cup in mockery.

"Tomorrow," Shien promised him.

They forded two shallow rivers, one at dawn and one at noon. Vanye reckoned well now where they were, nearing the Gate that stood in Azeroth. He grew afraid, as it was impossible not to fear contemplating that power, which could drink in substance and ravel it.

But no sign of the Gate was yet visible, not in the long ride they made that afternoon. There were few rests; Shien had promised that they would come to Hetharu's camp in this day and seemed determined on it if it exhausted them. Vanye said nothing to Shien as the distance wore away under the horses' hooves. Shien had nothing more to say to him, save now and again to gaze at him brooding speculation. He reckoned again what his chances were if he yielded on the Shiua lord's terms, and averted his face from temptation.

They did not stop at dusk, even to rest, and the night turned bitterly cold. He asked them for a cloak, but they refused it, though the guard who had lent it before would not wear it himself; they took pleasure in refusing. After that he bowed his head, trying to ignore them. They taunted him with threats which this time Shien did not silence, but he said nothing, caring nothing for them.

Then there appeared a glow on the horizon . . . cold, like the moon; but the moon was aloft, and the light was far brighter.

The Gate of Azeroth, that Men called the Fires.

He lifted his face, staring at that terrible presence, seeing now where they were bound, for nearer at hand were the dimmer red lights of woodfires, and ungainly shapes: tents and shelters.

They passed sentries who sat their posts concealed in shelters of grass; and rode past picket lines, where horses stood . . . few in proportion to the vast sprawl of the Shiua camp . . . the camp of a nation spread over the vast plains under the Gate; of more than a nation: of the remnant of a world.

And it aimed at the heart of Shathan.

*Morgaine and I have done this thing,* he could not forbear thinking. *My doing as much as hers. Heaven forgive us.*

They passed the fringes of the camp. Suddenly Shien put the company to a gallop, passing the sprawling shelters of grass and cloth which hemmed them about on all sides.

Men stared at their passage . . . dark shapes, small: true Men, of Shiuan's marshes. Vanye saw the stares and went cold as someone sent up a thin, hysterical cry.

*"Her* man. *Hers!"*

Men rushed out to bar their way, scattered from the hooves of the horses when the *khal* kept coming. The marsh-landers knew him, and would gladly tear him limb from limb if he fell among them. The *khal* whipped their horses and thundered through, reckless of human lives, and into a quieter portion of the camp, where demon-helms quickly parted and shut a barricade of brush and sharpened stakes, and backed it with a row of barbed pikes.

The mob no longer pursued; the gate sufficed. They slowed, the horses blowing and panting in exhaustion, stretching at the reins and seeking air. They rode slowly up to a sprawling shelter, the largest in the compound.

The structure was patched, cobbled together of various bits of cloth and bundles of reeds and grass, and part of it was a tent. Light blazed within, showing through the canvas; and there was music, but not such as the *arrhendim* had played. They halted there, and guards came to take the horses.

They lifted him down from the saddle. "Be careful," said Shien when one of them jerked at him. "This is a very valu-able Man."

And Shien himself took him by the elbow and brought him toward the door of the tent. "You were not wise," Shien said.

He shook his head, uncertain whether he had rejected a trap that would have killed him or whether he had rejected the only hope he had. It was impossible. A *khal* would scarcely keep faith with *khal*. That one would keep faith with a Man was not to be believed.

He blinked, suddenly thrust into the light and warmth within.

# Chapter Eight

Hetharu.

Vanye stopped, with Shien at his back, steadied himself on his wounded leg; and of all in that gathering, he recognized that tall, black-clad lord. The music died away with a hiss of

strings, and noble lords and ladies of Shiuan stopped what
half-clad diversions they were practicing and came to slow,
studied attention where they lounged on sacks and cushions
within the tent, against walls of bound reeds.

Of sacks and brocade cloaks was the throne to which
Hetharu settled. A cluster of halfling guards was about him,
some far gone in stupor, others alert, armored and armed. A
naked Woman shrank into the shadows of the corner.
Hetharu stared at the intrusion, blank with amazement for
the instant, and then pleasure grew on his countenance . . .
thin and shadow-eyed that face, the more startling for the human eyes which looked darkly out from what were otherwise
pure *qhalur* features. His white hair lay lank and silken on
his shoulders. His black brocade was somewhat worn, the
lace frayed; the ornate sword that he wore still looked serv-
iceable. Hetharu smiled, and about him settled the miasma of
all that was Shiuan, drowning and rotting at once.

"Nhi Vanye," Hetharu murmured. "And Morgaine?"

"That matter must be cared for by now," said Shien.
Vanye clenched his jaw and stared through all of them, trying to use his wits; but that callous reckoning of Morgaine's
life hit him suddenly with more force than he had yet felt.

Kill Hetharu? That was one of the thoughts that he had
entertained over recent days; and suddenly it seemed useless,
for here were thousands like him. Gain power among them?
Suddenly it seemed impossible; he was a Man, and what else
was here of humankind crouched naked and ashamed and
weeping in the corner.

He took a step forward. Though his hands were bound, the
guards were uneasy; pikes inclined marginally toward him.
He stopped, sure that they would not be careless with him.

"I hear," he said to Hetharu, "that you and Roh have
quarreled."

That set them back. There was an instant's silence, and
Hetharu's face was whiter than usual.

"Out!" Hetharu said suddenly. "All of you who have no
business here, out."

That included many: the Woman, the majority of the *khal*
who had disported themselves about the fringes of the gathering. One half-conscious lordling reclined at Hetharu's side,
leaning against the sacks and the brocade with unfocused
gray eyes and a dreaming smile that mocked all reality. A
middle-aged *khalur* woman remained; and a handful of lords;
and all the guards, although some of them were far-departed

in dreams, and knelt near Hetharu and about the other lords with their eyes distant and their hands loose on their weapons. Enough still remained who had all their wits about them. Hetharu leaned back in his makeshift throne and regarded him with old and familiar hate.

"Shien, what have you been telling this Man?"

Shien shrugged. "I have been pointing out his situation, and his possible value."

Hetharu's dark eyes swept over Shien narrowly. "Knowledge such as Roh has? Is that your meaning?"

"It is possible that he has it. He is reticent."

"He," said the woman suddenly, "might be more reasonable than Roh has been. After all, the human rabble hates him bitterly, and he cannot gain any followers among them. That is one sure advantage over Roh."

"There are personal issues," Hetharu said, and the lady laughed unpleasantly.

"We know the truth of those. Do not waste a valuable source, my lord Hetharu. Who here cares about the past . . . things done and not done? Shiuan is behind us. Here is important. You have an opportunity to rid us of the so-named halfling and his followers. Use it."

Hetharu was not pleased by that, but the lady spoke as one who was accustomed to be heard, and she was of the old blood, gray-eyed and white-haired, with guards about her none of whom were hazy in their look. One of the hold-lords, Vanye reckoned her: not Sotharra like Shien, but perhaps of Domen or Marom or Arisith. The Shiua lords were not firmly held in Hetharu's hand.

"You are too credulous, lady Halah," said Hetharu. "This Man is quite capable of turning in the hand that holds him. He surprised Roh, who should know him; and my lamented brother Kithan. And would you not attempt to surprise us in the same way, Man?"

Vanye said nothing. Debate with Hetharu could win nothing. The hope was rather in playing one and the other of his subordinates against him.

"Of course you would," Hetharu answered for him, and laughed. "And you plan to. You are not the sort who will ever thank us for the handling you have had . . . at my hands and now at Shien's. —Beware this one, Shien. He is not hand-broken, though he may try to let you think so. His cousin says that he does not know how to lie; but he does know how to keep secrets, do you not, Vanye of the Chya?

Morgen-Angharan's—" and he used a word that Vanye did not know; but he suspected, and set his jaw the harder, looking through Hetharu. "Ah, glare at me. We are better acquaintances than the others, you and I. So this Morgen is missing. Where?"

He did not answer.

"Over by the great river," Shein said. "In the midst of our deepest penetration into the forest, with a Hiua arrow in her. Our riders have her trail, and if they have not found her by now, she will scarcely survive the wound. My lord, there was a *khal* with her, and another human. And that is another thing this prisoner does not like to talk about."

"Kithan?"

Vanye bowed his head and concealed his surprise, for Hetharu's brother had not come through, then, and he would have reckoned otherwise . . . *my lamented brother*, Hetharu had said. He was sorry to know Kithan not in the camp, for with him there might have been some hope; that Kithan would have joined them instead was a natural conclusion for Hetharu. He shrugged.

"Find him," Hetharu ordered. There was a frantic edge to his voice, more disturbance than Hetharu was wont to show. *Morgaine's weapons*, Vanye thought suddenly; *here is a man scarcely clinging to his position.*

"My lord," said Shien, "my men are trying to do so. Perhaps they have."

Hetharu was silent then, biting at his lip, and what passed between him and Shien was plain enough.

"I brought you this one alive," Shien said very softly. "And I had to pull him out of the Hiua's keeping. Else he would be in other hands, my lord."

"We are grateful," Hetharu said, but his eyes were dead, cold. They traveled back to lock with Vanye's. "Well. You are in a sorry position, are you not, Nhi Vanye? There is not a human in that camp out there but would skin you alive if he set hands on you; they know you well, do you see? And there are the Hiua, who are Roh's dogs. And your mistress is not coming here, if ever she comes anywhere again. You can hardly look for friendship from Chya Roh. And you know what love we bear you."

"Yet you must keep Roh's favor, must you not, Shiua lords?"

Anger flared in the others; and guards fingered the hafts of their weapons. Hetharu only smiled.

"Now," said Hetharu, "there are things we could do, regarding Chya Roh. But since he has been the only storehouse of the information we want, why, we have handled him with utmost respect. He is dangerous. Of course we know that. But now you have given us some latitude, have you not? You know what Roh knows, and you are not, now, dangerous. If we should happen to lose your life in the process, why—we still have Roh. So we can dice with it, can we not? —You are dismissed, Shien, with our—thanks."

There was no stir of movement. Hetharu lifted his hand and the pikes inclined.

And Shien and his men strode out. One of the lordlings gave a low laugh. The others relaxed, easing back into comfort, and Hetharu smiled tautly.

"Did he try to persuade you to his cause?" Hetharu asked.

Vanye said nothing, his heart sinking with the knowledge that he had turned from one who might have done what he promised. Hetharu read his silence, and nodded slowly.

"You know the choice we give you," Hetharu said. "You may volunteer that information . . . and you may live . . . while Roh will someday be surprised to discover that we do not need him. Now if you will do that, you will be wise. Or we can seek it against your will, and you will be sorry for that. So make your choice, Man."

Vanye shook his head. "There is nothing I could tell you, only show you. And I need to be present at the Gate to do that."

Hetharu laughed, and so did his men, for that was transparent. "Ah, you would like to find yourself there, would you not? No, what you can demonstrate, you can tell. And tell us you shall."

Again he shook his head.

Hetharu's hand crept to the shoulder of the *khal* who dreamed, eyes open, at the side of his seat. He urged at that one gently until the dazed face lifted to his. "Hirrun, give me a double portion of what you have . . . aye, I know you have more with you. And give it to me—if you are wise."

A mean and ugly look came on Hirrun's handsome face, but he flinched under the grip of Hetharu's fingers, and dug in his belt-pouch, brought forth something which he offered with shaking hands into Hetharu's palm. Hetharu smiled and gave it to the guard next to him.

Then he looked up. "Hold him," he said.

Vanye understood then, and moved, flung himself backward, but others were behind him and he had no chance. The splinted leg lost its footing, and he sprawled along with his guards. They weighed him down and forced his jaws apart, rammed the pellets down his throat. Someone poured liquor after, to the laughter of the others, a sound that pealed like bells. He tried to spit them out, but they held him until it was swallow or choke. Then they let him go, amid much laughter, and he rolled onto his side and tried to vomit the drug up, but it was too late for that. In a moment he began to feel the haze of it—*akil,* that vice too common among the *khal* and the marshlanders who provided it to them, that stole his sense and sent a horrid languor over him. It was strange; it did not diminish the fear, but it sent it to some far place where it did not influence what he did. A warmth stole over him, and a curious lack of pain, in which the touch of anything was pleasurable.

"No!" he screamed in outrage, and they laughed, a gentle and distant rippling of sound. He screamed again, and tried to turn his face from them, but the guards gathered him up and held him on his feet.

"There is more," said Hetharu, "when that fades. Let him stand, let him stand."

They let him go. He could not move in any direction. He feared for his balance. His heart was beating painfully and there was a roaring in his ears. His vision was hazy save in the center of focus, and there was a blackness between him-self and that center. But worst was the warmth which crawled over him, destroying all sense of alarm; he fought that with all the mind that was left to him.

"Who is the *khal* who rode with you?"

He shook his head, and one of the guards seized his arm, distracting him so that he could not recall anything. The guard hit him, but the blow was nothing but bewildering. The blackness that centered upon Hetharu abruptly slipped wider. It seemed ready to tear asunder and drop him into it.

"Who?" Hetharu repeated, and shouted at him. "WHO?"

"Lellin," he answered in his startlement, and knew what he was doing and that he must not. He shook his head and re-called Mirrind, and Merir, and all that he could betray to them. Tears ran down his face, and he pulled away from the guard and stumbled, caught his balance.

"Who is Lellin?" Hetharu asked someone else, and the voice echoed in the emptiness. Others answered that they did not know. "Who is Lellin?" Hetharu asked of him, and he

shook his head and shook it again, desperately, trying to hold
to the fear that was his life, his sanity.

"Where were you going when the Hiua ambushed you?"

Again he shook his head. They had not asked him that before, and the answer of it was deadly; he knew it, and knew
that they could shake that out of him as well.

"What is the knowledge you have of the old powers?" the
woman Halah asked, a female voice which confused him in
this gathering.

"Where were you going?" Hetharu asked, shouting at him,
and he flinched from that horrid sound and stumbled against
the guards.

"No," he said.

And suddenly the wall of the tent went back. Men stood
there . . . Fwar, and others, with drawn bows. The pikes
swung about to face that intrusion; but the bowmen parted
slightly, and Roh walked out of the dark into the light of the
tent.

"Cousin," Roh said.

The voice was gentle; that kinsman's face looked concerned for him, and kind. Roh held out his hand, and no
*khal* dared forbid him. "Come," Roh said, and again:
"Come."

He recalled why he should fear this man: but Roh's human face promised something more honest than surrounded
him. He came, trying not to see the dark at the edges. Roh's
hand caught him by the arm, helped him walk as Fwar's
bowmen closed to guard their retreat, a human curtain between them and the *khal*.

Then the cold wind outside hit him, and he had not even
the control of his limbs to shiver.

"My tent is this way," Roh said, bearing him on his feet.
"Walk, curse you."

He tried, although the splinted leg was the only steady one.
It was a long blank time until he found himself lying against
a wall of bound reeds in Roh's shelter. A ring of Hiua a
Roh's shoulder leaned on their bows and stared down at
him, shadows in the dim light of a fire, the smoke of which
curled up to an opening in the roof. Fwar was there, foremost of them.

"Go, get out of here," Roh bade the Hiua. "All of you.
Keep an eye on the *khal*."

They went, though Fwar lingered last . . . gave him a
broad and disturbing grin before he went out the door.

Then Roh dropped down on his heels. He put forth a hand to his face, turned it to him and stared him in the eyes. *"Akil."*

"Yes." The haze of it was too thick to fight any longer. He turned his face away, shuddering, for the warmth made the touch like that on a burn . . . not painful, but too sensitive.

"Where is Morgaine? Where would she have gone?"

That alarmed him. He shook his head vehemently.

"Where?" Roh repeated.

"The river . . . Fwar knows."

"The control is there, is it not?"

The question shot through all his refusals. He looked at Roh and blinked, and realized afterward that his reaction had betrayed the truth.

"Well," Roh said, "we have suspected it. We have been searching all that area. She dares not come back here, Master Gate though this is . . . aye, I know that too; and therefore she must have that which controls the Gate. She will seek that point, reliable as a lodestar . . . if she is not dead. Do you think that she is?"

"I do not know," he admitted, and the tears surprised and overwhelmed him, flowing down his face. He could not stop them, nor tell how much or what he had said that he ought not; all his sense was undone, and, he feared, his memory with it.

"She was badly hurt, Fwar said."

"Yes."

"What worries me now is the thought of that sword of hers. Think of that in Hetharu's gentle hands. That must not happen. That must not happen, Vanye. You must prevent that. Where would she go?"

The words were reasoning, the touch gentle and pleasant. He drew back from it and shook his head, swore. Roh's hand fell and Roh rested on his heels staring at him as at a perplexing problem, his face, so like a brother's to him, furrowed between the brows with distress. He shut his eyes.

"How much did they give you? How much of the *akil?*"

He shook his head, not knowing the answer. "Let me be. Let me be. It has been days since I rested; Roh, let me sleep."

"Stay awake. I fear for you if you do not."

That had not the incongruity it might have held; it was not the first time he had seen this face of his enemy, that which had been his cousin. He blinked with dull perception, trying to think through Roh's words, flinched as Roh put his hands on his splinted knee.

"Fwar told me that a horse went down on you. And these other hurts?"

"Fwar knows."

"I thought so." Roh took the knife from his belt—hesitated as Vanye saw it and recognized it. "Ah, yes. You carried it . . . to return to me, I do not doubt. Well, it is back. Thank you." He cut the binding on the splint, and that plain stabbed even through the *akil*, touching all other nerves. But Roh felt of the joint with great gentleness. "Swollen . . . torn. Probably not broken. I will do what I can with it. I will free your hands—or not, as you will have it. You tell me."

"I will make no trouble for the meanwhile."

"Sensible man." Roh bent him forward and cut the cords, then sheathed the blade and massaged his torn hands until some life returned to his swollen and discolored fingers. "You are clear-minded enough to know where you are, are you not?"

"The Gate," he recalled, and recalled what had befallen Roh at such a place. Panic took him. Roh's fingers bit into his wrist, stopping him from a wild move, and the leg shot fire through the arch of the knee, pain and the *akil* almost taking his senses.

"You are going nowhere, crippled as you are," Roh hissed into his ear, and thrust his arm free. "What do you expect? That anyone could want the carrion they have left of you? I have no such designs. Use your wits. I would not have let you free if I had."

He blinked, trying to think clearly, trying to flex the life back into his fingers. He was shaking, sweat cold on him.

"Be still," Roh said. "Believe me. Body-changing is nothing pleasant. The one I have suffices . . . although," he added in cold mockery, "one of the Hiua might find yours an improvement. Fwar, for instance. His face gives him no joy."

He said nothing. The *akil* set even this at distance. The pain faded back into the warmth.

"Peace," Roh said softly. "I assure you, you are safe from that."

"Which are you? Liell now, is it not?"

Roh's face smiled. "More than not."

"Roh—" he pleaded, and the smile faded and the frown came back, an indefinible shift of the eyes.

"I say I will not harm you."

"Who is 'I,' Roh?"

"I—" Roh shook his head and rose. "You do not understand. There is no separation, no division. I—" He went across the shelter, there dipped up a pan of water . . . and on an apparent other thought, poured some into a handle-broken cup and brought it back to him. "Here."

He drank, thirstily. Roh knelt and took the cup back when he was finished, tossed it aside into the straw, then dipped a cloth into the pan of cold water and began, very gently, to wash the dirt from his wounds, starting with his face. "I will tell you how it is," Roh said. "At the first is utter shock . . . and then a few days that are like a dream. You *are* both. And then part of the dream begins to fade, and you know that it was once there, but you cannot recall it in daylight. I was Liell once. Now I am Chya Roh. I think that I like this shape well. But then I probably liked the other. And the others before that. I am Roh now. Everything that he is, all that he remembers—all that he loves or hates. All, in short—that he is or ever was—I contain."

"Except his soul."

A touch of irritation came over Roh's face. "I would not know about that."

"Roh would have."

Roh's hands resumed the gentle ministering they had for an instant ceased, and he shook his head. "Cousin—sometimes—there is a perverseness in me that I cannot help. I would not harm you, but do not prick at me. Do not. I do not like it when I have done such a thing."

"Oh Heaven, I pity you."

The cloth found a raw spot and he winced. "Do you prick at me," Roh repeated between his teeth. The touch gentled again. "You do not know what trouble you have caused me . . . this whole camp. You know the marshlanders are across that barricade trying to figure how to get their hands on you."

He gazed at Roh, distantly.

"Wake up," Roh insisted. "They have put too much of that into you. What did you tell them?"

He shook his head, confused. For a time he truly did not remember. Roh seized his shoulder and forced his attention.

"What, confound you? Will you have them to know and not me? Think it through."

"They asked—asked me to tell what I knew of the Gates. They are tired of relying on you. They said—that because the

Men in this camp want to kill me, they would have more
hold on me than on you . . . that was Shien's thought . . .
or someone's . . . I cannot remember. But Hetharu . . .
meant to have what I know—and not to tell you until a time
suited him—"

"What you know. And what do you know of Gates. Has
she given you knowledge enough to be dangerous?"

He thought over the hazard of truth with Roh. Nothing
would focus.

"Have you such knowledge?" Roh asked.

"Yes."

"And what did you tell them?"

"Nothing. I told them nothing. You came."

"I heard that they had brought you in. I guessed as much
as you have told me."

"They will cut your throat when they can."

Roh laughed. "Aye, that they will. And yours, sooner,
without my protection. What do you know that you did *not*
tell them?"

Panic flashed through him, muddled with the *akil*. He
shook his head desperately, not trusting to speak.

"I will tell you what I suspect," Roh said. "That Morgaine
has had help staying out of sight. She has been in a certain
village; I have learned that much: Hetharu knows it too. Men
live here, elusive as they are, and there are others too, are
there not?"

He said nothing.

"There are. I know that. And I think that there are *qhal*—
are there not, cousin? And you have friends. Perhaps that is
who rode off with her, when she fled. Allies. Native allies.
And she thought to go to the high place and seize control of
the Gate and destroy me. Well, is that not her purpose? It is
the only sane course for her. But I am less worried about
what Morgaine will and will not, in the state she must be in
now, than I am worried for who has his hands on that
weapon of hers. A *qhal* and a Man are with her. So Fwar reports. And who are they, and what would either of them do
with such a weapon as that sword in his hands?"

The thoughts tumbled chaotically about him: *Merir*, he
thought. *Merir would use it well*. But then he doubted, and
recalled that he and Morgaine held purposes at odds with the
*arrhendim*.

"Fwar brought me something," Roh said. "Oh, he did not
want to give it, but Fwar has a great respect for my anger,

and he most readily gave it up for his health's sake." He drew from his belt a silver circlet on a chain . . . Merir's gift. "You wore this. I find it very strange workmanship, nothing like home, nor even like Shiuan. See, it is written over with *qhalur* runes. *Friendship* is the inscription. Whose friend are you, Nhi Vanye?"

He shook his head and his eyes hazed. He was exhausted. Of a sudden the fear that had stayed remote began to trouble him, nearer and nearer, stalking him.

"Hardly honorable . . . to worry at you when you are full of that foul stuff—is it? You are easy as a new-written page. Well, I shall not, any more. But I do tell you this that you may think on when you are sober again . . . that what I have asked of you I have not asked with purpose to harm you. And you must stay awake, Vanye. Come, keep your eyes clear. Look at me with sense."

He tried. Roh hit him, enough to sting, but not with malice. "Stay awake. I will make you angry with me if that is what it takes. Your eyes are still hazed with that drug, and until that goes, you will stay awake, whatever I have to do to keep you that way. I have seen men die of it in this camp. They sleep to death. And I want you alive."

"Why?"

"Because I have put my neck on the block for you tonight and I want reward of it."

"What do you want?"

Roh laughed. "Your company, cousin."

"I warned you—warned you that you would not find your companions grateful when you joined them. You are a Man, and they hate you for it."

"Am I?" Roh laughed again. "You admit it then, that I am your cousin."

"A *qhal* . . ." —*told me*, he almost said, *what it was like for you*. But he was not quite hazed enough to let it slip, and stopped himself in time. Roh looked at him strangely, and then shrugged and let it pass, beginning again to wash at his injuries. Roh's touch hurt, and he winced: Roh swore softly.

"I cannot help it," Roh said. "Thank Fwar for this. I am as careful as I can be. Be glad of the *akil* for a while."

Roh was indeed careful, and skilled; he cleaned the wounds and dressed them with hot oil, and tended those that were fevered. He put hot compresses on the knee, changing them often. In time Vanye let his head fall. Roh disturbed him to look at his eyes, and finally let him sleep, rousing him only when he changed the compresses. It was far into the night, Vanye judged at one of these wakings, and yet Roh disturbed him again, putting heat on the knee. "Roh?" he asked, perplexed by this.

"I would not have you lame."

"Someone else might see to it."

"Who? Fwar? I am scant of servants in this grand hall. Go to sleep, cousin."

He did so, a quiet sleep, for the first time since Carrhend. This last and better effect the *akil* left on him, that its passing exhausted him and he was able to rest.

# Chapter Nine

Roh roused him again with daylight flooding through the door and hazing through the smoke from the opening overhead. There was food; Vanye bestirred himself and took it, bread and salted fish and a little of Shiuan's sourish drink— for the first time in days, enough to eat, poor though it was and foul with the memory of Shiuan.

His jaw hurt in eating, and there was little of him elsewhere that was not bruised or wounded. But the knee had freedom of movement this morning, and the pain there, which had become so constant he had ceased even to realize it, had somewhat abated. He did not dress again, but sat with a length of cloth wrapped about him, and Roh saw to it that the hot compress stayed on the knee even at breakfast, a bit of rag constantly aboil in a pot on the fire, one and then the other.

"Thank you," Vanye said in sum of everything.

"What, honest gratitude? That is more than I had of you in our last meeting. I think you meant to cut my throat, cousin."

"I have sense enough to know what I owe you."

Roh smiled a twisted smile and poured another panful of

water into the pot on the fire, then settled and poured himself a cup of the Shiua liquor. He drank of it and grimaced. "Because I did not take advantage of you as I could have done? They would have gone on and on with that drug until you had no sense left what you were doing, and if they had had long enough—well, you would have handed them everything you know, and that would have been enough to save your life . . . of sorts. You would have lived—perhaps . . . so long as humiliating you amused them. You do well to thank me. But of course I had to get you out of there; it was only practical. You would have ruined me. For the rest, well, you do owe me, do you not? At least you owe me better than to turn on me."

Vanye turned up his scarred palm, that was Morgaine's mark, sealed in blood and ash. "I cannot say that, and you know it. Whatever I have done and will do—is under *ilin*-law. No promise of mine is binding where it crosses that; I have no honor."

"But you have enough to remind me of it."

He shrugged, troubled, as Roh had always been able to seize his heart and turn it in him. "You should have looked well on what was happening in that tent last night. They dare not lay hands on you—yet. But they will find a way someday."

"I know. I know how far I can trust Hetharu, and we passed the borders of that territory long ago."

"So you surround yourself with the likes of Fwar. You know surely that he and his kindred served Morgaine once. They turned on her when they did not gain of her what they wanted. They will do the same for you the first time you cross their wishes. And that is not my hate speaking. That is the truth."

"I expect it daily. But the fact remains that Fwar and his men had rather serve me than the *khal*, reckoning how much the *khal* love them. The *khal* have alienated every human in this camp, Hiua, marshlanders—all who have any experience of independence; but the marshlanders do not love Fwar, no, not in the least. Fwar and his Hiua lads are few, hard Men as they are, and he knows that if ever he slips, the marshlanders will put his face in the dirt. Fwar loves power. He must have it, many as his enemies have become. He joined Morgaine while he thought that she would give it to him, while it looked likely that he could remain her lieutenant and lord it over conquests. He joined me only when it was clear that he could not deal with the *khal* and when he realized that I am also a power in this camp. Fwar keeps the marshlanders under his heel and that is useful to me. He is essential to my survival here; he is nothing without me and he knows it . . . but so long as I have him in my employ, the *khal* do not rule Hiua or marshlanders in this camp. And arrogant as the *khal* are, they do realize that they are outnumbered, and that the Men who still serve them are cattle, of their own making. No Shiua human is a match for marshlander or Hiua, and of course not all the Men who have lived under the *khal* truly love their masters, not even those Men who wear the brand on their faces. The *khal* are really quite terrified of their own servants, and so they redouble their cruelties to keep them cowed . . . but that is not a thing to say openly. For one thing, it would not be good to have Men find it out, would it? —Another bit of bread?"

"I cannot."

"Things among them have changed since Hetharu came to power," Roh continued with a shake of his head. "There was an urge to decency in some of these folk. But in the passage, only the strongest survived; they were generally not the fittest to live."

"You chose Hetharu for your ally . . . when you had other choices."

"I did, yes." Roh refilled both their cups. "To my lasting sorrow, I chose him. I have always been unfortunate in my allies. —Cousin . . . *where* do you reckon Morgaine is?"

Vanye swallowed at a bit suddenly gone dry and reached for the cup, drank deeply and ignored the question.

"The place she attempted to reach over by the river," Roh said, "is surely the control itself . . . I believe so; Hetharu surely does. Hetharu's patrols will scour that area . . . will have been doing so in searching for her. Hetharu wants the Hiua sent back out on her trail. I am not eager to send Fwar from me, for obvious reasons; Fwar himself is not at all anxious to go, but that even he sees the danger if that weapon of hers goes to Hetharu's men. Hetharu himself is terrified, I do not doubt, of someone like Shien . . . of even his own folk getting possession of it. I do not, I confess, like to think of Fwar holding it either. Of course Fwar should have let you lie under that horse and gone after her; he realizes that now, in cold blood, but . . . he is afraid of her: he has faced her weapons before, and it was fear that obscured his good sense—fear and his obsessive hate of you. He dared an arrow against her at distance, but facing *Changeling* . . . well, that is quite another matter, at least in his thought of the moment. Fwar sometimes needs time to reckon clearly where his advantage truly lies; his instincts for survival on the instant sometimes overwhelm those for the long range. He regrets that choice now; but the moment has passed—saving your help, of course."

"Then it has passed," he said; the words almost choked him. "I will not help you."

"Peace, peace, I advise you against any attack on me. And put *khalur* tactics from your mind; I could have done the same as they last night, if I would. No, I am the only safety you have here."

"Liell tended to allies like Fwar: bandits, cutthroats—a hall that would have had fit place in Shiuan, for all it was human-held. I find you unchanged—and my chances equal, here and there."

Roh's eyes clouded, cleared again slowly. "I do not blame you. I loathe my companions, as you warned me I would . . . but you forced me to them. They will kill me when they can; of course they will. You are safe here just as I am . . . only because Hetharu still fears a rising in the human camp if he comes and tries to take you; I could do that to him, and he fears it. Besides, he has reason to wait."

"What reason?"

"The hope that at any hour one of his patrols may ride in bearing Morgaine's weapons . . . and in that hour, my friend, we are both dead men. And there is yet another danger: that perhaps you and I and Morgaine are not the only ones in this land who can use the power of the Gate; perhaps there is knowledge to be had elsewhere in this land. And if that is so— Is it so, Vanye?"

He said nothing, trying to keep all reaction from his face.

"I suspect that there could be," Roh said. "Whatever else we have to fear, the sword is beyond doubt. It was madness ever to have made such a thing. Morgaine knows it, I am sure. And the thought of that . . . I know what is written in the runes on that blade, at least the gist of it. And that should never have been written."

"She knows it."

"Can you walk? Come here. I will show you something."

He strove to rise, and Roh lent his hand and steadied him as he limped across the shelter to the far side where Roh wished to lead him. There Roh flung back a ragged curtain, and showed him the horizon.

And there was the Gate, afire with shimmering colder than moonlight. Vanye gazed at it, and shuddered at that nearness, at the presence of that power that he had learned to dread.

"It is not good to look at, is it?" Roh asked. "It drinks up the mind like water. It hovers over us here. I have lived in that presence until it burns through the curtains and the wall. There is no peace with that thing. And the Men who live here, and the *khal*—feel it. Because of *her* they have feared to leave it; and now they are beginning to fear to stay near it. Some may leave it and go out. Those who do stay here . . . will go mad."

Vanye turned from it, would have left Roh's help and risked falling, but Roh went with him and helped him down on the mat by the fire.

Roh sank down then on his heels, arms folded across his knees, and settled further, crosslegged. "So you see the other source of insanity in this place, deadlier than the *akil*. And far more powerful." He picked up his cup and drank it to the last, shuddered and swallowed heavily. "Vanye, I want you to guard *my* back for a time, as you have guarded hers."

"You are mad."

"No. I know you. There is no man more reliable. Save that other oath of yours, I know that any promise you give freely will be kept. And I am tired, Vanye." Roh's voice broke suddenly, and pain was in the brown eyes. "I ask only that you do this until it crosses your oath to her."

"That might be at any time I decide it is. And I owe you no warning."

"I know. Still I ask you. Only that."

He was bewildered, and turned the thing over and over in his mind, finding no trap in it. At last he nodded. "Until then, I will do what I can. As I am—that is little. I do not understand you, Roh. I think you have something in mind, and I do not trust you."

"I have said what I want. For now—I will leave awhile. Sleep; do what you choose, so long as you stay in this shelter. There is clothing there if you must have it, but do not walk on that leg; keep the compresses on it, if you have any sense."

"If Fwar comes within my reach—"

"He would not come alone; you know him. Do not look for that kind of trouble. I will keep my eye in Fwar's direction, and you will not have to worry where he is." He gathered himself up and slung on his sword, but he left his bow and quiver.

And as he left he dropped the flap that curtained the door, taking most of the daylight.

Vanye lay down where he was and curled up to sleep, drawing a blanket over him. None did come to trouble his rest; and after a long while Roh returned, with no word of what he had been doing, though his face was weary.

"I am going to sleep," Roh said, and flung himself down on his unused pallet. "Wake me if it is necessary."

It was a strange vigil, to know the Gate on one side and *khalur* enemies on the other, and himself keeping watch over the kinsman he had sworn to kill. And he had leisure to think of Morgaine, counting the days since their parting . . . the fourth day, now, when any wound would have reached and passed its crisis, one way or the other.

Through the day he kept the compresses on the knee, and in late afternoon, Roh changed the dressings on his wounds and left him again a time, returning with food. Then Roh let him sleep, but waked him midway through the night and wished him to sit awake again while he slept.

He looked at Roh, wondering what was afoot that Roh dared not have them both asleep; but Roh cast himself down on his face as if the weariness on him were unbearable, as if it were more than last night that he had not slept securely. He stayed awake until the dawn, and drowsed the next morning, while Roh pursued his own business outside.

He waked suddenly, at a footstep. It was Roh, and there was commotion in the camp. He looked in that direction, questioning, but Roh sat down and laid his sword on the mat beside him, then poured himself a drink. His hands were shaking.

"It will settle," Roh said finally. "There has been a suicide. A man, a woman, and two children. Such things happen here."

He looked at Roh in horror, for such things did not happen in Andur-Kursh.

Roh shrugged. "One of the *khal's* latest. They pushed the man to it. And that is only the edge of evils here. The Gate—" He shrugged again, that became a shudder. "It broods over all here."

The curtain of the doorway was thrust back, and Vanye

saw their visitors: Fwar and his men. He reached for the jug of liquor, not to drink; Roh's hand clenched on his wrist, reminding him of sense.

"It is settled," Fwar said, avoiding Vanye's eyes, staring at Roh. "The *khal* gave grain; the kin have begun to bury their dead. But it will not stay settled. Not while this other matter has them stirred up. Hetharu is pushing at us. We cannot have men there and here. We are not enough to be in both places."

Roh was silent a moment. "Hetharu is playing a dangerous game," he said in a still voice. "Sit down, Fwar, you and your men."

"I will not sit with this dog."

"Fwar, sit down. Do not try my patience."

Fwar considered it long, and sullenly sank down at the fireside, his cousins with him.

"You ask too much of me," Vanye muttered.

"Have peace with them," Roh said. "On your word to me: this is part of it."

He inclined his head sullenly, looked up at Fwar. "Under Roh's peace, then."

"Aye," Fwar answered gracelessly, but Vanye gave it no more belief than he would have given Hetharu's word . . . less, if possible.

"I will tell you why you will keep peace," Roh said. "Because we are all about to perish, between the *khal* and the marshlanders. Because *that*—" He hooked a gesture over his shoulder to the wall which concealed the Gate, and the glances that went that way were uncomfortable. "—*That* is a thing that will drive us mad if we stay here. And we need not. Must not."

"Where, then?" Fwar asked, and Vanye set his jaw and stared at the mat to conceal his own startlement. He was afraid, suddenly, mind leaping ahead to unavoidable conclusions; he trusted nothing that Roh did, but he had no choice but to accept it. Fwar was the alternative; or the others.

"Nhi Vanye has a certain usefulness," Roh said softly. "He knows the land. He knows Morgaine. And he knows his chances in this camp."

"And with the likes of *them*," Vanye said, and there was almost a dagger drawn, but Roh snatched up his sheathed longsword and thrust it at Trin's middle, stopping that with cold threat.

"Peace, I say, or none of us will live to get clear of this camp . . . or survive the journey afterward."

Fwar motioned at Trin, and the dagger went back solidly into its sheath.

"There is more than you think at stake," Roh said. "That will become clear later. But prepare for a journey. Be ready to ride tonight."

"The Shiua will follow."

Follow they may. You have itched for killing them. You will have your chance. But my cousin is another matter. Keep your knives from his back. Hear me well, Fwar i Mija. I need him, and so do you. Kill him, and the Shiua will be on one side and the folk of this land on the other, and that is a position no better than we have now. Do you understand me?"

"Aye," Fwar said.

"Start seeing to things quietly. As for me, I am not involving myself in any of your preparations. The Shiua have been urging me to send you out on a certain mission; if you are challenged, say that you are going. And if you stir up trouble—well, avoid it. Go to it."

They gathered themselves up. Vanye did not look at them, but stared into the fire, and glanced up only when he had heard the last of them walk away.

"Whom do you betray, Roh? Everyone?"

Roh's dark eyes met his. "All but you, my cousin."

The mockery chilled. He looked down again, unable to meet that stare, which challenged him to doubt, and to do something about it.

"I will go with you."

"And guard my back?"

He glared at Roh.

"It is from Fwar that I need most guarding, cousin. I will guard you, and you, me—when Fwar and his folk hold watch during the night. One of us will be awake, and seem asleep."

"You have been planning this journey—from the hour you took me from Hetharu."

"Aye. I could not leave the Gate before, for fear of Morgaine. Now I cannot stay here, for fear of her . . . now I know what I needed to know; and you will aid me, Nhi Vanye i Chya. I am going to Morgaine."

"Not with my guidance."

"I have run out of allies, cousin. I shall go to her. It is possible that she is dead; and then we shall see—we two—what we shall do then. But she does not die easily, the witch of Aenor-Pyvvn. And if she lives, well, I shall take my chances with her all the same."

Vanye nodded slowly, a tautness in his stomach.

"You want your chance at Fwar," Roh said. "Be patient."

"Weapons."

"You will have them. Your own; I gathered everything back that the Hiua had of yours. And I will splint that knee of yours. You cannot bear the ride we must make, otherwise. There are clothes there . . . better than the Hiua rags you and I will have to wear to ride out of here."

He edged over to the bundle that Roh pointed out, gathered up his own boots, and what else he needed, and dressed: they were of a size, he and Roh. He avoided looking at Roh, holding what he did in his mind: Roh knew he meant to turn on him; Roh *knew*, by his own clear warning, and yet armed him. And there was no sense in it that pleased him, nothing.

Roh rested in the corner against the grass wall, staring at him from half-lidded eyes. "You do not believe me," Roh observed.

"No more than the devil."

"Believe this at least: that out of this camp you trust me and keep your pledge to me, or Mija Fwar will have both our skins. You can bring me down . . . but I promise you it will not profit you."

The commotion did not die away. It rose up again within the hour, and Trin thrust his head inside the shelter and hung there against the doorway, hard-breathing. "Fwar says get ready now. No waiting until dark. There is talk now of coming up here. The marshlanders want *him*, slow-cooked; him they could have, for my opinion . . . but if they once pass those guards, with the *khal* on this side—well— If you want those horses brought through, we have a chance of doing it now, quick, while they talk down there; when it gets to more than talk, we have no hope of doing it."

"Get to it," Roh said.

Trin spat in Vanye's direction, and left. Vanye sat still, his breathing choked with anger.

"How long will we need them?" he asked then.

"You may have to endure worse than that." Roh threw a bundle of cloth at him; he caught it, but did nothing more, blind with anger. "I mean it, cousin; armed you may be, but you will do nothing. You gave me a pledge, and I assume you will keep it. Smother that Nhi temper of yours and keep your head down. Leave your avenging to me until the time comes . . . act the part of an *ilin* to the letter. You still remember how, do you not?"

He was shaking, and expelled several short breaths. "I am not yours."

"Be so for a few days. Bitter days. But by that means you may survive them, and so may I; and your surviving them . . . does that not serve *her*?"

That argument shot home. "I will do it," he said, and started pulling on the Hiua garments over his own; Roh did likewise.

There were two more bundles. Roh gave one to him, and it was incredibly heavy. "Your armor," Roh said. "All your belongings, as I promised. Here is your sword." And he unwrapped that and tossed it over, belt and all. Vanye set down the other and buckled it only about his waist, for to fasten it at the shoulder spoiled the Hiua garments and galled his wounds. Roh looked less Hiua than he, he reckoned, for Roh's hair was twisted at the nape in the warrior's knot, in the fashion of a hall-lord of Andur, and Roh was clean-shaven. His own face, bruised as it was, had not known a razor in days; and his hair, shorn in his loss of honor, had grown shoulder-length and a little beyond: usually that was held from his face by helm or coif, but now it went where it would, and he let it, which hid some of his bruises. He considered the bearing of the Hiua, and assumed in his mind their gracelessness, their hangdog manner: there was a nakedness in the prospect of going outside the shelter that chilled the blood in him.

Roh gathered up his own weapons, chiefest of which was a fine Andurin bow; the shafts his quiver carried were mostly long, green-fletched Chya arrows. He had the bone-handled Honor-blade at his belt, and bore sword and axe as well, the latter for the saddle. *Hall-lord,* Vanye thought in vexation; *he cannot seem anything else.*

And when the horses came thundering to the front of the shelter, with the shouts of Men audible in the distance, there was Roh's tall black mare, conspicuous among the smaller Shiua mounts: no hope of concealment; the alarm was surely passed . . . Chya wildness—Vanye cursed it aloud, and flung himself for the saddle of the bow-nosed sorrel allotted him, . . . cursed again as the leg shot fire up the inside when he threw it over. He shook the hair from his eyes and looked up—saw a cluster of *khalur* riders bearing down on them from the center of the camp.

"Roh!" he shouted.

Roh saw it, wheeled the black mare about and plunged through the Hiua, drawing them face-about, nigh forty riders, Hiua and a scattering of renegade marshlanders.

"We will shake them from our heels," Roh cried. "There is no luck for them in this direction."—For they were headed for the sprawl and clutter of the human camp, where a thin row of demon-helms manned the barricade, barring the way of trouble coming out of it.

The guards saw them coming, hesitated in confusion. Roh drew rein, shouted an order to open the barricade, and Hiua sprang down to do it—Roh passed at the least opening, and Vanye stayed with him, raking his leg on the barrier: it was all too quick, the guards without orders, not resisting. More Hiua poured through, and they plunged for the midst of the human camp at a dead gallop, aimed for the mob gathered there.

Swords whipped out; the mob lost its nerve at the first shock and scattered from their charge, with only a few missiles flying. One man was hit and unhorsed, and they took him . . . for what fate was not good to think. But they broke through by sheer impetus and shock, with the open plain before them and a scatter of futile stones pelting from behind. Vanye kept low; he had not blooded his sword, not on men's backs, not on the side of Hiua.

Roh laughed. "The *khal* will ride into a broken hive."

He looked back then, and there was not a Man in sight; no more stones, no fight; the human folk had gone to cover, armed, and there was no sight of the Shiua riders behind them either. Either they would seek some exit that avoided the human camp, or they would make the mistake of trying to ride through, and either would take them time.

"When Hetharu knows we are gone," Roh said, "as he must by now—then there will be no shaking them from pursuing us."

"No," said Vanye, "I do not think there will be."

He looked again over his shoulder, past the dark mass of Hiua riders, and it dawned on him what should have before, that his flight with Roh would stir all the camp into action . . . the whole army would mass and move.

He said nothing, seeing finally the trap into which he had

fallen—he had wanted to live, and therefore he had blinded himself to things other than his own survival.

*Mirrind*, he thought over and over, grieving. *Mirrind and all this land.*

# Chapter Ten

They pushed the horses to the limit, and it was dark before they stopped, a fireless camp, one that they would break before dawn. Vanye slid down from the saddle holding to the harness and found himself hardly able to walk; but he cared for his horse, and took his gear and limped over to Roh's side, head bowed as he passed through the midst of the men. He thought that if one of them should set hands on him he would turn and kill that man; but that was madness and he knew it. He endured one man shouldering his horse past deliberately, and kept his head down as Roh had said . . . assumed an *ilin's* humility like a garment.

When he reached Roh's side he flung his pack down and stayed standing, for it was painful to rise once down. "I would like to change clothes," he said.

"So shall I. Do so."

He stripped off the Hiua garments with distaste, and stood only in shirt and breeches, Shiua, of fine-spun cloth: the haqueton he put on, against the chill, and meditated putting on the mail-shirt as well, but the stiffness of his shoulders decided otherwise. He put on his cloak, no more. And Roh also rid himself of the disguise; and paused in that to give orders to Fwar.

"We will want sentries watching all horizons. There are Shiua riders behind us without doubt; but there could be some returning from the forest edge, and we cannot risk that meeting either.

Fwar made a sound that might be agreement, turned, and with his foot hooked Vanye's good leg.

Vanye sprawled, his knee awash with pain, and rolled and started up as best he could; but Roh was on his feet in the instant, his sword drawn. "Do that again," Roh said, "or lay any hand on him and I will have the head from your shoulders."

"For *this?*"

Vanye struggled to his feet, but Roh laid a hand on his arm and thrust him back, turned on him when he resisted, and struck him hard across the face. "You forget yourself. Morgaine's patience was longer than mine. Cause me trouble and I will give you to them."

Anger blinded him for the moment; and then he understood and bowed his head and sank down again—for good measure performed the full obeisance as an *ilin,* an awkwardness with a stiff leg. Then he sat down, head bowed. It amused the Hiua mightily. He did not react to the laughter, which, ugly as it was, lightened the air.

"He is *ilin*," Roh said. "Is that in the old songs? Perhaps you have forgotten that custom; but he is not a free man. He is outlawed . . . Morgaine's servant, no more than that. By Andurin law, he is free of any blood he sheds: Morgaine is guilty. Now he is in my service, and he stays, Myya Fwar. Or would you rather kill him and lose our only hope of surviving? That is your choice. You are playing games with our own lives. Cripple or kill him and we have no guide, no safe passage. Hetharu is behind us. Why do you think? For me? No. I could ride out and Hetharu would bear that as he has everything else I have done, because he dares not kill me: I have the knowledge that provides him safety in this land . . . knowledge of the Gates and of *power*, my Myya friends, that is greater than Hetharu himself suspects. And because you serve me, Hetharu has feared us both. But listen to me now and I will tell you what has driven Hetharu and me to this parting of ways, why he has taken arms against us—and he has done so, if any of you care to ride back and find out. It is because he had a chance to question this man, and he knows enough now to fear my getting my hands on him. He knows that with this man I can overthrow the *khal* . . . and seize control of all this land."

There was dead silence. All the men had gathered, hearing this, and Vanye turned his face aside and kept his head bowed, his hand clenched on his sword.

"How?" Fwar asked.

"Because this man has knowledge of the forest, of its

people, and of Morgaine. The *khal* have not found her. He
can. And he is the means by which we can gain her weapons,
and absolute control of the Gates. You have been trying to
plunder *villages*. But with that power in hand, do you not
think the *khal*-lords know what we will be then? They will
risk everything to stop us. They are not anxious to be ruled
by Men. But we will settle with them. No one . . . *no one*
. . . is to set hands on this man. I have promised him his life
for his help. The *khal* could get nothing from him . . . nor
could you, my friends, where they failed. But me he will listen to; he knows I keep my word. Now if that is too great a
matter for you to bear, ride off now and join Hetharu . . .
take your chances you will survive that. But if you will stay
with me, then keep your hands off him or go through life
one-handed. He is too valuable to me."

"He will not always be," someone said.

"My oath," Roh shouted at that man. "Put it from your
mind, Derth. Put it from your mind!"

There was sullen agreement. Derth spat on the ground, but
nodded. Others muttered assent.

"Four days," Roh said, "and we will be within reach of all
you came into my service to have. Does that not content
you? Four days."

"Aye," Fwar said suddenly, and the rest of the pack fell in.
"Aye, lord," the rest agreed, and the camp settled again, with
mutterings of what would be done with the *khal*-lords when
they had gained power over them.

Vanye swallowed heavily and looked up as Roh settled by
him. Roh said nothing for a moment.

"Are you hurt?" Roh asked then. He shook his head for reply, stared at Roh with an uneasiness he could not shake. He
dared not question; Fwar's cousins sat within earshot. This
would be so for the duration of their journey. Roh could not
be expected to reassure him, to do anything which would betray agreement between them. And he could not help wondering if he had not just heard Roh tell the truth.

Roh's hand clenched on his arm. "Get some sleep, cousin."

Vanye wrapped his cloak about him and lay down where
the blanket was spread; he slept, but not quickly.

Roh nudged him in the mid of the night; he opened his
eyes then and stayed awake while Roh closed his, as their
agreement was. All about them were the sounds of men
breathing, the sometime shifting of the horses, the strangeness

of such a combination of men and purposes. It oppressed him.

At the first hint of dawn the camp stirred, the sentries passing among the blanketed shapes and kicking this man and that . . . no more grace had they among their own folk than with strangers. Vanye did not abide that manner of waking, but reached and shook at Roh, disappointing the Hiua who was coming this way—sat up and began putting his armor on. Already there were men saddling their horses and cursing the dark and the chill, for the Hiua went unarmored save where they had plundered somewhat from the *khal*-lords. Fwar had a scale-shirt under his Shiua-cloth garments: Vanye had already marked that for a time yet to come. He eased on his own ring-mail with a protest of his scabbed shoulders and laced up, put on the coif as well as his helm, to keep his hair from his eyes. And Roh had included a dagger for his belt, not a proper Honor-blade, but a Shiua knife.

"You carried mine so long and faithfully," Roh mocked him out of the dark, "I hate to deprive you of it."

"Avert," he said, crossing himself fervently.

"Avert," Roh echoed him, and made the gesture too, and laughed afterward, which gave him no comfort at all.

He slid the hostile weapon into place at his belt and went to seek the horses, walking through the Hiua, as he must ride among them and sleep beside them and endure them for days more. They did not lose whatever chance they could find to trouble him. He bowed his head and took the abuse, choked with anger, reminding himself that he had grown too proud. It was no more than baiting, though uglier wishes lay beneath it. They hoped to provoke anger from him, which would bring Roh's wrath down on him . . . *Cause me trouble,* Roh had said in their hearing, *and I will give you to them.* They longed for that. But their baiting was only what an *ilin* in Andur-Kursh might endure under a harsh lord. Morgaine's service had been otherwise, even from the beginning, however hard it had been in other ways. He recalled her face and voice suddenly, and the gentleness she had given him, and thrust the memory away at once, for he could not afford to grieve.

She was not dead. He was not forever bound to the likes of these, in a world where she did not exist. His sanity insisted to believe it.

"Lord," someone said, and pointed south, in the direction

of the Gate. There was a second dawn on that horizon, a glimmering of red brighter than the true one.

"Fire." The word hissed through the company on many lips.

Roh stared at it, and suddenly gestured for them to move. "The *khal* must have settled the trouble we started in the camp; there is no hope it could be any other way. That fire is their means of dislodging the lower camp and moving them on; we have seen that tactic before. They are behind us now, and their outriders will have moved out long before now. We have to ride hard hereafter. They are coming, all of them."

The smudge of smoke on the horizon was evident in full dawn, but it soon burned itself out and dissipated on the winds: the wind was steadily from the north . . . had it been otherwise, it would have been a fire perilous in the extreme. "It has come up against the south river," Roh surmised, on one occasion that he turned in the saddle to look back. "I am relieved. Their madness might have swept down on all of us on this plain."

"Their riders will not come much slower than the fire would have," Vanye said, and looked back also; but all that was to be seen was Fwar's troop, and their faces were a sight he cared for as little as Hetharu's own. He turned about again, and spoke little to Roh thereafter, reckoning that much friendliness apparent between them could make things no better for Roh.

He tended Roh's horse at rests, and did all such things as he would have done for Morgaine. The Hiua were uncommonly quiet in their malice by daylight, where all that was done had to be done under Roh's witness. There were only spiteful looks, and once Fwar smiled broadly at him and laughed. "Wait," Fwar said, and that was all. He glared steadily at Fwar, reckoning that his principal danger was a knifing in the bcak when the time came. Fwar was one that wanted facing all the time.

And once thereafter he saw Fwar looking at Roh's back, with quite another look than he gave to Roh's face.

*This is a man*, Vanye thought, *who never forgives; some cause he has with me; and perhaps with Roh—another*.

*Guard my back*, Roh had wished him, knowing well the men of his service.

They crossed the two rivers in the morning and the noon. Their bearing was to the north and slightly easterly, toward the ford of the Narn. Vanye chose their direction, for he rode at the head of the company with Roh and Fwar and Trin, and he bore as he would, while Roh adjusted his course to suit his at each small jostling of the horses, and Fwar and his men followed Roh's leading.

There was, he recalled, that camp of Hetharu's men or Fwar's due north, and he did not want to encounter that; there was the ford of the Narn itself, which he wanted less. But between the two, the expanse of a night's hard ride, there was a patch of forest that did not love Men, and that he chose, knowing it might be the end of them.

But having heard Roh's talk with the Hiua, he was determined on it, rather than to guide them all near Morgaine. He lived in the hourly anticipation that Fwar would discover where they were bound, and who was truly leading them, for Fwar had been in that region and might well know the danger . . . but it did not happen. He made himself as inconspicuous in his position as possible, bowing his head on his chest and feigning to give way to his wounds and to exhaustion. In fact, he did sleep a little while they rode, but not long; and he pretended hardly to be aware of what direction they took.

"Riders," Trin said of a sudden.

Vanye looked up and followed the pointing of Trin's arm. His heart pounded in sudden fright at the cloud that rose on the northwesterly horizon. "A Shiua camp was there," he said to Roh. "But they cannot yet know you have fallen out with Hetharu."

"They would know *him* quickly enough," Fwar said. "Get some covering round that armor, quick."

Fwar's advice or no, it was worth taking. Vanye slipped off his helm and unlaced his coif, shaking his hair free as the Barrows-men wore theirs. Fwar stripped off his tunic of coarse wool and gave it to him. "Put that on, Roh's bastard cousin, and drop back of us."

He did so, shrugged the unwashed garment down over his own leather and mail and reined back into the center of Fwar's pack of wolves where he was less conspicuous. His face was hot with rage for the taunt Fwar had flung at him . . . an old one, and one which only Roh could have told them, concerning the proper degree of their kinship. It disturbed him the more because the Roh he had known was his mother's close kin, and the taunt was not one that did honor to clan Chya or Roh's house.

Fwar's riders made close formation about him. Their hair was dark, and none were so tall. He made his stature as little obvious as possible. There was little more to be done. The riders were coming on them at speed now, having seen the dust they raised, and surely meant to meet them.

"The Sotharra camp," a man at his left muttered. "Shien's folk, those."

Roh and Fwar rode ahead to meet the riders at distance from the company, a wise maneuver if it were Shien. The oncoming riders slowed, breaking from a charge to an approach, and finally came to a halt, but for their three leaders, who kept riding. In Fwar's band, bows were strung and arrows readied, but there was no show of them.

It was indeed Shien. Vanye recognized the young *khal*-lord and thanked Heaven for the distance between them. The horses snorted and fretted wearily under them. There was a time that everything seemed peaceful. Then voices were raised, Shien's bidding them turn and follow his lead to his camp.

"I do not want your Barrows-scum riding where they please and cutting through our territory. They are hindrance as much as help. They take no orders."

"They take mine," Roh returned. "Out of my way, lord Shien. This is my path and you are in it."

"Go on, go on, then, but you are coming up against forest soon. Your men are no loss, but you are. Nothing has come alive out of that area, and I will use force to stop you, lord Roh. You are too much to risk."

Roh lifted his arm. Hiua bows lifted and bent. "Ride off," Roh said.

Shien stared incredulously, dazed by the sight of human defiance. "You are quite mad."

"Ride off. Or discover the limits of my insanity."

Shien backed his horse, and his escort with him; with a sudden jerk he wheeled about and rode back to his own troop, which glittered with scale-armor and pikes. One of the Barrows-men softly entreated protection of his several gods.

Roh started moving, Fwar and Trin beside him. The company moved forward, passing the Shiua riders, who stood still watching them. First their flank and then their backs were exposed to the Shiua, who remained motionless. Eventually the

Shiua dwindled in the distance, and Roh started them to a gallop, which they kept until the horses could stay it no more. Even so it was well after dark before they stopped and flung down from their horses.

Fwar asked his tunic back. Vanye surrendered it gladly enough, and tended his horse and Roh's . . . and Fwar's, for the Barrows-man flung him the reins as Roh had done, to the general laughter of the company; they mocked him: *bastard* was a taunt they had all taken up, seeing how it pricked at him.

He averted his face from their tormenting, and settled the horses and passed through the Hiua company back to Roh, where Fwar sat.

And he had no more than sat down than Fwar grasped his shoulder and pulled him roughly about.

"You are our guide, are you? The lord Roh says it. So what did Shien mean about hazards in the forest?"

He thrust off Fwar's hand. "There are," he said carefully, though rage nearly choked him, "there are hazards everywhere in the forest. I can guide you through them."

"What sort?"

"Others. *Qhal.*"

"Fwar scowled and looked at Roh.

"Morgaine has allies," Roh said softly.

"What kind of trap have you led us into? We trusted *her* once and learned. I have no trust in this now."

"Then you are in a bad situation, are you not? Hetharu on one side and Shien on the other, and the forest that none of us yet have found a way to travel safely——"

"Your arranging."

"I will talk with you privately. Vanye, get out of here."

"See he does, Trin."

Vanye gathered himself up; Trin was quicker, and seized him by the arm and drew him away to the far side of the camp, where the horses were picketed.

They stopped there. Fwar and Roh spoke together, out of hearing, two shadows in the dark. Vanye stared at them, trying to hear all the same, trying to ignore his guard, who suddenly seized his collar from behind and wrenched. "Sit down," Trin advised him, and he did so. Trin stood over him and kicked several times gently at his splinted knee, naught but casual malice. "We will get you away from him sooner or later," Trin said.

He answered nothing, planning that meeting in his own way.

"Thirty-seven of us—all with reason enough to settle with you."

He still said nothing, and Trin swung his foot again. He seized it and wrenched, and Trin went down, startling the horses, crying out for help. Men poured toward them. Vanye hit the Hiua, staggered up from Trin's prostrate form and came up on one leg, whipped out his dagger and slashed a tether. The horse shied back; he seized its mane and swung up as the dark tide reached him.

The horse screamed and plunged—went over as the Hiua overwhelmed it, other horses shying and screaming and tearing at their tethers. Vanye cleared the falling animal and sprawled into a yielding mass of Hiua almost under other hooves. He slashed blindly and lost the dagger as that arm was held and strained back nearly to breaking.

They drew him up then, and one snatched him by the harness on his chest and wrenched him forward. He would have struck, but for the glitter of mail, that showed him who it was. Roh cursed him and shook him, and he flung the hair from his eyes, ready to fight the rest of them. One tried to come at him—Trin, alive, with dark blood on his face and a knife in his hand.

Fwar stopped the man, took the knife, thrust the rest of the mob back. "No," Fwar said. "No. Let be with him."

The Hiua gave back sullenly, began to move away. Vanye shivered convulsively from his anger and caught his breath. Roh had not let him go. He reached for Roh's hand and disengaged it.

"Trying to run?" Roh asked him.

He said nothing. It was obvious enough what he had tried.

Roh seized his wrist and turned his hand up, slammed the hilt of his dagger into it. "Put that away and thank me for it."

He went to the ground and performed the obeisance, and Roh stood staring at him for a moment, then turned and walked away, Fwar lingered Vanye gathered himself up, expecting Fwar's malice, recalling to his confusion that it had been Fwar who pulled his men back.

"Someone go catch that horse," Fwar said then. A man went, walking out to the horse that had stopped its flight a little distance from the picket line.

Vanye started back to Roh. Fwar took him by the arm.

"Come along," Fwar said, and guided him through the standing crowd.

No hand was laid on him else. Trin threatened; but Fwar
took him aside and spoke to him in private, and Trin returned pacified. The whole camp settled.

Vanye looked about him at this sudden tolerance, and at
Roh, who averted his face and began to prepare himself for
the night's rest.


# Chapter Eleven


They moved out yet again before dawn, and by the time
day came full upon them, the dark line of Shathan bowed
across their northern horizon.

During that day a strange tension lay over the company,
which had riders dropping back to the rear by twos and
threes and talking together a while before riding forward
again.

Vanye saw it plainly enough, and reckoned that Roh did
. . . dared not call it into question, for there was Fwar, as
ever, at his side. *I am mad*, he kept thinking, *to have any
trust left in him.* He was afraid, with a gnawing apprehension
which Shathan's nearness did nothing to allay: to ride into
that darkness . . .

He flexed the knee against the splints, and estimated that
with the horse under him he was a whole man and without it
a dead one. To ride with any speed through that dark maze
of roots and uneven ground was impossible; to run it afoot,
lame as he was, held no better hope—and the question was
how far he could lead this band, before someone called halt
and challenged him.

Yet Roh let him guide them still, even after Shien's warning, and what mutterings Fwar had made about it were
silenced. All objections were stilled. There were only the
whisperings in the back of the column.

In the afternoon they stopped and sat down with tether lines in hand, letting the horses rest, themselves taking a little food and drink, unpacking nothing which was not at once replaced, ready to move on in any instant. A gambling game started up, using knives and skill, and imaginary stakes of *khalur* plunder; that grew loud, and swiftly obscene. Roh sat unsmiling. His eyes shifted to Vanye's, and said nothing.

And suddenly flickered, fixed beyond his shoulder. Vanye turned and saw through his horse's legs a haze of dust on the southern horizon.

"I think we should move," Roh said.

"Aye," he murmured. There was no doubt what that was, by its direction: Hetharu—Hetharu with his riders, and the Shiua horde in his wake.

Fwar swore blackly and ordered his men to horse. They sprang up from their game and checked girths, adjusted bits, took to the saddle with feverish haste. Vanye swung up and reined about, taking another look.

It was more than one point of the horizon now: it was an arc that swept toward them from south and west, hemming them half about. "Shien," he said. "Shien has joined with them."

"That dust will be seen in the Sotharra camp," Fwar judged, and swore. "There and among the ones out on Narnside. They will lose no time riding this way either."

Roh made no answer, but set spurs to the black mare. The whole company rode after him in haste, driving their horses to desperate flight. Spur and quirt could not keep the weaker with the pace; already the company was beginning to string back. The Shiua animals, journey-worn, could not keep the Andurin mare's ground-eating stride, much as their riders belabored them. Vanye nursed his sorrel gelding as he had done from the beginning . . . an unlovely animal, burdened with a bigger man than the Hiua, and him armored; but the beast had had at least a horseman's care on the journey, and he held his own at the rear . . . not important now to be in the lead, only to be with the rest, to keep the animal running for that green line ahead of them. The *khalur* riders were gaining: he looked back and saw the glint of metal through the dust of their own riding; doubtless the *khal*, better mounted, would kill their horses if need be to overtake them, seeing the forest ahead as well as they did.

Roh's lead was now considerable, and only a few of the Hiua could keep with him. Vanye guided the sorrel around a bit of brush another rider had gone over, reckoning the land and the easiest path. He passed three of the Hiua, though he had not changed his pace. He bit at his lip and kept the gelding to what he had set.

Now there was a cloud of dust not only behind them, but eastward, closer there, ominously closer.

Others looked that way eventually, saw that force that sprang bright and glittering as if by magic over a swell of the land. The Hiua cried out in alarm, and spurred and whipped their horses near to exhaustion, as if that would help them— rode them over ground that was fit to lame them even at a slower pace.

A horse went down, screaming, in the path of another. Vanye looked back; one of the riders was a marshlander, and a comrade dropped back for that man: three gone, then. The man picked up the one rider and overtook them again, leaving the other; but soon the overburdened horse broke stride and fell farther and farther behind.

Vanye cursed; Kurshin that he was, he loved horses too well to enjoy what was happening. Roh's doing, Roh's Andurin callousness, he thought; but that was because he had somewhere to place the anger for such cruelty. He consented in it and rode, although by now the little gelding was drenched in sweat, and his own gut and joints felt every bruise the land dealt them.

The forest was all their view now, though the *khlaur* riders were almost within bowshot. Arrows flew, fell short; that was waste. Archery slowed the force that fired, to no profit at this range.

He no longer rode among the last: three, four more horses that had been near the fore broke stride and dropped behind him, even within reach of the forest. The others might make it.

*"Hai!"* he shouted, and used the spurs suddenly; the gelding leapt forward, startled—passed others, began to close the gap with the foremost, gaining on Roh's Andurin mare. Vanye bent low, although the arrows still flew amiss, for now the forest lay ahead. Roh disappeared into that green shadow, and Fwar, and Trin; he came third and others followed, slowing at once in that thickening tangle. One rider did not, and a horse rushed past riderless.

Vanye ducked a limb and pressed the exhausted gelding past to the fore. "Come," he gasped, and none disputed.

The gelding was surefooted despite that it was so badly

spent; Vanye wound his way this direction and that with an eye to the ground and the tangle overhead, as rapidly as the horse could bear—down one leaf-covered slope and up another.

More riders crashed after them, horses breaking a way where there was none, either their own companions or the most reckless of their pursuers. A man screamed somewhere behind them, and Vanye did not look back, caring nothing who it was. The horse's breathing between his legs was like a bellows working, the beast's legs communicating an occasional shudder of exhaustion which he felt through his own body. He tapped it with his heels, talked to it in his own tongue as if all horses understood a Morij accent. It kept moving. He looked back and Roh was still there, and Fwar and Trin a little farther, and a third and fourth man; brush crashed somewhere that he could not see. A horse broke through a screen of branches even as he watched, and labored downslope; Minur was that rider, and the horse could scarcely make the gentle climb up again.

There was a stream, hardly with water enough to cover the horse's hooves. His wanted to stop; he did not allow it, drove it up the slope, found the trail he had thought to find. He put the horse to no more speed, only enough to maintain the pace. The shadow thickened, not alone of the forest, but of the declining sun. He turned in the saddle and saw Roh with him, Fwar and Trin and Minur, others, about three near, more farther back. Fwar looked back too, and the look in his eyes when he turned showed that finally, finally he understood.

Vanye drove the spurs in, ducked low and rode, shouts pursuing him, the thunder of hooves with him still and close. The trail dipped again, where a tree was down. The gelding measured that slope, refused it, and Vanye reined about in the same move, whipped his sword from sheath.

Fwar rode into it, his own sword drawn: Vanye remembered the scale-armor and cut high. Fwar parried; Vanye rammed the spurs in and defended in turn, cut downward as the gelding shied up. Fwar screamed, tumbled under the hooves of his own backing mount as a second horse plunged past, riderless: horses collided, went down on the slope, and Fwar was somewhere under them.

A third: Minur. Vanye spun the staggering gelding about and parried with a shock that numbed his fingers, whipped the blade about and across Minur's with a desperation Minur should have moved to counter: he had not. There was only his head in the longsword's path, and the Barrows-man died without a sound, sped before he left the saddle.

"Hai!" Vanye shouted, and spurred past blind at the others, cut right and cut left and emptied two saddles, he knew not whose. The gelding brought up short as one of the horses shouldered it, staggered. He drew rein and saw Roh in his path; but Roh faced the other way, still ahorse, and his bow was bent and one of his green-fletched shafts was trained down that dark aisle of trees, which was held only by dead men.

"Roh," Vanye called to him.

The shaft flew. Roh reined about and spurred toward him: a hail of arrows pursued, white-feathered, and none of them accurate. Vanye turned, and drove the gelding back toward the slope, weaving through the trees to avoid the obstacle at the bottom. The black mare stayed close behind.

An outcry rang out behind them, rage and anguish. Vanye took the gelding up the other slope, hearing brush break in the distance. The gelding reached the top and staggered, kept going a little farther and faltered badly. It was the end for it. Vanye slid down and slashed the leather that held the girth-ring, freeing it of the saddle, and he tore off its bridle and hit it a good slap to drive it farther. Roh did the same for the black mare, though it could have borne him farther—turned and nocked one of his god Chya shafts.

"We did not lose enough of them," Vanye said, in what of breath remained to him; he clenched the bloody sword in his fist and regretted bitterly the bow that was lost with Mai.

The sound of pursuit crashed nearer down the trail—and stopped, simply stopped. There was silence, save for their own hard breathing.

Roh swore softly.

A man cried out, and another. All through the forest there were thin outcries, and of a sudden a crash of brush near them that nearly startled Roh into firing. A riderless horse broke through and kept going, mad with terror. There were screams of horses and brush crackled in every direction.

Then silence.

Brush whispered about them. Vanye let his sword drop to the dry leaves, stood still, gazing into the shadowing dark with the hair prickling at his nape.

"Put down your bow," he hissed at Roh. "Drop it, or we are dead men."

Roh did so, nothing questioning, and did not move.

Shadows moved here and there. There was a soft chittering.

"Their weapons are poisoned," Vanye whispered. "And they have had bitter experience of Men of our breed. Stand still. Stand still whatever they do."

Then very carefully, arms wide, he limped a little apart from Roh, in the midst of the trail where they had turned at bay. He stood still a moment, then carefully turned, faced every quarter of the wood until he saw the strange shadow that he sought . . . not on the ground. It sat like a nest of old moss in the crotch of a tree. Enormous eyes were centered on him, alive in the midst of that unlikely shape.

He signed to it as Lellin had done. And when that brought no reaction, he bent his good leg and awkwardly knelt, hands still far from his sides, that it might see he held no weapon.

It moved. It was incredible how it descended, as if it had no need of branches, but clung to the wood of the trunk. It stood then watching him, tall and stilt-limbed. Voices chittered now from all sides, and all about them in the dusk, shadows moved, stalking into the pathway.

They towered over him as he knelt. They stayed absolutely still, and they put their hands on his shoulders and arms . . . slender, powerful fingers that tugged strangely at his garments and his armor. They closed and drew him to his feet, and he turned and stared up into their faces, shivering.

They spoke to him, and tugged at his clothing; there was anger in their rapid voices.

"No," he whispered, and signed at them carefully: *friend, friend,* hand to his heart.

There was no response. Slowly he lifted his arm and pointed down the trail in the direction he wished to go, and saw that others considered Roh, who stood deathly still in their unhuman hands.

He tried to leave those about him and walk in that direction, but they would not let him walk free: they brought him to Roh, holding him firmly. His eyes roved the area, counting: ten, twenty of them. Their faces, their dark, fathomless eyes, seemed all immune to reason or passion.

"They are *harilim,*" he said to Roh softly. "And they are of the forest . . . *of* it, entirely."

"Morgaine's allies."

"No one's allies."

It was fully night now; the last twilight faded, and the

shadows thickened. More and more of the *harilim* arrived, and all began to speak at once, in chittering rushes of sound that thundered like falling water; debate, perhaps, or chanting. But at last came other stalking shadows that simply stood and watched, and silence fell, so suddenly it numbed.

"The amulet," Vanye said. "Roh. The amulet. Do you still have it?"

Roh reached very slowly into his collar and drew it forth. It shone in the starlight, a silver circle trembling on Roh's hand. One of the *harilim* reached and touched it, and chirred softly.

Then one of the tall late-comers stalked forward with that heron-like gait, which halted several times and did not hurry. It too fingered the amulet, and touched Roh's face. It spoke, and the sound was deeper, like frog-song.

Tentatively Vanye lifted his arm yet again, pointing to the path that they wanted to go.

There was no response. He tried a step and none forbade. He took another, and another, and stooped very carefully and gathered up his sword and put it in its sheath. He edged back yet farther. Roh took his lead then, and moving very carefully, picked up his bow. There was no sound from the *harilim*, none anywhere in the forest. Step after step they were allowed.

A hail of twigs came down from overhead. They kept walking, and still none prevented them. They passed down the trail and met the stream again, where the trail ceased and they had only the streamcourse to guide them. Reeds rustled behind them. A chittering came from the trees.

"You planned this," Roh said hoarsely. "Shien understood. I would that I had."

"What did you plan for me?" he returned, half a whisper, for sound was fearsome in this place. "I promised only to go with you and guard your back—*cousin*. But what did you contrive with Fwar that so well pleased him?"

"What do you suppose I promised him?"

He answered nothing and kept walking, limping heavily over tangles of roots and washes in the mossy earth. The stream beside them promised water they dared not stop to drink, not until the breath was raw in their throats.

Then he fell to one knee and gathered a cold double handful to his mouth, and Roh did likewise, both of them taking what they could. Leaves rustled. A hail of twigs flew about them, leaves and debris hitting the water. They gathered themselves up as larger pieces began to fly. Shadows moved in the forest. They started walking and the shaking of branches stopped.

There came a time that they had to rest. Vanye sank down, hands clasped to his aching knee, and Roh flung himself down among the leaves, heaving with sobs for breath. They had left the stream for a trail that offered itself. There was only dark about them.

Of a sudden the shaking of branches began. A piece of wood cracked; a branch crashed dangerously near them, breaking young trees in its fall. Vanye reached for support and clawed his way to his feet, Roh springing up hardly slower. A scattering of twigs hit them. They began walking and it ceased.

"How far will they drive us?" Roh asked. His voice shook with exhaustion. "Is there a place they have in mind?"

"Til morning . . . and out of their woods." He caught the bad leg and stumbled, recovered with an effort that blurred his eyes. Almost he would have defied them and flung himself down to see whether they meant their threats, but he was too sure that they did. The *harilim* had done much, indeed, not to have killed them among the others . . . save that they might—at least one or two of them—recall him as a companion of the *qhal* . . . if they had memories at all, if anything like the thoughts of Men existed behind those huge dark eyes.

Cruel, cruel as any force of nature: they would have their way, their forest cleared of outsiders. He reckoned that their freedom to walk was the utmost of the *harilim's* mercy and went blindly. Once they met another, broader trail, started to take it, but a hail of twigs came down on them, in their faces, and the chittering began to be angry.

"Go back," he said, pushing at Roh, who was minded otherwise, and they turned and struggled the other, the harder trail, which took them deeper into the woods.

He fell. The leaves skidded slickly under his hands and for a moment he simply lay there, until the chittering nearby warned him, and Roh put a hand under his arm and cursed him. "Get up," Roh said, and when he had his feet under him again, Roh flung an arm about him and kept him moving until he had recovered his senses.

Day was beginning, a first grayness. The shadows which stalked them became more and more visible, sometimes moving along beside them with more rapidity than a Man could manage in the brush.

Then as the light increased a hush fell, and nothing now disturbed the trees, as if their herders had suddenly become one with bark and moss and limb.

"They are gone," Roh said first, and began to slow, leaned against a tree. Vanye looked about him, and again his senses began to leave him. Roh caught his arm, and he sank down where he was and sprawled on the dry leaves, numb and blank for a time.

He woke with a touch on his face, realized he was on his back now, and Roh's hand, cold and wet, bathed his brow. "There is another stream just beyond those trees. Wake up. Wake up. We cannot spend another night in this place."

"Aye," he murmured, and moved, groaned aloud for the misery in body and limbs. Roh steadied him to rise on his good leg, and helped him climb down to the water. There he drank and bathed his aching head, washed the dirt from him as best he could. There was blood on his hands and his armor: Fwar, he recalled, and bathed that off with loathing.

"Where are we?" Roh asked. "What do you expect to find here? Only their like?"

He shook his head. "I am lost. I have no idea where we are."

"Kurshin," Roh said, like a curse. Roh was Andurin, in all his lives, and forest-bred, as Kurshin were of the mountains and valley plains. "At least that way is the river." He pointed to the downstream of the brook. "And the ford where she was."

"Which lies across the *harilim* woods, and if you choose that route, go to it; I will not. It was your imagining to use me for a guide. I never claimed for myself what you claimed for me to Fwar."

Roh regarded him narrowly. "Aye, and yet you knew accurately enough how to cast us to those creatures, and you have travelled here. I think you are shading the truth with me, my Kurshin cousin. Lost you may be, but you know how to find yourself. And Morgaine."

"Go to blazes. You would have thrown me to the Hiua if the hour had needed it."

"A kinsman of mine? I fear I am too proud for that kind of bartering. Is that a reasoning you understand? No, I promised you to them, when we should have taken Morgaine . . . but I can shade the truth too, cousin. I would have

shaken them from my track. I heard Shien's warning. I could
have turned aside. I trusted to you. Are not a Kurshin and an
Andurin match for Hiua in the woods? Do you think that I
would ever have found them comfortable allies? Fwar hated
me almost as he hated you. He meant to knife me in the
back the moment Morgaine was no longer a threat and he
had you in his hands, disarmed. That was the anticipation
that sweetened his disposition. He thought he had everything
he wanted, me to deal with Morgaine, and half-witted enough
to strip myself of the only man who might give me warning
if they went for my back. Fwar saw himself as master of this
land if he only tolerated us for a time; that I could give my
trust to you, who had been my enemy—Fwar was not such a
man, and therefore he could not imagine it in others. And it
killed him. But you and I, Vanye—we are different men. You
and I—know what honor is."

Vanye swallowed heavily, uneasily reckoning that it might
remotely be truth. "I promised to guard your back . . . no
more than that. I have done so. It was your own saying, that
you would find Morgaine and try to speak with her. Well, do
it without my help. Here our agreement ends. Go your own
way."

"For a cripple, you are very confident to dismisss me."

Vanye scrambled awkwardly to his feet, hand jerking his
sword from its hook; he almost fell, and braced his back
against a tree. But Roh still knelt, unthreatening.

"Peace," Roh said, turning empty hands palm up. A mocking smile was on his lips. "In fact, you do think you can
manage without me in this woods, and I would know why.
Crippled as you are, cousin, I should hate to abandon you."

"Leave me."

Roh shook his head. "A new agreement: that I go with
you. I want only to speak to Morgaine . . . if she is alive;
and if she is not, cousin . . . if she is not, then you and I together should reconsider matters. You evidently have allies in
this forest. You think that you do not need me. Well, that is
the truth, more than likely. But I shall follow you; I promise
you that. So I may as well go with you. You know that no
Kurshin can shake me from his trail. Would you not rather
know where I am?"

Vanye swore, clenched his hand on the sword he did not
draw. "Do you not know," he asked Roh hoarsely, "that
Morgaine set me under orders to kill you? And do you not
know that I have no choice where it regards that oath?"

That took the smile from Roh's face. Roh considered it, and shrugged after a moment, hands loose across his knees. "Well, but you could hardly out-fence me at the moment, could you?—save I gave you a standing target, which would hardly be to your liking. I shall go with you and abide Morgaine's decision in the matter."

"No," he pleaded with him, and Roh's expression grew the more troubled.

"What, is that keeping faith with your liege—to warn her enemies that she is pitiless, that she is unbending, that she understands no reason at all where it regards a threat to her? My oldest memories are dreams, cousin, and they are long and full of her. The Hiua call her Death, and the Shiua *khal* once laughed at that. No longer. I know her. I know my chances. But the *khal* will not forgive what I have done. I cannot go back; I would have no freedom from them. I saw what they did to you—and I am quick to learn, cousin. I had to leave that place. She is all that is left. I am tired, Vanye, I am *tired*—and I have bad dreams."

Vanye stared at him. Gone was all semblance of pride, of mockery; Roh's voice trembled, and his eyes were shadowed.

"Is it in your dreams . . . what Liell would have done with me and with her?"

Roh looked up. Horror was in his eyes, deep and distant. "Do not call those things up. They come back at night. And I doubt you want the answer."

"When you—dream those things: how do you feel about it?"

"Roh hates it."

Vanye shuddered, gazing into the wildness in Roh's face, the war exposed. He sank down again on the bank of the stream, and for a time Roh wrapped his arms about himself and shivered like a man fevered. The shivering stoppped finally, and the dark eyes that met his were whole again, quizzical, mocking.

"Roh?"

"Aye, cousin."

"Let us start walking."

They walked the streamside, which in Shathan was no less than a road . . . more reliable than the paths, for all the habitations of Men in Shathan were set near water. They must struggle at times, for the way was overgrown and at times the trees arched over the little stream or grew down to the very margin, or some fallen log damned it, making deep places. They had no lack of water, hungry as they were . . . and there were fish in the stream that they might devise to take when they dared stop: not favored fare for a Kurshin, but he was not fastidious, and Roh had fared on much worse.

He limped along with Roh at his back, saying nothing of how he guided himself, though perhaps Roh could guess; he had found himself a staff and leaned on it as he walked, though it was less the knee that troubled him than other wounds, which covered the most of his body and at times hurt so that the tears came to his eyes . . . an abiding, never-ceasing misery that now had the heat of fever.

He sank down toward noon and slept, not aware even that he chose to do so. He simply came to himself lying on the ground, with Roh asleep not far from him. He rose up and shook at Roh, and they both stood up and started walking.

"We have slept too long," Roh said, anxiously looking skyward. "It is halfway through the afternoon."

"I know," he said, with the same dread. "We cannot stop again."

He made what haste he could, and several times dared whistle aloud, as close to Lellin's tones as he could manage, but nothing answered him. There was no sight of game, hardly a flicker of a bird's wings through the trees, as if they were all that lived in this section of Shathan. No *qhal* were near . . . or if they were, they chose to remain silent and unseen. Roh noted it; whenever he looked back he saw Roh's anxious shift of eyes over their surroundings and agreed with Roh's uneasiness. They walked through something utterly unnatural.

They came upon an old tree, corded with white. It was rotten at the heart, lightning-riven.

"Mirrind," Vanye said aloud, his pulse racing, for now he knew completely where he was, to what place the little stream had guided them.

"What is that?" Roh asked.

"A village. You should know it. The Shiua murdered one of its people." Then he repented his words, for they were both at the end of their strength and their wits, and he needed no quarrel with Roh. "Come. Carefully."

He sought the rutted road and found it, concealed as it was now by brush. He walked as quickly as he could with his limping stride, for the night was coming fast on them. From this place, he thought, he might try to find Merir's camp . . . but he was not sure of the way, and the chance was that

Merir would have broken camp and left the place even if he could find it. He was noly anxious now to put the *harilim* behind them before the dark came on them again.

Through the trees suddenly appeared a haze of open space, and when they had reached that edge there were only shells of stone and burned skeletons of timber where Mirrind had stood. He swore when he saw it, and leaned against one of the trees by the roadside. Roh wisely said nothing at that moment, and he swallowed the tightness from his throat and started forward, keeping to the shadow of trees and ruins.

The crops still grew, although weeds had set in; and the ruins of the hall were mostly intact. But the desolation, where beauty had been, was complete.

"We cannot stay here," Roh said. "This is within reach of the Sotharra camp. Shien's men. We have come too far. Use some sense, cousin. Let us get out of the open."

He lingered yet a moment, staring about him, then turned painfully and began to do as Roh had advised.

An arrow hit the dirt at their feet, quivered there, brown-feathered.

# Chapter Twelve

Roh started back from the arrow as from a serpent, reaching for his own bow. "No," Vanye said, holding him from flight.

"Friends of yours."

"Once. Maybe still. —*Arrhendim, lher nthim ahallya Meriran!*"

There was no response. "You are full of surprises," Roh said.

"Be still," he answered. His voice shook, for he was very tired, and the silence dismayed him. If the *arrhendim* themselves had turned against him, then there was no hope.

"*Khemeis.*" The voice came from behind him.

He turned. A Man stood there, a *khemeis*. It was not any that he knew.

"Come."

He began to do so, bringing Roh with him. The *khemeis* melted back into the forest, and when they had reached that place there was no sign that he had stood there. They walked farther into the shadow.

Suddenly a white-haired *qhal* shifted into their view, from the shadow of the trees. His bow was bent, and a brown-feathered arrow was aimed at them.

"I am Lellin Erirrhen's friend," Vanye said. "And *khemeis* to Morgaine. This man is my cousin."

The arrow did not waver. "Where is Lellin?"

Then his heart sank, and he leaned on his staff, little caring whether the arrow was fired.

"Where is Lellin?"

"With my lady. And I do not know. I hoped that the *arrhendim* would."

"Your cousin bears lord Merir's safe-passage. But that is good only for him who bears it."

"Take us to Merir. I have an accounting to give him for his grandson."

Slowly the arrow was lowered and eased from the bow-string. "We will take you where we please. One of you does not have leave to be here. Which?"

"I," Roh confessed, lifting the amulet from his neck. He gave it into Vanye's hand.

"You will both come with me."

Vanye nodded when Roh looked question at him; and he hung the amulet again about his neck and, heavily, limped in the *qhal's* wake.

There was no stopping until long after dark; and then the *arrhen* halted and settled among the roots of a large tree. Vanye sank down, Roh beside him, tucked his good leg up and rested against it, exhausted. But Roh shook at him after a moment. "They offer us food and drink," Roh said.

Vanye bestirred himself and took it, small appetite as he had now; afterward he leaned against the base of a tree and gazed at the *arrhendim* . . . two now, for the *khemeis* had joined them.

"Do you know nothing of where Lellin or my lady is?" Vanye asked them.

"We will not answer," said the *qhal*.

"Do you count us enemies?"

"We will not answer."

Vanye shook his head and abandoned hope with them, rested his head against the bark.

"Sleep," said the *qhal*, and spread his cloak and wrapped in it, becoming one with the tree against which he leaned; but the *khemeis* vanished quietly into the brush.

There was a different *qhal* and a different *khemeis* in the morning. Vanye looked at them, blinked, disturbed that they had shifted about so silently. Roh cast him a sidelong glance no less disturbed.

"I am Tirrhen," said the *qhal*. "My *khemeis* is Haim. We will take you farther."

"Nhi Vanye and Chya Roh," Vanye replied. "Where?"

The *qhal* shrugged. "Come."

"You are more courteous than the last," Roh said, and took Vanye's arm, helping him rise.

"They are Mirrind's guardians," Tirrhen replied. "Would you expect joy of them?"

And Tirrhen turned his back and vanished, so that it was Haim who walked with them a time. "Be silent," the *khemeis* said when Roh ventured to speak; it was all he said. They walked all the day save brief rests. and Vanye flung himself down at the mid-afternoon stop and lay still a good moment before he had caught his breath, eyes blurred and half-closed.

Roh's hand touched his. "Take the armor off. I shall carry it. You are done, otherwise."

He rolled over and began to do so, while Roh helped him. The *khemeis* watched, and finally offered them food and drink although they had had a little at noon.

"We have sent for horses," Haim said. Vanye nodded, relieved at that.

"There is no word," Vanye said again, trying another approach, "what became of my party."

"No. Not that we know. And we know what there is to be known in this part of Shathan."

"But others might have contact elsewhere." Hope sprang up in him, swiftly killed by Haim's grim look.

"What there is of news is not good, *khemeis*. I understand your grief. I have said too much. Get up and let us be going."

He did so, with Roh's help. The lack of the armor was relief. He made it until nightfall before he was utterly winded and halted in his tracks.

It was Tirrhen with them now, and not Haim; and Tirrhen

showed no intention of stopping. "Come," he said. "Come on."

Roh flung an arm about him and steadied him. They followed Tirrhen until Roh himself was staggering badly.

Then a clearing lay ahead of them in the starlight, and four *arrhendim* waited with six horses. "They mean we should keep going," Roh said, and his voice nigh broke.

Vanye looked, and knew none of them. He was helped to one of the saddleless horses, which was haltered only, and led by one of the *arrhendim*. Roh mounted the other without their help, and silently the party started to move.

Vanye leaned forward and rested against the horse's neck, instinct and habit keeping him astride over rough ground and through winding trails. The pain subsided to something bearable. The horse's patient strength comforted him. He slept at times, though once it cost him a bruise on a low branch: he bent back under it and slumped forward again, little the worse for it among so many other hurts. They moved through the night like shadows, and by morning they had reached another clearing, where more horses waited for them, with another escort.

He did not even dismount, but leaned, grasped a mane, and drew himself to the other horse. The party started forward, with no offering to them of food or water. Vanye ceased even to care, although such was finally offered at noon, without stopping. He rode numbly, silent as their escort was silent. Roh was still there, some distance behind . . . he saw that when he would look back. *Arrhendim* rode between them so that they could not speak to each other. They had not been disarmed, he realized at last, which heartened him; he trusted that Roh still had his armor and his weapons, for Roh had his own. He himself was beyond using any, and wished only for a cloak, for he was cold, even in daylight.

He asked finally, recalling that these were *qhal,* not Hetharu's halfling breed, and not by nature cruel. He was given a blanket to wrap himself in as they rode, and they offered him food and drink besides, all with little delay in their riding. Only twice in the day did they dismount even for a moment.

At nightfall there was another change of horses, and new guides took over. Vanye returned the blanket, but the *qhal* gently put it back about him and sent him on into the night with the new escort.

The *arrhendim* who had them in charge now were more

than gentle with them, as if their condition aroused pity in them; but again at dawn, mercilessly, they were passed to others, and both of them now had to be helped to mount.

Vanye had no memory of how many changes there had been; it all merged into nightmare. There were always whistles and sounds about them now, as if they rode some well-marked highroad in the wood, one well-watched . . . but none of those watchers came into their view.

The trees here loomed up monstrous in size, of different sort than they had seen. The trunks were like walls beside them, and the place existed in shade that made it always twilight.

Night settled on them in that place, a starless dark beneath that canopy of branches; but there was the scent of smoke in the air, and one of their horses whinnied a greeting to another.

Light gleamed. Vanye braced his hands on the horse's moving shoulders, and stared at that soft glow, at the assemblage of tents gathered amid those great trunks, color showing in the firelight. He blinked through tears of exhaustion, fragmenting the image.

"Merir's camp?" he asked of the Man who led his horse.

"He has sent for you," that Man said, but no more would he say.

Music drifted to them, *qhalur* and beautiful. It died at their coming. Folk left the common-fire and stood as a dark line of shadows along the course that they rode into camp.

The *arrhendim* stopped and bade them dismount. Vanye slid down holding the mane, and needed the bracing of two *arrhendim* to keep his feet as they guided him, for his legs were weak and the ceaseless motion of the horses still ruled his senses, so that the very earth seemed to heave under him.

*"Khemeis!"*

A cry went up. A small body impacted his and embraced him. He stopped, freed a shaking hand and touched the dark head that rested against his heart. It was Sin.

"How did you come here?" he asked the boy, out of a thousand questions that he wondered, the only one that made clear sense.

The wiry arms did not let him go; small hands clenched in the sides of his shirt as the *arrhendim* urged him to start walking, and drew him on. "Carrhend moved," Sin said. "Riders came. It burned."

"Go away, lad," said the *khemeis* at the right—gently. "Go away."

"I came," Sin said; his hands did not unclench. "I went into the forest to find the *qhal*. They brought me here."

"Did Sezar come back? Or Lellin?"

"No. Ought they? Where is the lady?"

"Leave him," said the *khemeis*. "Lad—do as you are told."

"Go away from me," Vanye said heavily. "Sin, I am not in good favor with your people. Go away as he tells you."

The hands relaxed, withdrew. Sin lagged behind. But then as he walked Vanye caught sight of him, staying to one side, trailing them forlornly. He walked, for they would not let him do otherwise, to Merir's tent. They brought him at once inside, but Roh was left behind: he did not realize that until he was faced about in front of Merir's chair.

The old *qhal* sat wrapped in a plain gray cloak, and his eyes were sad, glittering in the light of the lamps. "Let him go," Merir said; they did, gently, and Vanye sank down to one knee and bowed himself to the mat in respect.

"You are sorely hurt," Merir said.

It was not the opening he had expected of the old lord, whose grandson was lost, whose line was threatened, whose land was invaded. Vanye bowed again, shaking with exhaustion, and sat back. "I do not know where Lellin is," he said hoarsely. "I want leave to go, my lord, to find him and my lady."

Merir's brows contracted. The old lord was not alone in the tent; grim armed Men and *qhal* were about him, force at need; and there were the elders, whose eyes were darkened with anger. But Merir's frown held more of pain than of wrath. "You do not know the state of things here. We know that you crossed the Narn. And after that, the *harilim*, the dark ones . . . have severed us from the region. Is it not so, that you went to find Nehmin?"

"Yes, lord."

"Because your lady would have it so, against my wishes. Because she was set on this thing; and warnings would not deter her. Now Lellin is gone, and Sezar; and she is lost; and war is upon us." The anger did come, and stilled, and the gray eyes brooded in the lamplight, lifted slowly once more. "I saw all these things in her. I saw in you only what I see now. Tell me, *Khemeis*, all that happened. I shall hear you. Tell me everything and spare no detail. It may be that some tiny scrap of knowledge will help us understand the rest."

He did so. His voice failed him in the midst of it, and they gave him drink; he continued, in their stark silence.

There was silence even after he had finished.

"Please," he asked of Merir, "give me a horse and one for my cousin too. Our weapons. Nothing more. We will go and find them."

The silence continued. In the weight of it, he reached to his neck and lifted off the chain that bore the amulet, tendered it to Merir. When Merir made no move to take it, he laid it on the mat before him, for his hand could not hold it longer without shaking.

"Then let us go out as we are," Vanye said. "My lady is lost. I want only to go and find her and those with her."

"Man," said Merir at last, "why did she seek Nehmin?"

He was dismayed by the question, for it shot to the heart of things that Morgaine had withheld from their knowledge. "Does it not control Azeroth?" he countered. "Does it not control the place where our enemies are?"

"Were," said another.

He swallowed, clenched his hands in his lap to keep them from trembling. "Whatever is amiss out there is my doing. I take responsibility for it. I told you why they came; they pursued me, and Nehmin has nothing to do with that. My lady is hurt. I do not know if she is still alive. I swear to you that she is not at fault in bringing attack on you."

"No," said Merir. "Perhaps she is not. But never yet have you told us all the truth. She asked truth of me. She asked trust. And trust have I given, to the very edge of war and the loss of our people's lives and homes. Yes, I see your enemies for what they are; and they are evil. But never yet have you told us all the truth. You and she crossed through the *harilim*. That is no small thing. You dared use the *harilim* in escaping your enemies; and you survive . . . and that amazes me. The dark ones hold you in uncommon regard—Man that you are. And now you ask us to trust you once more. You wish to use us to set you on your way, and never once have you told us truth. We shall not harm you, do not fear that; but loose you again to work more chaos in our land . . . no. Not with my question still unanswered."

"What will you ask, lord?" He bowed again to the mat, trembling, and sat back. "Ask me tomorrow. I think that I should answer you. But I am tired and I cannot think."

"No," said another *qhal*, and leaned on Merir's chair to

speak to the old lord. "Will a night's rest improve the truth? Lord, think of Lellin."

Merir considered a moment. "I ask," he said at last, though his old eyes seemed troubled at the unkindness. "I do ask, *khemeis*. In all cases your life is safe, but your freedom is not."

"Would a *khemeis* be asked to betray his lord's confidence?"

That told upon all of them; there were doubtful looks among these honorable folk. But Merir bit his lip and looked sadly at him.

"Is there something then to betray, *khemeis*?"

Vanye blinked slowly, forcing the haze away, and shook his head. "We never wished you harm."

"Why Nehmin, *khemeis*?"

He tried to think what to answer, and could not; and shook his head yet again.

"Do we then guess that she means some harm to Nehmin? That is what we must conclude. And we must be alarmed that she has had the power to pass the *harilim*. And we must never let you go."

There was nothing else to say, and even silence was no safety. The friendship that they had enjoyed was gone.

"She wished to seize Nehmin," Merir said. "Why?"

"Lord, I will not answer you."

"Then it is an act which aims at us . . . or the answer would do no harm."

He looked at the old *qhal* in terror, knowing that he should devise something to say, something of reason. He pointed vaguely and helplessly back toward Azeroth, from which he had come. "We oppose that. That is the truth, lord."

"I do not think we have truth at all until it involves Nehmin. She means to seize power there. No. Then what else might she intend? *'The danger is to more worlds than this one . . .'* Her words. They sweep much wider than Azeroth, *khemeis*. Do I dare guess she means to destroy Nehmin?"

He thought that he must have flinched. The shock was evident too in the faces that watched. There was heaviness in the air such that it was hard to draw breath.

*"Khemeis?"*

"We . . . came to stop the Shiua. To prevent the kind of thing that has come on you.". .

"Aye," said Merir after a moment, and breath was held in

that place; none stirred. "By destroying the passage. By taking and destroying Nehmin."

"We are trying to save this land."

"But you fear to speak the truth to those who live in it."

"That out there . . . *that* . . . is the result of the opening of your Gate. Do you want more of it?"

Merir gazed down on him. His senses blurred; he was shaking convulsively. He had lost the blanket somewhere; he could not remember. Someone put a cloak about him, and he held it close, shivering still.

"This Man, Roh," Merir said then. "Bring him in."

It was a moment before Roh came, and that not willingly; but he seemed too weary to fight, and when he was brought to face Merir Vanye looked up and whispered to him: "Lord Merir, cousin; a king in Shathan, and worth respect. Please. For my sake."

Roh bowed: hall-lord and clan-lord himself, although they had taken his weapons and insulted him, he maintained his dignity, and when he had bowed, he sat down crosslegged on the floor . . . the latter a courtesy to kinsman rather than to Merir, for he should have demanded a seat on Merir's level or remained standing.

"Lord Merir," Roh said, "are we free or no?"

"That is the question, is it not?" Merir's eyes shifted to Vanye's. "Your cousin. And yet you have warned us before now what he is."

"I beg you, my lord—"

"Chya Roh." Merir's eyes flashed. "Abomination among us, this thing that you have done. Murder. And how many times have you so done?"

Roh said nothing.

"Lord," Vanye said. "He has another half. Will you not remember that?"

"That is to be reckoned . . . for he is both the evil and its victim. I do not know which I see."

"Do him no harm."

"No," said Merir. "His harm is within him." And Merir wrapped his cloak the more tightly about him and brooded in silence. "Take them," he said at last. "I must think on these things. Take them and lodge them well."

Hands settled on them, gentle enough. Vanye struggled to rise and found it beyond his strength, for his one leg was stiff and the other would scarcely hold him. *Arrhendim* helped him, one on a side, and they were led away to a neighboring tent, where there were soft skins still warm from someone's body. Here they were left, unrestrained, able to have fled, but that they had no strength left. They sprawled where they were let down, and slept.

Day came. A shadow stood against the light in the doorway of the tent. Vanye blinked. The shadow dropped down, and became Sin, squatted with his arms folded across his bare knees, patiently waiting.

A second presence breathed nearby. Vanye turned his head, saw a *qhalur* lad, his long white hair and clear gray eyes strange in a child's face; delicate, long hands propped his chin.

"I do not think you should be here," Vanye whispered to Sin.

"We may," said the *qhalur* child, with the absolute assurance of his elders.

Roh stirred, sat up reaching for weapons that were not there. "Be still," Vanye said. "It is all right, Roh. We are safe with such guards."

Roh dropped his head against his hands and drew a slow breath.

"There is food," said Sin brightly.

Vanye rolled over and saw that all manner of things had been provided them, water for washing, cloths; a tray of bread. and a pitcher and cups. Sin crawled over and sat down there, gravely poured frothing milk into a cup for him and offered it . . . offered a cup to Roh when Roh held out his hand for it. They breakfasted on butter and bread and a surfeit of goat's milk, the best fare they had had in many days.

"He is Ellur," said Sin, indicating his *qhalur* friend, who settled crosslegged near him. "I think that I may be *khemeis* to him."

"Yes. It is mending. I shall take that off soon."

Ellur soberly inclined his head.

"Are you all right?" Sin asked, touching his splinted knee with great care.

"Yes. It is mending. I shall take that off soon."

"This is your brother?"

"Cousin," said Roh. "Chya Roh i Chya, young sir."

They inclined their heads in respect as men might.

"*Khemeis* Vanye," said Ellur, "is it true what we have heard, that many Men have come behind you against Shathan?"

"Yes," he said, for there was no lying to such children.

"Ellur has heard," said Sin, "that—Lellin and Sezar are lost; and that the lady is hurt."

"Yes."

The boys were silent a moment, both looking distressed. "And," said Ellur, "that if you go free, then there will be no *arrhendim* by the time we are grown."

He could not look away. He met their eyes, dark human and gray *qhal*, and his belly felt as if he had received a mortal wound. "That could be the truth. But I do not want that. I do not want that at all."

There was long silence. Sin gnawed at his lip until it seemed he would draw blood. He nodded finally. "Yes, sir."

"He is very tired," Roh said after a moment. "Young sirs, perhaps you should speak to him later."

"Yes, sir," said Sin, and rose up, gently reached out and touched Vanye's arm, bowed his head and exited the tent, Ellur shadowing him like a small pale ghost.

It was a mercy equal to any Roh had ever shown him. He felt Roh push at him, and lay down, shivering suddenly. Roh flung a cover over him, and sat there wisely saying nothing.

He drowsed at last, found respite in sleep. It did not last. "Cousin," Roh whispered, and shook at him. "Vanye."

A shadow fell across the doorway. One of the *khemi* crouched in the opening. "You are awake," he said. "Good. Come."

Vanye nodded to Roh's questioning look, and they gathered themselves out of the cramped confines of the tent, stood and blinked in the full daylight outside. There were four *arrhendim* waiting there.

"Will Merir see us now?" Vanye asked.

"Perhaps today; we do not know. But come and we shall see to your comfort."

Roh hung back, doubting them. "They can do what they will," Vanye said in his own tongue, and Roh yielded then and came. He limped heavily, loath to be moved anywhere, for he was dizzy and sore; but what he had told Roh was the very truth: they had no choice in the matter.

They came to an ample tent, and entered into it, where sat an old *qhalur* woman, robed in gray, who regarded them with bright stern eyes and looked them up and down, sorry as they were and filthy. "I am Arrhel," she said in a voice that cracked with authority. "Wounds I treat, not dirt." She ges-

tured to the young *qhal* who stood in the rear corner. "Nthien, take them into the back and deal with what you may;
*arrhendim*, assist Nthien where needful."

The young *qhal* parted the curtain for them, expecting no
argument. Vanye went, pausing to bow to the old woman;
Roh followed, and their guard trailed them.

Hot water was already prepared, carried steaming through
an opening at the rear of the tent. At Nthien's urging they
stripped and washed, even to the hair . . . Roh must unbind
his, which was shame to any man; but so was it to be unwashed, so he only frowned displeasure and did so. Vanye
had no such pride left.

The water stung in the wounds, and Vanye felt fever in his
which must be dealt with; Nthien saw that at a glance and a
touch, and began to make preparations in that direction.
Vanye watched him with dread, for there was likely the
cautery for the worst of them. Roh's injuries were scant, and
a little salve sufficed for him, and a linen bandage to keep
them clean; afterward Roh settled, wrapped in a clean sheet,
on a mat in the corner, braiding his hair back into the warrior's knot and watching Nthien's preparations with mistrust
equal to his own.

"Sit down," Nthien said then to Vanye, indicating the
bench where he had set his vessels and instruments. There
was no cautery at all. Nthien's gentle hands prepared each
wound with numbing salve; some he must open, and he kept
the *arrhendim* coming and going with instruments to be
washed, but there was little pain. Vanye simply shut his eyes
and relaxed after a number of the worst were done, trusting
the *qhal's* skill and kindness. The numbness preceeded from
the most painful to the least of his hurts, and afterward there
was no bleeding; clean bandages protected them.

Then Nthien examined the knee . . . called in Arrhel, to
Vanye's consternation, who laid her wrinkled hands on the
joint and felt it flexing. "Leave the splint off," she said, then
touched her hand to his brow, pressed his face between her
hands, making him look at her. Regal she was in her aged
grace, and her gray eyes were surpassing kind. "You are fevered, child."

He almost laughed in surprise, that she could call him
child; but *qhal* lived long, and when he looked into those
aged eyes, so full of peace, he thought that perhaps most
Men to her years were children. She left them, and Roh

gathered himself up off the mat, staring after her with a strangely disturbed expression.

*His kind*, Vanye thought, and his skin prickled at the thought. *Liell's kind . . . the Old Ones.* He was suddenly frightened for Roh, and wanted him quickly out of this place.

"We are done," said Nthien. "Here. We have found you both clean clothing."

The *khemi* offered it to them . . . soft, sturdy clothing such as the *arrhendim* wore, green and brown and gray, with boots and belts of good workmanship. They dressed, and the clean cloth next the skin was itself a healing thing, restoring pride.

Then the *arrhendim* held back the curtain and showed them again into Arrhel's presence.

Arrhel was standing at the tripod table which had not been there before. She stirred a cup, which she brought then and offered Vanye. "For the fever. It is bitter, but it will help." She gave him a small leather pouch. "Here is more of it. Once daily as long as the fever lasts, drink this steeped in water, as much as covers the center of your palm. And you must sleep much and ride not at all, nor wear armor on those wounds; and you must have wholesome food and a great deal of it. But it seems that this is not in anyone's plans. The supply is for your journey."

"Journey, lady?"

"Drink the cup."

He did so; it was bitter as promised, and he grimaced as he gave it back to her, uneasy at heart. "A journey to or from where I asked lord Merir to go?"

"He will tell you. I fear I do not know. Perhaps it depends on what you say to him." She took his hand in hers, and her flesh was soft and warm, an old woman's. Her gray eyes looked into him, so that he could not look away.

Then she let him go and turned, sat down in her chair. She set the cup on the tripod table beside her, and looked at Roh. "Come," she said; and he came, knelt when with her open hand she indicated a place before her—hall-lord though he was, he did so—and she leaned forward and took his face between her hands, gazing into his eyes. Long and long she stared, and Roh shut his eyes finally rather than bear that longer.

Then she touched her lips to his brow, and yet did not let him go. "For you," she whispered, "I have no cup to drink.

There is no healing that my hands can work. I would that I could."

Her hands fell. Roh thrust himself away and to his feet and came against the warning hand of the *khemeis* who kept the door, stopped cold.

Vanye cast a look back at Arrhel, remembered courtesy and bowed; but when the lady then dismissed them, he made haste to take Roh from that place. Roh did not look back or speak, not then nor for a long time after, when they were settled again in their own tent.

Merir sent for them in the afternoon, and they went, escorted by the same several *arrhendim*. The old lord was wrapped in his feather-cloak, and bore the circlet of gold about his brow; armed Men and *qhal* were about him.

Roh bowed to Merir and sat down on the mat; Vanye knelt and performed the full obeisance, and settled as much as he could off his injured leg. Merir's face was grave and stern, and for a long time he was content only to stare at them.

"*Khemeis* Vanye," Merir said at last, "your cousin much troubles what little peace I have found in my mind. What will you that I do with him?"

"Let him go where I go."

"So Arrhel has told you that you are leaving."

"But not where, lord."

Merir frowned and leaned back, folding his hands before him. "Much evil has your lady loosed on this land. Much harm. And more is to come. I cannot wish this away. The wishes of all the folk of Shathan cannot turn this away. Even yet I fear you have not told me all that you know . . . yet I must heed you." His eyes flicked to Roh and back again. "The ally that you insist to take: would your lady approve him?"

"I have told you how we came to be allies."

"Yes. And yet I think she would warn you. So do I. Arrhel vows she will not sleep soundly for days for his sake, and she warns you. But you will not listen."

"Roh will keep his word to me."

"Will he? Perhaps. Perhaps you know best of all. See that it is so, *khemis* Vanye. We will go to find your lady Morgaine, and you will go with us . . . So will he, since you insist; I will reserve my judgment. I have misgivings—for many things in this—but go we shall. Your weapons, your belongings, all are yours again. Your freedom, your cousin's. Only you must return me assurance that you will ride under my authority and obey my word as law."

"I cannot," Vanye said hoarsely, and turned his scarred palm toward Merir. "This means that I am my lady's servant, no one else's. But I will obey you while obeying you serves her; I beg you take that for enough."

"That is enough."

He pressed his brow to the mat in gratitude, only then daring believe they were free.

"Make ready," Merir said. "We leave very shortly, late in the day as it is. Your belongings will be returned to you."

Such haste was what he himself desired; it was more in all respects than he had dared hope of the old lord . . . and for an instant suspicion plucked at him; but he bowed again and rose, and Roh stood with him to pay his respect.

They were let out, unguarded, the *arrhendim* withdrawn.

And in their tent they found all that they owned given back to them, as Merir had said, weapons and armor, well-cleaned and oiled. Roh gathered his bow into his hand like a man welcoming an old friend.

"Roh," Vanye said, suddenly apprehensive at the dark look.

Roh glanced up. For an instant the stranger was there, cold and menacing, for all the affront the lord Merir had offered him.

Then Roh slowly shed that anger, as if he willed it so, and laid the bow down on the furs. "Let us leave off wearing the armor, at least until the next day on the trail. There is no need to bear that weight on our aching shoulders, and doubtless we are not immediately in range of our enemies."

"Roh, deal well with me and I will deal so with you."

Roh gave him a hard look. "Worried, are you? Abomination. Abomination I am to them. How kind of you to speak for me."

"Roh—"

"Did you not tell them about *her,* about your half-*qhal* liege? What else is she? Not pure *qhal*. Nor human. Doubtless she has done what I have done, no higher nor nobler. And I think you have always known it."

Almost he struck . . . held his hand, trembling with the effort; there were the *arrhendim* outside, their freedom at hazard. "Quiet," he hissed. "Be quiet."

"I have said nothing. There is much that I could say, and I have not, and you know it. I have not betrayed her."

It was truth. He stared at Roh's distraught face and reckoned that it was no more and no less than Roh believed. And
Roh had not betrayed them.

"I know it," he said. "I will repay that, Roh."

"But you are not free to say so, are you? You forget what
you are."

"My word is worth something . . . among them, and with
her."

Roh's face tautened as if he had been struck. "Ah, you do
grow proud, *ilin,* to think that. And you trade words with *qhal*-
lords in their own language, and dispose of me how you will."

"You are lord of my mother's clan. I do not forget that. I
do not forget that you offered me shelter, in a time when others of my kin would not."

"Ah, is it 'cousin,' now?"

There was no appeal to that hardness. It had been there
since Arrhel gazed at him. Vanye turned his face from it. "I
will do what I said, Roh. See you do the same. If you ask
apology as my clan-lord, that I will give; if as my kinsman,
that will I give; if it galls you that *qhal* speak civilly to me
and not to you . . . that involves another side of you that I
have no reason to love; with *him* there is no dealing, and I
will not."

Roh said nothing. Quietly they packed their belongings into
what would be easy to carry on the saddles. They put on only
their weapons.

"I will do what I said," Roh offered finally.

It was Roh again. Vanye inclined his head in the respect
he had withheld.

In not a long time, *khemi* came to summon them.


# Chapter Thirteen


The company was forming up outside Merir's tent . . . six
*arrhendim,* all told: two younger; two older, the *khemeis'*
hair almost as white as his *arrhen's,* with faces well-weathered

by time; and an older pair of *arrhendim*, women of the *arrhend* . . . not quite as old, for the *khemein* of that pair had hair equally streaked with silver and dark, while her *arrhen*, like all *qhal*, aged yet more slowly and had the look of thirty human years.

Horses had been readied for the two of them, and Vanye was well-pleased with them: a bay gelding for him and a sorrel for Roh, both deep-chested and strong, for all their gracefulness. Even the herds of Morija would have been proud of such as these.

They did not mount up; one horse remained riderless, a white mare of surpassing beauty, and the party waited. Vanye heaved his gear up to his saddle and bound it there, found also a waterflask and saddlebags and a good gray blanket, such things as he would have asked had he dared press at their charity. A *kehmeis* from the crowd came offering them cloaks, one for him and one for Roh. They put them on gratefully, for the day was cool for their light clothing.

And when all that was done, they still waited. Vanye stood scratching the bay's chin and calming his restiveness. He felt himself almost whole again, whether by Arrhel's draught or by the touch of a horse under his hands and his weapons by him . . . fretting to be underway, to be beyond intervention or recall, lest some circumstance change Merir's mind.

One of the *khemi* brought a chain of flowers, and bound it in the mane of the white horse; and came others, bringing such flower chains for each of the departing *arrhendim*.

But it was Ellur who brought a white one for Roh's horse, and Sin came bearing a chain of bright blue. The boy reached high to bind it into the black mane, so that they swung there like a chain of tiny bells. And then Sin looked up at him.

Premonition came on him that he was looking on the boy for the last time, that there would be—one way or another— no return for him from this ride. Sin seemed to believe it too this time. Tears brimmed in his eyes, but he held them; he had been through Shathan: he was no longer the boy in Merrind.

"I have no parting-gift," Vanye said, searching his memory for something left that he owned but his weapons; and never had he felt his poverty as much as in that moment, that he had nothing left to spare. "Among our people we give something when we know the parting will be long."

"I made this for you," said Sin, and drew forth from his

shirt a carving of a horse's head. It was made of wood, small, of surpassing skill, as there were so many talents in Sin's hands. Vanye took it, and thrust it within his collar. Then in desperation he cut a ring from his belt, plain steel and blue-black; it had once held spare leather, but he had none of that left either. He pressed it into Sin's hand and closed his brown fingers over it. "It is a plain thing, the only thing I have to give that I brought from home, from Morija of Andur-Kursh. Do not curse my memory when you are grown, Sin. My name was Nhi Vanye i Chya; and if ever I do you harm, it is not from wanting it. May there always be *arrhendim* in Shathan, and Mirrindim too. And when you are *arrhendim* yourselves, you and Ellur, see that it is so."

Sin hugged him, and Ellur came and took his hand. He chanced to look up at Roh, then, and Roh's face was sad. "Ra-koris was such a place," Roh said, naming his own hall in forested Andur. "If I had no reason to oppose the Shiua for my own sake, I would have now, having seen this place. But for my part I would save it, not take from it the only thing that might defend it."

The boys' hands were clenched in either of his; he stared at Roh and felt defenseless, without any argument but his oath.

"If she is dead," Roh said, "respecting your grief, cousin, I shall not even say evil of her—but you would be free then, and would you still carry out what she purposed? Would you take that from them? I think there is some conscience in you. They surely think so."

"Keep silent. Save your shafts for me, not them."

"Aye," Roh murmured. "No more of it." He laid his hand on his horse's neck, and looked about him, at the great trees that towered so incredibly above the tents. "But think on it, cousin."

There was a sudden murmuring in the crowd; it parted, and Merir passed through—a different Merir from the one they had seen, for the old lord wore robes made for riding; a horn bound in silver was at his side, and he bore a kit which he hung from the saddle of the white horse. The beautiful animal turned its head, lipped familiarly at his shoulder, and he caressed the offered nose and took up the reins. He needed no help to climb into the saddle.

"Be careful, Father," said one of the *qhal*. "Aye," others echoed. "Be careful."

Arrhel came. Merir took the lady's hand from horseback. "Lead in my absence," he bade her, and pressed her hand before he let it go. The others were beginning to mount up.

A last time Vanye bade the boys farewell, and let them go, and climbed into the saddle. The bay started to move of his own accord as the other horses started away; and before he had ridden far he was drawn to look back. Sin and Ellur were running after him, to stay with him while they could. He waved at them, and they reached the edge of the camp. Trees began to come between. His last sight of them was of the two stopped forlornly at the forest margin, fair-haired *qhalur* lad and small, dark boy, alike in stance. Then the green leaves curtained them, and he turned in the saddle.

The company rode mostly in silence, with the two young *arrhendim* in the lead and the eldest riding close by Merir. Vanye and Roh rode after them, and the two *arrheindim* rode last . . . no swords did they bear, unlike the *arrhendim,* but bows longer than the men's, and their slim hands were leathered with half-glove and bracer, old and well-worn. The *khemein* of that pair often lagged behind and out of sight, serving apparently as rearguard and scout as the *khemeis* of the pair in front tended to disappear ahead of them to probe the way.

Sharrn and Dev were the names of the old *arrhendim;* Vanye asked of the *arrhen* Perrin, the *qhalur* woman, who rode nearest them. Her *khemein* was Vis; and the young pair were Larrel and Kessun, cheerful fellows, who reminded him with a pang of Lellin and Sezar whenever he looked on them together.

They rested briefly halfway to dark. Kessun had vanished some time before that stop, and did not reappear when he ought; and Larrel paced and fretted. But the *khemeis* came in just as they were setting themselves ahorse again, and bowed apology, whispering something to lord Merir in private.

Then from somewhere in the far distance came the whistled signal of an *arrhen,* thin and clear as birdsong, advising them that all was well.

That was comforting to hear, for it was the first signal they had heard in all that ride, as if those who ranged the woods hereabouts were few or frightened. Lightness came on the *arrhendim* then, and a smile to Merir's eyes for a moment, though they had been sad before.

Thereafter Larrel and Kessun both parted company with them, and rode somewhere ahead.

Nor did they appear at night, when they could no longer see their way and stopped to set up camp.

They were settled near a stream, and brazenly dared a fire
. . . Mirer decided that it was safe enough. They sat down
together in that warmth and shared food. Vanye ate, although he had small appetite: he felt the fever on him after
the day's riding, and drank some of Arrhel's medicine.

He would gladly have sought his blanket then and gone to
sleep, for his wounds pained him and he was exhausted from
even so short a journey; but he refused to leave the fireside
with Roh able to say what he would, to use his cleverness
alone with the *arrhendim*. Chances were that Roh would keep
his word; but he did not think it well to put overmuch temptation in Roh's way, so he rested where he was, bowed his head
against his arms and sat savoring at least the fire's warmth.

Merir gave some whispered instruction to the *arrhendim*,
which was not unusual in the day; quietly the *arrhendim*
moved, and Vanye lifted his head to see what was happening.

It was Perrin and Vis who had withdrawn, and they
gathered up their bows where they stood, deftly strung them.

"Trouble, lord?" Roh asked, frowning and tense. But the
*arrheindim* made no move to depart on any business.

Merir sat unmoved, wrapped in his cloak, his old face
gaunt and seamed in the firelight. All pure *qhal* had a delicate look, almost fragile; but Merir was like something
carved in bone, hard and keen. "No," Merir said softly. "I
have simply told them to watch."

The old *arrhendim* still sat at the fire, beside Merir; and
something in the manner of all of them betokened no outside
enemies. The *arrheindim* quietly put arrows to their strings
and faced inward, not outward, though no bow was drawn.

"It is ourselves," Vanye said in a still voice, and a tremor
of anger went through him. "I believed you, my lord."

"So have I believed you," Merir said. "Put off your
weapons for the moment. I would have no misunderstanding
—Do so, or forfeit our good will."

Vanye unbuckled the belts and shed the sword and the
dagger, laid them to one side; and Roh did likewise, frowning. Dev came and gathered them all up, returned to Merir's
side and laid them down on that side of the fire.

"Forgive us," said Merir. "A very few questions." He
arose, Sharrn and Dev with him. He gestured to Roh. "Come,
stranger. Come with me."

Roh gathered himself to his feet, and Vanye started to do
the same. "No," said Merir. "Be wise and do not. I would not
have you harmed."

The bows had drawn.

"Their manners are marginally better than Hetharu's," Roh said quietly. "I do not mind their questions, cousin."

And Roh went with them willingly enough, possessed of knowledge enough to betray them thoroughly. They withdrew along the bank of the stream, where trees screened them from view. Vanye stayed as he was, on one knee.

"Please," said Perrin, her bow still bent. "Please do not do anything, *sirren.* Vis and I, we seldom miss even small targets separately. Together, we could not miss you at all. They will not harm your kinsman. Please sit down so that we may all relax."

He did so. The bows relaxed; the *arrheindim's* vigilance did not. He bowed his head against his hands and waited, with fever throbbing in his brain and desperation seething in him.

The *arrhendim* led Roh back finally, and settled him under the watchful eye of the archers. Vanye looked at Roh, but Roh met his eyes but once, and his look said nothing at all.

"Come," Sharrn said, and Vanye rose up and went with them, into the dark, down where the trees overhung and the brook splashed among the stones.

Merir waited, sitting on a fallen log, a pale figure in the moonlight, wrapped in his cloak. The *arrhendim* stopped him at a few paces' distance, and he stood, offering no respect: respect had been betrayed. Mirer offered him to sit on the ground, but he would not.

"Ah," said Merir. "So you feel misused. And yet have you been misused, *khemeis,* reckoning all things into the account? Are we not here, pursuing a course you asked of us—and in spite of the fact that you have not yet been honest with us?"

"You are not my sworn lord," Vanye said, his heart sinking in him, for he was sure now that Roh had done his worst. "I never lied to you. But some things I would not say, no. The Shiua," he added bitterly, "used *akil,* and force. Doubtless you would too. I thought you different."

"Then why did you not deal with us differently?"

"What did Roh say to you?"

"Ah, you fear that."

"Roh does not lie . . . at least not in most things. But half of him is not Roh; and half of him would cut my throat and I know it. I have told you how that is. I have told you. I do not think anything he would have told you would have been friendly to me or to my lady."

"It is so, *khemeis,* that your lady bears a thing of power?"

Had it been daylight, Merir must have seen the color wash from his face; he felt it go, and fear gathered cold and small in his belly. He said nothing.

"But it *is* so," said Merir. "She could have told me. She would not. She left me and sought her own way. She was anxious to reach Nehmin. But she has not done so . . . I know that much."

Vanye's heart beat rapidly. Some men claimed Sight; it was so in Shiuan . . . but something there was in Merir's hardness which minded him less of those dreamers than of Morgaine herself.

"Where is she?" he demanded of Merir.

"And do you threaten? Would you?"

He sprang to seize the old *qhal* to hostage before the *arrhendim* could intervene; and all at once he felt that thickness of sense that a Gate could cause. He caught at the *qhal*-lord, and as he did so his senses swam; he yet held to the robes, determined with all that was in him. Merir cried out; the dizziness increased; for a moment there was darkness, utter and cold.

Then earth. He lay on dew-slick leaves, and Merir with him. The *arrhendim* seized him—he hardly felt the grip—and drew him back. Weakly Merir stirred.

"No," Merir said. "No. Do not harm him." Steel slid back into sheath then, and Sharrn moved to help Merir, lifted him gently, set him on the log; but Vanye rested still on his knees, lacking any feeling in hands or feet. The void still gaped within his mind, dazing him, as it surely must Merir.

Gate-force. An area about the *qhal*-lord—charged with the terror of the Gates. *I know,* Mirer had claimed; and know he must, for the Gates were still alive, and Morgaine had not stilled their power.

"So," Merir breathed at last, "you are brave . . . to have fought that; braver surely than to sink to violence against one so old as I."

Vanye bowed his head, tossed the hair from his eyes and met the old lord's angry stare. "Honor I left long and far from here, my lord. I only wish I could have held you."

"You know such forces. You have passed the Fires at least twice, and I could not frighten you." Merir drew from his robes a tiny case and carefully opened it. Again that shimmering grew about his hand and his person, although what rested inside was a very tiny jewel, swirling with opal colors. Vanye flinched from it, for he knew the danger.

"Yes," said Merir, "your lady is not the only one who holds power in this land. I am one. And I knew that such a thing was loose in Shathan . . . and I sought to know what it was. It was a long search. The power remained hidden. You fit well into Mirrind, invisibly well, to your credit. I was dismayed to know that you were among us. I sent for you, and heard you out . . . and knew even then that there was such a thing unaccounted for in Shathan. I loosed you, hoping that you would go against your enemies; I did believe you, you see. Yet she would seek Nehmin . . . against all my advice. And Nehmin has defenders more powerful than I. Some of them she passed, and that amazes me; but she never passed the others. Perhaps she is dead. I might not know that. Lellin should have returned to me, and he has not. I think Lellin trusted you somewhat, else he would have returned quickly . . . but I do not even know for certain that he lived much past Carrhend. I have only your word. Nehmin stands. Perhaps the Shiua you speak of have prevented her . . . or others might. You cast yourself back into our hands as if we were your own kindred—in some trust, I do think; and yet you admit with your silence what it was she wished in coming here . . . to destroy what defends this land. And she is the bearer of the power I have sensed; I know that now, beyond doubt. I asked Chya Roh why she would destroy Nehmin. He said that such destruction was her function and that he himself did not understand; I asked him why then he sought to go to her, and he said that after all he has done, there is no one else who will have him. You say he rarely lies. Are these lies?"

A tremor went through him. He shook his head and swallowed the bile in his throat. "Lord, *he* believes it."

"I put to you the same questions, then. What do you believe?"

"I—do not know. All these things Roh claims to know for truth . . . I do not; and I have served her. I told her once that I did not want to know; she gave me that—and now I cannot answer you, and I would that I could. I only know *her,* better than Roh knows—and she does not wish to harm you. She does not want that."

"That is truth," Merir judged. "At least—*you* believe that it is so."

"I have never lied to you. Nor has she." He strove to gain his feet; the *arrhendim* put their hands on him to prevent him, but Merir gestured to them to let him be. He stood, yet sick and dizzied, looking down on the frail lord. "It was Morgaine who tried to keep the Shiua out of your land. Blame me, blame Roh that they came here; *she* foresaw this and tried to prevent it. And this I know, lord, that there is evil in the power that you use, and that it will take you sooner or later, as it took the Shiua . . . this thing you hold in your hand. To touch that—hurts; I know that; and she knows best of all . . . she hates that thing she carries, hates above everything the evil that it does."

Merir's eyes searched over him, his face eerily lit in the opal fires. Then he closed the tiny case, and the light faded, reddening his flesh for a moment before it went. "One who bears what Roh describes would feel it most. It would eat into the very bones. The Fires we wield are gentler; hers consumes. It does not belong here. I would she had never come."

"What she brought *is* here, lord. If it must be in other hands than hers—if she is lost—then I had rather your hand on it than the Shiua's."

"And yours rather than mine?"

He did not answer.

"It is the sword—is it not? The weapon that she would not yield up. It is the only thing she bore of such size."

He nodded reluctantly.

"I will tell you this, Nhi Vanye, servant of Morgaine . . . that last night that power was unmasked, and I felt it as I have not felt it since first you came into Shathan. What would it have been, do you think?"

"The sword was drawn," he said, and hope and dread surged up in him—hope that she lived, and agony to think that she might have been in extremity enough to draw it.

"Aye, so do I judge. I shall take you to that place. You stand little chance of reaching it alone, so bear in mind, *khemeis,* that you still ride under my law. Ride free if you will; attempt Shathan against my will. Or stay and accept it."

"I shall stay," he said.

"Let him walk free," Merir said to the *arrhendim,* and they did so, although they trailed him back to the fire.

Roh was there, still under the archers' guard; the *arrhendim* signalled them, and the arrows were replaced in their quivers.

Vanye went to Roh, anger hazing his vision so that Roh was all the center of it. "Get up," he said, and when Roh would not, he seized him and swung. Roh broke the force with his arm and struck back, but he took the blow and drove one through. Roh staggered sidewise to the ground.

The *arrhendim* intervened with drawn swords; one drew blood, and he reeled back from that warning, sense returning to him. Roh tried to rise to the attack, but the *arrhendim* stopped that too.

Roh straightened and rose more slowly, wiped the blood from his mouth with a dark look. He spat blood, and wiped his mouth a second time.

"Henceforth," Vanye said in Andurin, "I shall guard my own back. Take care of yours, clan-lord, cousin. I am *ilin*, and not your man, whatever name you wear. All agreements are ended. I want my enemies in front of me."

Again Roh spat, and rage burned in his eyes. "I told them *nothing*, cousin. But have it as you will. Our agreement is ended. You would have killed me without asking. Nhi threw you out. Clan-lord I still am, and for my will. *Chya* casts you out. Be *ilin* to the end of your days, kinslayer, and thank your own nature for it. I told them nothing they did not already know. Tell him, lord Merir, for his asking: What did I betray? What did I tell you that you did not first tell me?"

"Nothing," said Merir. "He told us nothing. That is truth."

The anger drained out of him, leaving only the wound. He stood there with no argument against Roh's affront, and at last he shook his head and unclenched his bloody hand. "I bore with everything," he said hoarsely. "*Now* I strike back . . . when I am in the wrong. That is always my curse. I take your word, Roh."

"You take nothing of me, Nhi bastard."

His mouth worked. He swallowed down another burst of anger, seeing how this one had served him, and went away to his pallet. He lay down there, too distraught for sleep.

The others sought their rest; the fire burned to ash; the watch passed from Perrin to Vis.

Roh lay near him, staring at the heavens, his face set and still angry, and when Roh slept, if ever that night, he did not know it.

The camp came to slow life in the daylight, the *arrhendim* beginning to pack up and saddle the horses. Vanye rose among the first, began to put on his armor, and Roh saw him and did likewise, both silent, neither looking openly toward the other. Merir was last to rise, and insisted on breaking their fast. They did so; and quietly, at the end of the meal, Merir ordered their weapons returned to them both.

"So you do not break the peace again," Merir cautioned them.

"I do not seek my cousin's life," Vanye said in a faint voice, only for Merir and Roh.

Roh said nothing, but slipped into his sword harness, and rammed the Honor-blade into place at his belt, stalking off to attend to his horse.

Vanye stared after him, bowed courtesy to Merir empty reflex . . . and went after him.

There were no words. Roh would not look at him but with anger, making speech impossible, and he turned instead to saddling his horse.

Roh finished; he did, and started to lead his horse into line with the others that were mounting up. And on a last and bitter impulse he stopped by Roh's side and waited for him.

Roh swung to the saddle; he did the same. They rode together into line, and the column started moving.

"Roh," he said finally, "are we beyond reasoning?"

Roh turned a cold eye on him. "You are worried, are you?" he asked in the language of Andur. "How much did they learn of *you*, cousin?"

"Probably what they did of you," he said. "Roh, Merir is armed. As she is."

Roh had not known. The comprehension dawned on him slowly. "So that is what unnerved you." He spat painfully to the other side. "And there is something here, then, that could oppose her. *That* is why you are so desperate. It was a bad mistake to set me at your throat; that is what you least need. You should not have told me. That is your second mistake."

"He would have told you when he wished; now I know that you know."

Roh was silent a time. "I do not know why I do not pay you what you have deserved of me. I suppose it is the novelty of hearing a Nhi say he was wrong." His voice broke; his shoulders sagged. "I told you that I was tired. Peace, cousin, peace. Someday we shall have to kill one another. But not . . . not without knowing why."

"Stay with me. I will speak for you. I said that I would, and I still mean it."

"Doubtless." Roh spat again to the side, wiped his mouth and swore with a shake of his head. "You loosened two of my teeth. Let it wipe out other debts. Aye, we will see how things stand . . . see whether *she* knows the meaning of reason, or whether these folk do. I have a fancy for an Andurin burial; or if things turn out otherwise, I know the Kurshin rite."

"Avert," he murmured, and crossed himself fervently.

Roh laughed bitterly, and bowed his head. The trail narrowed thereafter, and they rode no more together.

Larrel and Kessun returned; they were simply standing in the way as they rode around a bending of the trail, and met and talked with Merir.

"We have ridden as far as the Laur," Larrel said, and both the *arrhendim* and their horses looked weary. "Word is relayed up from Merrind: no trouble; nothing stirs."

"This is a strange silence," Merir said, leaning on his saddle and casting a look back. "So many thousands—and nothing stirs."

"I do not know," said Vanye, for that look shot directly at him. "I would have expected immediate attack." Then another thought came to him. "Fwar's men. If any who fell behind were not killed—"

"Aye," Roh said. "They might have given warning what that forest is, if any came out again; or Shien might. And perhaps others of Fwar's folk could do us harm enough by talking."

"Knowledge where *she* is to be sought?"

"All the Shiua know where she was lost. And having lost us . . ."

"Her," Merir concluded, taut-lipped. "An attack near Nehmin."

The sword was drawn, Vanye recalled, two nights ago. There was time enough for the horde to have veered to Narnside. A fine sweat broke out on him, cold in the forest shadow. "I pray you haste."

"We are near the *harilim's* woods," Merir said, "and there is no reckless haste, not for our lives' sake."

But they kept moving, the weary *arrhendim* falling in with them, and they rested as seldom as the horses could bear, save that they stopped at midafternoon and rested until twilight; then they saddled up again, and set out into a deeper, older part of the woods.

Dark fell on them more quickly under these monstrous old trees; and now and again came small chitterings in the brush that frightened the horses.

Then from the fore of their party flared an opal shimmer

that made Merir's horse shy the more, horse and rider for a
moment like an image under water. The flare died.

For a moment the forest was utterly quiet. Then the *harilim* came, stalking, rapid shapes. The first gave a chirring
sound, and the horses threw their heads and fought the bits,
dancing this way and that in a frenzy to run.

Then Merir led them forward, and their strange guides
went about them, melting away into shadow after a time until
there were only three left, which walked with Merir, chittering softly the while. It was clear that the master of Shathan
had safe-passage where he would, even of these: they reverenced the power of the Fires which Merir held in his naked
hand, and yielded to that, although the *arrhendim* themselves
seemed afraid. Of a sudden Vanye realized what his chances
had truly been, trifling with these creatures, and he shuddered
recalling his passage among them: they served the Fires in
some strange fashion, perhaps worshipped them. In his ignorance he had sought a passage in which even the lord of
Shathan moved carefully and with dread . . . and one of
them at least must have recalled him as companion to another who carried the Fires. Surely that was why he and Roh
lived: the *harilim* had recalled Morgaine.

His heart beat faster as he scanned the dark, heron-like
shapes ahead of him on the trail. *They may know*, he
thought. *If any living know where she is, they may know.*
He entertained a wild hope that they might lead them to her
this night, and wished that there were some way that a human tongue could shape their speech or human ears understand them. Even Merir was unable to do that; when he did
consult with them, it was entirely with signs.

The hope faded. It was not to any secret place that the
*harilim* led them, but only through; they broke upon the
Narn at the last of the night . . . black and wide it showed
through the trees, but there was a place which might be a
crossing, sandbars humped against the current. The *haril*
nearest pointed, made a sign of passing, and as suddenly began to leave them.

Vanye leaped down from his horse, caught his balance
against a tree and tried to stop one of them. *Three persons,*
he signed to the creature. *Where?* Perhaps it understood
something. The vast dark eyes flickered in the starlight. It lingered, made a sign with spidery fingers spread, hand rising.
And it pointed riverward. The third gesture fluttered the fin-

gers. And then it turned and stalked away, leaving him helpless in his frustration.

"The Fires," said Sharrn. "The river. Many."

He looked at the *ghal*.

"You took a chance," said Sharrn. "It might have killed you. Do not touch them."

"We could learn no more of them," said Merir, and started the white mare down the bank toward the water.

The *harilim* were gone. The oppression of their presence lifted suddenly and the *arrhendim* moved quickly to follow Merir. Vanye swung up to the saddle and came last but for Roh and Vis. The anxiety that gnawed at him was the keener for the scant information the creature had passed. And when they went down to water's edge he looked this way and that, for although it was not the place they had been ambushed, it was the same situation and as likely a trap. The only difference was that the *harilim* had guided them right up to the brink, and perhaps still stood guard over them in the coming of the light.

There was need of care for another reason in crossing at such a place, for quicksands were well possible. Larrel gave his horse into Kessun's keeping and waded it first; at one place he did meet with trouble, and fell sidelong, working out of it, but the rest of the crossing went more easily. Then Kessun rode the way that he had walked, and Dev followed, and Sharrn and Merir and the rest of them, the women last as usual. On the other side the young *arrhen* Larrel was soaked to the skin, shivering with the cold and with the exhaustion of his far-riding and his battle with the sands. *Qhal* that he was, he looked worn to the bone, thinner and paler than was natural. Kessun wrapped him in his dry cloak and fretted about fevers, but Larrel climbed back into the saddle and clung there.

"We must get away from this place," Larrel said amid his shivering. "Crossings are too easily guarded."

There was no argument from any of them in that; Merir turned them south now, and they rode until the horses could do no more.

They rested at last at noon, and took a meal which they had neglected in their haste of the morning. No one spoke; even the prideful *qhal* sat slumped in exhaustion. Roh flung himself down on the sun-warmed earth, the only patch of sun in the cover they had found in the forest's edge, and lay like

the dead; Vanye did likewise, and although the fever he had
carried for days seemed gone, he felt that the marrow had
melted from his bones and the strength that moved them was
dried up from the heat. His hand lying before his face looked
strange to him, the bones more evident than they had been,
the wrist scabbed with wounds. His armor was-loose on his
body—sun-heated misery at the moment where it touched
him; he was too weary even to turn over and spare himself
the discomfort.

Something startled the horses.

He moved; the *arrhendim* sprang up; and Roh. A whistle
sounded, brief and questioning. Merir stood forth to be seen,
and Sharrn answered the signal in such complexity of trills
and runs that Vanye's acquaintance with the system could
make no sense of it. An answer came back, no less complex.

"We are advised," Merir said after it fell silent, "of threat
to Nehmin. *Sirrindim* . . . the Shiua you fled . . . have come
up the Narn in great numbers."

"And Morgaine?" Vanye asked.

"Of Morgaine, of Lellin, of Sezar . . . nothing. It is as if a
veil has been drawn over their very existence. Alive or dead,
their presence is not felt in Shathan, or the *arrhendim* this
side could tell us. They cannot. Something is greatly amiss."

His heart fell then. He was almost out of hopes.

"Come," said Merir. "We have no time to waste."

# Chapter Fourteen

The trouble was not long in showing itself. Movement
startled birds from cover in the thickets of the Narn's other
bank, and soon there were riders in sight, but the broad Narn
divided them from the enemy and there was no ford to give
either side access to the other.

The enemy saw them too, and halted in consternation. It
was a *khalur* company, demon-helmed, scale armored, on the

smallish Shiua horses. Their weapons were pikes; but they carried more than those . . . ugly opponents. And the leader, whose white mane flowed evident in the wind of his riding when he led them forward to the water's edge: the *arrhendim* were appalled at the sight of him, one like themselves, and different . . . fantastical in his armor, the *akil*-dream elaborations of *khalur* workmanship.

"Shien!" Vanye hissed, for there was no one in the Shiua host with that arrogant bearing save Hetharu himself. The *khal* challenged them, rode his horse to the knees in water before he was willing to heed his men-at-arms and draw back.

Their own company kept moving, opposite to the direction of the Sotharra band; but Shien and his riders wheeled about and paced them, with the broad black waters of the Narn between. Arrows flew from the Sotharra side, most falling into the water, a few rattling on the stones of the shore.

The *qhal* Perrin reined out to the river's very brink and shot one swiftly aimed shaft from her bow. A demon-helmed *khal* screamed and pitched in the saddle, and his comrades caught him. A cry of rage went up from that side, audible across the water. And Vis raced her horse to the brink and shot another that sped true.

"Lend me your bow," Vanye asked then of Roh. "If you will not use it, I will."

"Shien? No. For all the grudge you bear him—he is Hetharu's enemy, and the best of that breed."

It was already too late. The Shiua lagged back of them, out of bowshot of the *arrheindim*, having learned the limits of their own shafts and the deadly accuracy of the Shathana. They followed at a distance on that other side, and there was no way to reach them and no time to stop. Perrin and Vis unstrung their bows as they rode, and the *arrhendim* kept tight formation about Merir, scanning apprehensively the woods on their own side of the river. It was speed they sought now, which ran them hard over the river shore, with nothing but an occasional wash of brushheap to deter them.

Then Vanye chanced to look back. Smoke rose as a white plume on the Shiua side.

Perrin and Vis saw the fix of his eyes and looked, and their faces came about rigid with anger.

"Fire!" Perrin exclaimed as it were a curse, and others looked back.

"Shiua signal," said Roh. "They are telling their comrades downriver we are here."

"We have no love for large fires," Sharrn said darkly. "If they are wise, they will clear the reach of that woods before night comes on them."

Vanye looked back again, at the course of the Narn which slashed through Shathan, a gap in the armor, a highroad for Men and fire and axes . . . and the *harlim* slept, helpless by day. He saw the dark shadow of distant riders, the wink of metal in the sun. Shien had done his mischief and was following again.

Again they rested, and the horses were slicked with sweat. Vanye spent his time attending this one and the other, for kindly as the *arrhendim* were with their mounts, and anxious as they were to care for them, they were foresters and the horses had come from elsewhere into their hands: they had not a Kurshin's knowledge of them.

"Lord," he said at last, casting himself down before Merir, "forest is one thing; open ground is another. We must not press the last out of the horses, not when we may need it suddenly. If the Shiua have gotten into the forest on our side and press us toward the river, the horses will not have it left in them to carry us."

"I do not fear that."

"You will kill the horses," Vanye said in despair, and left off trying to advise the old lord. He departed with an absent caress of the white mare's shoulder, a touch on the offered nose, and cast himself down by Roh, head bowed against his knees.

In a few moments more they were bidden back to the saddle, but for all Merir's seeming indifference to advice, they went more slowly.

*Like Morgaine,* he thought bitterly, *proud and stubborn.* And then he thought of her, and it was like a knife moving in a wound. He rode slumped in the saddle, cast a look back once, where Shien and his men still paced them, out of range. He shook his head in despair and knew what that was for: that they were apt to meet a force on their side of the Narn up by the next crossing, and Shien meant to be there to seal them up.

Roh rode close to him, so that the horses jostled one another and he looked up. Roh urged one of the *arrhendim's* journeycakes on him. "You did not eat at the stop."

He had had no appetite, nor did now, but he knew the sense of Roh's concern, and took it and washed it down with

water, though it lay like lead in his stomach. Small dark Vis
rode up on his other side and offered another flask to him.

"Take," she said.

He drank, expecting fire by the smell of it, and it was,
enough to make his eyes sting. He took several more swal-
lows, and gave it back to Vis, whose dark eyes were young in
her aging face, and kindly. "You grieve," she said. "We all
understand, we that are *khemeis,* we that are *arrhen.* So we
would grieve too." She pressed the flask back into his hand.
"Take it. It is from my village. Perrin and I can get more."

He could not answer her; she nodded, understanding that
too, and dropped behind. He hung the flask to his saddle, and
then thought to offer some to Roh, which Roh accepted, and
passed it back to him.

Night-shadow began to touch the sky. The sun burned over
the dark rim of Shathan across the river, and from the east
there was silence, no comforting whistles out of the dark
woods, nothing.

They kept moving while there was still twilight to guide
them, and bent into the forest itself, for a river barred their
way, flowing into the Narn.

It was not a great river; quickly it dwindled until the trees
that grew on its margin almost sufficed to span it.

And suddenly about them stealthy shadows moved, and a
chittering warned them of *harlim.*

One waited on the riverside, like some large, ungainly bird
standing at the water's shallow edge. It chirred at them as
that kind would in perplexity, and backed when Merir would
have approached it on horseback. Then it beckoned.

"We cannot go another such journey," Sharrn protested.
"Lord, *you* cannot."

"Slowly," said Merir, and turned the white mare in the
direction that the creature would have them go: breast-high
she waded, but the current was very weak, and all of them
followed, up the other bank, into wilder places.

The *haril* wanted haste: they could not. The horses
stumbled on stones, faltered going up the slopes of ravines.
The trees were old here, and the place beneath them much
overgrown with brush. *Harilim* moved all about them, finding
passage that the horses could not.

And suddenly there was a white shape before them in the
dark, an *arrhen,* or like unto one, afoot and clothed in white,
not forest green. His hair was loose, his whole aspect like and

unlike one of the *arrhendim*, seeming more wraith than flesh in the starlight.

Lellin.

The youth lifted his hand. "Grandfather," he saluted Merir, softly. He came and took Merir's offered hand, reaching up to the saddle. Solid he was, yet there was a change on him, a sad quiet utterly unlike the youth they knew. "Ah, Grandfather, *you* should not have come."

"Why should I not?" Merir answered him. The old lord looked frightened. "What madness has taken you? Why this look on you? Why did you not send the message you promised?"

"I had no means."

"Morgaine," Vanye said, forcing his horse past Sharrn's to Lellin. "Lellin—what of Morgaine?"

"Not far." Lellin turned and lifted his arm. "A stony hill, the other side—"

He used the spurs, broke free of them and bent low, caring nothing for their protest, for *harilim* warnings. He would not bring Merir on her without warning. His horse stumbled under him, recovered; brush opposed, branches caught at him and snapped on his armor. He clung low to the saddle and the horse stayed on its feet, upslope and down, shying from this side and that as it sensed *harilim*. Pursuit was on his heels: the *arrhendim* . . . he heard them coming.

Suddenly there was a broad meadow in the starlight, and the low hill that Lellin had named hove up. He broke through a thin screen of young trees and rode for that place.

White figures appeared before him in the starlight, white robes, white hair flying in the wind, aglow like foxfire. He saw the shimmer, tried to rein over at the last instant and could not avoid it.

There was dark.

*"Khemeis."*

A touch fell on his shoulder. He heard a horse near . . . sensed still the numbing oppression of Gate-force in the air.

*"Khemeis."*

*Lellin.* Coarse grass was under his hands. He strove to push himself up. Another hand reached to help him rise. He looked into Sezar's face . . . Sezar likewise in white such as Lellin's, neither of them armed. He cast a dazed look about him, at white-robed *qhal*, at the two who had once been *ar-*

*rhendim* . . . one of the *qhal* held the reins of his horse, which stood with legs braced as if it were still dazed.

And others . . . Merir, who dismounted and took his place among the *qhal* in white robes, a taint of gray among them. Roh was there at a distance, among the *arrhendim*, who grouped together as if in great fear.

"You are permitted," Lellin said, pointing toward the hill. "She sends for you. Go, now, quickly."

A moment he looked a second circuit of him, looking on the white figures, feeling the silence. His senses still swam. Gate-force worked at his nerves. He turned suddenly and went, overwhelmed with anxiety. One of them shadowed him, pointed the way that he should take up the hill, where a trail began among the trees which marched up its side. He did not run, but he wished to.

It was not a high hill, hardly more than a rocky upthrust amid the forest. At either side of him were trees aged and warped, twisted by wind or Gate-force, strange shapes in the starlight. He climbed that path carefully, his heart frozen in dread of the thing that he might find in this smothering silence.

The path bent, and she was there, a white figure like the others, as Lellin had been, standing among the rocks. Wind tugged at her white hair and her thin garments . . . unarmored and unarmed she was, when never willingly would she part from *Changeling*.

*"Liyo,"* he said in half a voice, and stopped . . . human, and feeling it mortally. He did not want to come closer and find her changed; he did not want to lose her like that.

But she came to him, and there was no difference but the clothing: the strength was there, and the recklessness. Wraith she seemed, but this wraith scrambled down from the rocks with Morgaine's energy, a hand to this side and the other to catch herself, and a hand to him at the bottom. He seized her as if she might prove illusion after all, and they flung arms about each other with the desperation of sanity returned.

She said nothing. It was long before he thought of saying anything. But then he thought of her wound, and realized how thin she was, and that he might be hurting her. He drew her aside to the rocks and gave her a place to sit, cast himself to a lower stone beside her. "You are well," he breathed.

"We saw the smoke . . . from here. I hoped . . . hoped that you were somehow the cause of that alarm. I sent word,

such as the *harilim* can bear. And I saw you coming . . .
from this hill. I could not prevent them. I shouted, but in the
wind, they did not hear, or heed. Lellin . . . Lellin found
you, did he not?"

"Down near the river." His voice failed him and he rested
his head against the stones at his side. "Oh Heaven, I did not
know how I would find you."

"Sezar found Mai dead on the riverbank. And traces of
horses about her. They searched further . . . but there were
Shiua aswarm in that area and they had to come back. What
happened?"

"Trouble enough." He reached for her hand, held it tightly,
to assure himself she was solid and with him. "What of you?
What are these folk? What are we amid here?"

"*Arrha.* Keepers of Nehmin, among other things. They are
dangerous. But without them I would not have survived,
whatever else we have to do one with the other."

"Are you free?"

"That is a question yet to be tried. There is nowhere to go
from here. Three nights ago the marshlanders tried our defenses. They are still out there. We held them then. Lellin
. . . Sezar . . . the *arrha.* I have tried to stay back from it,
to avoid having them know me . . . but then I could not.
Even so it was close."

A host of questions pressed on him. He felt her hand, how
thin and fragile it had become. "Are you all right? Your
wound—"

She moved her hand to her hip, where the leg joined.
"Mending. The *arrha* are skilled healers. It was a bad one. I
came close enough to dying. I do not remember the last of
that ride, but that Lellin and Sezar knew where they were going . . . or thought they did. And the *arrha* . . . let us pass."

"If you had not stayed ahorse . . ." He did not finish the
thought, sickened by it.

"Aye. I had the same thought for you. But you reached
Merir after all. And yet you sent me no message."

He was confused for a moment, realizing then how she
had misconstrued things. "Would my course had been that
direct," he said, and a sudden fear possessed him, reluctance
to admit what had happened . . . most of all to have her
know he had been in the enemy's hands. Gate-force could
change men: Roh was proof enough of that; and he recalled
a time when she would have killed out of hand for any such
doubt of a companion. "Forgive me," he said. "I have used

allies in getting here that you will curse me for taking. And Merir knows both what you hold and what you have come to do . . . what *we* came to do. Forgive me. I trust too easily."

She was silent a moment. Fear touched her eyes. "The *arrha* know both by now, then."

"There is more, *liyo*. One of the men out there is Roh."

She drew back.

"I have been to the Gate and back again," he said hoarsely, refusing to let her go. "*Liyo*, on my soul, I had no choice; and I would not be here but for Roh."

"What of an oath you swore? What of that? You were not to let him live. And you have brought him to me?"

"He has helped us both. He asked only to see you; that was his condition. I warned him . . . I confess that I warned him and tried to persuade him to run. But—he would come. He has run out of friends. And without him—. Will you not hear him?"

She looked down. "Come with me," she said, and rose, still with her hand in his. He rose and walked with her among the rocks, down the other slope of the hill, by yet another trail. "Our camp is here," she said as they walked. "Extraordinary dispensation: no axe touches Nehmin . . . but the *arrha* brought wood from the outside, and built this for us. In some regards they have been more than kind."

A wooden shelter was almost hidden among the tall trees; a ghostly horse grazed beside it . . . Siptah. He recognized the gray Baien stud with a pang of relief, for Morgaine loved that horse, and had she lost him, she would have grieved . . . as much, he thought, as she might for him, for the gray horse had come with her farther and longer. Two other horses grazed slightly apart: Lellin's and Sezar's, one conspicuous for its white stockings. All of them looked sleek and well-cared for.

"Roh," she murmured as they descended toward the shelter. "The *arrha* meant to hold all of you from me at least overnight, to ask their own questions, I do not doubt. But they understand the bond of *khemeis* and *arrhen*, and when I accused them of harming you, they let you come, out of shame, I suppose. Roh's presence . . . that concerns me. I would not have him giving witness of me."

"We might try to break out of here."

She shook her head. "I fear our choice is in the Shiua's hands. They are on two sides of us at least." She drew back the curtain of the shelter, gray gauze like the *harilim's* veils, like old moss, many layered. It swung against his face as he entered, and he did not like the feel of it.

Morgaine bent and touched a reed to a brazier of coals and transferred that tiny flame to a single-wicked lamp, so that a dim light surrounded them. "The *harilim* do not like fire," she said. "But we are very careful. Drop the curtain. Shed the armor. No enemies can come at us here without a great deal of trouble, and as for the *arrha* . . . they are of a different sort. I will find out what we have about here to eat—"

He stood motionless in the center of the small shelter as she searched through the collection of jars in the corner. There was Siptah's harness, and that of Lellin's and Sezar's horses; there were three pallets, with gray gauze veils dividing one off for privacy; Morgaine's armor, laid neatly in the corner; and *Changeling* . . . as if it were only another sword, leaned by it. Even to have walked up to the hilltop without that fell thing was something incredible in her . . . a dulling of cautions by which she had survived. There was after all a change about her, something alien and distant. In this place of familiar things . . . she was the difference. He watched her in the dim light, slender and delicate as the *qhal* in the white garments . . . and her features when she looked up at him: the tautness of pain had been there recently. *So close,* he thought with sudden anguish, *so very close to losing her; perhaps that is the mark on her.*

"Vanye?"

He reached for the straps of his armor, worked at them clumsily, managed them. She helped him pull it off, received the two-stone weight of mail into her hands and laid it aside. He unlaced the haqueton and shed it, sank down onto the mat with a sigh. Then she gave him water to drink, and bread and cheese of which he could eat only a few bites. He was more content simply to lean against the support of the shelter and rest. It was warm; she was there. It was for the moment, enough.

"Do not worry about the others," she said. "Lellin and Sezar will give warning if anything threatens us, and the *arrha* refuse to lay hand on them or me. —Oh, it is good to see thee, Vanye."

"Aye," he murmured, for his voice was too taut to say more.

She sat on the mat beside the brazier, locked her hands

about one knee. A moment she gazed at him, as if taking in
small details. "You have been hurt."

"It passes."

"Your fall out there—"

"I rode into that blind." He grimaced. "I thought to warn
you . . . of my company."

"You succeeded." Her face grew the more concerned,
deeply distressed. "Vanye. Will thee—tell me what happened?"

"Roh, you mean."

"Roh. And whatever else thee thinks good for me to
know."

He glanced down, up again. "I have gone against your orders. I know that. I could not kill him. I confess to you . . .
it has not been the first time. I agreed with him that I would
speak to you . . . he asked nothing more, not even that
much, but I told him that I would; I owed him. He is out of
allies, out of hope, except to come here."

"And you believe him."

"Yes. In that—I do believe him."

Her hands clenched on her knee until the knuckles were
white. "And what do you expect me to do?"

"I do not know. I do not know, *liyo.*" He made the pro-
found obeisance, which gesture she ordinarily hated, but the
time demanded it. "I told him that I would speak with you.
Will you let me do so, and hear me? I set my word on that."

"Do not hope that it will make any difference. My choices
are not governed by what I would or you would."

"All I ask is a hearing. It is not easy to explain. In any
sense, it is not easy. And I have asked few things of you,
ever."

"Aye," she said softly, drew a long breath and let it go. "I
will listen. I will at least listen."

"For long?"

"As long as you wish. Til the sun rises, if that is what you
want of me."

He bowed his head against his hands a moment, gathering
his thoughts. Nothing would make sense except from the beginning . . . and there he began, far off the matter of Roh.
She looked perplexed at that . . . but she listened as she had
said she would do; her gray eyes lost their anger and bore
only on what he haltingly told her: things of himself, and his
home, small things that she had not known of him, some of
which were agony to tell . . . what it was for a half-Chya lad

in Morija, what constant war Nhi and Chya had known, and how he came to be a Nhi lord's bastard. And there were things even of times that they had travelled together, things which he had seen and she had not . . . of Liell; and Roh; of the night they had spent in Roh's hall at Ra-koris; and another with him in the woods near Ivrel, when she had slept; or in Ohtij-in of Shiuan, unknown to her. He watched understanding flicker into sometime anger, and puzzlement return; she said nothing.

And he told her the rest: Fwar, and Hetharu's camp; and Merir's; and their way here. He spared nothing, least of all his pride; at the last he did not look at her, but elsewhere, close to choking on the words . . . for half of him was Nhi, and Nhi were proud, and not given to such admissions as he made.

Her hands were clenched when he had done. She loosed them after a moment, as if she had only then realized it. It was a moment before she looked up.

"Some things I would that I had known at the time."

"Aye, and some things I would that you did not know now."

"Nothing that you have told me troubles me, not on your account. Only—Roh . . . *Roh.* I did not reckon on that. I swear that I did not."

"You saw him. But—but perhaps—I do not know, *liyo.*"

"It cannot make any difference. It changes nothing."

"*Liyo.*"

"I warned you it could not make any difference . . . Roh or Liell; no difference."

"But Roh—"

"Let me alone a time. Please."

His control came close to breaking. He had said too much, too painful things, and she shrugged them off with that. "Aye," he said thickly, and thrust his way to his feet, seeking the cold, sane air outside. But she rose and prevented him with a grip on his wrist. He would hurt her if he struck out in his anger; he stood still, and the tears broke his control. He averted his face from her.

"Think of something," she hissed fiercely. "*Think* of something that I can do with this gift you have brought me."

He could not. "His word you would never take. And that is all there is . . . his word, and my faith that it is worth something. And that is nothing to you."

"You are unfair."

"I make no complaint of you."

"Keep him prisoner? He knows too much . . . more than you, more perhaps than Merir . . . in some things more than I, perhaps. I cannot trust that much knowledge . . . not with Liell's instincts."

"At times . . . at times, I think there is only Roh. He said the other was only in dreams; and perhaps the dreams are stronger than he is when there is nothing near him that Roh remembers. He says that he needs me. —But I have no knowledge of such things. I only guess. Perhaps I am the one who forced him to come here to you, because when he is with me . . . he is my cousin. I only guess."

"Perhaps," she said after a moment, "your instinct in that guess is not so far amiss."

There was a clutching pain in him. He turned and looked at her, looked into her gray eyes, the face that was utterly *qhalur*. "Roh has said . . . again and again . . . that you know all these things very well—and by your own experience."

She said nothing, but stepped back from him. He did not mean to let it go this time.

"I do not know," she whispered at last. "I do *not* know."

"He says that you are what he is. I am asking you, *liyo*. I am only *ilin;* you can tell me never to ask; and the oath I took to you does not question what you are. But *I* want to know. *I* want to know."

"I do not think you do."

"You said that you were not *qhal*. But how do I go on believing that? You said that you had never done what Liell has done. But," he added in a still voice difficult to force against the distrust in her eyes, "if you are not *qhal*—*liyo*, are you not then the other?"

"You are saying that I have lied to you."

"How can you have told me the truth? *Liyo*, a little lie, even a kindly lie at the time . . . I could understand why. If you had told me you were the devil, I could not free myself of the oath I had given you. Perhaps you mean it for kindness in that hour. It was. But after so long, so many things—for my peace—"

"Would it give you peace?"

"To understand you—yes. It would. In many ways."

The gray eyes shimmered, pained. She offered her hand to his, palm up; he closed his over it, tightly, a manner of pledge, and he marked even in doing so that her fingers were

long and the hand narrow. "Truth," she said faintly. "I am
what Hetharu is: halfling. A place long ago and far from Andur-Kursh . . . closed now, lost, no matter. The catastrophe
did not come only on the *qhal;* they were not the only ones
swept up. There were their ancestors, who made the Gates."
She laughed, a lost and bitter laugh. "You do not understand.
But as the Shiua are out of my past, I am out of theirs. It is
paradox. The Gate-worlds are full of that. Can what I have
told you give you peace?"

Fear was in her look . . . anxiety, he realized numbly, for
*his* opinion, as if she needed regard it. He half understood
the other things, the madness that was time within gates. That
anything could be older than the *qhal* . . . he could not grasp
such age. But he had hurt her, and he could not bear to have
done that. He let go her fingers, caught her face between his
hands and set a kiss beside her lips, the only affirmation of
trust he knew how to give. He had believed her a liar, had
accused her, assuming so, so surely that he could dimiss such
a lie and forgive, understanding her.

And he did not. A pit opened at his feet, to take in all his
understanding.

"Well," she said, "at least thee is still here."

He nodded, knowing nothing to say.

"Thee surprises me sometimes, Vanye."

And when he still found no answer, she shook her head
and turned away across the little shelter, her arms folded
tightly, her head bowed. "Of course you came to that conclusion; there was nothing else you could think. Doubtless Roh
himself believes it. And for whatever small damage it could
do—Vanye, I beg you keep it to your knowledge, no one
else's. I am not *qhal.* But what I am no longer has any meaning, not in this age. Not in Shathan. It no longer matters."

*"Liyo—"*

"I would not have you believing that I knew Roh's nature.
I would not have you thinking I sent you against him, knowing that. I did not. I did *not,* Vanye."

"Now you have me between two oaths. Oh Heaven, *liyo.* I
was thinking of Roh's life, and now I am afraid of winning
it. I do not . . . I swear I do not try to pull against your
good sense. I do not want that. *Liyo,* protect yourself. I
should never have questioned you; this is not how I would
have persuaded you. Do not listen to me."

"I know my own mind. Do not shoulder everything." She
tossed her head back, thin-lipped, and looked at him. "This is

Nehmin. You will see it as I have seen it; I am not anxious
to spill blood in this place. We are far from Andur-Kursh
. . . far from every grudge it had . . . and I pity him. I pity
him, even as Liell—though that is harder: I knew his victims.
Give me time to think. Go to sleep a while. Please. There is
at least something of the night left, and you look so tired."

"Aye," he agreed, though it was less for weariness than
that he would not dispute her, not now.

She gave him the mat by the east wall, her own. He lay
down there with no real desire of sleep; but the ease it gave
sent a sudden heaviness on him, so that he cared not even to
move. She drew the blanket farther over him, and sat down
on the mat beside him, leaned there against the post, her
hand over his. He shivered for no reason—if he had taken a
chill he was too numb to feel it. He let his breath go, flexed
his fingers against hers, enclosed them.

Then he slept, a hard, swift darkness.

# Chapter Fifteen

She was gone in the morning. There was food there, milk
and bread and butter, and slices of cold meat. Written in a
dab of butter on the side of the pitcher was a Kurshin sym-
bol, the glyph that began *Morgaine*.

*Safe*, she meant. He ate, more than he had thought he
could; and there was water heated for him over the coals. He
bathed, and shaved . . . with his own razor, for his personal
kit was there: they had recovered it from Mai, surely; and his
bow was laid there with his armor, and other things that he
had thought forever lost. He was glad—and dismayed, to
think that they might have risked themselves, she and Lellin
and Sezar, to recover them.

But her own weapons were still standing in the corner, and
it began to trouble him that she stayed so long, unarmed. He

went outside, unarmored, to see whether she was in sight:
Siptah was gone too, though the harness was not.

Then a movement caught his eye, and he saw her coming
back, riding down the slope, bareback on the gray horse, a
strange figure in her white garments. She slid down and
wrapped the tether-line over a branch, for she had been riding with only the halter. Her face had held a worried look for
an instant; but she put on a different face when she looked
up at him . . . he saw it and answered it with a faint smile,
quickly shed.

"We have a little trouble from the outside this morning,"
she said. "They are trying us."

"Is that the way to go looking for it?" He had not meant
his voice to be so sharp, but she shrugged and took no affront. The frown came back to her eyes, and they fixed beyond, back the way she had come.

He looked. Three *arrha* had followed her, and a Man
walked with them, a tall man in green and brown, coming
from the shadow of the trees.

It was Roh.

They brought him to the front of the shelter and stopped:
they laid no hand on Roh in their bringing, but he had
no weapons either. "Thank you," Morgaine told the *arrha*,
dismissing them; but they withdrew only as far as the rocks
near the shelter.

And Roh bowed, as lord visiting hall-lord, with weary
irony.

"Come inside," Morgaine bade him.

Roh came, passed the curtain which Vanye held aside for
him. His face was pale, unshaven—and afraid, although he
tried not to show it. He did not look as if he had slept.

"Sit down," Morgaine invited him, herself settling to the
mat by the brazier, and Roh did so on the opposite side,
crosslegged. Vanye sank down on his heels at Morgaine's
shoulder, an *ilin's* place, which said what it might to Roh.
*Changeling*, he thought uneasily, for the sword was unattend-
ed in the corner, and Morgaine unarmed: he had at least
placed himself as a barrier between Roh and that.

"Chya Roh," Morgaine said softly. "Are you well?"

A muscle jerked in Roh's jaw. "Well enough."

"It took me some argument to bring you here. The *arrha*
were minded otherwise."

"You usually obtain what you want."

"Vanye did speak for you—and well. None could be more persuasive with me. But counting all that—and my gratitude for your help to him, Chya Roh i Chya—are we other than enemies? Roh or Liell, you have no love for me. You hate me bitterly. That was so in Ra-koris. Are you the kind of man who can change his mind that thoroughly?"

"I hoped you would be dead."

"Ah. Truth from you. That does surprise me. And then what would you?"

"The same that I did. I would have stayed . . ." His eyes shifted to Vanye's and locked, and his voice changed. "I would have stayed with you and tried to reason with you. But . . . that is not how it came out, is it, cousin?"

"And now?" Morgaine asked.

Roh gave a haggard grin, made a loose gesture of the hands. "My situation is rather grim, is it not? Of course I offer you my service. I should be mad not to. I do not think that you have any intention of accepting; you are hearing me now to satisfy my cousin's sensibilities; and I am talking to you because I have nothing left to do."

"Because Merir and the *arrha* turned a deaf ear to you last night?"

Roh blinked dazedly. "Well, you did not expect me not to try that, did you?"

"Of course not. Now what else will you try? Harm Vanye, who trusts you? Perhaps you would not; I almost believe that. But me you never loved, not in any shape you have worn. When you were Zri you betrayed your king, your clan, all those men . . . when you were Liell, you drowned children, and made of Leth such a plague-spot, such a sink of depravity—"

Terror shot into Roh's eyes, horror. Morgaine stopped speaking, and Roh sat visibly shivering . . . gone, all pretense of cynicism. Vanye looked on him and hurt, and set his hand on Morgaine's shoulder, wishing her to let him be; but she did not regard it.

"You do not like it," she murmured. "That is what Vanye said—that you had bad dreams."

"Cousin," Roh pleaded.

"I shall not call it back for you," she said. "Peace. Roh . . . *Roh* . . . I shall say nothing more of it. Be at peace."

Roh's hands, shaking, covered his face; he rested so a moment, white and sick, and she let him be. "Give him drink," she said. Vanye took the flask she indicated with a glance, and knelt and offered it to him. Roh took it with trembling hands, drank a little. When he was done, Vanye did not leave him, but held to his shoulder.

"Are you all right now?" Morgaine asked him. "Roh?" But he would not look at her. "I have done you more harm than I wished," she said. "Forgive me, Chya Roh."

He said nothing. She rose then, and took *Changeling* from the corner . . . withdrew from the shelter entirely.

Roh did not look at that, nor at anything. "I can kill him," he breathed between his teeth, and shuddered. "I can kill him. I can kill him."

For a moment it made no sense, the rambling of a madman; and then Vanye understood, and kept hold of him. "Cousin," he said in Roh's ear. "Roh. Stay with me. Stay with me."

Sanity returned after a moment. Roh breathed hard and bowed his head against his knees.

"Roh, she will not do that again. She saw. She will not."

"I would be myself when I die. Can she not allow me that?"

"You will not die. I know her. I *know* her. She would not."

"She will manage it. Do you think that she will ever let me at her back where you stand, or rest when I am near her? She will manage it."

The veil shadowed, went back. Morgaine stood in the doorway. "I am afraid I hear you," she said quietly. "The veils do not stop much."

"I will say it to your face," Roh said, "syllable by syllable if you did not get it clear. —Will you not return the courtesy, to me—and to him?"

Morgaine frowned, rested *Changeling* point down on the floor before her. "I will say this: that there is some good chance it will make no difference what I will and will not." She nodded vaguely westward, at the other wall. "If you want to walk through that woods and take a look at the riverside, you will find enough Shiua to make any quarrel we have among ourselves quite pointless. What I say I would say if Vanye were not involved. The kindnesses I attempt generally come to worse than my worst acts. But murder sits ill with me, and, . . ." She lifted *Changeling* slightly from the floor and rested it again. "I have not the options of fair fight that a man has; nor would I put that burden on Vanye, to deal with you in that fashion. You are right; I cannot trust you as I do him. I do not think I could ever be persuaded to that. I do not want you at my back. But we have mutual enemies out there. There is a land about us that does not deserve that plague on it . . . and you and I made it, did we not? You and I created that horde. Will you share in stopping it? The fortunes of war—may make it unnecessary to concern ourselves about our . . . differences."

Roh seemed dazed a moment . . . and then he set his hands on his knees and laughed bitterly. "Yes. Yes, I would do that."

"I will not ask an oath of you or take one, no great one: it would bind me to an honor I cannot afford. But if you will give your simple word, Roh—I trust *you* can bind your other impulses."

"I give it," Roh said. He rose, and Vanye with him. "You will have what you want of me. *All* . . . that you want of me."

Morgaine's lips tightened. She turned and walked to the far wall and laid down *Changeling*, gathering up her armor. "Do not be too forward in it. There is food left, probably. Vanye, see he has what he needs."

"My weapons," Roh said.

She looked at him, scowling. "Aye, I will see to that." And she turned again and began working into her armor.

"Morgaine kri Chya."

She looked up.

"You . . . did not bring me from Ra-koris; I brought myself, I. You did not aim that horde at this land. I did, no other. And I will not take food or drink or shelter of you, not—as matters stand. If you insist, I must; but if not—then I will take it elsewhere, and not inflict any obligation on myself or on you."

She hesitated, seeming stunned. Then she walked over and flung back the veil to the outside, waved a signal at the *arrha* who waited there. Roh left, pausing to offer a bow of courtesy; Morgaine let fall the veil after him, and lingered there, leaning her head against her arm. After a moment she swore, in her own tongue, and turned away, avoiding his eyes.

"You," Vanye said into that silence, "you did as much as he would have asked of you."

She looked up at him. "But you expect more."

Vanye shook his head. "I regard you too much, *liyo*. You are risking your life in giving what you have. He could kill you. I do not think so, or I would not have him near you. But he is a risk; and I know how you feel. Maybe more so.

He is my cousin. He brought me here alive. But . . . if . . . he is overmuch tempted, *liyo,* then he will lose. I know that. What is more, he does. You have done the best thing you could do."

She bit her lips until the blood left them. "He is a man, your cousin. I will give him that."

And she turned and gathered up the rest of her armor, put it on with a grimace of discomfort. "He will have his chance," she said then. "Armor and bow: little use for anything else if this is like the last time . . . until they reach the rock itself. We are in no small danger."

"They are prepared?"

"Some of them are well up the Silet, the tributary river to our south; the force at Narnside began moving across to our bank at dawn."

"You permit this?"

She gave a bitter laugh. "I? Permit? I fear I am not in charge here. The *arrha* have permitted it, step by step, until we are nigh surrounded. Powerful they are, but their whole mind, their whole conception of the problem, is toward defense, and they will not hear me. I would have done differently, yes, but I have not been able to do anything until recently. Now it comes to the point that the only thing I can do is help them hold this place. It has never been a matter of what I would choose here."

He bent and gathered his armor from where he had left it.

They saddled the horses, not alone Siptah, but Lellin's and Sezar's, and gathered up all that they might need if it came to flight. What was in Morgaine's mind remained her own; but he reckoned in his own thoughts what she had told him, the isolation by wood and water of the area that was Nehmin, and the Shiua possessing the rivers that framed their refuge.

All the area about them was tangled and wooded, and that was a situation no Kurshin could find comfortable; there was no place to maneuver, no place to run. The horses were all but useless to them, and the hill was too low to hold.

They rode up the slope of the hill and among the twisted trees, down again by the winding trail among the rocks, so that they came out again on the meadow.

"No sight of them," Vanye muttered, looking uneasily riverward.

"Ah, they have learned a slight caution of this place. But it will not last, I fear."

She turned Siptah to the right hand, and warily they rode away from that vicinity into the woods, through brush, into an area where the trees grew very large. A path guided them . . . *and our enemies next*, Vanye thought dismally. Horses had been down it recently.

"*Liyo*," he said after a space. "Where do we go? What manner of thing have you in mind?"

She shrugged, and seemed worried. "The *arrha* have withdrawn. And they are not above abandoning us to the enemy. I am concerned for Lellin and Sezar. They have not reported back to me. I do not like to take their horses from where they expect to find them, but likewise I do not want to lose them."

"They are out there—toward the enemy?"

"That is where they should be. At the moment, I am concerned that the *arrha* are not where they should be."

"And Roh."

"And Roh," she echoed, "though in some part I doubt he is the center of this matter. He may himself be in danger. Merir . . . Merir is the one who deserves watching. Honorable he may be—but thee learns, Vanye, thee learns . . . that the good and virtuous fight us as bitterly as those who are neither good nor virtuous . . . more so, perhaps—for they do so unselfishly, and bravely . . . and we must most of all beware of them. Do you not see that I am what the Shiua name me? And would a man not be entitled to resist that . . . for himself—most of all for what the *arrhend* protects? —Forgive me. Thee knows my darker moods; I should not shed them on thee."

"I am your man, *liyo*."

She looked at him, surprised out of the bitterness that had been her expression.

And around the bending of the trail there stood one of the *arrha*, a young *qhalur* woman. Silent, she stood among the branches and ferns, light in green shadow.

"Where are your fellows?" Morgaine asked of her.

The *arrha* lifted her arm, pointed the way that they were going.

Morgaine started Spitah forward again, slowly, for the trail wound much. Vanye looked back; the *arrha* still stood there, a too-conspicuous sentinel.

Then they passed into another space where few trees grew,

and in that open space there were horses; the *arrhendim* were there, seated . . . the six who had gone out with Merir, and Roh. Roh gathered himself to his feet as they came.

"Where is Merir?" Morgaine asked.

"Off that way," Roh said, and pointed farther on. He spoke in Andurin, and looked up . . . shaven, washed, he looked more the *dai-uyo* he was, and he bore his weapons again. "No one is doing anything. Word is the Shiua are closing on us from two sides, and the old men are still back there talking. If no one moves, we will have Hetharu in our midst before evenfall."

"Come," said Morgaine, and slid down from the saddle. "We leave the horses here." She wrapped Siptah's reins about the branch, and Vanye did the same for the horse he rode and the ones he led.

None of the *arrhendim* had done more than look up.

"Come," she bade them; and in a stronger voice: "Come with me."

They looked uncertain; Larrel and Kessun stood up, but the elder *arrhendim* were reluctant. Finally Sharrn did so, and the six came, gathering up their weapons.

Wherever they were bound, Morgaine seemed to have been this way before; Vanye stayed at her shoulder, that Roh should not walk too near her, watching either side and sometimes looking back at the *arrhendim* who trailed them on this suddenly narrower path. He was far from easy in his mind, for they were all too vulnerable to treachery, for all the power of the weapons Morgaine bore.

Gray stone confronted them through the tangle of vines and branches . . . lichen-spotted, much weathered, standing stones thrust up among the roots of trees, closer and closer, until the stones formed an aisle shadowed by the vast trees.

Then they had sight of a small stone dome at the end of that aisle. *Arrha* guarded the entry of it, one on either side of the doorway that stood open, but there was no offer to oppose their coming.

Voices echoed within, echoes that died away at their tread within the doorway. Torches lit that small dome within; *arrha* sat as a mass of white on stone seats that encompassed more than half the circuit of the walls: the center of the floor was clear, and there Merir stood. Merir was the one who had been speaking and he faced them there.

One of the *arrha* arose, an incredibly old *qhal*, withered and bent and leaning on a staff. He stepped down onto the floor where Merir stood.

"You do not belong here," that one said. "Arms have never come into this council. We ask that you go away."

Morgaine did nothing. A look of fear was on all the *arrha* . . . old ones, very old, all those gathered here.

"If we contest for power," said another, "we will all die. But there are others who hold the power we have. Leave."

"My lord Merir." Morgaine walked from the doorway to the center of the room; Vanye followed her: so did the others, taking their place before that council. His distress was acute, that she thus separated herself from the door. There were guards, *arrha*, bearing Gate-force, he suspected. He could not prevail against that. If it came to using her weapons she needed him close to her, where he was able to guard her back . . . where he was not in the way of what had taken at least one comrade of theirs. "My lords," she said, looking about her. "There are enemies advancing. What do you plan to do?"

"We do not," said the elder, "admit you to our counsel."

"Do you refuse my help?"

There was deep silence. The elder's staff rang on the floor and echoed, the slightest tap.

"My lords," she said. "If you do refuse my help, I *will* leave you. And if I leave you, you *will* fall."

Merir stepped forward half a pace. Vanye held his breath, for the old lord knew, knew utterly what she meant, the destruction of the Gate which gave them power, in her passing from this world. And surely he had told the others.

"That which you bear," said Merir, "is greater than the power of all the *arrha* combined. But it was fashioned as a weapon; and that . . . *that* is madness. It is an evil thing. It cannot be otherwise. For fifteen hundred years . . . we have used our power gently. To protect. To heal. You stand here, alive because of it . . . and tell us that if we do not bow to your demands, then you will turn that thing against us, and destroy Nehmin, and leave us naked to our enemies. But if we do as you wish—what, then? What are your terms? Let us hear them."

There was no sound or movement after.

But suddenly other footfalls whispered on the stones at the doorway.

Lellin, and Sezar.

"Grandfather," Lellin said in a hushed voice, and bowed.

"Lady . . . you bade me come when the enemy had completed their crossing. They have done so. They are moving this way."

A murmur ran the circuit of the room, swiftly dying, so that the tiniest movement could be heard.

"You have been out doing her bidding," Merir said.

"I told you, Grandfather, that I went to do that."

Merir shook his head slowly, lifted his face to look on Morgaine, on all of them, on the *arrhendim* who had come with Morgaine, and all but Perrin lowered their eyes, unable to meet his.

"You have already begun to destroy us," Merir said. His voice was full of tears. "You offer your way . . . or nothing. We might have been able to defeat the Shiua, as we did the *sirrindim* who came on us long ago. But now we have come to this, that armed force has entered this place, where arms never have come before, and some have faith in them."

"Lellin Erirrhen has said," the elder *arrha* declared, "that he is *hers,* lord Merir. And therefore he insists on coming and going at her bidding, refusing ours."

"Else," Morgaine said in a loud voice, "the council would keep me blind and deaf. And Lellin and Sezar in their service to me have kept me from taking other action, my lords. They know what you do not. By serving me . . . they have served you."

Merir's lips made a taut line, and Lellin looked at the old lord, bowed to him very slowly, and to Morgaine . . . faced his grandfather again. "Of our own choice." Lellin said. "Grandfather—the *arrhendim* are needed. Please. Come and look. They cover the riverside like a new forest. Come and look on this thing." He cast an anguished glance about at all the *arrha*. "Come out of your grove and see this horde. You talk of taking it into Shathan. Of peace with it . . . as we found with the remnant of the *sirrindim.* Come and look on this thing."

"One more dangerous to us," said the elder, "is already here." And Gate-force flared, making the air taut as a drawn string. It shimmered about the elder.

And it grew. One and another of the *arrha* began to bring forth that power, until the *arrhendim* flinched back against the wall, and the whole dome sang with it.

"*Liyo,*" Vanye murmured, and whipped his sword from its sheath, for two of the *arrha* barred the doorway, and the air between them shimmered with the barrier they formed.

"Cease!" Morgaine shouted.

The elder stamped the heel of his staff on the floor, a sound almost drowned in the taut air; his half-blind eyes were set rigidly. "Six of us have invoked the power. There are thirty-two. Surrender that which you bear."

*"Liyo—"*

Morgaine slipped *Changeling's* ring and dropped the sword to her hip. Vanye looked about him, at the elders, at the frightened *arrhendim* . . . and Roh, whose face was pale, but whose hands stayed from his weapons.

"Two more," said the elder. The singing in the air grew louder, numbing hearing, and Morgaine lifted her hand.

"You know what the result will be," she cried.

"We are willing to die, all of us. The passage we open here may be wide enough to work ruin on the enemies of Shathan as well. But you who do not love this land . . . may not be willing to become part of that. One by one we shall add to the force. We do not know how many of us will be needed before the passage is complete, but we shall discover it. You cannot leave. You can try your other weapons. If you do, we will answer you with all we have. Or you can draw that sword and complete the passage beyond any doubt: its force with ours is sufficient beyond any argument. It will drink us all up, and more besides. But surrender that weapon and we shall deal well with you. Our word is good. You have nothing to fear from us."

Gate-force keened in the air. Another joined it.

*"Liyo,"* Vanye said. Very small his voice sounded in that power. "Your other weapon—"

She said nothing. He dared not look at what was happening before her, but kept his eyes to the *arrhendim,* who were at her back and armed; and Roh, Lellin and Sezar were apart from the others, fear in their faces, but they stood with arms folded and had never moved.

"My lords!" Morgaine exclaimed suddenly. "My lord *arrha!* We are gaining nothing by this. Only your enemies gain."

"We have made our choice," said Merir.

"You sat here—sat here until I should become desperate enough to try to come stir you out of it. A trap of your working, lord Merir? It is a well-devised one."

"We are utterly willing," said Merir, "to perish. We are old. There are others. But there is no need of it, unless you value power more than your own life. If we add many more jewels to the web, lady Morgaine, it will be accomplished. You sense that. So do I." He held up his hand, with the jewel-case upon it. "Here is another mote of that power you hold. Perhaps this will complete it. It is that near. Shall I add it to the others?"

"Enough! Enough. I see that you are capable of doing it. No more."

"Surrender the sword."

She unhooked it and grounded it point-down before her. "My lords of the *arrha!* Lord Merir is right . . . that is an evil thing. And there is only one of it, and that itself is a great evil, and subtle. You hold your power divided into many hands; whoever takes this, that one will be more powerful than all the others. Which? Who of you seeks it?"

None answered.

"You have never seen a Gate opened," Morgaine said. "You have never summoned that power entire, counting that passage dangerous. You are right. Shall I show you? Damp that which you hold: I shall show you my meaning. Let me show you *why* Nehmin must cease to exist. You value reason, my lords; then listen to me. I have no terms. I come not to possess Nehmin by the threat of destroying it. I come to destroy it, whether or not the enemy is stopped. I do not want any power over you."

"You are mad," said the elder.

"Let me show you. Damp the jewels. If I do not convince you, the unveiling of only a few of them while *Changeling* is unsheathed will be sufficient for your purposes . . . and mine. You do not well reckon . . . that I also am willing to die for what I do."

The elder stepped back, bewilderment in his look. Merir made a helpless gesture. "She says well," Merir said, "We can always die."

The force ebbed, more suddenly than it had grown, jewel after jewel winking into cover. And when it was utterly gone, Morgaine eased *Changeling* forth, crystal is the jewels, which were only motes that human flesh itself could obscure unharmed. Opal fire flowed along *Changeling's* runes, and suffused the blade, and darkness flared at the tip of it, where the wind began. Someone cried out. Its light bathed all their faces. She moved it, and the wind grew stronger, whipping at the torches, tugging at hair and robes and howling within the dome. Vanye stepped back from her side, not even aware that he moved until he found himself near Lellin.

"Here is the passage you would form!" Morgaine shouted over the roar of the wind. "Here it is open before you. Look into it. Have you courage now to add your jewels to that? A few of them would suffice, and this whole dome will be else-where, with us in it. The shock of air will level all the trees hereabouts, and perhaps, as you say, take a good part of the enemy with us. Or more than that, if the force leaks through to this side of here and now. This is the power that your fa-thers' fathers' fathers trifled with. You do well to avoid it. But what will your children do? What, when someday some-one less wise than yourselves takes it up again? What, if I surrender the sword to you, and someday one of your folk draws it? On it is written the knowledge of the Gates . . . and it cannot be destroyed, save by one who will carry it un-sheathed within a Gate, into the Fires. Who of you wants to go in my place? For any man who loves this world, for any man who holds this weapon and has anything of virtue left in him—there is only one choice in the end—and that is to take it out of this world, outside this world, and to keep going from world to world, forever. Is not a calamity written in your legends? The same calamity fell everywhere that such power has been . . . and it will come again, and again. That power must have an end. Does one of you want the sword? Does one of you want to carry it under those conditions?"

She held it aloft, and the void gaped and howled. Roh was at her back; Vanye saw him, never took his eyes entirely from him. Roh's face was rigid, his eyes reflecting that opal light.

And suddenly Roh moved, fled, thrusting aside Sezar and Lellin, rushed past the *arrha* guards . . . the two of them too dazed to react. Vanye realized his sword was still in his hand. He looked on the others, on faces pale and drawn . . . turned and saw Morgaine. Her arm trembled from that force which numbed body and soul. Sweat stood on her face.

"You must seal it off," she said. "Let me take this out of your world and seal the passage forever after me. Your other choice is not one that Shathan can survive. *This—this*—does not love living things."

"Put it away," Merir said hoarsely. "Put it away, now."

"Have you seen enough? I always questioned the wisdom that made this thing. I know the evil of it. Its maker knew And perhaps that is its only virtue: that it is shaped as what it is . . . it is something that you can see and know exacly as it is. There is no ambiguity here, no yes and no. This thing ought not to exist. Those delicate jewels of yours . . . are nothing other than this. Their beauty deludes you. Their usefulness deludes you. Someday someone will gather them together and you will know that they were all aspects of *this*. Look. Look at it!"

She swung it in a great arc, faster and faster, and the wind grew until it pulled at them, until the light blazed white, until the void widened and there seemed little air in the room. Cold numbed the skin, and the *arrha* held to their chairs, those standing staggered to the walls as if their own weight could not anchor them.

"Stop it!" the elder cried.

She did so, and returned it to sheath. The winds stopped; the howling died; the dark void and the blazing light went together, leaving the dome darkened, the light of the torches sucked out, only a shaft of daylight reaching them from the door. She grounded the sword, sheathed, before her.

"That is the power you hold, *arrha*. You have but to combine your tiny jewels into one. Did you not know that? We are armed . . . alike. And I make you free gift of that knowledge now—for someday one will discover it, and you will have to use them that way."

"No."

"Can you forget what I have told you?" she asked in a low voice. "Can you forget what you have seen? Can you take the sword and keep it forever sheathed, when the *sirrindim* rise up with cities and threaten you, when Men increase and you are few? Some evil, *qhal* or Man, someday . . . will draw it. And unlike your jewels, which will fade when the Gate is sealed, the sword is knowledge to build more such Gates."

There was deathly silence. Some of the *arrha* wept, their heads bowed into their hands.

"Give it up," Morgaine urged them. "Or leave Nehmin, and come my road, the passage that I must take. I have told you truth. I have shown you. And while Nehmin remains open, that truth will always gape at your feet to swallow you up. Seal up the passage; seal Nehmin and the stones lose their fire and Shathan stands . . . unbarriered, but living. Keep Nehmin open, and you will fall to it one day. But whatever you choose, I have no choice. I must take this sword out of the world. More than Shathan is at hazard. More than your lives. More than this world alone. The evil is as wide as all the passages that ever existed. And it is most dangerous when you think it tamed and secure. Those little stones are more

evil than *Changeling* . . . because you do not see them for
what they are: fragments of a Gate. Joined, they will drink
you in and ruin more than your own world: they will reach
to others."

The elder trembled, and looked on the others, and on
Merir. Lellin wept, and Sezar, the both of them bowed to the
floor; and two by two their brother *arrhendim* joined them.

"We have heard truth," Merir said. "I think we have heard
the truth my grandson was quicker to hear."

The elder nodded, his hands trembling so that the staff
rattled against the floor. He looked at all the *arrha* about
him. There was none to say otherwise.

"Do as you will," he said then to Morgaine. "Pass. We will
seal Nehmin behind you."

Morgaine let go a long slow breath, and bowed her head.
After a moment she gathered *Changeling* to her side and
hooked it there, drew it to her shoulder. "We have a number
of Shiua to clear from our path to Azeroth. The enemy, my
lords of the *arrha,* is still advancing from the river. What will
you do about it?"

There was long silence. "We—must hold, this place and
Nehmin. Nehmin is surrounded. The enemy has already
taken all the area. We can speak to the *arrha* who hold
Nehmin itself; and within the hold of Nehmin, they can work
what you ask. You may ride from here. We can give you
seven days . . . to reach Azeroth and pass; and then we may
kill the power."

"You would fall. Shathan would be utterly open to the Shiua horde."

"We fought the *sirrindim,*" said Merir. "The *arrhend* will
drive these invaders back too."

Morgaine stared at them, one after another, scanning all
the company. And at last she folded her arms and looked at
the floor, glanced up at Vanye. He tried to say nothing with
his expression. She turned last to Merir. "Will you take my
help? I would not leave you with such a gift as waits out
there. Aye, Vanye and I could slip past, go another route
. . . reach Azeroth in seven days. But what sits out there
is—mine. I do not want to leave you to that."

The elder approached her slowly, leaning on his staff. He
bowed, deeply, and gazed at her when he straightened, like a
man looking into the Gates themselves. "There have been—
many passages for you."

"Yes, elder. I am older than you."

"Much so, I suspect." The frail hand reached, touched Vanye's arm, and the dim gray eyes turned to his. "*Khemeis* to such an *arrhen* . . . We sorrow for both of you. For both of you." He looked at Lellin, and bowed, and to Sezar and the other *arrhendim;* and lastly at Merir and Morgaine once more. "You are experienced in wars. We are not. We need you. If you are willing, we need you."

"This, at least, must be on my terms. We consult together."

"We accept that," said Merir.

"You say that you can signal those who now hold Nehmin. Bid them expect us, and soon. You shall hold here, as you can; and they must hold Nehmin until we can reach them. My lord Merir——" she nodded to him to join her, and started to the door, unsteady suddenly; at her side, Vanye felt her lean against him, and took her arm, lending his strength. The sword took, of body and soul; he had held it, and knew the pain of it. "Roh," she said suddenly, distractedly. "Where is Roh?"

He had that worry on him too; there were too many things random, too much slipping their grasp.

But Roh waited outside, a huddled figure at the base of the third standing stone, arms tucked about him. He saw them coming, and rose, torment in his eyes.

"They let you go," he said. "They let you go."

"They agreed," Morgaine said, "to seal Nehmin themselves. That was their choice."

The look went stricken, dazed; they walked past, and Roh followed after.


# Chapter Sixteen


They found the horses still safely in the clearing, with some of the *arrha* watching over them—your *qhal,* male and female, dressed in white, with faces which still were innocent of what had passed in the dome. The *arrha* offered neither courtesy nor resistence, but backed from them in seeming distress as they came close—perhaps there was a mark on all of them, Vanye thought, for there was a grimness about the *arrhendim*, the same fey desperation which had troubled him in Lellin and Sezar: he understood now that bleak, lost manner . . . that of men who had seen the limits of their world.

And of all the *arrhend*, it rested most heavily on Merir.

"My lord," said Morgaine to him. "The *arrhendim*—must be brought here. If we are to save this place—they must be brought. Can you do it?"

The old lord nodded, turned, the reins of the white horse in his hand, and stared in the direction of the river. Even through the trees the roar of many voices could be heard, shouts raised; the horde was on the march.

"I would see this thing," Merir said.

It was madness. But not even Morgaine opposed it. "Aye," she said. "Lellin, Sezar?"

"The hill is still ours," Lellin said. "Or was, lately."

*Arrha* stood sentinel in the woods, and farther on, in the meadow. "Do not stay here when they come," Morgaine said to the last. "You will only lose your lives. Take shelter with our elders."

They bowed, after their silent fashion. Perhaps they would heed and perhaps not. There was no dispute with men who did not speak.

There rose their own goal, the stony hill at the side of the meadow, and the trail which wound among the trees. The shouts of the horde sounded very near to this place, hardly beyond the screen of trees at the far side of the hill.

They climbed the height on horseback, and rode farther, Morgaine guiding them among the trees which crowned that slope and far to the other side. Rocks were frequent here, a tumbled basalt mass which became a naked promontory, highest of all points hereabouts.

Here Morgaine drew rein and slid down, leaving Siptah to stand. The rest dismounted and tied their horses among the aged trees, and followed her.

Vanye looked back; the last of them rode in, Roh, who left his horse too, and came. Roh might have fled. *Do so,* Vanye wished him with part of his heart; but that which loved the man knew why he had stayed, and what he sought, that was his soul.

But he did not wait for Roh; what battle Roh fought was

his own, and he feared to intervene in it. He turned instead and followed after Sharrn and Dev, up among the rocks.

The hill gave them view across the open meadow, higher than it had seemed, for it overtopped most of the trees at this one point, which upthrust broken fingers of stone. Slabs stood like standing stones on this crest, no work of *qhal,* but of nature. Morgaine and Merir stood between two of them, sheltered there, with the others of their company.

Vanye moved up carefully past Dev to the very brink next Morgaine, and gained a view which spanned the river and showed far across into the *harilim's* woods, so subtly did the ground hereabouts slope. Trees extended into gray-green haze on all sides of this place, on this side of the river and the other, and even part of the curve of a clearing was visible.

And nearer . . . ugliness moved. It was as Lellin had said, like a new forest grown upon the shores of the Narn, a surging mass bristling with metal-tipped pikes and lances of wood, dark and foul. Occasionally there showed a small *khalur* band, conspicuous in the sunlight glancing off their armor . . . most of those were horsemen. The horde filled all the shore and surged up the throat of the low place that led to the meadow, moving steadily and in no haste. Their voices roared as if from a common throat.

"They are so many," breathed Vis. "Surely there are not so many *arrhedim* in all Shathan. We cannot find that many arrows."

"Or time to fire them," said Larrel.

Morgaine stepped closer to the edge. Vanye seized her arm, anxious, although the distance was far and the chance was small of being seen in this sheltered point against the rocks. She regarded his warning and stopped. "This place," she said, "is impossible to hold, even if we would. The slope on the other side is too wide. This height would become a trap for us. But the enemy's circle is not yet closed. If the *arrhendim* could be brought . . . before they start to work at us with fire and axe, and if we could keep the horde from breaching Nehmin's gates . . ."

"It can be done," said Lellin. "Grandfather, it must."

"We cannot fight," said Merir, "not after their fashion, armored and with horses. We are not like them, of one mind and one voice."

"Yet we must have help," Morgaine said, "of whatever fashion."

"Do not trust—" Roh said, edging forward; Vanye

whipped out his dagger and Roh stopped still a distance from Morgaine, leaning against the slanting rock. "Listen to me. Do not trust appearances with the Shiua. I taught them. Hetharu took the whole north of Shiuan in a matter of days. He is a student more apt than his teacher."

"What do you reckon of them?"

Roh looked toward the river, grimacing into the wind and the light. "Eight, ten thousands there, if they extend much beyond that point of the trees. What they have coming in on the other side of Nehmin . . . three times that many. Probably more coming up that little river north of here, until they have us framed. Any riders of ours who try to escape this wedge of land now—will be cut down. They are screened in brush and on every side of us. This—*show*—is to distract us."

"And the higher crossings of the Narn? How many are we dealing with?"

"Believe that Shiua will have reckoned first of those crossings. Every possible escape will be held. And the whole number of the horde . . . that is uncounted; even the *khal* do not know. But they reckon a hundred thousands—all fighters, killers. Even the young ones. They plundered their own land and killed their own kind to come here into this one. A man who falls even to the children will be cut to pieces. Murder is common among them; murder, and theft, and every crime. They will fight; they do that well when they think their enemy helpless."

"Shall we," asked Merir, "believe that advice this one gives?"

Morgaine nodded. "Believe," she said softly, "that this man wishes you well, my lord Merir. His own land was such as Shathan, even more so in the age before him, which he may remember—in his better dreams. Is it not so?"

Roh looked at her, shaken, and reached forth a hand to the rocks, leaning there.

"My lord," said Morgaine, "I do not think even the *arrhendim* could fight with more love of the land than this man."

A moment Merir looked on him. Roh bowed his head, looked up with eyes glittering with tears.

"Aye," Merir said, "aye, I do think so."

The voices from the lower meadow chanted the louder. The sound began to strike them with immediacy, reminder of their danger.

"We cannot stay here," Vanye said. *"Liyo—"*

She stepped back; but Merir lingered, and unslung the

horn which he carried . . . silver-bound and old and much cracked.

"Best you get to horse," said the old lord. "We are bound to attract notice. —It is a strange law we have, stranger-friends, . . . that no horn shall ever be blown in Shathan. And yet we do keep them, silent though they have been these fifteen hundred years. You asked the *arrhendim* be summoned. Get you to horse."

She looked beyond him, to the horde which swarmed toward the hill. Then she nodded, started back quickly with the others. Only Lellin and Sezar stayed.

"We shall not leave them," said Sharrn.

"No," Morgaine agreed. "We shall not. Ready their horses for them; I think we shall have a hard ride leaving this place."

They reached the horses and mounted up in haste.

And of a sudden came a low wailing that grew to the bright, clear peal of a horn. Vanye looked back. On the height they had quitted Merir stood, and sent forth a blast which rang out over the meadow . . . exhausted, he ceased, and gave the horn to Lellin, who lifted it to his lips. Uncertain the sound was at first, in the raging shout of the horde who took it for challenge. Then it rang out louder than all the voices of the enemy, woke echoes from the rocks, and sounded again and again and again.

There was silence for a moment; even the voices of the horde were stilled by that.

Then from far away came another horn-call, faint as the wind in leaves. A howl from the enemy drowned it, but the faces of the *arrhendim* were wild with joy.

"Come!" Morgaine shouted at the three, and now they left the high rocks, Lellin and Sezar helping the old lord.

Vanye led the white mare across their path, gave Merir the reins as the two youths helped him into the saddle; then Lellin and Sezar ran for their own horses as Morgaine turned them all for the trail off the hill.

They ran, weaving in and out the trees of the grove, around the rocks; and sudden and chilling came a howl on their right, on the gentle slope of the hill. Shiua were pouring up it toward them.

"*Angharan!*" the cry went up, *Angharan! Angharan!*" —That to them was Death.

A bolt of red fire came from Morgaine's hand, a single arrow from Perrin's bow. Several of the horde fell, but Morgaine did not stay for more, and Vanye spurred his horse between her and them, bent low for the hazard of branches and answering fire. The down-trail was before them. They hurtled down that winding chute, the horses twisting and turning at all the speed they could manage.

The enemy had not yet reached the point of the hill; at the bottom of the trail Morgaine bent low and headed Siptah for the forest and the path concealed there, and in that moment Vanye cast a look over his left shoulder. There were Shiua aplenty running up the slope of the meadow, foot and riders, demon-helms with barbed pikes and lances.

Sharrn and Dev, Perrin and Vis and Roh: they rode rear-guard, and sent a few arrows back. Larrel and Kessun were with Merir, guard to him, for Lellin and Sezar bore no weapons . . . all too vulnerable they were, with three of their number unarmed. But into that arrow-fire which shielded them the Shiua were less than willing to ride.

Vanye had his sword in hand: vanguard, he and Morgaine, and there was no use for his bow in head-to-head meeting. Morgaine would pull ahead of him . . . insisted so, for fear of taking him as she had taken one of their comrades: the black weapon and the sword needed freedom for their effective use; and in *ilin's* place at his lord's left hand, shield-side. Vanye kept there now, as best he could, while they rode a mad course through land that demanded more caution. Branches raked them; horses jostled one another avoiding obstacles or making the turns. But the *khalur* riders, less skilled, hampered with their barbed lances and half-blinding helms, could not follow so swiftly here, and in time the sounds of pursuit faded into distance behind them.

There was a flash of white in the woods; they rounded a curve in the trail and Morgaine drew up suddenly, for there stood two of the *arrha*, young women.

The *arrha* waved them past.

"No," Morgaine said. "You waste yourselves. Even the force of the jewels cannot hold back what is behind us."

"Obey her," Merir said. "Climb up with us. We have need of you."

It was Lellin and Sezar who took them up, being unarmed and least likely to involve them in fighting. The *arrha* took their hands and scrambled lightly to the rear of the saddles. Morgaine started off again, at reckless pace as they crossed the small clearing, quickly slowed by undergrowth as they veered aside from the aisle of stones and the dome.

"This way!" It was the only time that Vanye had ever heard an *arrha* speak; but the young *qhalur* woman behind Sezar pointed them another direction, and Morgaine reined instantly off upon that track.

Swiftly it became a broad way among the trees of an aged grove, cleared ground where their horses could find easy passage, without brush to hinder.

They ran then, weaving when they must, until the horses were blowing with the effort and the trees, darkening their way, grew wider spaced. The Shiua seemed now to have lost their trail. They walked for a time to rest the horses, ran again, slowed again, making what time they could without completely winding the horses.

And suddenly they burst through upon cleared ground, a vast open space, and Vanye forgot all their haste in that instant. Two hills upthrust, the farther of incredible steepness, although all the clearing else was naked and flat, hazy with distance and the westering sun. A vast hold sat atop that high place, dominating all the land round about, looking down on clearing and on forest, square, a cube such as the great holds of power tended to be.

Nehmin.

And before them on the flat of the vast clearing was mustered the host of Shiuan, the glitter of arms ascending the side of the rock of the fortress, shining motes, rare in the dark tide of Men, all misty with afternoon haze.

Morgaine had drawn rein yet within the cover of the woods. Dismay seldom touched her face, but it did now. The number of those about Nehmin seemed that of the stones at Narnside. They stretched as a gray surging mass across the floor of the clearing in the far distance, stretched up the farther hill like the waves of Shiuan's eroding seas beating at the rock, tendrils of humanity which straggled among the rough spires and wound constantly higher toward the stronghold.

"*Liyo,*" Vanye said, "let us work round the side of this place. To be caught between that and what already pursues us . . . little appeals to me."

She reined Siptah about so that her back was to the clearing and her face toward the woods from which they had come. There was audible again the distant sound of pursuit. "They *have* us between," she said. "There is ambush everywhere; they have come in by all three rivers. Days—*days*—before the *arrhend* can match this kind of force."

Merir's face was grim. "We will never match it. We cannot fight but singly. In time, each will come, each fight."

"And singly die," Vanye said in despair. "That is madness, to go by twos against that force."

"Never *all* die," said Sharrn. "Not while Shathan stands. But it will take time to deal with that out there. The first to oppose them will surely die, ourselves surely among them . . . and thousands may die, in days after. But this is our land. We will not let it fall to the like of these."

"But Nehmin may fall," said Morgaine. "Enough force, enough weight of bodies and doors will yield and even the jewel-force cannot long stop them. Their ignorance—let loose in Nehmin—amid the powers *it* holds——no. No, we do not wait here for that to happen. Where, lord, is the access to Nehmin?"

"There are three hills, not apparent from this view: there is the Lesser Horn, there to the side of the greatest hill, a fortress over the road itself: gates within it face this way and the far side . . . that is the way up. Then the road winds high to the Dark Horn, which you cannot see from here, and then to the very doors of Nehmin. We cannot hope to reach more than this nearest and least, the White Hill, before they come on us."

"Come," she said. "At least we shall not be waiting here for them. We shall try. Better that then sitting still."

"They will know that horse of yours, even at distance," Roh said. "There is none such in their company, yours or Lord Merir's."

Morgaine shrugged. "Then they will know me," she said. There was distrust in her look suddenly, as if she had sudden reckoned that Roh, armed, was at her back in a situation where none could prevent him.

But the sound of pursuit was almost upon them, and she touched the spurs to Siptah and led them forward, circling within the fringe of trees, riding the bow of the clearing.

She meant a run with the White Hill between her and Nehmin, Vanye realized; it was what he would have done, running at the horde on the flat from an angle such that they had cover for at least a portion of their ride.

"They are on us!" Kessun cried; they looked back and the foremost of their pursuers had broken through, riders stringing out in wild disorder, cutting across the open to head them off while they still rode the arc.

But at the same moment Morgaine veered out into the

open, and meant to lead them from under the face of that
charge, riding for the White Hill.

"Go!" she shouted. "Lellin, Sezar, Merir, ride while you
can. We will shake these from our heels and overtake you.
The rest of you, stay by me."

*Well-done,* Vanye thought; the unarmed five of their party
had cover enough in which to gain ground; the nine armed
had cover in which to deal with these rash pursuers. He dis-
dained the bow: he had no skill at firing from horseback. He
was Nhi when he fought, and whipped out the Shiua
longsword, at Morgaine's left. Perrin and Vis, Roh, Sharrn,
Dev, Larrel and Kessun: their arrows flew and riders went
down; and Morgaine's lesser weapon laced red fire across the
front of the charge which met them. Horses and riders went
down, screaming, and even so a handful broke through,
demon-helms, their barbed lances lowered, with a straggling
horde of marshlands foot panting behind.

The charge reached them: Vanye fell to the side Nhi-style,
simply not there when the lance passed, and the good horse
held steady as he came thrusting up again, blade aimed for
that rider. The *khal* saw it coming, horrified, for the lance
point was beyond and his sword inside the defense. Then his
point drove into the undefended throat and the *khal* pitched
over his horse's rump, carried on the force of it.

"*Hai!*" he heard at his side, and there was Roh, longsword
flashing through *khalur* defense—no plains-fighter, the Chya
lord, but there was an empty saddle where there had been a
*khal* about to skewer him.

Others came on them; one rider pitched from the saddle
short of them, a red streak of fire for his undoing. Vanye
trusted to Morgaine's aim and took the gift, aiming for the
rider hard behind, whose half-helmed face registered horror
to find an enemy on him before he expected and his own
guard breached. Vanye cut him down and found himself and
Roh enmeshed in marshlands rabble. That dissolved in terror
at what fire Morgaine sent across their mass, cutting down
men indiscriminately, so that dying fell on dead. Grass was
burning. The trampling of feet put it out as the horde turned
in panic. *Arrhendur* arrows and Morgaine's bolts pursued
them without mercy, cutting down the hindmost in windrows
of dead and dying.

Vanye wheeled to turn back, chanced to look on Roh's
face, which was pale and grim and satisfied. And he turned
farther and saw Larrel on the ground with Kessun bending

over him. From the amount of blood that covered him and Kessun there was no hope he could live; a *khalur* lance had taken the young *qhal* in the belly.

Even as he watched, Kessun sprang up with bow in hand and sent three shafts in succession after the retreating Shiua. Whether they hit he did not see; the *khemeis'* face ran with tears.

"Horses!" Morgaine shouted. "*Khemeis*—get to horse! Your lord needs you!"

Kessun hesitated, his young face twisted with grief and indecision. Then Sharrn ordered him the same, and he sprang to the saddle, leaving his *arrhen* among the Shiua dead. The shock had not yet hit Kessun. Vanye hurt for him, and remembered at the same time that they had two horseless members of their company . . . one, now: Perrin had caught Larrel's.

And Roh came up leading one of the Shiua mounts, even as they started to move. They struck a gallop and held it, and Kessun rode ever and again looking back.

The White Hill lay before them, and their party neared it. Morgaine gave Siptah his head and the gray stretched out and ran with a speed which none of the *arrhendur* horses could match. Vanye dropped back in despair, but he looked on that craggy hill which rose so strangely out of the flat and of a sudden chill hit him as he considered how it seemed to stand sentinel to this approach.

Morgaine wanted the others stopped short of arrowflight of that hill; Merir's group was nearly there, moving at the best speed they could make with two horses carrying double, but she and the gray horse closed on them rapidly, the while they behind labored to stay with her. And she had their attention; the five waited at the last, seeing her desperate to overtake them, and in moments they all closed ranks, out of breath.

"Larrel," Merir mourned, seeing who it was who had fallen. Vanye recalled what Merir had said of a *qhal* dying young, and grieved for that; but he grieved more for the stricken *khemeis* who sat his horse with his hands braced on the saddle and his head bowed in tears.

"Mount up," Morgaine bade the *arrha* shortly; the young women scrambled uncertainly to the ground and Sezar helped them to the horses they were offered. Their handling of the reins was that of folk utterly unused to horses.

"The horses will stay with the group," Roh told them. "Keep the reins in your hands and do not pull back on them. Hold to the saddle if you think you will fall."

The *arrha* were frankly terrified. They nodded understand-

ing, and held on at once when they started to move, the
horses hardly more than loping. Vanye looked on the women
and cursed, showed them how to turn and how to stop, thinking with horror of what must befall the helpless creatures
when they rode full tilt into the Shiua horde. It was all there
was time to give them. He shook his head at Roh, and received back a grim look.

"Larrel was only the first," Roh said; and that took no
prophecy, for the *arrhendim* were not armed or armored for
hand-to-hand. Only he, Roh, Morgaine could fight that sort of
battle. Vanye rode closer to Morgaine, taking his place by
habit as much as clear thought; and it was impossible now to
avoid the sight that faced them. Gray indistinct lines
stretched across their whole horizon, the great rock of
Nehmin behind. Their coming was not yet remarked or not
yet known for attack: they might as well have been Shiua
riders for all the main forces knew. The skirmish had not
been seen because of the hill . . . and the approach of thir-
teen riders to that countless host could hardly seem threatening.

"Look!" cried one of the *arrha,* gazing back, for there was
a signal fire lit on the White Hill, a plume of smoke trailing
out on the wind.

And that was enough.

The sound that went up from the Shiua horde was like that
of the waves of the sea, and their number—the number was
unimaginable even to a man who had seen forces in the field
and knew how to estimate them: all that the camp on
Azeroth had spilled forth, the refuse and scourings of a
drowning world. *Khalur* riders poured out toward them, a
troop of demon-helms, a cold sheen of metal and a forest of
lances in the fading daylight.

Then Vanye doubted their faintest hope of survival, for
even if the marshlanders would flee and confound themselves
by their own numbers, the Shiua riders would not: the *khal*
knew what they attacked, had made up their minds, and
came at Morgaine for hate. A hundred riders, two hundred,
three hundred deep and twice that wide; a shout went up,
drowned in the thunder of hooves.

And of a sudden Merir drew even with them in the lead,
the white mare easily matching strides with Siptah and the
bay. "Fall behind," the old lord urged them. "Fall back. Here
the *arrha* and I am worth something, if anywhere."

Morgaine began to do so, falling back more and more,

though Vanye shuddered at the sight of the old lord out to the fore of them, and the frail white-robed *arrha* joining him in the face of those lances. Merir and his companions spread wide, and the horses shied with the *arrha* as Gate-force suddenly shimmered about them; one lost her seat and fell, a stunning blow; but the one on the horse which had been Larrel's rode still with Merir.

The downed *arrha* scrambled for her feet, scraped and shaken, childlike in her size and her helplessness. Vanye rode down on her and in a desperate maneuver leaned from the saddle and seized the back of the clothing as they seized the prize in riders' games in Kursh . . . dragged the bemused girl belly-down across his saddle and kept going. Morgaine cursed him bitterly for his madness, and he flung her back a look of anguish.

"Stay with me," Morgaine shouted at him. "Throw her off if you must; stay with me."

"Hold on," Vanye begged of the *arrha;* he could not do more for her. His horse was already laboring with that added burden. But the frail child struggled to rise, pounding her taut fist on his leg, until at last he realized that she yet held the jewel and wished him to know it. She was sore hurt; he thrust his sword into sheath and hauled her up with one hand by her robes, knowing what pain the saddle must be giving her. Thin arms went about his neck, held desperately: she dragged at one side and he leaned to the other. She flung a leg across his, relying on his balance with more courage than he had expected. The Shathana horse held steady with this shifting, staggered only a little, and when she had gained a hold he suddenly felt the queasiness of Gate-force about them: the *arrha* had unleashed the power of her jewel.

He knew then what she wanted of him, and used the spurs, aimed himself forward with all the speed the horse had left . . . defying Morgaine's direct order for one of a few times in their partnership. He pulled out to the side at the interval of Merir and the other *arrha,* hearing someone coming hard yet farther over; and it was, as he had thought . . . Morgaine.

He gasped and the horse staggered as they joined that bridge of force, but the little *arrha* held tightly and he blinked his eyes clear as the serried line of lances came at them, near and distinct, like a forest horizontal.

It was madness. They could not hit that mass and live.

Senses denied it, even while the terror of Gate-force ripped
the air along the line they held. He thought of *Changeling*
added to that, and that frightened him the more; but Morgaine did not draw it. The red fire of her lesser weapon laced
across the charge, merciless to horse and rider. Animals went
down in a line; those behind tumbled after in a screaming
tangle; and others went round them, some falling, but not
enough. The lances came into their very faces.

Vanye leaned aside as the Gate-force hit the rank like a
scythe, tumbling horses and riders in the area of crossing
forces; but the few riders nearest stayed ahorse, unaffected,
flashing past most too dazed to strike well. Vanye could but
lean and evade. A blade rang on his helm and shoulder as he
bowed over the saddle and shielded the *arrha* as best he
could. The horse stumbled badly, recovered by a valiant effort, and they rode over corpses and the unconscious; he was
hit more than once, and then they broke into the clear, the
horses running. Morgaine drew ahead of him, Siptah taking
free rein for a space, with the marshlanders ahead of her.
The rabble tried to hold their ground; a hedge of braced
spears barred her way. Then *Changeling* flashed into the
open, a force that hit his nerves and sent the horse staggering
even at this distance. It stopped; the *arrha* had shielded her
own. For an instant he thought himself clear.

Then a hoarse shout warned him. He hurled the *arrha* off
as he wheeled and leaned, holding to the mane only. Roh was
there, and Lellin, and the rider that thundered past spun off
over his horse's tail. More Shiua came on. Vanye gained his
seat and whipped out his sword, feeling his backing horse
stumble over a body, recover under the brutal drive of the
spurs.

Hetharu. He saw the *khal*-lord coming down on him ahead
of a trio of riders, and tried to gather himself to meet that
charge. But Roh was already flashing past him, sword to
sword with the *khal* with a shock of horse and metal, and
Vanye veered instead for the rider at Hetharu's right—
swordsman likewise. The halfling shouted hate and cut at
him; Vanye whipped the sword aside and cut for the neck,
knowing the man at the last instant: Hetharu's *akil*-drugged
minion. He grimaced in disgust and reined about for the two
that had sped behind him, expecting attack on his flank, but
*arrhendur* arrows had robbed him of those. Roh needed no
help; in his jolted vision he saw Hetharu of Ohtij-in flung
nigh headless from the saddle, and themselves suddenly in a

wide area where only corpses remained, corpses, a scattering of dazed men and horses only beginning to recover, and a handful of *arrhendim,* and the main body of the horde yet hazy with distance.

He reined full about in desperation, seeking Morgaine— but he saw her then beyond them, she, and Merir, and a wide area where no dead lay and their enemies were in confused retreat. *Changeling's* shimmer glowed moon-pale in the twilight, and his arm ached in sympathy, for he knew well what it was to wield it.

Then he recalled another companion, and looked right, turning his horse . . . saw with a pang of shame the little *arrha,* her white garments torn and bloody, who had gained her feet and caught one of the dazed horses. She could not reach the stirrup; the horse shied from her. Sezar reached her before any other, reached across the saddle from the other side and pulled her up. Then Vanye called to the rest of them and they started moving forward anxious to close the interval between themselves and Morgaine and Merir, for the Shiua were recovering themselves and their clear space was about to be invaded.

But Morgaine did not delay for them. Once she saw them coming she reined about and spurred Siptah into a charge, knifing toward the regrouping Shiua foot, driving them before her as they had scattered the first time. Arrows flashed about them, brief and short of the mark; the fleeing Shiua did not delay to fire again.

The Lesser Horn loomed now distinct and near, rising out of the twilight; a road led up to it, and marshlanders and Shiua humans scattered off it as they came. Some lingered to die, whirled away into that darkness at *Changeling's* tip; more fled, even casting down weapons in their terror, scrambling down the rocks at the side of the road.

A vast gateway was open before them, and a dark interior with yet another open gate beyond, showing road and rocks in the fading light. Morgaine rode for that narrow shelter, and Merir beside her, the rest of them following in desperate haste, for arrows began to rattle on the stones about them. Then they gained the refuge, finding it empty—a fortress, of which the doors were splintered and riven, the near ones and the far. The horses skidded on the stone floor, hooves bringing echoes off the high arch above them, and stopped, hard breathing. Roh came in; and Lellin and Sezar; and Sharrn and Kessun and Perrin, the *arrha* with them. Vis came last and late. Perrin leaned from the saddle to embrace her, over-whelmed with relief, though the *khemein* was bloody and hurt.

"Dev is not coming," said Sharrn; tears glistening on the old *arrhen's* face. "Kessun, we must make a pair now, we two."

"Aye, *arrhen,*" said Kessun steadily enough. "I am with you."

Morgaine rode slowly to the gate by which they had en-tered, but the Shiua seemed to have hesitance to charge the fortress, and had fallen back again. She found *Changeling's* sheath and despite the tremor of her arm, managed to slide the blade in and still the fire. Then she leaned forward on the saddle, almost fell. Vanye dismounted and came to her side, reached up and took her down into his arms, overwhelmed with fear for her.

"I am not hurt," she said faintly, though sweat beaded her face. "I am not hurt." He sank down on his knees with her and held her tightly until the trembling should leave her. It was reaction, the pain of the sword. They all settled, content for the moment simply to draw breath. The old lord was al-most undone, and the little *arrha* lay down quietly sobbing, for she, like Sharrn and Kessun, was alone.

"Doors." Morgaine murmured suddenly, trying to gather herself. "Better see if there is any stir outside."

"Rest," Vanye said, and rose and left her, picking his way back to the riven farther door of the fortress. There was little means to close those gates now, little left of them but splin-tered wreckage. He looked at what lay farther, a road up the height, winding turns indistinct in the gathering dusk. Sight of enemies there was none.

"Lellin," Morgaine said elsewhere, and timbers crashed. She was on her feet by the other doorway, that by which they had entered, trying to move it alone. Lellin rose to help her; Vanye came to assist; others gathered themselves up, ex-hausted as they were. Down on the flat, in the gray distance across the clearing, there was a force massing, riders gather-ing, sweeping up the horde of foot and forcing them on, driv-ing them rather than leading.

"Well," Roh said hoarsely, "they have learned. That is what they should have done before now, put the weight of bodies against us. Too late for Hetharu. But some other leader has taken them now, and they care not how many hu-man folk they lose."

"We must get these doors closed," Morgaine said.

The hinges were broken; the doors, thick at the edges as a man's arm, grated over stone and bowed alarmingly close to coming apart as they threw their strength against them. They moved the other valve as well, and that was too free at one point, for one hinge still held, but it too grated into place, with daylight between.

"That big timber," Roh said, indicating a rough, bark-covered log which had been an obstacle in the hall, amid the other fallen beams. "Their ram, doubtless. It can brace the center."

It was the best they had. They heaved it up with difficulty, braced it hard; but the broken gates could hardly stand long at any point if the Shiua brought another ram against it. The doors were a lattice of splinters, and though they braced them up with beams and debris from the rear doors, they could not stop them from bowing at their weak points, even to one man's strength.

"It is not going to hold," Vanye declared in despair, leaning head and arms against it. He looked at Morgaine and saw the same written on her face, exhausted as she was, her face barred with the half-light that sifted through their barricade.

"If," she said in a faint voice, "if those higher up this hill have not attacked us down here it can only be for one cause: that they see the others coming. They are waiting for that, to hit us from both sides at once and pin us here. And if we do not stop them from attacking Nehmin itself, then ultimately they can batter down its gates. Vanye, we have no choice. We cannot hold this place."

"Those down below will be on our heels before we can engage those above."

"Should we sit and die here, to no account at all? I am going on."

"Did I say I was not? I am with you."

"Get to horse, then. It is getting dark, and we dare not waste the little time we have."

"You cannot go on wielding that sword. It will kill you. Give it to me."

"I shall carry it while I can." Her voice went hoarse. "I do not trust it near Nehmin. There is danger that you might not feel, a thing one senses in the sound and feel of it . . . a limit of approach. A mistake would kill us all. If it comes to you—avoid the jewels . . . avoid them. And if someone stirs up the forces channelled through the fortress—I hope you

feel it in time. It would tear this rock apart, unsheathed." She
thrust herself from the gateway and sought Siptah's side, took
up the reins. "Stay with me."

Others began to go to their horses, weary as they were, determined to come with them. Morgaine looked about at them
and said nothing. Only at Roh she looked long and hard. In
her mind surely was Nehmin itself—and Roh for their companion.

Roh averted his eyes and looked instead toward their fragile barricade. The sounds of the horde were louder, the enemy almost at the foot of the road, by the sound of it. "I can
keep a ram away from that barrier a little time. At least they
will not be on your backs. That will give you a chance."

Vanye looked at Morgaine, wishing otherwise, but Morgaine slowly nodded. "Aye," she said, "you could do that."

"Cousin," Vanye said, "do not. You can buy too little time
for your life."

Roh shook his head, desperation in his eyes. "You mean
well; but I will not go up there while there is any use for me
here. If I went up there, near *that* . . . I think I would
break my word. There is some use for me here . . . and you
underestimate my marksmanship, Nhi Vanye i Chya."

Vanye understood him then, and embraced him with a
great pain in his heart, then turned and hurled himself into
the saddle.

Sezar cried out sudden warning, for there was the sound of
a force advancing not only up out of the valley, but down off
the height, coming down upon them.

Only Perrin and Vis stayed afoot, leaning on their bows.
"Here is work for more than one bowman," Perrin said.
"Three of us just might be able to change their minds;
besides, if some pass you, we can keep them from Roh's
back."

"Your blessing, lord," Vis asked, and Merir leaned down
and took the *khemein's* half-gloved hand. "Aye," he said, "on
you all three."

Then he broke away, for Morgaine turned Siptah's head
and rode into the gathering dusk. Vanye followed closely, too
wrapped now in their own fate to mourn others. Even for
them it was a matter of time: Lellin and Sezar were with
them, weaponless; the little *arrha* rode with them, bloodied
and scarcely clinging to her saddle, but she stayed with
Merir; and Sharrn and Kessun with their bows . . . the only
two armed now but themselves.

"How far?" Morgaine asked of the *arrha*. "How many turns before the Horn? How many from there to the fortress of Nehmin itself?"

"Three before the Dark Horn; more after . . . four, five; I do not clearly remember, lady." The *arrha's* voice was hardly audible in the sounds about them, a painful breach of habitual silence. "I have only been here once."

Rocks hove up on either side of them in the near-darkness, making a wall on their left, sometimes falling away sharply to the right, so that they looked down a darkening fall to the flat. There was no more sound from above them, while shouts came distantly from the gray masses which surged toward the Lesser Horn.

Then the rocks began to rise on their right as well as on their left, and they must venture a steep, dark winding.

"Ambush," Vanye muttered as they approached that. Morgaine was already reaching for *Changeling*.

Suddenly rock hurtled down, bounding and thundering from above, and the horses shied in terror. *Changeling* whipped the air and wind howled, cold, sucking at them in that narrow chute. The moaning drank the thunder: the only rock to come near them plummeted down on their very heads and went elsewhere. Sweat ran down Vanye's sides beneath the armor.

Siptah leaned into a run; they pressed forward with arrows hailing down like invisible wasps, but the overhang of the cliff and *Changeling's* wind sheltered them from harm.

It was when they made the turning and faced the height that the arrows came truly; Morgaine held the fore, and the sword shielded them all, hurling the arrowflight into nothingness, the winds sucking such few as passed into forceless impacts. Men with wooden spears opposed them and Morgaine hit those ranks with a sweep that cleared Men and weapons elsewhere, flung them screaming into dark, and what remained Vanye caught, closer to *Changeling's* howling dark than ever he liked to come: he felt the cold himself, and Morgaine struggled to press Siptah as close to the outer margin of the road as she could, rather than risk him.

Panic seized the Shiua remaining; they turned their backs and began to flee up the road, and on them Morgaine had no mercy: she pursued them, and in her wake no bodies remained.

Blackness waited beyond the turn, the shadow of the Dark

Horn itself, upthrust against the sky, a wide flat a bowshot across where the road turned and enemies massed.

Suddenly Kessun cried warning at a rattle of rock behind, for enemies poured off the rocks at their left flank, cutting them off from retreat.

Witch-sword and plain steel: they held an instant; then Morgaine began to back against the rock of the Horn. These Shiua did not break and run: *"Angharan!"* they cried, knowing Morgaine, voices hoarse with hate. With pike and staff they pressed forward, demon-helms on the one side and marshlands rabble on the other.

There was no more retreat. Lellin and Sezar, Sharrn and Kessun, had snatched themselves weapons such as they could of the dead, wooden spears and barbed lances. They set their backs against the jumbled rock of the Horn, the horses backed almost against it, and held, the while *Changeling* did its dread work.

Then there was respite, a falling back, the enemy seeming exhausted, dazed by the lessening of their ranks, and raw abrasion of Gate-force loose in the area: hearing dimmed, skin seemed raw, breath seemed close. A man could bear that only so long.

So could its wielder. Vanye spurred forward as the retreat spread, thinking Morgaine would attempt it, but she did not; he checked his impulse at once, appalled when he saw her face in the opal light. Sweat beaded her skin. She could not sheath the sword. He pried it from her fingers and felt the numbing force in his own bones, worse than it was wont to be. With that gone, she simply slumped against Siptah's neck, undone, and he stayed beside her, the sword yet naked, for he wished to give their enemies no encouragement by sheathing it.

"Let us try," said Merir, moving up beside. "Our force added to yours. We might have distance enough here."

Morgaine sat up and shook her white hair back. "No," she exclaimed. "No. The combination is too dangerous. It might still bridge, take us all, perhaps. No. And stay back. Your kind of barrier cannot turn weapons. We have seen that. You and the *arrha*—" She looked about, for the *arrha* was not with Merir. Vanye cast a quick look back too, and saw the small white figure poised halfway up the black rock, perched there forlornly . . . horse lost in the melee. "Send she stays there," Morgaine said. "Lord, go back, go back against the rock."

Then came a booming from far below, echoing up the height. Even the murmur of the enemy fell silent, and the faces of the *arrhendim* were for an instant bewildered.

"Ram," Vanye said hoarsely, shifting his grip on *Changeling's* dragon-hilt. "The Lesser Horn will fall quickly now."

A shout arose from the enemy; they had also understood the sound and the meaning of it.

"They will wait now," Lellin judged, "til they can come at us with the help of those from the flat."

"We ought to carry the attack to these uphill of us," Morgaine said. "Sweep them from our path and try to reach Nehmin's doors."

"We cannot," Vanye said. "Our backs are at least to rock and we can hold that turning. Higher up—we have no guarantee there is a place to stand."

Morgaine nodded slowly. "If they grow cautious of us, we may last a little time—maybe long enough to make a difference for the *arrhend*. At least we carry food and water. Matters could be worse."

"We have not eaten today," Sezar exclaimed.

Morgaine laughed weakly at that, and others smiled. "Aye," she said. "We have not. Perhaps we should take the chance."

"A drink at least," said Sharrn, and Vanye realized the parchment dryness of his own throat, his lips cracked. He sipped at water of the flask Morgaine offered him, for he did not sheath the sword. And another flask went the rounds, fiery stuff that lent a little false warmth to shock-chilled bodies. In their lasting freedom from attack, Sezar broke a journeycake or two which they passed about; and Kessun went over to the *arrha* on her lonely perch, but she accepted only the drink, refusing the food.

Anything of substance lay cold in the belly, indigestible; only the *arrhendur* liquor lent any comfort. Vanye wiped his eyes with the back of a bloody hand and suddenly became aware of silence.

The ram had ceased.

"Soon now," Morgaine said. "Vanye, give me back the sword."

"*Liyo—*"

"Give it to me."

He did so, hearing that tone; and his arm and shoulder ached, not alone from the shocks they had endured, but from the little time he had held it. It was worse than ever it had been. *Jewel-force,* he thought suddenly, *in the fortress above us. Someone has one unmasked.*

And then with comforting clarity: *They know that we are here.*

Not yet did the enemy come on them. There was a growing murmur from below, from the part of the trail which wound below the Dark Horn. The sound came nearer and louder, and now their enemies above rallied, waiting eagerly.

"We simply hold," Morgaine said. "Stay alive. That is all we can do."

"They come," Kessun said.

It was so. The dark mass of riders thundered up the road in the dark. *They have erred,* Vanye thought with grim joy; *they choose speed over numbers.* And then he saw the number of them and his heart sank, for they packed the road, filled it, coming on them leftward as the marshlanders surged forward on the right, slower than the riders who plunged between.

Demon-helms, white-haired riders, and pikes and lances beyond counting in the moonlight . . . and there was one bareheaded.

"Shien!" Vanye shouted in rage, knowing now who it was who had broken Roh's defense, though Roh had spared him once. He checked his impulse on the instant: he had other concern, Shiua arrows on their flank. Morgaine fended those away, though one hit his mailed ribs and nigh drove the breath from him. Sharrn and Kessun spent their last several shafts in the other direction, into the riders . . . spent them well; and Lellin and Sezar gave good account of themselves with Shiua pikes. But constantly they were forced back against the rocks.

A charge surged at them. Shien was the heart of it, and he came hard, seeing them without retreat. Horsemen plunged about them and Morgaine drove Siptah for the midst of them, aimed at Shien himself. She could not; man and rider *Changeling* took, but there were ever more of them, more pouring up the road, deafening clamor of steel and hooves.

They were done. Vanye kept at her side, doing what he could; and only for an instant in the shying of a demon-helm from attack was there an opening. He rammed the spurs in with a manic yell and took it, broke through, swung an arm which itself was lead-weighted with sword and armor, but he was suddenly without hindrance.

Shien knew him: the *khal*-lord's face twisted in grim pleasure. The blade swung, rang off his, his off Shien's in two passes. His exhausted horse staggered as Shien spurred forward and he lurched aside and felt the blade hit his back, numbing muscles. His left arm fell useless. He drove up straightarmed with his blade with force enough to unseat his elbow, and it grated off armor and hit flesh. Shien cried a shriek of rage and died, impaled on it.

Gate-force swept near, Morgaine by him. The wind out of the dark took the man who came at him; the face went whirling away into dark, a tiny figure and lost. He reeled in the saddle, and while the reins were still tangled in the fingers of his left hand, the arm was lifeless, the horse unguided. Siptah shouldered it back; it staggered and turned with that shepherding as Morgaine tried to set herself twixt him and them.

Then her eyes fixed aloft, toward the Horn.

"No!" she cried, reining back. Vanye saw the white-robed *arrha* who stood with one arm thrust up, the shapes of men crawling up the height to reach her; but the *arrha* looked not at them, but to Morgaine, fist extended, white wraith against the rock.

Then light flared, and dark bridged from *Changeling's* tip to the Horn, cold and terrible. Rocks whirled away vast and then eye-wrenchingly small; and riders and horses, debris sucked screaming into a starry void. The white form of the *arrha* glowed and streamed into that wind, vanished. Abruptly light went, all save *Changeling* itself, while the earth shook and rumbled.

Horses shied back and forward, and part of the road went. Rock rumbled over the side, taking riders with it; rock tumbled from the height, and poured over the edge. Those riders nearest cried out in terror, and Morgaine shrieked a curse and whipped a blow that took the man nearest.

Few Shiua remained; they fled back, confounding themselves with the marshlanders. And Vanye cast his sword from his bloody fingers; with his right hand he dragged the reins from his useless left and kept with her.

Some of the enemy attempted the slide itself, scrambling down the unstable rocks to escape; some huddled together in desperate defense, and a few of their own arrows returned from *arrhendur* bows shattered that.

There was silence then. The balefire of *Changeling* lit a place of twisted bodies, riven rock, and seven of them who survived. Kessun lay dead, held in Sharrn's arms: the old *ar-*

*rhen* mourned in silence; the *arrha* was gone; Sezar had taken hurt, Lellin trying with shaking hands to tear a bandage for the wound.

"Help me," Morgaine asked in a broken voice.

Vanye tried, letting go the reins, but she could not control her arm to give him the sword; it was Merir who rode to her right, Merir alone of them unscathed; and Merir who took the sword from her fingers, before Vanye could prevent it.

Power . . . the shock of it reached Merir's eyes, and thoughts were born there that were not good to see. For a moment Vanye reached for his dagger, thinking that he might hurl himself across Siptah—strike before *Changeling* took him and Morgaine.

But then the old lord held it well aside, and asked the sheath; Morgaine gave it to him. The deadly force slipped within, and the light winked out, leaving them blind in the dark.

"Take it back," Merir said hoarsely. "That much wisdom I have gained in my many years. Take it back."

She did so, and tucked it against her like a recovered child, bowed over it. For a moment she remained so, exhausted. Then she flung her head back and looked about her, drawing breath.

It was utter wreckage, the place where they had stood. No one moved. The horses hung their heads and shifted weight, spent, even Siptah. Vanye found feeling returning to his back and his fingers, and suddenly wished that it were not. He felt of his side and found riven leather and parted mail at the limit of his reach; whether he was bleeding he did not know, but he moved the shoulder and the bone seemed whole. He dismounted and limped over to pick up his discarded sword.

Then he heard shouting from the distance below, and the heart froze in him. He returned to his horse and mounted with difficulty, and the others gathered themselves up, Sharrn delaying to take a quiver of arrows from a marshlander's corpse. Lellin gathered up a bow and quiver, armed now as he preferred. But Sezar was hardly able to get to the saddle.

The sound was coming up from the foot of the road. It roared like the sea on rocks, as wild and confused.

"Let us ride higher," Morgaine said. "Beware ambush; but that rockfall may or may not have blocked off the road below us."

They rode slowly, the only strength they and the horses

had left, up the winding turns, blind in the dark. Morgaine would not draw the sword, and none wished her to. Up and up they wound, and amid the slow ring of the horses' shod hooves there were sounds still drifting up at them out of the night.

A great square arch loomed suddenly before them, and a vast hold built of the very stone of the hill. Nehmin: here if anywhere there should be resistence, and there was none. The great doors were scarred and dented with blows, a discarded ram before them, but they had held.

Merir's stone flashed once, twice, reddening his hand.

Then slowly the great doors yielded inward, and they rode into a blaze of light, over polished floors, where a thin line of white-robed *arrha* awaited them.

"You are she," said the eldest, "about whom we were warned."

"Aye," Morgaine said.

The elder bowed, to her and to Merir, and all the others inclined themselves dutifully.

"We have one wounded," Morgaine said wearily. "The rest of us will go outside and watch. We have advantage here, if we do not let ourselves be attacked by stealth. By your leave, sir."

"I will go," said Sezar, though his face was drawn and seemed older than his years. "You shall not," Lellin said. "But I will watch with them for you."

Sezar nodded surrender then, and slipped down from his horse. If there had not been an *arrha* close at hand, he would have fallen.

# Chapter Seventeen

Cold wind whipped among the rocks where they sheltered, and they wrapped in their cloaks and sat still, warmed by hot drink which the *arrha* brought out to them—fed, although they were so bloody and wretched that food was dry in the mouth. *Arrha* tended their horses, for they were hardly fit to care for themselves; Vanye interfered in that only to assure himself that at least one of them had some skill in the matter, and then he returned to Morgaine.

Sezar joined them finally, supported by two of the young *arrha* and wrapped in a heavy cloak; Lellin arose to rebuke him, but said nothing after all, for joy that he was able to have come. The *khemeis* sank down at his feet and Sharrn's and rested against their knees, perhaps as warm as he would have been inside and fretting less for being where they were.

Morgaine sat outermost of their group, and looked on them little; generally she gazed outward with a bleak concentration which made her face stark in the glare from Nehmin's open doors. Her arm was hurting her, perhaps other wounds as well. She carried it tucked against her, her knees drawn up. Vanye had moved into such a position that he blocked most of the wind, the only charity she would accept, possibly because she did not notice it. He hurt; in every muscle he hurt, and not alone with that, but with the anguish in Morgaine.

*Changeling* had killed, had taken lives none of them could count; and more than that—it had taken yet another friend; that was the weight on her soul now, he thought: that and worry for the morrow.

There was still the tumult on the field below . . . sometimes diminishing, sometimes increasing as bands surged toward the rock of Nehmin and away again.

"The road must surely be blocked with the stonefall," Vanye observed, and then realized that would remind her of the *arrha* and the ruin, and he did not want to do that.

"Aye," she said in Andurin. "I hope." And then with a shake of her head, still staring into the dark: "It was a fortunate accident. I do not think we should have survived otherwise. Fortunate too . . . there were none of us in the gap twixt *Changeling* and the *arrha*."

"You are wrong."

She looked at him.

"Not fortunate," he said. "Not chance. The little *arrha* knew. I bore her across the field down there. She had great courage. And I believe she thought it through and waited until it had to be tried."

Morgaine said nothing. Perhaps she took peace of it. She turned back to the view into the dark, where cries drifted up fainter and fainter. Vanye looked in that direction and then back at her, with a sudden chill, for he saw her draw her Honor-blade. But she cut one of the thongs that hung at her belt-ring and gave it to him, sheathing the blade again.

"What am I to do with this?" he asked, thoroughly puzzled.

She shrugged, looking for once unsure of herself. "Thee never told me thoroughly," she said, lapsing into that older, familiar accent, "for what thee was dishonored . . . why they made thee *ilin*, that I know; but why did they take thy honor from thee too? I would never," she added, "*order* thee to answer."

He looked down, clenching the thong taut between his fists, conscious of the hair that whipped about his face and neck. He knew then what she was trying to give him, and he looked up with a sudden sense of release. "It was for cowardice," he said, "because I would not die at my father's wish."

"Cowardice." She gave a breath of a laugh, dismissing such a thought. "Thee?—Braid thy hair, Nhi Vanye. Thee's been too long on this road for that."

She spoke very carefully, watching his face: in this grave matter even *liyo* ought not to intervene. But he looked from her to the dark about them and knew that this was so. With a sudden resolve he set the thong between his teeth and swept back his hair to braid it, but the injured arm would not bear that angle. He could not complete it, and took the thong from his mouth with a sigh of frustration. "*Liyo*—"

"I might," she said, "if thy arm is too sore."

He looked on her, his heart stopped for a moment and then beginning again. No one touched an *uyo*'s hair, save his closest kin . . . no woman except one in intimate relation with him. "We are not kin," he said.

"No. We are far from kin."

She knew, then, what she did. For a moment he tried to make some answer, then as it were of no consequence, he turned his back to her and let her strip out his own clumsy braiding. Her fingers were deft and firm, making a new beginning.

"I do not think I can make a proper Nhi braid," she said. "I have done only my own once and long ago, Chya."

"Make it Chya, then; I am not ashamed of that."

She worked, gently, and he bowed his head in silence, feeling what defied speaking. Long-time comrades, she and

he; at least in distance and time as men measured it; *ilin* and
*liyo*—he thought that there might be great wrong in what had
grown between them; he feared that there was—but conscience in this area grew very faint.

And that Morgaine kri Chya set affection on anything vulnerable to loss—he knew what that asked of her.

She finished, took the thong from him and tied it. The warrior's knot was familiar and yet unaccustomed to him, setting
his mind back to Morija in Kursh, where he had last been entitled to it. It was a strange feeling. He turned then, met her
gaze without lowering his eyes as once he might. That was
also strange.

"There are many things," he said, "we have never reckoned with each other. Nothing is simple."

"No," she said. "Nothing is." She turned her face to the
dark again, and suddenly he realized there was silence below
. . . no clash of arms, no distant shouting, no sound of
horses.

The others realized it too. Merir stood and looked out over
the field, of which only the vaguest details could be seen. Lellin and Sharrn leaned on the rocks to try to see, and Sezar
struggled up with Lellin's help to look out over the edge.

Then from far away came thin cries, no warlike shouts,
but terror. Such continued for a long time, at this point of
the horizon and that.

Afterward was indeed silence.

And a beginning of dawn glimmered in the overcast east.

The light came slowly as always over Shathan. It sprang
from the east to touch the gray clouds, and lent vague form
to the tumbled rocks, the ruin of the great cliffs of Nehmin,
and the distant breached gate of the Lesser Horn. The White
Hill took shape in the morning haze, and the circular rim of
the grove which ringed them about. Bodies of men lay thick
on the field, blackening areas of it. Birds came with the
dawn. A few frightened horses milled this way and that,
riderless, unnatural restlessness.

But of the horde . . . none living.

It was long before any of them moved. Silently the *arrha*
had come forth into the daylight, and stood staring at the
desolation.

"*Harilim*," said Merir. "The dark ones must have done this
thing."

But then the distant call of a horn sounded, and drew their

eyes northward, to the very rim of the clearing. There was a
small band gathered there, which began their ride to Nehmin
even as they watched.

"They came," said Lellin. "The *arrhend* has come."

"Blow the answer to them," Merir said, and Lellin lifted
the horn to his lips and sounded it loud and long.

The horses began in their far distance, to run.

And Morgaine gathered herself up, leaning on *Changeling*.
"We have a road to open," she said.

It was a grisly ruin, that tumbled mass on the lower road
which had been the Dark Horn. They approached it carefully, and perhaps the *arrhendim* had vision of setting hands
to that jumble of vast blocks, for they murmured dismay; but
Morgaine rode forward and dismounted, drew *Changeling*
from its sheath.

The blade shimmered into life, enveloped stone after stone
with that gulf at its tip, and whirled them away otherwhere
. . . no random choice, but carefully, this one and the next
and the next, so that some rocks fell and some slid over the
brink and others were taken. Even yet Vanye blinked when it
was done, for the mind refused such vision, the visible dimi-
nution of that debris whirled away into the void, carried on
the wind. When even a small way was cleared, it seemed yet
impossible what had stood there before.

They went past it fearfully, with an eye to the slide above
them, for Morgaine had taken some care that it be secure,
but the whole mass was too great and too new to be certain.
There was enough space for them to pass; and below, cau-
tiously, they must venture it again on the lower windings of
the road.

The carnage was terrible in this place: the road had been
packed with Shiua when the Horn came down, here and in
other levels. In some places Morgaine must clear their way
through the dead, and they were wary of stragglers, of ambush, by arrow or stonefall, at any moment; but they met
none. The lonely sounds of their own horses' hooves rolled
back off the cliff and up out of the rocks of the Lesser Horn
as they wound their way down to that breached fortress.

This Vanye most dreaded; so, surely, did they all. But it
had to be passed. Daylight showed through the broken doors
as they rode near; they rode within and found death, dead
horses and dead Men and *khal*, arrow-struck and worse.
Beams and timbers from the shattered doors were scattered

so that they must dismount, dangerous as it was, and lead the
horses among Shiua dead.

There lay Vis, her small body almost like a marshlander's
for size, fallen among her enemies, hacked with many
wounds; and by the far gates was Perrin, her pale hair spilled
about her and her bow yet in her dead fingers. An arrow had
found her heart.

But of Roh, there was no sign.

Vanye dropped the reins of his horse and searched among
the dead, finding nothing; Morgaine waited, saying nothing.

"I would find him," he pleaded, seeing the anger she had
not spoken, knowing he was delaying them all.

"So would I," she answered.

He thrust this way and that among the bodies and the broken planks, the crashes of disturbed timbers echoing off the
walls. Lellin helped him . . . and it was Lellin who found
Roh, heaving aside the leaf of the front gate which had fallen
back against the wall, the only one of the four still half on its
hinges.

"He is alive," Lellin said.

Vanye worked past the obstacle, and put his shoulder
beneath it, heaved it back with a crash that woke the echoes.
Roh lay half-covered in debris, and they pulled the beams
from him with care, the more so for the broken shaft which
was in his shoulder. Roh's eyes were half open when they had
him clear; Sharrn had brought his water flask, and Vanye
bathed Roh's face in it, gave him a sip to drink, lifting his
head.

Then with a heaviness of heart he looked at Morgaine,
wondering whether having found him was kindness at all.

She let Sipth stand and walked slowly over in the debris.
Roh's bow lay beside him, and his quiver that held one last
arrow. She gathered up both out of the dust and knelt there,
frowning, the bow clasped in her arms.

Horses were coming up the road outside. She rose then and
set the weapons in Lellin's keeping, walking out into the gateway; but there was no alarm in her manner and Vanye
stayed where he was, holding Roh on his knees.

They were *arrhendim*, half a score of them. They brought
the breath of Shathan with them, these green-clad riders,
fair-haired and dark, scatheless and wrapped in dusty daylight from the riven doors. They reined in and dismounted,
hurrying to give homage to Merir, and to exclaim in dismay

that their lord was in such a place and so weary, and that *ar-rhendim* had died here.

"We were fourteen when we came into this place," said Merir. "Two of the nameless; Perrin Selehnnin, Vis of Amelend, Dev of Tirrhend, Larrel Shaillon, Kessun of Obisend: they are our bitter loss."

"We have taken little hurt, lord, of which we are glad."

"And the horde?" Morgaine asked.

The *arrhen* looked at her and at Merir, seeming bewildered. "Lord—they turned on each other. The *qhal* and the Men—fought until most were dead. The madness continued, and some perished by our arrows, and more fled into Shathan among the *harilim*, and there died. But very, very many—died in fighting each other."

"Hetharu," Roh whispered suddenly, his voice dry and strange. "With Hetharu gone—Shien; and then it all fell apart."

Vanye pressed Roh's hand and Roh regarded him hazily. "I hear," Roh breathed. "They are gone, the Shiua. That is good."

He spoke the language of Andur, thickly, but the brown eyes slowly gained focus, and more so when Morgaine left the others to stand above him. "Thee sounds as if thee will survive, Chya Roh."

"I could not do even this much well," Roh said, self-mocking, which was Chya Roh and none of the other. "My apologies. We are back where we were."

Morgaine frowned and turned her back, walked away. "*Arrhendim* can tend him, and we shall. I do not want him near the *arrha*, or Nehmin. Better he should be taken into Shathan."

She looked about her then, at all the ruin. "I will come back to this place when I must, but for the moment I would rather the forest, the forest . . . and a time to rest."


They made an easier ride this time across Azeroth, attended by old friends and new. They camped last beyond the two rivers, and there were *arrhendur* tents spread and a bright fire to warm the night.

Merir had come . . . great honor to them; and Lellin and Seza and Sharrn, no holding them from this journey; and Roh: Roh, sunk much of the time in lonely silence or staring bleakly elsewhere. Roh sat apart from the company, among the strange *arrhendim* of east Shathan, well guarded by them, although he did little and said less, and had never made attempt to run.

"This Chya Roh," Merir whispered that night, while the remnant of the company shared food together, all but Roh. "He is halfling, aye, and more than that—but Shathan would take him. We have taken some even of the Shiua folk who have come begging peace with the forest, who have some love of the green land. And could any man's love for it be greater than his, who has offered his life for it?"

He spoke to Morgaine, and Vanye looked on her with sudden, painful hope, for Roh's fate had blighted all the peace of these last days. But Morgaine said nothing, and finally shook her head.

"He fought for us," said Lellin. "Sezar and I will speak for him."

"So do I," said Sharrn. "Lady Morgaine, I am alone. I would take this Man, and Dev would not reproach me for it, nor would Larrel and Kessun."

Morgaine shook her head, although with great sadness. "Let us not speak of it again tonight. Please."

But Vanye did, when that night they were alone, in the tent which they shared. A tiny oil lamp lent a faint glow among the shadows. He could see Morgaine's face. A sad mood was on her, and one of her silences, but he ventured it all the same, for there was no more time.

"What Sharrn offered . . . are you thinking of that?"

Her gray eyes met his, guarded at once.

"I ask it of you," he said, "if it can be given."

"Do not." Her voice had a hard edge, quiet as it was. "Did I not say: *I will never go right or left to please you?* I know only one direction, Vanye. If you do not understand that, then you have never understood me at all."

"If you do not understand my asking, hopeless as it is, then you have never understood me either."

"Forgive me," she said then faintly. "Yes. I do. Thee must, being Nhi. But consider him, not your honor. What did you tell me . . . regarding what struggle he has? How long can he bear that?"

He let go his breath and clenched his hands about his knees, for it was true; he considered Roh's moodiness, the terrible darkness that seemed above him much of the time. The Fires were near dying. The power at Nehmin had been set to fade at a given day and hour, and that hour was evening tomorrow.

"I have ordered," Morgaine said, "that his guards watch him with special closeness this night."

"You saved his life. Why?"

"I have watched him. I have been watching him."

He had never spoken with her of Roh's fate, not in all the days that they spent in the forest about Nehmin, while Roh and Sezar healed, while they rested and nursed their own wounds, and took the gentle hospitality of Shathan's east. He had almost hoped then for her mercy, had even been confident of it.

But when they had prepared to leave, she had ordered Roh brought with them under guard. "I want to know where you are," she had told Roh; and Roh had bowed in great irony. "Doubtless you have stronger wishes than that," Roh had answered, and the look of the stranger had been in his eyes. The stranger was much with them on this ride, even to this last night. Roh was quiet, morose; and sometimes it was Roh and as often it was not. Perhaps the *arrhendim* did not fully see this; if any suspected this shifting, it was likely Merir, and perhaps Sharrn, who knew fully what he was.

"Do you doubt I consider what pain he suffers?" Vanye asked bitterly. "But I have faith in the outcome of this mood of his; and you always have faith in the worst. That is our difference."

"And we would not know until the Fires were dead, whether we should believe one thing or the other," Morgaine said. "And thee and I cannot linger this side to find it out."

"And you do not take chances."

"I do not take chances."

There was long silence.

"Never," she said, "have I power to listen to heart more than head. Thee's my better nature, Vanye. All that I am not, thee is. And when I come against that . . . Thee's the only—well, I would miss thee. But I have thought it over . . . how perhaps if I should harm this man, thee would hate me; that thee would, finally, leave me. And thee will do what thee thinks right; and so must I, thee by heart, I by head; and which of us is right, I do not know. But I cannot let myself be led by wanting this and wanting that. I must be right. It is not what Roh can do that frets me; once the Fires are dead—I hope . . . I *hope* that he is powerless."

*I know what is written in the runes on that blade,* Roh had said; *at least the gist of it.* The words shot back into his mind out of all the confusion of pain and *akil,* turning him cold to the heart. Little of that time he did remember clearly; but this came back.

"He knows more," he said hoarsely. "He has at least part of *Changeling's* knowledge."

A moment she stared at him, stark-stricken, and then bowed against her hands, murmured a word in her own lost language, over and over.

"I have killed him," Vanye said. "By telling you that, I have killed him, have I not?"

"It was long before she looked up at him. "Nhi honor," she said.

"I do not think I will sleep well hereafter."

"Thee also serves something stronger than thyself."

"It is as cold a bedfellow as that you serve. Perhaps that is why I have always understood you. Only keep *Changeling* from him. What wants doing—I will do, if you cannot be moved."

"I cannot have that."

"In this, *liyo,* I do not care what you will and will not."

She folded her arms and rested her head against them.

The light eventually burned out; neither of them slept but by snatches, nor spoke, while it burned. It was only afterward that Vanye fell into deeper sleep, and that still sitting, his head upon his arms.

They slept late in the morning; the *arrhend* made no haste to wake them, but had breakfast prepared when they came out, Morgaine dressed in her white garments, Vanye in the clothing which the *arrhendim* had provided. And still Roh did not choose to sit with them, nor even to eat, though his guards brought him food and tried to persuade him. He only drank a little, and sat with his head bowed on his arms after.

"We will take Roh," Morgaine said to Merir and the others when they had done with breakfast. "Our ways must part now, yours and ours; but Roh must go with us."

"If you will it so," said Merir, "but we would go all the way to the Fires with you."

"Best we ride this last day alone. Go back, lord. Give our love to the Mirrindim and the Carrhendim. Tell them why we could not come back."

"There is also," said Vanye, "a boy named Sin, of Mirrind, who wants to be *khemeis.*"

"We know him," said Sharrn.

"Teach him," Vanye asked of the old *arrhen*. He saw then a touch of longing come to the *qhal's* gray eyes.

"Aye," said Sharrn. "I shall. The Fires may go, but the *arrhend* must remain."

Vanye nodded slowly, comforted.

"We would come with you," said Lellin, "Sezar and I. Not to the Fires, but through them. It would be hard to leave our forests, harder yet to leave the *arrhend* . . . but—"

Morgaine regarded him, and Merir's pain, and shook her head. "You belong here. Shathan is in your keeping; it would be wrong to desert it. Where we go—well, you have given us all that we need and more than we could ask. We will fare well enough, Vanye and I."

*And Roh?* The question flickered briefly into the eyes of the *arrhendim*, and there remained dread after. They seemed then to realize, and there was silence.

"We had better go," Morgaine said. From her neck she lifted the chain, and the gold medallion, and gave it back into Merir's hands. "It was a great gift, lord Merir."

"It was borne by one we shall not forget."

"We do not ask your forgiveness, lord Merir, but some things we much regret."

"You do not need it, lady. It will be sung *why* these things were done; you and your *khemeis* will be honored in our songs as long as there are *arrhendim* to sing them."

"And that is itself a great gift, my lord."

Merir inclined his head, and set his hand then on Vanye's shoulder. "*Khemeis,* when you prepare, take the white horse for your own. None of ours can keep up with the gray, but only she."

"Lord," he said, dismayed and touched at once. "She is yours."

"She is great-granddaughter to one who was mine, *khemeis;* I treasure her, and therefore I give her to you, to one who will love her well. The saddle and bridle are hers; Arrhan is her name. May she bear you safely and long. And this more." Merir pressed into his hand the small case of an *arrha's* jewel. "All these will die in this land as the Fires die. If your lady permits, I give you this . . . no weapon, but a protection, and a means to find your way, should you ever be parted."

He looked at Morgaine, and she nodded, well-pleased.

"Lord," he said, and would have knelt to thank him, but the old lord prevented him.

"No. We honor *you. Khemeis,* I shall not live so much longer. But even when our children are dust, you and your lady and my small gift to you . . . will be yet upon your journey, perhaps not even across the simple step you will take this evening. Far, far travelling. I shall think of that when I die. And it will please me to be remembered."

"We shall do that, lord."

Merir nodded, and turned away, bidding the *arrhendim* break camp.


They armed with care for this ride, in armor partly familiar and partly *arrhendur,* and each of them had a good *arrhendur* bow and a full quiver of brown-fletched arrows besides. Only Roh went unarmed; Morgaine bound his bow, unstrung, upon her saddle, and his sword was on Vanye's.

Roh seemed not at all surprised when told that they required him to ride with them.

He bowed them, and mounted the bay horse which the *arrhend* had provided him. He yet moved painfully, and used his right hand more than his left, even in rising to the saddle.

Vanye mounted up on white Arrhan, and turned her gently to Morgaine's side.

"Goodbye," said Merir.

"Goodbye," they said together.

"Farewell," Lellin offered them, and he and Sezar were first to turn away, Merir after; but Sharrn lingered.

"Farewell," Sharrn said to them, and looked last on Roh. "Chya Roh——"

"For your kindness," Roh said, almost the first words he had spoken in days, "I thank you, Sharrn Thiallin."

Then Sharrn left, and the rest of the *arrhendim,* riding quickly across the plain toward the north.

Morgaine started Siptah moving south, in no great haste, for the Fires would not die until the night, and they had the day before them with no far distance to ride.

Roh looked back from time to time, and Vanye did, until the distance and the sunlight swallowed up the *arrhendim,* until even the dust had vanished.

And no word had any of them spoken.

"You are not taking me with you," said Roh, "through the Gate."

"No," said Morgaine.

Roh nodded slowly.

"I am waiting for you," said Morgaine, "to say something in the matter."

Roh shrugged, and for a time he made no answer, but the sweat beaded on his face, calm as it remained.

"We are old enemies, Morgaine kri Chya. Why this is, I have never understood . . . until late, until Nehmin. At least—I know your purpose. I find some peace with that. I only wonder why you have insisted on my survival this far. Can you not make up your mind? I do not believe at all that you have changed your intentions."

"I told you. I have a distaste for murder."

Roh laughed outright, then flung his head back, eyes shut against the sun. He smiled, smiled still when he looked at them. "I thank you," he said hoarsely. "It is up to me, is it not? You are waiting for me to decide; of course. You bade Vanye carry that Honor-blade of mine, long since hoping. If you will give it back to me, I think that—outside the sight of the Gate—I shall have the strength to use that gift. Only— *there*—I could not say what I would do, if you bring me close to that place. There are things I do not want to remember."

Morgaine reined to a halt. There was nothing but grass about them, no sight yet of the Gate, nor of the forest, nor anything living. Roh's face was very pale. She handed across to him the bone-hilted Honor-blade, his own. He took it, kissed the hilt, sheathed it. She gave him then his bow, and the one arrow that was his; and nodded to Vanye. "Give him his sword back."

Vanye did so, and was relieved to see that at the moment the stranger was gone and only Roh was with them; there was on Roh's face only a sober look, a strangely mild regret.

"I will not speak to him directly," Morgaine said at Roh's back. "My face stirs up other memories, I think, and perhaps it is best he look on it as little as possible under these circumstances. He has avoided me zealously. But do you know him, Vanye?"

"Yes, *liyo*. He is in command of himself . . . has been, I think, more than you have believed."

"Only with you . . . in Shathan. And with difficulty . . . now. I am the worst possible company for him; I am the only enemy Roh and Liell share. He cannot go with us. Chya Roh, you have knowledge enough it is deadly to leave you here; all that I do would rest on your will to rule that other nature of yours. You might bring the Gate to life again in this land, undo all that we have done, work ruin on us, and on this land."

He shook his head. "No. I much doubt that I could."

"Truth, Chya Roh?"

"The truth is that I do not know. There is a remote chance."

"Then I give you choice, Chya Roh. That you have the means with you and the strength to leave this life: choose that, if you think that safest for you and for Shathan; but if you choose . . . if you can for the rest of your years be strong enough . . . choose Shathan."

He backed his horse and looked at her, shaken for the first time, terror on his face. "I do not believe you could offer that."

"Vanye and I can make the Gate from here; we will wait here until we see you over the horizon, and then we will ride like the wind itself and reach it before you could. There we will wait until we know that you cannot follow. That eliminates the one chance. But the other, that you might do harm here—that rests on Chya Roh. I know now which man is making the choice: Roh would not risk harm to this land."

For a long time Roh said nothing, his head bowed, his hands clenched upon the sword and the Chya longbow which lay across his saddle.

"Suppose that I am strong enough?" he asked.

"Then Sharrn will be glad to find you coming after him," said Morgaine. "And Vanye and I would envy you this exile."

A light came to Roh's face, and with a sudden move he reined about and rode—but he stopped then, and came back to them as they watched, bowed in the saddle to Morgaine, and then rode close to Vanye, leaned across and embraced him.

There were tears in his eyes. It was Roh, utterly. Vanye himself wept; a man might, at such a time.

Roh's hand pressed the back of his neck, bared now by the warrior's knot. "Chya braid," Roh said. "You have gotten back your honor, Nhi Vanye i Chya; I am glad of that. And you have given me mine. Your road I do not truly envy. I thank you, cousin, for many things."

"It will not be easy for you."

"I swear to you," said Roh, "and I will keep that oath."

Then he rode away, and the distance and the sunlight came between.

Siptah eased up next Arrhan, quiet moving of horse and harness.

"I thank you," Vanye said.

"I am frightened," Morgaine said in a still voice. "It is the most conscienceless thing I have ever done."

"He will not harm Shathan."

"And I have set an oath on the *arrha*, that should he stay in this land, they would guard Nehmin still."

He looked at her, dismayed that she had borne this intention secret from him.

"Even my mercies," she said, "are not without calculation. You know this of me."

"I know," he said.

Roh passed out of sight over the horizon.

"Come," she said then, turning Siptah about. He reined Arrhan around and touched heel to her as Siptah sprang forward into a run. The golden grass flew under their hooves.

Soon the Gate itself was in sight, opal fire in the daylight.

## Epilogue

*It was a late spring . . . green grass covered all of Azeroth's plain, with wildflowers spangling areas gold and white.*

*And it was an unaccustomed place for* arrhendim.

*Four days the two had ridden from Shathan's edge, to this place where the land lay flat and empty on all sides and the forest could not even be seen. It gave them a curious feeling of nakedness, under the eye of the spring sun.*

*Loneliness came on them more when they came within sight of what they had come to find.*

*The Gate towered above the plain, stark and unnatural. As they rode near, the horses' hooves disturbed stones in the tall* grass, bits of old wood, mostly rotted, which remained of a great camp that had once sat at the base of it.

They drew rein almost beneath the Gate, in a patch of sun which fell through the empty arch. Age-pitted it was, and one of the great stones stood aslant, after only so few years. The swiftness of that ruin sent a chill upon them.

The khemeis of the pair dismounted . . . a smallish man, his dark hair much streaked with silver. An iron ring was on his finger. He looked into the Gate, which only looked through into more of the grassland and the flowers, and stood staring at that until his arrhen came walking up behind him and set his hand on his shoulder.

"What must it have been?" Sin wondered aloud. "Ellur, what was it to look on when it led somewhere?"

The qhal had no answer, only stared, his gray eyes full of thoughts. And at last he pressed Sin's shoulder and turned away. There was a longbow bound to the saddle of Sin's horse. Ellur loosed it and brought it to him.

Sin took the aged bow into his hands, reverently handled the dark, strange wood, of design unlike any made in Shathan, and strung it with great care. It was uncertain whether it had the strength to be fired any longer; it had been long since its master had set hand to it. But one arrow they had brought, green-fletched, and Sin set that to the string, drew back full, aimed it high into the sun.

It flew, lost from sight when it fell.

He unstrung the bow and laid it within the arch of the Gate. Then he stepped back and gazed there a last time.

"Come," Ellur urged him. "Sin, do not grieve. The old bowman would not wish it."

"I do not," he said, but his eyes stung, and he wiped at them.

He turned then, and rose into the saddle to put the place behind him. Ellur joined him. Four days would see them safe in forest shadow.

Ellur looked back once, but Sin did not. He clenched his hand upon the ring and stared straight ahead.

Presenting MICHAEL MOORCOCK
in DAW editions

### The Elric Novels

## DAW PRESENTS MARION ZIMMER BRADLEY

"A writer of absolute competency . . ."—Theodore Sturgeon

☐ **THE FORBIDDEN TOWER**
"Blood feuds, medieval pageantry, treachery, tyranny, and true love combine to make another colorful swatch in the compelling continuing tapestry of Darkover."—**Publishers Weekly.** (#UJ1323—$1.95)

☐ **THE HERITAGE OF HASTUR**
"A rich and highly colorful tale of politics and magic, courage and pressure . . . Topflight adventure in every way."—**Analog.** "May well be Bradley's masterpiece."—**Newsday.** "It is a triumph."—**Science Fiction Review.** (#UJ1307—$1.95)

☐ **DARKOVER LANDFALL**
"Both literate and exciting, with much of that searching fable quality that made **Lord of the Flies** so provocative."—**New York Times.** The novel of Darkover's origin.
(#UW1447—$1.50)

☐ **THE SHATTERED CHAIN**
"Primarily concerned with the role of women in the Darkover society . . . Bradley's gift is provocative, a topnotch blend of sword-and-sorcery and the finest speculative fiction."—**Wilson Library Bulletin.** (#UJ1327—$1.95)

☐ **THE SPELL SWORD**
Goes deeper into the problem of the matrix and the conflict with one of Darkover's non-human races gifted with similar powers. A first-class adventure. (#UW1440—$1.50)

☐ **STORMQUEEN!**
"A novel of the planet Darkover set in the Ages of Chaos . . . this is richly textured, well-thought-out and involving."—**Publishers Weekly.** (#UJ1381—$1.95)

☐ **HUNTERS OF THE RED MOON**
"May be even more a treat for devoted MZB fans than her excellent Darkover series . . . sf adventure in the grand tradition."—**Luna.** (#UW1407—$1.50)

---

To order these titles,

use coupon on the

last page of this book.

## ANDRE NORTON

### in DAW BOOKS editions